The Tears
Book One of All The Silences

Geneviève Montcombroux

Dedicated to all those who rose up to fight against Nazi oppression so that I and others could live in a free world.

To the memory of Rose Ernstberger who, in Germany, and I in France as children suffered the hunger, the cold and the fear during WWII.

Acknowledgments

My grateful thanks to June for her enthusiasm, to Tanis for her endless support, and friendship.

And last but not least to my husband Michael who relentlessly encouraged me to write this book when I was plagued by doubts.

All The Silences
Book One – The Tears

Notes

All the historical facts are meticulously researched and include fragments of diaries and other original documents. The language used corresponds to the era. So do the behaviors. Situations and incidents are based on true stories although the characters are fictional. This book is not a romance, and it is not about the exploits of some fictitious heroine and hero during WWII in France. It is about what life was like for the everyday people, particularly women, what they did because they wanted to do something, yet not knowing what, and how they were drawn into actions they had never planned on doing and never thought they were capable of.

Life in France under German occupation changed dramatically, in particular for women who were left alone to provide and care for children. Even those, whose husbands had returned, were still responsible for managing the household and seeing to their children's needs.

Women had no status – they didn't have the vote – and were considered feeble. The man of the household had undisputed authority.

A woman's role was not recognized. In fact women became the scapegoat of head of state Marshal Pétain who accused them of not having produced enough children, not having raised the children in the spirit of a work ethic. Pétain blamed women who worked outside the home for not keeping the family unit together. Of course, those working outside the home were working-class women and their income was essential to the welfare of the family, as men often had low wages, often reduced by drinking. Marshal Pétain, who had no children himself, failed to understand that WWI had removed over a million men from the population, leaving many women unmarried. Those unmarried women became the object of his scorn, as did couples who had no children.

Women were not recognized as a major part of keeping the country together. Nor were women recognized when they actively participated in the Résistance. Medals and honors went to men. Yet without the women who acted as couriers – a most dangerous work – who trained with the

SOE and parachuted into France, without the women who took over the leadership of resistance networks when the male leader was caught by the Gestapo, the Résistance may not have grown as it did and become a major help to the Allies in June 1944. General Eisenhower said: "The French Résistance was the equivalent of ten divisions."

This was life during the Occupation of France, mostly in this series, in Paris, where I lived throughout that period.

The novel starts when the phoney war ends on April 10, 1940. At first, life wasn't much different. People were hesitant, shocked, wondering "what now?" Not until toward the end of 1940 did real change happen. The shift in public opinion began later, in the winter of 1941 and reached its culmination in the summer of 1942.

Characters of importance at the start of 1940

Gontrand & Bérangère, patriarch & matriarch of the de Montregard family, live in a mansion: Le Manoir

First son: Philippe m. to Madeleine = Mireille 20, Pierrette 18, François 16

Second son: Bernard m. to Marie-Ange = Paul 10, Micheline 8

Daughter Agnès, mentioned, no active role

Third son: Rodolphe = Lyse-May 3 (or 4 the family doesn't know)

Fourth son: Sylvain m. to Julie = Claire 3

Fifth son: Florent 18

Arnaud (Gontrand's brother) supports Pétain, m. to Huguette, supports de Gaulle = Matthieu, Jean-Jacques, live in Montauloup, family country home, in the Auvergne

Eugène (Gontrand's brother) m. to Berthe, support de Gaulle, live in Suresnes

Camille, Bérangère's sister, m. to police captain Hilaire Malleville = Christophe, live in Pontcharra, near Grenoble (Alps)

Lorraine (Gontrand's sister) m. to Jean-Luc Bourgmestre, print shop owners = Yolande 27, Hughes 15

Brigitte (close friend to the de Montregards) m. to Hubert Marchand = Damien 7, Estelle 5, Sylvestre 2, Christiane newborn

Charmaine (close friend to the de Montregards) m. to Alexandre Lebeau, photographic studio owners = Marianne 12, Baptiste 10

Gus, assistant to Charmaine and Alexandre

Maude Pleynet, Bérangère's best friend

Jacques Werner, commandant of the Paris gendarmerie, Gontrand's friend

Léonie Bodénan, Julie's close friend

Xavier Despins, escapee, becomes friend of the family

Madame Durand, Julie's concierge

General Reynard von Trennen, requisitions the Manoir. Aide-de-camp Captain Gerhardt Langen, + orderly Günter Klein, driver Karl Froeder + groom (no active role)

SS-Obersturmbannführer Kurt Meinhard, Julie's hated former suitor

Luftwaffe Oberleutnant Ernst Lohse, Yolande Bourgmestre's boss at the Ritz Hotel

Lars Gunnarsson, neutral Swede involved in smuggling Jewish children

Baron Dieter von Hauffen, Mireille's lover

Rose Sauter, son Helmut, German refugees, friends of the family

Pedro & Elissa Poveda, Spanish refugees in Montauloup

Dédé Dumonteil, m. to Gertrude = Francine, Lucette, Robert 15, farmers in the Auvergne

Claude Auzello, m. to Blanche, Director of the Ritz Hotel

Monsieur Biquette of Fromageries Biquette (cheese business) passeur on the demarcation line

Émile, aka Mimile, passeur to Switzerland

Chapter One

War destroys roads, railroads, houses and bridges. This is told in history books. War also destroys families. This is never mentioned.

Paris, Wednesday, April 10, 1940

"No, don't go!" Julie pounded her fists on her husband's uniformed chest.

Sylvain tightened his embrace. One hand traced her spine. "Let's not have a scene, ma chérie. I have to protect you and baby Claire."

"Then stay with us."

He clenched his jaw. His teeth ground audibly. "Be your usual rational self, *mon amour*. You know I have to go. It's my duty. I'm a soldier. I can best protect you by doing my bit to prevent the Huns from crossing our borders."

"You sound like one of those awful news readers on the wireless."

"My darling sweetheart, don't listen to the T.S.F." He rubbed his chin over her fragrant hair and closed his eyes to imprint the memory in his mind. "Women don't understand war."

"Oh, yes we do. I understand war. Men die. Women die. Children die."

Sylvain repressed a sigh. "I had a long leave while nothing happened during that phoney war. Well, *la drôle de guerre* is now over. Nothing I can do about that."

She released the breath she'd been holding. "I know. But what about our famous Maginot line?"

How could he tell his wife without scaring her half to death that when the Germans turned their attention to France, the Maginot line wouldn't be of much help. "Chérie, the Maginot Line isn't long enough."

"That's stupid."

"The French government wanted to respect Belgian neutrality. They didn't drive the line all the way to the North Sea. Don't worry, the mountainous Ardennes forest is a formidable obstacle."

"A forest! That wouldn't stop a boy scout troop, never mind a trained army, and nothing, least of all Belgian neutrality, is going to stop Hitler from threatening France, if I believe what I heard on the T.S.F. and some of the things you said."

Eyes half-closed, Sylvain let a wave of despair wash over him. Although he tried not to talk about the politics of war during his leave, he had done his best to explain some of it in reassuring terms. But his beloved wife grasped situations quickly, just in a different way. He admitted to himself that she was right and the generals wrong.

Because he made no reply, Julie asked, "Why do I get the feeling I'll never see you again?"

He shrugged. Soldiers are supposed to accept death. He did. Only, it wouldn't touch him because he had a loving wife and a beautiful three-year-old daughter to return to. "You'll see me again. I fully intend to come back."

Julie wound her arms around his neck and raised herself on tip-toe to reach his lips. A wildfire of need ran through him. His nerves began to slip. "If the front is breached and France is invaded, promise me you'll take Claire and go to your parents in New York."

"I married you for better or for worse. I'll wait for you here. Anyway, my father's contract finishes at the end of this academic year. So they'll be back."

Her stubbornness worried him, but he spoke quickly. "I think they have more sense than to return to a country in the middle of a war."

"Mother hates it in the States. She wants to be home. Now that dad is retired from the diplomatic service, they're going to settle back here."

Her slender form molded against him and created havoc with his self-control. Nobody mentioned this part of soldiering, when a woman got a man aroused with no time to deal with it. Unless... "I don't have to leave this very minute."

There was no need for words. A look, a heartbeat, that's all the habit of making love required. Seconds later they were lying on the Persian rug. Her fingers combed through his short brown hair with calculated slowness to remember his shape, his softness, all of him. She looked into his dark eyes. "I love you."

"I'll carry your love with me as my talisman. Keep my love in your heart."

"Always, I promise."

Gone was the usual banter after lovemaking. A seriousness stifled them both, as the war's grim reality insinuated itself between them.

"Papa?"

Her face framed by tousled blond curls, Claire stood thumb-in-mouth in the open doorway. Her other hand clutched her teddy bear. A wide grin illuminated her pixie face. Her blue eyes sparkled. She flung herself at her parents and snuggled between them.

Sylvain buried his face in the toddler's soft hair. The warmth of her tiny body penetrated his own, awaking in him an immense feeling of love and a fierce resolution to protect her. He wished more than anything that he could freeze this moment, full of ineffable tenderness, in the infinity of life. In silent haste, they readied themselves.

"Let's go."

"Don't go, papa."

"I have to, my little rose."

A giggle escaped her throat. "Sing it again, papa."

"*Mignone, allons voir si la rose est éclose.*"

The toddler's crystalline laugh filled the room. Throat constricted, Sylvain murmured the words of the song once more. Sweetie, let's go and see if the rose has flowered. It was the song he always sang when entering Claire's room to see if she was awake. And Claire always pretended to be asleep before laughing. He wondered if he'd really come back to sing it again.

"Maman says you're going to kill the bad people."

"Yes, my sweetie pie."

"All of them?"

"Sure."

"After that you come back?"

"Absolutely. You wait for me."

Words evaporated. After German troops had marched into Norway and Denmark, he received orders to rejoin his regiment. The previous day, all leave was cancelled. The Wehrmacht had unleashed its Blitzkrieg. The French army could only hope to stop them. He shook his head thinking of his company so poorly equipped.

In mute acceptance of his fate, and with Claire on one arm, Sylvain shouldered his pack. Strange how a soldier's belongings could fit in one modest canvas bag. Julie gathered up her purse and their gas masks. At the door, he turned his head for one last look at the love nest they had created in the comfortable nineteenth century apartment. The high ornate ceilings and plaster moldings must have witnessed countless departures. A man needed a few memories to make war more bearable.

Once on the sidewalk, he lifted his face and felt the light rain falling like tears. He took a deep breath. Since yesterday, he was consciously garnering scraps of his family life. He was filing them in a recess of his mind to be able to lean on them during the inevitable hard days that lay ahead, when fear and bloodshed would surely sap the morale.

With the knowledge born of deep love, Julie slipped her hand in his and together they set out to walk to the Métro, but at the end of the street where it joined the Avenue Henri-Martin, Julie hailed a slowly cruising taxi. The aging driver jumped out and held the door open. He stuffed the soldier's gear in the trunk and climbed back behind the wheel. He threw his cigarette out of the window. "Gare de l'Est, mon lieutenant?"

"Gare de l'Est, yes."

On this day there was only one destination for soldiers.

"I was in the First, you know. In the trenches at Douaumont."

Sylvain leaned forward. Douaumont, the fort that'd been crucial to Verdun's survival. "Then, you're one of the brave men that saved Verdun. I'm honored to meet you."

A silence fell as the cab negotiated the traffic. Claire filled the void with her birdlike chattering. At the magnificent station, the cab pulled up at the curb. The driver took the pack out of the trunk. Sylvain reached for his wallet.

The old man held up a hand. "*Non, mon lieutenant*, there's no charge for soldiers."

"Thanks, my good man."

"No, it's me who thank you. Go and beat the hell out of the Boches and send them packing."

Lieutenant de Montregard offered his hand, which the visibly moved driver shook. Inside the terminal, the crowd opened up and swallowed the young family. All around them rose the odd hum of thousands voices, cries smothered by propriety, tears and held-back emotions that pervaded the station concourse. Young women's anxious eyes searched the crowd for a boyfriend or a fiancé.

The identical mask of the sheer agony of waiting, of the unknown toward which young men would travel, was written on faces everywhere.

An attendant opened the gate to allow Sylvain, his wife and daughter onto the platform where a train was preparing to leave, its locomotive already belching smoke and steam. No need for tickets. On this day, the bottle-green uniform was the only pass required, its dark tones contrasting with the spring-like field of pastel print dresses. But no one took note of this bucolic image set against the drab gray concrete. They only saw a beloved man going away, perhaps forever.

The pungent smell of hot metal and superheated steam assailed the nostrils and enveloped the knots of waiting families. This characteristic odor would indelibly be seared into their collective memory. The odor of departure.

Soldiers held children in their arms. Wives clung to husbands. Adolescent boys stomped their feet, impatient to grow up and go to fight. Older women stood straight and dignified, holding back tears, tears they had shed when their husbands had left for the First. Fathers too old to fight, chewed their lips to prevent them from trembling. Those old men, haunted by the visceral images of the Great War, the war to end all wars, stared stubbornly at the faded green and brown train cars as though seeing so many gigantic caskets. And now, the same horrors they had endured twenty years ago were about to be visited on their sons.

"Well, it's over," a voice said.

The seven months of static war had ended. And along with it all hopes for peace. A faded bit of humor that had prevailed in September 1939 still showed on one car, *Paid holidays*.

Overhead, oblivious to the drama being enacted below, sleek swallows darted through the smoke-filled air in the hunt for pieces of fluff to build their nests. Sparrows chirped and foraged along the edge of the platform for crumbs thrown by children, before retreating to their perch high amid the station's canopy of delicate iron tracery. Magnified birds' trills resonated like the din of marching drums and fifes. The shrill shriek from the locomotive ripped through the peace, a painful reminder that war awaited.

On the platform, Sylvain and Julie met the family. He greeted his brother Bernard, a stretcher-bearer and ambulance driver. The young men's laughter lightened the atmosphere. Madeleine and her husband Philippe, in civilian clothes, stood slightly apart. Philippe was exempt from serving as he was the director of the family's factory and its essential work for the war effort. Gontrand de Montregard, the family patriarch, leaned more than usual on Bérangère, his wife of forty-two years, and threw a dark look toward his non-combatant son.

"Good God! The whole army was on leave!" An air of disgust settled on Gontrand's features. "Is there anyone left to fight?"

"Father, there has been no fighting until now. We just sat and waited. Soldiers who get bored get rowdy. Young men with nothing to do get into trouble. It was best to give leave to as many as possible," Bernard said.

Gontrand shook his gray head. "*Drôle de guerre.* In the First we fought all the time."

"Bernard is right. Nothing was happening during that phoney war because both sides waited for the order to fire. Neither wanted to be the first to shoot, for political reasons," Sylvain said.

"Politics, politicians! They should all be put in prison."

"This time it's for real, father," Sylvain said. What he didn't say was that this time there was blood and death at the end of the line.

Behind him, Bernard's wife, Marie-Ange, held her three-year-old niece Lyse-May by the hand. The little girl's father was no longer part of the family, and they didn't know whether he was in the army or not.

As if impatient to be off, their locomotive belched a jet of steam. Unlike the gray September of 1939, when the station resonated with defiant cries, now, in April 1940, a collective hush contained the fear and resignation of the soldiers recalled from leave.

Young children clung to their parents. Older children stood in forlorn knots. The warm spring air wafted through the station. Sylvain glanced around and saw the youngest of the de Montregard family in earnest conversation with a pretty girl. Eighteen-year-old Florent, too young to join in 1939 but now just a few months later old enough, had attracted girls since elementary school. Sylvain smiled at the tender scene. A smile. That was what was expected from the soldiers. Look happy and enthusiastic about the imminent slaughter.

Madame Maude Pleynet, Bérangère de Montregard's closest friend and Bernard's godmother, came to stand beside Hubert Marchand, tall and proud in his blue air force uniform. He was on leave on compassionate grounds for the birth of his fourth child. Eager to rejoin his squadron, he had refused the exemption granted to fathers of large families.

"My heart weeps," Madame Pleynet said to him, "for little Lyse-May. She looks utterly lost. Isn't it dreadful to be kidnapped by her own father?" A quick thrust of her chin in the direction of the little girl holding Marie-Ange's hand directed Hubert's look.

Bernard and Sylvain approached their best friend. "He didn't kidnap her, Maude. When he brought her to the Manoir, he said his wife couldn't take care of her." Bernard made a circular motion to his temple with his index finger. "You know... gone in the head."

"Don't believe what he says. It was kidnapping," Maude said.

"She went crazy," Bernard said.

"That's what your brother said. So who knows? We weren't there. Rodolphe abandoned her for a whore, then took the child away in the middle of the night. He knew his wife wouldn't be allowed to cross the Spanish border."

"Speculation, dear auntie, speculation. There's much we don't know," Sylvain said.

Maude frowned. "Lyse-May is a smart child, far too advanced for a three-year-old. She told me it was night and how she had to hide behind the suitcases in the train and pretend to be asleep so no one would know she was there."

"He should never have gone to Spain in the first place. Then get embroiled in that civil war which had nothing to do with him," Bernard said.

Maude pinched her lips. "Rodolphe is one slippery character. Your mother tried hard to dissuade him from going in the first place." She added, "Before their war."

"And now father has thrown him out. In the meantime, my brother dumped his little girl on the family to be looked after," Bernard said.

Sylvain nodded. "Maybe having to fight for France will calm him down and he'll come back more rational."

"How do you know he's in the French army? He was such an admirer of Hitler and his policies when that dictator came to power. You can guess what camp he's going to choose." Maude just about spat on the ground.

The three men exclaimed NO in unison. With haste, Bernard diverted the conversation. "Lyse-May is a sweet girl. She loves little Claire."

Maude shrugged. "Much too quiet. Much too intelligent. Who's going to look after her?"

"She's been with mother and father, but taking care of a young child might be too much work. Mother has to contend with father's explosive moods. Maybe Julie could take over. Wouldn't be too difficult to add a bed in Claire's room," Sylvain said.

Bernard brushed an invisible speck from his uniform. "Marie-Ange would love to take care of her, but Paul and Micheline are already sharing a room. We were planning on getting a bigger apartment but this rotten war came along."

Bérangère stepped into the little group. "Lyse-May will stay with us. Gontrand loves having her around and when she is there, he doesn't get into arguments with Philippe over his exemption from the military."

"But it's nothing like being with her mother," Maude said. "I'll never understand why men always need to kill each other."

Unable to comment on such statement, Bernard hugged the friend they all called Auntie Maude. The family group fluctuated, dissolved and reformed to encompass other family members. Young Florent struck a martial pose and read aloud from a poster attached to one of the station's supporting pillars. "We will conquer because we are the strongest." A collective groan answered him. "Come'n, we're going to kick the Boches in the *cul*."

"Spoken like a true Frenchman," Gontrand said. "Kick them in the ass."

Sylvain shook his head. "When I think of all the diplomatic mumbo jumbo we went through to create a rapprochement with Germany. Now look at the bloody mess."

Sixteen-year-old François waved a hand in the air. "And I even went with Les Petits Chanteurs à La Croix de Bois to sing in Germany."

Philippe hugged his lanky son. "Boys' choirs singing together was great, but that was three years ago. Much has changed since then."

The patriarch bent his head. "Singing together. For all the good it did."

"I made a friend in Frankfurt, Wilhelm Fischer. We used to write to each other, but he can't anymore. He had to join the Hitlerjugend. He doesn't want the war. I don't either, but since Hitler has taken Austria and Poland and is trying to take others, we may as well go and sort the bastard out. Time to finish with the *Shitzkrieg*."

A shocked silence greeted his words. "The what?"

Surprised by the reaction, François continued, "I meant Sitzkrieg. The sitdown war. That's what they call the phoney war on the other side. I wish I was big enough to go and get them."

His grandfather stiffened with pride. "Amen. Hear, my sons. Out of the mouth of babes comes wisdom. The only thing you can do with barbarians is to crush them."

Bernard and Sylvain spoke together. "That's just what we're going to do."

The women exchanged glances, sad faces, heads tilted. Brigitte Marchand held her newborn in a sling against her chest.

"Here comes tante Charmaine!" François exclaimed.

With her two children in tow, an elegant, gorgeous brunette, breathing hard, joined the family. "Sorry, I'm so late. The Métro was packed. We had to wait a couple of trains. But I wanted to send off our men. Bernard, if you meet Alexandre, tell him I'm waiting for him."

Bernard hugged his best friend's wife. "I hope I don't meet him."

"Of course, how silly of me. You only deal with the wounded."

A brief silence while everyone mentally added, yes, and the dead.

"If only our government could get its act together! But no, it's dispute here, jealousy there, push and shove for power, bring down the government and get another one, and start everything over." François' sister Pierrette spoke for the first time to break the uncomfortable silence. Not as tall as most of her classmates, she often seethed about being treated like a child.

"What does an eighteen-year-old know about politics, hein?" Gontrand asked.

"I'm going to university in the fall to study political science."

Philippe sighed. "You're growing up too fast, ma fille. Daughters shouldn't get involved in politics."

At that moment a song burst from the rear of the train.

"Monte là-d'sus et tu verras Montmartre."

Bérangère turned to listen. "And what will that achieve, I ask you, to climb on whatever it is to see Montmartre?"

They laughed at the woman's logic.

Sylvain detected anger in his mother's tone. "Mother, it's only a song."

"You're right. People need to sing silly things to get over the wait... the uncertainty. What was it the English were singing?"

"*We'll hang our washing on the Siegfried Line.*"

Bérangère grimaced. "Providing Fritz doesn't walk over first to hang his on our Maginot Line."

Somewhere a voice rose, Allons enfants de la patrie... another joined in the national anthem. Moments later, the Marseillaise, picked up by a hundred throats, echoed throughout the whole station. A strident whistle punctuated the last word. A babble of voices resumed, now more subdued. Stifled sobs colored the forced gaiety of the soldiers' last farewells. The men did their utmost to conceal the true cost of boarding the train that would carry them to an almost certain death. Equally stoic, the women wanted husbands, brothers, sons to take with them the memory of tranquil and proud womenfolk.

Forgotten the Paris Fair, the huge international event with its eight thousands exhibitors. Forgotten the only life they knew. What they knew was that the departing train was about to change all that.

One final frantic kiss and those soldiers still on the platform leapt aboard the train. Steam billowed all around. The locomotive jolted. The train cars shuddered. Steel wheels grated against steel rails. With one turn after another turn of the wheels, faster and faster, the train irrevocably ferried its human cargo toward its destiny. A sea of white handkerchiefs unfolded, then fell limp as the train vanished from view, leaving empty rails stretching to infinity. Only the old men, the women and the children, eyes still fixed on a horizon they couldn't see, remained on the silent platform.

Tears make no noise.

Tall and with a regal bearing, Bérangère straightened even more. "Let's all go home. I got Marie to prepare lunch."

Maude Pleynet hugged her friend and turned to Julie, who had no car. "I'll drive you and Claire. Charmaine, want to squeeze in as well into the Berlingot?"

A burst of forced laughter greeted her words. The red and white hard candy was the nickname of her equally white and red Peugeot 202 sedan, and gave rise to much teasing. Being outrageous came naturally to Maude, a widow of the First War and a very independent woman.

"Thanks. I don't fancy another trip in the Métro."

"If you don't mind taking Claire with you, I'm going to see some of those refugees from the Netherlands and Belgium and interview them for my magazine," Julie said.

Cane in hand, Gontrand motioned the children to climb into his Mathis automobile. François grabbed toddler Sylvestre who was about to go and explore the tracks. Marie-Ange and Charmaine went with Maude in the Berlingot. Philippe and Madeleine ordered their reluctant adolescents, who were trying to squeeze in with their grandparents, into their Citroën Rosalie coupé.

A scared Madeleine, her incredibly beautiful face creased with worry, tugged on Julie's sleeve. "You'll ask the refugees if it's true they rape women and cut off little boys' right arms?"

"I don't know where those rumors come from. I don't think there's anything to them."

"But you'll ask?"

"Yes, Madeleine. I'll ask."

Bérangère had been listening. "I'll tell you where it comes from. It was in 1914. The people of the northern areas fled because the soldiers were raping women and girls. They were burning whole villages and putting women and children in front of advancing infantry units."

"I thought they were all in trenches," Julie said.

"When the trench was overtaken, they advanced in the open, until the next fortifications."

Julie glanced toward Madeleine fitting herself into the car. "So they'll do the same here, you think?"

Bérangère sighed. "I don't know. I don't know. How does anyone know? War is the ugliest thing that men inflict on each other. Why? Why can't governments get together to discuss things rationally?" She hurried toward her husband.

Notepad and pencil in hand, Julie pushed her way out through the crowd.

Slowly the cars made their way between buildings protected by sandbags. They stopped to let pass an assortment of miserably wet people, shoulders hunched against the rain, heading south with bicycles, carts and oxen.

"Same as in 1914," Bérangère said. "People from the north fleeing south to safety."

Chapter Two

The mansion, known in the district as Le Manoir, resonated with children's laughter and cries. François escaped to the music room at the end of the ballroom and carefully opened the case of the Guarneri violin. A smile spread over his boyish features. The warmth of the wood sent tremors throughout his body. He fine-tuned the instrument and drew the bow across the strings, oblivious to the hubbub in the great hall. The pure notes sang and took flight, reached the dining room and the kitchen, snuffing out the voices. In the kitchen, Marie Latour, head maid and cook, placed a finger on her lips but it was not needed. The young children listened, agape, to the heart-wrenching melody.

The last note echoed in the silence. François returned the violin to its case. Forks and spoons clattered, glasses clinked, young and old voices mixed in an indistinct wave of sound. He went to his place at the dining room table.

"That was beautiful, François," Charmaine said. "I didn't recognize the piece."

François shrugged. "I just played... It's nobody's music. It's the war. It's my uncles gone away to fight."

"Your improvisation was exceptionally good."

"With this war, will I still be able to go to the Conservatory in October?"

Philippe put down his glass. "I don't see why not." A sigh of relief shook François' chest, just as his older sister Mireille made a grand entrance.

"Sorry I'm late. Classes at the Sorbonne were disrupted. Some profs have been called up."

"They'll have to get profs out of retirement to come and teach, I suppose," Bérangère said.

Marie brought in dessert. "It's a bread pudding. I didn't think we should waste the stale bread."

"But the children feed it to the ducks." Pierrette spoke with caution. Food was being discussed by everybody. People feared there may be shortages. Already the restaurants were operating three days a week without meat, three days without pastries and three days without alcohol.

"I saved some crumbs for the little ones. They don't need much."

As it was Gontrand's habit, they adjourned to his study to listen to the wireless. The news was optimistic.

"If it is going so well, why are they telling people to evacuate?" Brigitte asked. She and Charmaine had been part of the family since they were little girls.

"So that civilians are not in the way of the army," Gontrand replied.

Pierrette curled her lips in the thoughtful way she had recently adopted. "It's the Blitzkrieg. Warsaw fell and it was horrible. Paris is next."

A wave of protests drowned her words. Gontrand's voice dominated the tumult. "The army will hold them back."

"Did you see the posters? Be careful. The Fifth Column is listening," Mireille said.

Bérangère came back to her seat. She'd been looking out of the window. "Some neighbors are already packing up."

"The city workers are blocking the Champs-Élysées and the Avenue of the Grande Armée to prevent planes from landing," Mireille announced.

"Enough defeatist talk. The Boches won't cross into France. The army will stop them long before that." Gontrand's bellow silenced the family.

Madeleine tugged on her husband's sleeve. "Time to go, Philippe."

One after the other, they took their leave.

Chapter Three

Paris, Friday, May 10, 1940

At the Manoir, Julie and Brigitte drew closer to the wireless to hear the news. Gontrand's roar filled the room. "The Ardennes! THE ARDENNES! The putain de Boches came through the Ardennes! Goddamned Boche!"

"The generals didn't think to put defenses there, the dummies," Julie said.

"The Germans can't have come through. It's impassable," Brigitte said.

Julie rolled her eyes. "Obviously not."

Bérangère shrugged. "Then, they're coming straight for Paris. I think the children should go to safety in Montauloup."

Gontrand gave a dismissive wave of his hand. "THE ARMY WILL HOLD THEM BACK! Like we did in '14!"

The women stopped talking and waited for Gontrand to calm down. Lyse-May came in and took his hand. Gontrand stopped in mid-sentence, picked up the child and sat down. The impersonal voice on wireless announced that the Franco-British armies were garnering military successes in Belgium. With an incredulous shrug, Gontrand reached to the set to switch stations. "I'll put it on Radio Luxemburg. It's better."

"Don't bother. It's been closed since the first few days of the war," Bérangère said.

Gontrand grumbled loudly. "Stupid generals. If we are in Belgium the Chleus will cut us off."

A hand on his shoulder, Bérangère spoke quietly. "We'll hear more tomorrow."

Julie stood up. "Brigitte, I'll help you take your children home."

Claire bounded to take Sylvestre's hand. The two-year-old leapt up and down. Seven-year-old Damien and Estelle, two years younger, ran ahead. Brigitte cradled her newborn in the sling. The little family stepped out into the balmy spring air and walked down the street to Brigitte's apartment.

"How are you getting home?"

"Claire and I will walk. It's not far at all."

"Ah, yes. Too bad she'd love to take the bus."

"She would indeed and chat up the ticket-collector." The two women laughed. "Usually they let her crank the handle to print the date on the ticket. But there are hardly any buses left in service. They've been requisitioned to transport more troops to the front."

Brigitte pursed her lips. "What do you really think about the German army going into neutral countries like Belgium and Luxemburg?"

"It doesn't look good, but it became clear what they were doing when they marched into neutral Denmark and Norway."

"Gontrand said the French army will hold and push back the Germans."

"I don't know, Brigitte. I don't know. Sylvain didn't want to talk about it, but he let out that the Germans have tanks."

"So we do, don't we?"

"That's what I asked him. He evaded the question. I think maybe we don't have enough. The politicians were too busy squabbling among themselves to pay attention to preparations for war."

Brigitte sighed. "Ah, men and their need to fight! Women ought to to take over and govern the world."

"You're right."

"Did you tell scary-poop Madeleine that the German soldiers don't rape and mutilate?"

"I did, the silly girl. I don't know what Philippe sees in her."

"She's stunningly beautiful, you have to admit. I'm envious of her so tiny waist when I look at mine."

"You've just had a baby. Give it time."

"I'll never be as slim as she is. Anyway, Philippe adores her."

"Which is good, and he protects her."

"She tends to be on the naïve side. But with a heart of gold."

"True." Julie sighed. "None of the refugees I talked to reported misbehavior on the part of the enemy soldiers. But it's well-known that rape and armies on the march go together. Right now they're too busy hurrying to Paris."

"Maybe they're quite civilized."

"The German people are. Look at all the music and literature Germany has produced, and that's only talking about the arts. All right, we're here." Julie hugged Brigitte and ushered the children inside. She took Claire's hand and turned in the direction of home.

Chapter Four

Paris, Sunday, May 13, 1940

Claire, pretty in a pink dress hemmed with a lace flounce, ran up to her cousin Sylvestre. The little boy looked smart in his suit and false bowtie. They'd arrived on the square in front of Église Saint-Honoré-d'Eylau. The light rain freshen the air. Claire's lace bonnet slid sideways. Julie straightened it.

"Steady, ma chérie. Sylvestre is only two. You don't want to knock him over." Marianne approached, equally elegant in a pale green pleated skirt and jacket, impeccably white knee socks and black patent leather shoes, "I'll stay with them, Auntie Julie, with my umbrella."

"Thanks. You look all grown up today."

"Well, I'm twelve now. Maman's busy with taking the photos."

"Yes, Charmaine's as good as your father."

"She's been running the photographic studio by herself since the war started."

A car came to a halt nearby and backfired, much to the general merriment. Maude, tall and slim, jumped out of her Berlingot, and Camille Malleville extricated herself from the passenger side while trying to open an umbrella. They both started talking at the same time.

"Traffic by the train station is horrendous with all the refugees. I thought I'd never spot Camille."

As tall and with as many dark curls as her sister, Camille kissed Bérangère, then had to do the rounds. "Phew, what a trip! I should have taken the car. People all over. I thought taking the train from Grenoble would be easier than driving, since we were told there are thousands of refugees on the roads. You'd think the trains going north would be empty, but they are full of panicky people."

"That bad?" Brigitte asked. She smoothed Christiane's christening gown that had been worn by every child of the family for three generations or more.

"Yes, and it's getting worse from what we saw at the railroad station."

"Now we're all here, let's go in. Monsieur le curé must be waiting to start the mass and the christening," Bérangère said.

The church was packed. The de Montregard family walked up to the front where a couple of pews had been reserved for them. The organist released a cascade of notes. The harmony swelled and flowed above the bowed heads, rushed around the pillars to return slight and spent under the magic of his hands. The priest was pronouncing the last words welcoming the infant into the kingdom of God when the air-raid sirens sounded their sharp, bone-chilling warning. Confused movement took place in the nave, but nobody left their seat. The priest turned back to the altar. The organist sent a storm of defiant music up to the roof timbers and down to the end pew.

The priest turned back to face the congregation. "*Ite missa est.*" He blessed the assembly.

With a hurried slowness, the attendees made their way to the door. An air of anxiety floated over the heads of women and a few older men. Serious faces looked at each other but didn't stop for the customary chat in the church square. A warden of the civil defence was urging the churchgoers to hurry to the shelter. Most obeyed.

Julie handed her umbrella to Bérangère. "Claire, chérie, go with mémée. I have to go to work."

"You're going to do your questions?"

"That's right, darling, I'm going to interview people."

"Bye."

The all-clear sounded. The rain eased somewhat. Pierrette and her brother François and their cousin Hughes, who had worn their guide and scout uniforms to church, waved goodbye.

"You're off to the refugee center?"

"Yes, Auntie Julie."

"Wait for me. I'm going too." Julie retrieved her notepad and pencils from Gontrand's Mathis car, and joined the adolescents. They made their way to the Métro. The rest of de Montregard family piled into their cars and went home to the Manoir.

Marie had prepared lunch. The nanny service had arrived. Two young women in blue uniforms greeted the children. They all climbed onto seats in the kitchen under the watchful eyes of the nannies and Marie, who began serving them. Marie-Ange and Madeleine carried the food to the dining room for the adults.

"Marie is a gem to cook such lovely dishes, considering the restrictions." Brigitte held out a bag of dragées. "Who managed to get these?"

Laughter met her words. "No christening without dragées. There are still a few available in the confiseries," Bérangère said.

"What will the candy stores do when they ration sugar?" Madeleine asked.

"They won't," Gontrand said. "The war will be finished in a few weeks.

A collective groan was the only answer.

"What? You don't believe me? Why do you think the government brought Maréchal Pétain out of retirement? Hein?"

"He wasn't exactly retired. He was ambassador to Spain," Bérangère said.

"There was nothing to do there. I tell you, he came back to sort out the Boche and put everything in order." Gontrand poured wine in their glasses. "Let's toast the victor of Verdun. Our soldiers will soon be home and that little upstart Hitler will run back to Berlin with his tail between his legs."

Before anyone could reply, the front door opened. François and his sister came in. They carefully inserted their wet shoes under the strap of the patins and glided across the hall, avoiding the children sprawled in various games under the nannies and Marianne's motherly supervision. François was having some trouble keeping his feet straight. "Damn felt pads!"

"Don't let anyone hear you swear. Just keep polishing the floor."

"Ah, that's why we have to use them. I thought it was to protect the floor."

"Shut up. Let's see if they saved us any food."

They pushed opened the glass door to the dining room. The adults were about to withdraw to the salon for coffee. "Come and sit. Food's coming."

Madeleine was already rushing to fetch food for her two adolescents. The others sat again.

"How was it?" Bérangère asked.

Pierrette straightened her navy-blue girl guide uniform before sitting. "It's pretty horrendous. People are arriving from all over the place, east, north and even from the Eure department."

"Sure, I was giving out sandwiches to people who said they'd walked from Évreux," François said. "I mean, that's only west of Paris, not near the battle zone. But they want to get on a train to the south and it was easier to come here than try from Évreux."

"My troop was assigned to making up beds, well not beds, but mats and blankets in the school préau. Poor people! Imagine, they have to make do under the covered playground and sleep on the cement floor with just a blanket or two. There weren't enough cots. Anyway, the assembly room was too small so we gave the cots to the pregnant women and mothers with babies."

François stuffed a piece of bread into his mouth and chewed quickly. "They're so dirty and wet and tired. Do you think we're going to have to go too?"

"Absolutely not!" his father said. "Paris is safe."

"We can't be so sure, Philippe," Bérangère said. "You heard the news. The German army is advancing fast."

"Blitzkrieg." François said.

Pierrette elbowed him. "Show off!"

"Well, that's what it means. Fast war."

"Not so fast, my boy. Our army is standing in their way. They'll be stopped." Gontrand punctuated his words by slamming his fist on the table.

"Like in the Ardennes?" Bérangère's sarcastic tone hushed the voices around the table.

Julie's arrival relieved the tension.

"Do you have enough information for your articles?" Maude asked.

"More than enough."

Marie brought a plate of food for Julie.

"What did you learn from the people you interviewed?" Brigitte asked.

"That the situation is grim. Some Parisians are already packing and trying to get on the trains."

"I wonder how I'll get back to Grenoble," Camille said.

"You can stay here, sister dear," Bérangère said.

"All right for a few days, but Hilaire is alone at home and you know how helpless he is. Hopefully he won't burn down the house trying to cook. He really wanted to come but being the *commissaire de gendarmerie,* he had to stay and work."

Julie smiled at her. "That's what happens to gendarmes when they're captains. They never get a holiday."

Gontrand was about to speak when the nearby air-raid siren wailed. They looked at one another. "Do we have to go down to the cellar?"

Brigitte ran out to grab baby Christiane. The nannies and Marie's husband Ernest, who carried Sylvestre, shepherded the children to the safety of the cellar under the turret.

"We should, too," Gontrand said.

Charmaine shrugged. "Nothing ever happens."

They sighed and got to their feet. In the basement, the children laughed as they bounced on the mattresses that Ernest and Marie Latour had installed around the first room of the large cellar... just in case. François inspected the space. He pointed to an arch. "Where does that lead to?"

"You don't need to know," Philippe said.

"Com'n, father. I'm not a child. So let me guess. The wine cellar?"

"Smarty pants!"

"And beyond, there's a passage into the old Parisian quarries," Pierrette whispered.

"How do you know?"

She threw a look around but no one was paying attention. Their father had joined the others seated on old chairs brought down from the attic.

"I sneaked in after I heard grand-papa talk about it a long time ago. This area is built on limestone, fairly chalky, and the builders just dug the stones from underground where it is best. That left vast quarries. Gontrand–"

"Don't call our grandfather Gontrand. It isn't polite."

"Who's talking, brother! I'm only talking about him, not addressing him. Anyway, he said the passage has been blocked up but that it would be easy to knock it down. You can travel a long way through those underground quarries."

"Great! Shall we go sometimes and open up the passage?"

"Better wait till the war is over."

"Chicken."

The all-clear sounded. The family returned to the larger salon. Soon, Marie brought coffee and green Chartreuse liqueur for the men in the sitting-room.

"I think we should send the children to Montauloup," Bérangère said.

François groaned. "There's nothing to do in that gloomy old château."

Philippe called his son to order.

Maude poked the youth in the ribs. "Better safe in an old castle than sorry."

"The fighting is getting close," Camille said.

"For sure, the Krauts will never get to Montauloup. It's so remote," Marie-Ange said.

Camille put her cup down. "Or we could take them to the chalet in Saint-Pierre-de-Chartreuse. It's so high in the Alps it'll be safe."

"There's no need to disrupt everything. The war won't last and the *putains de Boches* won't come marching anywhere near here." Gontrand's voice boomed across the room.

Mireille who had inherited her mother's good looks, and had been engrossed in a book ever since she'd finished her meal, jumped to her feet. "Oh, grand-papa, you scared me."

"Wait till the Germans roll in here to be scared." François' sarcastic tone made her shrug.

"Maybe the Germans will win," Philippe said. "And if they do get here, it might be a good thing for us."

With a roar, Gontrand was out of his chair. He grabbed his son by the collar and dragged him to the entrance, threw him out and slammed the door. Stunned, everyone, including the children in the hall, stopped talking. The nannies started a song and soon the brouhaha resumed. Bérangère heard the front door swoosh open and waited.

A sheepish Philippe sneaked back in. "Sorry, father, I spoke out of turn."

Gontrand grumbled something inaudible.

Philippe took a big breath. "It all came out wrong. That joke of a government we have is in total disarray. There are not enough guns, not even a rifle for every soldier."

Uninhibited, François spoke up. "That's what Uncle Sylvain said too."

The patriarch's voice rumbled. "But it's all going to change because Maréchal Pétain is the government now."

Gontrand's nephew, fifteen-year-old Hughes Bourgmestre, couldn't take his eyes full of admiration off his cousin François. His mother Lorraine, Gontrand's sister, unfolded her height to stand up.

"The christening was marvelous, and we had a nice day all together, but I have to prepare some printing for tomorrow. Business doesn't stop just because of a war. I've got to keep it going."

"I'll keep helping, maman. I think they're going to close the schools and the *lycées*, anyway."

Lorraine turned to her ever-silent daughter. "Yolande, are there any rumors floating around the Ritz Hotel?"

"Rumors and gossip are rife and totally without substance. Gabrielle Chanel is still there, and so is Prince Otto de Hasbourg. I don't think Coco Chanel is even aware there is a war going on. I must leave too. I start work early tomorrow. I have to supervise some new chambermaids. I'll take the Métro."

Bérangère turned to her sister-in-law. "If we decide to go to

Montauloup or Saint-¬Pierre-de-Chartreuse, will you come?"

"No. No matter what, I have to keep the printing business going."

"But Hughes can come with us." Madeleine said.

"Thanks, Auntie Madeleine, but I'll stay to help maman."

"Fine. Anyway, you ought to stock upon non-perishable goods, in case we get more alerts," Bérangère said.

Gontrand took his pipe out of his mouth. "The government warned everyone not to stockpile."

Philippe twirled a cigarette that he wasn't allowed to smoke in the house, though he badly wanted to. "Mother is right. If the alert lasts a long time, you sure would prefer to have food and wine in the cellar, non?"

With a commanding gesture of the hand, Gontrand lunged toward the wireless which had been on low in the background, and turned up the volume.

"...Sedan. We repeat, the front has been breached in the area of Sedan. Our valiant troops have fallen back to regroup. I repeat. The German army has captured Sedan." A collective wail rose from tight chests and died in a deathly stillness.

Maude broke the stunned silence. "Stupid generals, they think nothing has changed since the First, They had plenty of warning. That's what we have *intelligence* for, but they didn't listen."

Head lowered, Gontrand walked out without a word. This was the signal for everyone to collect their offspring and set off toward their homes, with worried looks on their faces.

Chapter Five

Julie helped a bubbly Claire dress. "Put your sweater on. It's cold today." She fixed a barrette and a blue ribbon in the girl's blond curls. "I have to go to work, ma chérie. Let's go to mémée. You can play with Lyse-May."

"Why I don't go with you?"

"Because I'm interviewing people at the refugee center this morning. It's very crowded and not very nice. But I'll come for you when I'm ready to hand in yesterday's article."

"Can I type on your machine?"

Julie kissed her daughter's nose. "Later."

Claire ran to the door and chattered all the way down the stairs. She paused on the ground floor to greet Madame Durand, the concierge who broom in hand, was about to clean the lobby.

At the Manoir, Claire kicked off her shoes and put on the slippers her mother had brought. Impatient, Lyse-May stood by. Then the two little girls scampered to the ballroom, their carefree laughter resonating happily. Julie went to the salon to greet her in-laws.

A frowning Gontrand dispensed with the greetings. "Did you hear? Did you hear! Belgium has surrendered!"

"*Oh, mon Dieu!*"

"Yes, I see you understand. Can you guess what will happen to the army now?"

Julie hesitated. "Are they going to be trapped on the border?"

"Not bad reasoning, for a woman... Hang on, more news." Gontrand turned up the volume on the wireless.

They listened in silence. Marie and her husband had come to the door. At the end of the report, Gontrand in a somber mood turned the dial until he got an English station. The news there was no better. He turned down the volume.

Julie looked at Gontrand. "The British Expeditionary Force and the French army are retreating to the coast, but do they have enough ships to get away?"

Gontrand kept shaking his head. "They're trying to get to Dunkirk. It's the only port to evacuate a whole army. The Germans have already taken thousands of prisoners. They're bombing the area. *Nom de Dieu!* What a bloody carnage! Good God, what a waste!"

"*On est foutu,*" Ernest said quietly.

"No, we are not finished." Bérangère straightened with a resolute air.

Gontrand looked at her and sighed. "Right. It's only a setback."

***

In the middle of the crush of panicked refugees, Julie had her notepad knocked from her hand. She made no attempt to find it. The refugees, too, had heard the news and found a sudden energy to set out on the road south.

Since no one was in any mood to talk to her, she walked home. She'd write her article about the mad rush of people toward the train station. There was no point in trying to take the Métro or find a bus, even less a taxi.

The sun had decided to heat the asphalt and she soon began sweating, but she didn't slow down. When she reached her apartment, she drank a big glass of water. In the coolness of the ancient stone building, she began to relax. It didn't take her long to type her article on her trusty Royal typewriter. Then she went to collect Claire. Gontrand insisted she take the Mathis car.

"Thanks, I wasn't looking forward to dragging Claire through the Métro."

"You can leave her here, you know. She's having a great time with Lyse-May."

"I heard the piano when I came in."

They laughed. The two little girls bounded into the petit salon. "Can we go with you?" More laughter.

"I guess it's been decided," Bérangère said.

At the wheel, a strange anguish gripped Julie. She listened to the animated chatter from the back seat and was thankful that the children were unaware of the war. But for how long would that blissful state last?

At the office of the *Pour Elles* magazine, Julie guided the girls to the second floor and the editorial department. The room was empty except for the editor-in-chief talking to Violette Leduc, another writer.

"Ah, Julie. Always punctual. But as you see, everybody's left. I don't know when we can next publish. Since you and Violette are here, I'll give you the money you're owed for this month. The accountant was kind enough to give me the combination of the safe."

Rendered ill at ease by the emptiness of the office, the two little girls stood clutching Julie's skirt.

"When do you think the staff will come back?" Violette Leduc asked.

"When the war is over. And considering the way it's going now, it might not be long before the Germans get here. So, girls, I appreciate your good work. Let's divide the funds in three parts. At least the Germans won't get it."

"You really believe the war is lost and the Germans will invade all of France?" Julie asked in disbelief.

"Look at what they've done so far. Everything folds in front of them. I don't know whether we'll have a magazine or even if we're going to be alive. Maybe with that money we can get away to the Americas."

Deeply troubled, Julie and Violette thanked their editor and left.

Chapter Six

Paris, Monday, June 3, 1940

Julie awoke to the air-raid siren that shattered the stillness of the night with its imperative wail. She threw aside the tangled sheet and groped for the light switch. Still numbed with sleep, her survival instinct kicked in. She swung her legs out of bed and pulled on a dress and woolen jacket over her nightclothes. It took mere seconds to bundle the still-sleeping Claire in her duvet and hoist her into her arms. On her way to the door, Julie snatched up her emergency bag and the ever-present gas masks. She took the stairs as fast as her precious burden allowed.

As she crossed the lobby, she heard the angry roar of the ack-ack guns opening up. From far away came the sickening thud of an explosion. Claire opened her eyes. "What's that, maman?"

"A bomb, chérie, but don't worry. We're safe here."

Madame Durand, who was also the shelter warden, stood at the top of the basement stairs, one hand holding open the door.

"Hurry up, now! You're the last one." The woman took Julie's bag and the gas masks, slammed the door shut behind them and hurried down the dimly lit stairs to where the other tenants stood huddled together, their faces etched with anxiety. "Phew, that was close!" Madame Durand said.

Wood and chain-link partitions formed storage areas at the far end of the basement to house the belongings the tenants didn't have room for in their apartments. Right from the start of the war, the tenants had been advised to prepare chairs, beds or mattresses and keep a supply of water and canned food on hand in cellars designated as shelters.

Léonie Bodénan saw Julie looking at the clutter of nondescript objects, along with civil defence paraphernalia, which lined one wall.

"Watch out for those shovels. They almost chopped my foot off when I knocked them over."

The woman resumed her conversation with Madame Bloch, the fourth-floor neighbor. Julie made Claire as comfortable as possible on a makeshift bed in their allotted storage area. In no time the child fell back to sleep, and Julie rejoined the group of women. For her, sleep was out of the question. "Is it going to last long, do you think?" Marguerite Bloch asked.

Madame Durand pulled a face. "I wouldn't know. What about you, madame Julie? What's your opinion?"

"Frankly, I don't know, either. The last news stated that the Germans had reached Amiens."

"On the River Somme. Surely, we'll stop them there, like we did in '14, non?"

"I hope so, with all my heart."

Another explosion interrupted the conversation. After a moment, Marguerite lowered her head. "Simon and I talked of leaving. Our daughter is in Nice with our grandson. She won't come back here. We only stayed because we thought the army would push the Germans back, but it doesn't look like that's happening."

"It isn't over, yet, madame," Léonie Bodénan said. "You must believe in the strength and valor of the French army."

"Oh, I do, but we're Jews."

"That doesn't matter. You're French."

Marguerite Bloch sighed. "Simon's great-grandfather came to France from Prussia. Simon, and his father fought for France during the Great War. That doesn't change us being Jews, even if we don't practice. You know what they're doing to the Jews in Germany..."

Julie nodded. "The Nazis are intolerant. They imprison Jews, gypsies, intellectuals and homosexuals."

The women gave a furtive look at the other tenants. Things of a sexual nature were not discussed openly, especially not by women. Fortunately, no one was paying them any attention. Just then, to everyone's relief, the all-clear siren sounded.

"I wonder where those bombs fell," Madame Durand said. "I'll go and find the block leader. He'll know."

***

In the morning, Julie and Claire greeted the concierge who was already outside sweeping the sidewalk, as if nothing untoward had taken place. Madame Durand smiled at the little girl. "Good morning, ducky. Had a good sleep?"

Claire bounced from one foot to the other. "I sleep good."

"Fortunately, she sleeps like a log. I heard on the news that some houses right here in the 16th arrondissement were hit and that the suburbs got it bad."

"According to the block leader, the 16th district to the south of us got serious damage. The factories in Boulogne-Billancourt got bombed. The planes were probably trying to hit the munitions depot in Puteaux. A bit too close for my liking. Are you going to view the damage?"

Julie shook her head. "I'm on my way to visit my father-in-law."

"Ah, oui, he has a factory in Suresnes."

"I'm worried. Suresnes also got bombed."

"What a mess!"

Claire scampered ahead of her mother, singing a counting-out rhyme. They arrived at the Manoir in the middle of a commotion. Berthe and Eugène, Gontrand's brother, were doing their best to calm a somewhat hysterical Madeleine. François and Pierrette were bringing suitcases from the Citroën Rosalie and dumping them into the great hall.

Julie looked at them and back to her niece and nephew. "What's going on?"

"Father asked Uncle Eugène to drive us here while he's inspecting the factory," François said. "It got bombed last night,"

"Maman doesn't want to stay in the house. She was so scared during the raid," Pierrette said. "She was frightened a bomb was going fall right on her head."

"How about you? Were you scared?"

Pierrette pulled a face. "Sure, it was pretty scary."

Julie smiled at her. Adolescents would never admit their fear. She sent Claire and Lyse-May to play in the ballroom and went to talk to Bérangère. "Is it badly damaged... the factory?"

Bérangère raised her arms in a gesture of despair. "Philippe phoned to say that the Citroën auto factories on Quai Javel and the Renault auto plant in Boulogne-Billancourt were hit first. Then it was our turn. He just said it's bad and that the fire crews were still on the scene The town hall also got damaged. There are some casualties. We'll hear the details later."

Berthe joined the conversation. "Bombs fell on the rail yards. Our house shook like a leaf in a hurricane."

"Of course," Julie said. "The rue de la Gauchère is only a stone's throw from the yards."

"Quite right." Bérangère then shook her head. "The Malakoff and Vanves districts got their share too. Madeleine and the children are going to stay here until Philippe finds them an apartment, either close by or out by Neuilly. She doesn't want to return to Suresnes. We have no way of knowing when the bombing's going to stop."

"I heard from a man I passed in the street," Julie said, "that the Germans were targeting the Orly and Villacoublay airfields as well as Le Bourget."

Bérangère shrugged. "It makes sense. They'd try to destroy the aircraft on the ground, at least, those that are not already at the front. Only a few remained to protect the city."

"Then, where were they last evening?" Julie asked.

All heads turned to Bérangère who said, "They'd been forewarned and had taken off."

"By whom?" François asked.

"The English, stupid!" Pierrette replied.

Gontrand finally spoke up in a gruff voice. "That's enough, you two."

At that moment Ernest opened the kitchen door. Dust plastered his clothes and hair.

"Come in, Ernest. Where were you on duty? Give us your news."

"I was stationed near the Porte de Saint Cloud, monsieur Gontrand. There was rubble from bombed buildings on rue Claude Terrasse and Boulevard Murat that needed clearing away to allow the rescue teams to get to the injured."

"As bad as that? Damn Krauts, dropping bombs on residential areas. We're not factories, *bon Dieu!*"

"Alas, some people were trapped in the collapsed buildings."

Bérangère shook her head. "What a tragedy! Go and have a glass of wine and something to eat, then rest. You've been up all night."

"Thank you, madame Bérangère."

Marie entered carrying a steaming dish. "Luncheon is ready."

"What about the children?"

"They've eaten already and have gone back to their game in the music room."

One note at a time, a nursery rhyme could be heard, which brought smiles to the faces of the adults, who followed the cook into the dining room.

When everyone was seated at the long table, Bérangère raised her hand. "I feel that we should give thanks for being together, safe and sound."

Gontrand stood and delivered the prayer. A silence followed, broken only by the muted clatter of knives and forks on plates.

Marie came in with dessert. "It's a strawberry tart. The first strawberries are ready in the garden. I used them for the tart just in case we were bombed before we could pick them."

Her words were met with a chorus of cries. "No, no, see how quiet it is here!"

Bérangère shushed everyone. "That was very thoughtful of you, Marie. Make sure you save a portion for yourself and Ernest."

"I want to listen to the wireless." Gontrand crossed the room and switched on the set.

The calm voice of the newsreader filled the room. "...as well as several buildings in the *seizième arrondissement*. The lycée Michelet, also in the sixteenth district, was damaged. Consequently, all classes have been cancelled. At this time there are more than two-hundred and fifty reported fatalities, including some twenty children, and more than six-hundred and fifty injured. We will communicate the final death toll when the civil defence workers finish sifting through the ruins."

Gontrand switched off. "No more shilly-shallying. The children must leave Paris and go to Montauloup. The Auvergne will be safe."

"Maybe we left it too late," Camille said. "I went to the station again yesterday and it's total chaos. I don't know how I'll get back to Grenoble and Pontcharra."

"You can stay here as long as it's necessary," Bérangère said.

Camille shook her head. "Thanks, but Hilaire needs me back home. His regular gendarmes have been called up. He's left with officers pulled out of retirement. Not an ideal situation and I've been here for three weeks now!"

Bérangère nodded. "In which case, we should gather everyone and discuss the best way to move everyone to safety. I'll send a pneu to Lorraine."

"Right," Gontrand said. "I'll write a note to Charmaine. Pierrette, write a note for Marie-Ange. She'll be at home, as her school classes must have been cancelled, too. François, get on your bicycle and take the notes to the post office for the pneumatic post."

Silence ensued while everyone set about their tasks.

Gontrand glanced at Pierrette hunched over a notepad. "Pierrette, don't write your memoirs, just a few words."

The girl looked up but dared not dispute Gontrand's military-style orders. She pulled a face when his back was turned and folded her note.

Lyse-May tugged Bérangère's sleeve. "What's the pneumatic post?"

"It's a special post. You write a letter, take it to the post office where they put it in a brass cylinder which takes it to the recipient. Do you know what a recipient is?"

"Yes. It's a person."

"That's good."

"It's very fast in an emergency," Camille said.

"How does it go to the people?"

Bérangère laughed. "You're persistent. The cylinder goes into a compressed-air tube straight to the nearest post-office. There, the telegraph boy jumps on his bicycle and delivers the message to the recipient. Just like a telegram."

"Is that all?"

"You always want to know everything."

"And she knows what compressed air is, too," Gontrand said. "She learned that when I pumped up the tires on her tricycle."

Bérengère smiled. "If she keeps this up, she'll pass her baccalauréat next year."

After the laughter subsided, Lyse-May asked, "What's the baccalauréat?"

Pierrette ruffled her young cousin's hair on her way to the door. "It's the school exam I have to pass if I hope to get into university this fall."

"What if the recipient is a long way away?"

"Then it goes into another tube to another post office."

Lyse-May was not finished. "Where are the tubes?"

"Underground. Along with the Métro, the sewer, the water pipes and the telephone lines."

"And through the underground quarries that Paris is built over," Camille said. "The ground is full of holes, just like Gruyere cheese. One of these days the town will cave in. You should all move to Grenoble and the mountains."

Lyse-May frowned to absorb the information. More laughter erupted from the grown-ups.

Julie turned to her father-in-law. "It usually takes two hours for a pneu to be delivered."

"Not that long. Lorraine's printing shop is in the rue du Sentier, virtually next door. As for Charmaine, the Boulevard Saint-Germain isn't far."

"You could phone her, beau-papa. She must already be in her photo studio."

"You think so?"

"Absolutely. She is super busy with all the people who want to leave and need photos for their identity papers."

Gontrand nodded and strode to his office where the telephone was located.

***

Pour Elles Magazine.

A Page in the Life of a Modern Woman column by Julie de Montregard,

Tuesday, June 4, 1940

My nephew and niece, who are in the Scouts and Girl Guides, have been busy helping with the refugees from the north. I didn't fancy handing out sandwiches, but I thought I ought to record the chaos at the railroad stations.

My father-in-law lent me his car. It's a Mathis Emy Fon6, rather big, and when I got near Gare Montparnasse, I had to leave it in a side street as it became impossible to drive without running someone over. Then, on foot, I joined the mass of humanity on the sidewalks.

Cars with mattresses on the roof tried to advance through the crush. Sometimes, drivers insulted the pedestrians who retorted with a few choice words of their own. All around me were people pushing baby carriages or bicycles piled high with various possessions. Small children hung to the sides, some crying, others complaining, or clung to their mothers' skirts. I saw only old men, burdened with bundles too heavy for them. All the younger men are at the front protecting us.

The spring temperature made everybody hot and sweaty. The smell was overpowering. I approached people but they refused to talk to me. Finally, I came alongside a young mother and her children, all sweating profusely, dressed as they were in their winter coats and hats.

I asked, "Where are you coming from?"

"Saint-Quentin."

"In the North. Tell me, why are you wearing winter clothes? It's far too warm."

"Dumb question, you must be a journalist. How else are we going to carry them? There's not enough room on the bicycle."

"I get it. Where are you heading?"

"No idea. As far away as possible."

This is what war does to women. It throws them out of their homes. They leave in fear as they try to reach safety, without knowing where safety is, not knowing even if there are any safe places.

How wrenching it must be to leave one's house behind. Will it be bombed or looted? Will they ever come back to it? What do people, who need to flee, pack to take with them? Their burdens look so haphazard, clothes, bedding, an alabaster lamp with a crushed shade and a goldfish bowl.

You can't plan when panic strikes. It looked like the women grabbed the closest thing they saw as they rushed out of their homes.

And the dogs. So many dogs running alongside people, stopping when they do, curling up next to children.

I took a few photos, but that proved difficult. I was constantly jostled and by the time I focused the camera on a scene, it had moved on. Some people simply said they came from Soissons, Compiègne or Amiens and asked directions to the nearest station.

When I arrived in front of Gare Montparnasse, a long line had formed, directed by gendarmes. The Red Cross had a van in the middle of the place. I could see Girl Guides handing out glasses of water to prostrate women and children. Tempers flared. Someone shouted, "Treason!" That was enough for a whole chorus to start.

"We've been betrayed!"

"It's the fault of the Jews!"

"Damn the Angliche."

That one wasn't surprising since we never forgave the English for having burnt Jeanne d'Arc at the stake.

"It's the government! Rich pigs in their big cars!"

When I heard that, I was glad I left my father-in-law's car in the rue Vaugirard. By then, I had seen enough and retraced my steps to the vehicle. Strange that they would swear at the English but not the Germans. I wonder why.

As soon as I got back to the house, my mother-in-law's sister, who had come for the christening of the latest member of the family, pounced on me. She lives near Grenoble and wanted to know if she could take the train back home. For the last two days, she had tried to go to the Gare de Lyon but hadn't been able to get anywhere near the ticket office.

I had to tell her the sad truth. "If you don't want to lose a limb, stay away from the station — any station. There were pregnant women fainting, old men yelling and swearing, kids screaming and even a few fist fights. Clearly, not all children have been evacuated."

Her mouth fell open. "Even though the government announced an early start to summer camps?"

It's obvious that not too many parents followed the instructions to evacuate the children.

I'll leave you now, dear readers, until next week for another Page in the Life of a Modern Woman.

Julie.

***

It was evening and the family had assembled at the Manoir for dinner. As usual, Marie had the children eat in the kitchen. Christiane was asleep in her baby carriage, while Sylvestre snoozed on a child's folding bed that Bérangère kept in the closet under the turret stairs. The older children were absorbed in a double-deck card game of Bataille. They didn't notice the irony of playing a battle game.

The heavy entrance door swung shut behind a grim-faced Philippe. He crossed the polished hall floor without taking the time to use the obligatory felt shoe pads.

"Father, we can't continue with the production of spare parts. That section of the factory is almost completely destroyed. All that's left is a couple of walls. The machinery that survived the inferno is buried under the debris."

"And the locator beacon prototypes?"

"Gone. I recuperated what I could of the plans from the office safe, which the bomb blasts had ripped open. Fernand was with me. He was devastated. We were so close to making a breakthrough in that project."

"As chief-engineer, he did most of the work. Can we rebuild?"

"We can... when this bloody war is over."

Normally, his oath would have invited a lesson on good manners, but these were not normal times. Bérangère raised her hand. "Let's have dinner, everyone. We'll talk about plans afterwards."

The wireless had been left on all day. For once the news was encouraging. The army was regaining lost ground.

The former soldier stiffened with pride. "I told you we'd send the Huns packing with their tails between their legs."

"Maybe we don't need to leave," Marie-Ange said.

Charmaine heaved a sigh. "Let's wait and see."

Long into the evening the debate continued back and forth over the merits of leaving or staying.

"Brigitte, stay here tonight," Bérangère said. "Damien and Estelle are fast asleep on the couch. I've already put a blanket over them."

"Merci, maman-Bérangère."

"Good, let's meet again here for lunch after church on Sunday," Gontrand said. "In the meantime, go to the bank and withdraw as much cash as you can."

Everyone nodded their agreement. Charmaine and Marie-Ange, together with Julie, rounded up their children and went home.

Chapter Seven

The de Montregard family didn't wait till the Sunday to gather again. The general air of urgency brought them back to the Manoir, their faces strained with anxiety "Stop fiddling with the wireless, François," his mother said.

"But listen. They're saying the Huns have broken through and have crossed the Somme. But, hey, a plane went and dropped bombs on Berlin!"

Gontrand shook his head, "My poor boy, a bomb or two on Berlin won't stop the German advance."

"At least, it shows we're not taking all that *merde* from the Krauts without—"

"François! Watch your language!"

"Sorry, but you know what I mean."

Smiles were quickly repressed.

"Frankly, I think we've left it too late to leave," Brigitte said.

At that moment. Bérangère entered with Sylvestre in her arms. "Go home and pack just enough for the journey to Montauloup. You'll have all the clothes you need once you get there."

"And take what canned food you have. Come back here to be ready to leave at dawn," Gontrand said.

"I have to close up the photo studio," Charmaine said.

"I'm going to stay. I don't want to shut down the printing shop," Lorraine said.

"In which case, I stay, too," Hughes said.

Gontrand stood up. "No, all the children are going with their mothers."

"I'm not a child, grand-papa. I'm fifteen."

"You can make your own choices when you reach twenty-one."

François groaned. "Who made twenty-one the age of majority? It's not fair, we can already do a man's work."

"In that case, both of you, go and help your mothers pack."

"Yes, sir," they replied in unison.

Gontrand turned to Madeleine. "Did you happen to bring any practical clothes in those ten suitcases of yours? No, maybe not. Stop laughing, Bérangère. Help your daughter-in-law sort out what she needs. Marie, make something to eat for them to take along."

He looked around the room. "François, where's Pierrette?"

"I'm here. Just arrived this minute. I'm exhausted and I've a headache. There were crowds of people and crying kids, everywhere. We ran out of places to put them at the refugee center."

Gontrand ran his fingers through his white hair. "Go with Brigitte and help her pack for her brood."

"Yes, sir."

"I'll help, too," François said. "Mother is in good hands with grand-maman. I'm just in the way."

Bérangère winked at him. He had already taken empty suitcases to his mother's room. Marie, with Marianne's help, was busy preparing supper as well as sandwiches for the journey.

"You're a good little housekeeper," Marie said.

"I have to be. Maman has to take care of the studio since papa's away at the war.

"You're so much more grown up than your boisterous cousins."

After dinner, Gontrand took charge of organizing the transport. "Madeleine and Marie-Ange don't drive. What about you, Lorraine?"

"I have a license, but I'm totally out of practice. I don't think I'm capable of driving any distance."

"That leaves us with three drivers and four cars. I don't think Brigitte should drive when she has to stop and feed the baby and watch Sylvestre too. Julie, you'll drive the Mathis with Brigitte and her kids, your Claire and Lyse-May. It's the biggest car and there's room for a folding baby carriage. Charmaine, you can drive the Citroën Rosalie with your Marianne and Baptiste, and Madeleine with François and Pierrette."

"That's too many people. I don't want to be squished all the way to the Auvergne," Pierrette said. I'm not going. I can stay with Mireille."

"Come to think of it, where's Mireille?"

"Helping Philippe at the factory to make an inventory of what's salvageable. Disaster victims face tons of government red tape. They'll leave later, together," Madeleine said.

"Don't look worried, Gontrand," Bérangère said. "She's no longer a child."

The old man shook his head. "It seems like only yesterday she was running around in pigtails."

Eugène signaled to his brother. "I can drive Marie-Ange with Paul and Micheline in her Peugeot 402."

"Good. Get the keys from your niece."

"Here they are." Marie-Ange handed him a bunch of car keys. "The carriage gate is unlocked and the suitcases are in the entrance hall as well as a cardboard carton of food. I was prepared."

Eugène hurried out. Rue de la Faisanderie was not far away.

"That leaves us with Brigitte's Juvaquatre." Camille spoke up. "I could take Pierrette in the Juva, along with Lorraine and Hughes, to Pontcharra."

"Good idea. Have I forgotten anyone? Oh, yes, Yolande. She can go with you."

Lorraine made a small grimace. "Look, Gontrand, my daughter's twenty-seven. Anyhow, I doubt if she'll want to quit her job at the Ritz Hotel."

Her brother bristled. "Does she think that because the hotel is Swiss owned, it's going to be treated as neutral? Bombs don't make any distinction."

Julie coughed. "All this is beautifully organized, beau-papa, but what about you and Bérangère?"

"My dear, we've been through one war already. My wife and I, are staying. We'll keep an eye on your houses and businesses."

***

Sunday, June 9, 1940

The household was astir at first light. Marie and Bérangère pulled back the living room blackout curtains and shutters.

At that moment, Madeleine entered and let out a shriek. "It's so dark outside! What's happened?"

"The sky is completely blotted out," Marie said. "It's smoke. Shut the window, quick."

Gontrand came out of his study and lifted the curtain. "That's thick smoke from an oil fire. It looks like the fuel tanks are burning."

In the dull light, they adjourned to the dining room where Marie had laid out bread, butter and jam, and bowls of coffee, which didn't take long to disappear. Gontrand paced back and forth, his unlit pipe clenched between his teeth.

Pierrette stood up. "Maybe we should put mattresses on the roofs."

Gontrand removed his pipe. "On the roofs? What for?"

"Refugees said planes were machine gunning them and that the mattresses on the car roof prevented the bullets from hitting them."

"Well, they're wrong. No mattress can stop a bullet. Ladies, are you ready to leave?"

"Julie, will you take the lead?" Charmaine asked.

"All right, if you want me to."

Gontrand let out a deep sigh. "Have all the drivers got maps?"

They nodded.

"Perfect. I suggest you leave the city by the Porte de Vanves and head for Malakoff to join up with Route National Twenty as far as Orleans. It might be less congested than the Route National Seven. Though I suppose everyone is making their way to Orleans, one way or another."

The goodbyes were quickly over. Gontrand checked that the jerrycans of gas were secured in the trunk of each car. Julie started the Mathis.

Lyse-May flattened her nose against the window. "Why there are no birdies flying?"

"They're hiding from that dreadful smoke," Brigitte said. She wouldn't tell the child they probably had been killed by the toxic fumes.

The small convoy of cars soon merged with other traffic. The metal rolling shutters of stores along the route hadn't been opened. To add to the eeriness, every house windows remained shuttered. They passed bombed-out buildings in Vanves and Malakoff. The women fell silent. Once they were clear of the built-up area, the column of cars and carts and bicycles thinned out. With the smoke behind them, Julie gave permission for the children to wind down the windows. Damien and Estelle cringed at Brigitte's sharp warning not to put their heads out.

In the middle of nowhere, gendarmes flagged them down and forced them to one side of the road to allow a regiment of motorized infantry to pass on its way north to the front. After which, the slow drive resumed. Overcome by the heat, the children became lethargic and slumped on the seats, immune to the shouting and swearing which from time to time broke the silence.

They advanced at a pace not much faster than that of those on foot. When they overtook one group, a man shouted in a hoarse voice, "Hey, you with the big car! You got plenty of room. Take my wife and children." The man gripped the handle of the passenger door.

Before Brigitte could speak, five tousled heads appeared in the window. Sylvestre tried to climb into the front. The man growled something and stepped back.

"At this speed, we're never going to make it to Orleans before lunch," Julie said.

"And I think we have to stop for a pee break."

Julie nodded in agreement and turned into the next farm entrance. She switched off the engine under the meager shade of a few gaunt trees. She and Brigitte led the children over to a grassy knoll. "We may as well have lunch here."

Brigitte unwrapped sandwiches, while the kids stretched their cramped limbs by running about. They had hardly bitten into the sandwiches when a high pitched noise deafened them. Explosions followed.

"That's bombs!"

Julie and Brigitte threw themselves over the children who shrieked, then burst out crying. The planes roared over their heads and disappeared as quickly as they had come. From farther north, along the road, screams rose.

"*Mon Dieu!* What happened?" Brigitte trembling from fright, tried to comfort her terrified two-year-old, while cradling Christiane, who was wailing as only a baby can.

Julie wrapped one arm around Lyse-May and the other around Claire in an effort to reassure them they were safe. Estelle sobbing quietly crawled into her lap. Damien still lay flat on the ground bawling his little heart out.

"They're dropping bombs on the people fleeing from the north. Innocent women, old men and children who just want to get away from the fighting. War is for soldiers, not civilians!" Julie spoke haltingly in an effort to dominate her frayed nerves.

At first they didn't notice the woman coming down the farm lane, with a big dog at her heels. She carried a bag and a jug of milk. The dog came up to the children and gently nosed them one after the other. The crying subsided. Hands reached out to pat the dog's golden hair.

"My goodness! What are we coming to! Here, little ones, I've brought you some bread and butter." From the bag, the woman pulled thick slices of country bread slathered in farm butter. She picked up the cups that had scattered and poured milk into them.

"Thank you so much. It was scary."

"Ah, we've got to help one another. You came from far away?"

"Paris. We're going to family in the Auvergne," Julie said. "Have you had many refugees stopping at your farm?"

"Just a few. But this is the second time those awful planes dropped bombs so close. I've been told they gun people down, too."

"We've heard that," Brigitte said.

"Thank you for bringing us this delicious bread and butter. I think now the children have eaten and recovered from their fright, we should go and try to stay ahead of the planes."

While Julie was talking, the farmwoman picked up the scattered sandwiches.

"There, a few bits of grass, but quite clean."

"May I pay you for the milk and bread?

"Good gracious, no." She lowered her voice. "Some refugees told me that at other farms they were charged three francs just for a glass of water. That's scandalous. These poor people are scared and they've got nothing, only what they can carry or fit onto a bicycle, even some with wheelbarrows."

After another round of thanks, and after the children insisted on kissing the dog, Julie and Brigitte shepherded the youngsters back to the car. A man was leaning against it, peering through the open windows. He took off when Damien, who had run ahead, got there to open the doors.

"That man was a thief," Damien said.

"That's possible, but you scared him off. Well done."

Dismayed, Julie pointed out to Brigitte several bullet holes in the hood and roof. The two women stared at each other, unspoken fear in their eyes. Back on the road, they could still hear shouts and cries.

Brigitte settled in the front seat and cradled Christiane. "You don't think we should go back and see what happened? See if we can help?"

"I thought of it. But we have six children to take care of. They're too young to be exposed to what I can only imagine."

"Charmaine and Eugène were behind us."

"I know. I lost sight of them after Vanves."

"It's so slow going."

"We have to trust they are all right. As for us, we have to ensure our children get to safety as quickly as possible."

At times the convoy of vehicles was stalled and those on foot overtook them. People trudged on in silence, bent over by their burdens of suitcases, bundles, and even the odd canary in a cage.

Night fell. They were nowhere near a town.

"We can't continue like this. We should do like those people, pull up under the trees and sleep," Julie said.

"I think you're right. We have enough food and water."

"I should try to fold the backseat down."

Brigitte secured Christiane on the front seat between their bags. "We can rearrange the back. We can't put anything outside, it might get stolen, but if we turn the jerrycans the other way and move the two suitcases, I can push the carriage bed for bébé over here. Then, the seat should go down a bit and give a little more room."

It worked out and the children fell into a tired sleep.

Julie took a blanket. "I'll sleep on the grass. You lie on the front seat."

"Wake me up later and we can switch."

The dawn painted the sky with brushstrokes pastel green and pink. Brigitte was already feeding Christiane when Julie resumed her place in the driver's seat. "We'll start while they're still sleeping," Julie whispered.

The long trek resumed. People stirred. The slow column of humanity moved off. Stop. Start. There seemed no end to it in the relentless heat.

Brigitte leaned across. "Do we have enough gas?"

"I'm hoping to find a pump at the next village. All we've seen so far are deserted houses and broken down gas pumps."

"Pass me the map."

Now and then delivery trucks rolled by, with a cyclist or two riding along with one hand on the tailgate. Occasionally, an impatient driver hurled abuse at pedestrians pushing baby carriages laden with goods and chattels down the center of the road. Horses plodded on, exhausted under heavy loads.

The late-afternoon shadows lengthened across the road, but brought no relief from the oppressive heat. On entering the village of Artenay, Julie spotted a garage that appeared open. She brought the car to a halt in front of the solitary gas pump. After some sharp words, the unwilling garage owner agreed to fill the gas tank. When they were once more on the road, Brigitte turned and asked, "Why did you pay the inflated price that rogue was asking? We've got two jerrycans in the back."

"We're nowhere near Orleans yet and there's no guarantee we can find gas up ahead. You saw all those abandoned cars on the road? They ran out of gas."

"I'm sorry. I don't have your cold analytical mind."

"You're trying to make me feel bad?"

"No, not at all. It's a compliment. You're good and generous, yet you can be as hard-nosed as that garage keeper. I admire your cool. We're caught up in this... this whirlwind of madness, with fleeing people all around us and the Germans overhead, bombing and shooting as they go. Me, I was ready to give away our spare gas to that family who tried to wave us down."

"I may sound selfish, but I'm just being pragmatic. I owe that to my American father. If we didn't have a bunch of youngsters in the back seat, I like to think I'd act differently."

Brigitte took a deep breath, then pointed up ahead. "That's an inn coming up."

Julie swung the Mathis off the road and into the inn courtyard. At that instant, the air was filled with the roar of aircraft engines. From out of the blue sky a line of German planes flew in low, sirens wailing, machine guns strafing the road where the car had been just moments before. The children screamed and flattened themselves onto the car floor. Brigitte and Julie, too stunned to react, watched bodies bounce off the pavement. Farther along, a car exploded in a ball of flames. A wounded horse screamed in agony.

The innkeeper carrying a gun dashed from the inn and ended the poor animal's sufferings. The innkeeper's wife came out and took the gun from him. On her return to the inn, she said, "That's the third horse. He's helping as best as he can."

Julie opened the car door. "I'm not sure what I can do but I'll go and see if I can help too. Stay with the children, Brigitte."

Other people came out of the inn to help care for the injured. Gendarmes and white coated stretcher-bearers arrived. Before they finished, the sun was setting in a blaze of purple and gold, draping the trees with cascades of precious stones.

With it, the heat began to subside. When everyone in need had been taken care of, dirty and tired, Julie returned to the car.

Brigitte stood watching the children lying flat on the ground. "The innkeeper lady said the children can't spend the night outside. She's giving us one room for all of us."

"That's good enough. First, I want to park in a less exposed spot."

The dazed passengers scrambled to the inn's front door. Damien helped Brigitte take out the folding baby carriage. The innkeeper himself showed them to a room. "But this is your bedroom, monsieur."

"Don't worry. The wife and I will sleep in the living room." He maneuvered the baby carriage inside. "You can put blankets on the floor for the youngsters."

His wife brought them a bucket of fresh water from the well. Julie thanked the couple. With the help of the innkeeper's wife, Brigitte had washed the diapers and put them through the ringer.

"Do you have enough until those dry?" the innkeeper asked.

"Yes, thank you. I'll lay those flat in the back of the car. It's so hot, they'll dry."

Finally, after the children had eaten the last of the bruised sandwiches, sleep overcame them.

Dawn came all too soon, but Julie was determined to be on the road to reach Orleans as soon as possible before too much traffic clogged the way.

The innkeeper refused payment for the room. He gave a resigned wave of the hand. "At times like this, everyone has to help."

His wife pressed a package into Julie's hand. "You've got to care of les petits. I made some sandwiches, and I filled up your bottles with water."

"Thank you so much, for everything." Julie noticed Brigitte slip a few bills under the hotel register open on the reception desk.

Once more back on the road, Brigitte fed Christiane. She turned to Julie. "I'm still half-asleep. You were up early."

"I wanted to get things ready for us to leave. We have to get to Orleans before they blow up the bridges."

"What? Why would they do that?"

"Just think about it. The Germans are not that far behind us. They need the bridges to cross the Loire. If I'm not mistaken, the French engineers would be planning to stop them by destroying the bridges."

"Mon Dieu, things are bad!"

With the sun appearing over the horizon, they approached Orleans.

Brigitte studied the map spread out on her knees. "It seems there are two bridges. The road ahead is dead straight."

"Merde!" Julie clapped her hand to her mouth. "Excuse me, *les gosses*."

Stifled giggles came from the youngsters. Damien shook his index at Julie's back.

"What I wanted to say is take a look at all the cars and people wanting to cross the river."

Brigitte shrugged. "At least the river forms a natural barrier, just like the Somme."

Julie sniffed in disdain. "And a fat lot of good that proved in holding back the Germans. Is there a side road we can take to get away from this crush?"

Again, Brigitte pored over the map. "Okay, take the next right and then the second road to the left. That might work. Unfortunately, the map is not very detailed."

After a few more detours, they reached a stone bridge from a side road. A mass of cars, bicycles and carts were already waiting from the main road. Brigitte gave a triumphal whoop. "That's got to be the George V bridge. But look, there are soldiers blocking the approach!"

Julie edged closer. "From their uniforms they look like cadets from the Saumur Military College."

She maneuvered the Mathis as close as she could through the protesting crowd.

A uniformed cadet came up. "Sorry, ma'am, you can't cross. The bridge has been rigged with explosives. Any moment now, we're expecting the order to blow it up. You'll do best to go back where you came from."

Julie shot him a cold look. She climbed out of the car and ran up to an officer.

"Captain, my husband is also a captain in the army. He's presently fighting on the frontline. I have six young children in the car, one a newborn. I have to get across. Otherwise we're going to be trapped in the fight between your troops and the advancing Germans. For the sake of the children, please let us through."

Fear knotted her insides but the firmness of her voice surprised her. Her husband was only a lieutenant but he had told her that on the front promotion came quickly and he'd be a captain like his father by the time he came back... if he did.

The officer looked her up and down, then walked with her over to the car. He glanced inside. "You've come from Paris?"

"Yes."

"In case you're interested, the news this morning said that Paris will be declared an open city tomorrow, meaning they are not going to put up an armed defense, to avoid needless destruction. As for you, where are you going?"

"To the Auvergne. We have family there."

"Fine, you can pass." He shouted an order to the soldiers at the barricade.

Julie wasted no time in putting the Mathis in gear and getting in line behind a couple of military vehicles which opened the way to the bridge among the protests of other stranded refugees.

On the other side of the bridge, she breathed a sigh of relief. Behind them, the bridge was once more blocked. Ahead, the traffic was sparse.

Brigitte gave her a questioning glance. "Our troops are going to fight there?"

"That's what it seems."

"What about all the people who didn't get across the way we did?"

"They'll take them to a refugee center."

"Phew, we were lucky, then! You're very persuasive."

The car quickly caught up with the last people to cross the bridge. Despite there being fewer pedestrians and vehicles, the going was still slow. The children became restless. Brigitte did her best to soothe baby Christiane.

"Quieten down, children," Julie said. "I know it's a long way and it's still too warm. But there's nothing we can do about it. Damien, take out the bag with the bread and give everyone a small piece. That'll hold you until we stop for lunch."

"Can we have a lump of sugar?" Estelle asked.

"Only if you say please."

This was met with a chorus of "Please!"

"All right, one cube for everyone."

Brigitte took advantage of the lull caused by the children's preoccupation with their piece of bread and sugar to breast-feed Christiane. She glanced over at Julie. "Are we far from Vierzon?"

"That's our next destination. At our rate of travel, I'd say we're half way there. Right now we're coming to the Sologne Forest."

Scarcely had she uttered the words when, from high overhead, came the unmistakable drone of enemy planes. All along the road, people dropped their possessions and dove for cover in the ditches. Before Julie and the others in the car had time to react, the sound receded into the distance.

"Thank God, they were not coming for us."

People emerged from the ditches and the forward procession resumed. A grocer's van overtook them and wove a path through the knots of people, its driver and passenger hurling insults as they sped ahead.

Julie focused her attention on driving, but Sylvestre hanging onto the back of the front seat kept jumping up and down. The child's rambunctiousness stretched her nerves to the breaking point. She gritted her teeth and reminded herself he was only a child. He was too young to know that he had to sit still in the overheated car. Behind him, Lyse-May and Claire chatted away like a couple of young magpies. Damien and Estelle lay crumpled against the other door in a fitful sleep.

Moments later, out of the calm sky, came the terrifying scream of sirens from a dive-bombing aircraft. Julie slammed on the brakes and jumped from the car. She wrenched open the passenger door. "Quick, get out! Run for the trees."

Lyse-May seized Claire by the hand. Julie took hold of Silvestre and raced for the nearby thicket of trees. The two girls fell down in the ditch. Julie pushed Sylvestre into the shelter of the trees. "Don't move!" She threw herself over the girls to protect them.

On the other side, Damien and Estelle, followed by Brigitte carrying Christiane, had already reached the trees.

The enemy planes flew low over the length of the road, firing their machineguns as they went. Lumps of turf flew in all directions. Earth and stones landed on Julie's back. Claire flinched. Julie didn't move. The planes banked, turned and came back, lower this time. The noise deafened her. A burning pain ripped through her outstretched arm.

Seconds later, the planes vanished from sight.

For several long moments silence reigned over the scene. Then all hell broke loose with the clamor of shouts and screams from the road.

Julie drew herself onto her knees. Her hair was caked with dirt. A trickle of blood ran down her arm. She watched a panicked horse gallop by, dragging the shafts of a broken cart.

A stunned and wide-eyed Lyse-May struggled to her feet. Next to her, Claire remained motionless. Julie reached down. "It's all over, ma chérie. The bad planes have gone away." As she lifted the child, the little girl's head flopped to one side revealing a long bloodied gash across the pale skin of her head, neck and shoulder. A spurt of blood ran onto the grass. Julie stared in disbelief. "NOOooo..."

Silvestre emerged, crying, from behind a tree. Lyse-May grabbed his hand and joined in his weeping.

With her eyes glued to the disfigured face framed by blond curls of her beloved child, Julie did not see Brigitte shepherding the children to the other side of the car. A long, plaintive wail escaped Julie's throat. She lost all sense of time and place and life.

A man came and knelt beside her. "I'm a doctor. Let me see her." He took Claire from her. A strange sound still coming from her, Julie didn't react. Her empty eyes stared ahead, unseeing.

"I'm afraid she's dead."

Brigitte, who had returned, handed the doctor a baby blanket. He wrapped the little corpse. On his mother's orders, Damien went and fetched the spade from the car and held it out for the doctor.

"Thank you, my young man. Be brave. Go and take care of your brother and sisters." He looked at Brigitte and motioned to Julie. "Stay with her. I'll dig a grave."

"She's injured," Brigitte said.

"A minor scratch. I'll attend to it in a moment." An arm around Julie's shoulders, Brigitte clenched her jaw to keep her composure. On the road, people began gathering up their belongings. Anything that was becoming too heavy or too cumbersome, they threw in the ditch. In several places, men and women were digging graves. Elsewhere, people walked past dislocated bodies that had no one to bury them.

The doctor threw the last spadeful on the tiny mound. With the spade he lopped off a couple of small branches and stuck them in the earth at the head of the grave. "Like that, you'll be able to find it again, later. Poor little tyke didn't have a chance. The bullet entered through the top of her head."

While speaking, he dabbed Julie's arm with mercurochrome. Helped by Brigitte, he carried Julie back to the car and settled her in the front passenger seat. He picked up his medical bag and left to help others. Unable to utter more than a thank-you, Brigitte looked about her and saw Damien trying to extricate the baby carriage from behind the back seat. At that moment her seven-year-old son had suddenly aged twenty years. A shudder went through her.

"Well done, Damien, that was smart thinking. We'll put Christiane in it for the remainder of the trip."

She wedged the carriage bed as best as she could into the well between the bench seats. She hugged and kissed Lyse-May, who was as white as a sheet. The little girl sat huddled in the corner. Brigitte kissed Estelle. The child climbed in and sat next to Lyse-May, her feet against the edge of the carriage bed. Damien slipped into the middle and held the exhausted Sylvestre.

With some trepidation, Brigitte sat behind the wheel. She adjusted the rearview mirror and turned on the ignition. She pressed her foot to the clutch pedal, took a long breath and put the car into first gear. The Mathis purred and eased onto the road.

Chapter Eight

Brigitte drove with mounting confidence. From time to time, she glanced at Julie still prostrate on the seat. Closed up houses and shops lined the road in small villages. Out of the corner of her eye, she saw some men force open the door of a house whose shutters were closed.

"What are they doing?" Damien asked.

"I believe they are looting houses whose owners have left to go to safety, like us."

"They are bad."

She swallowed. "Yes, mon chéri. They are very bad." She had to ram her grief all the way into the farthest recesses of her heart. She had to be normal and strong to help the children understand and surmount their own grief. Her own tragic background came to the fore again reminding her that contrary to the adults' saying, children do not forget. They grieve, even if they appear to play happily. They are just different.

Farther off in the fields, distraught cows with full udders lowed. There was no one near the wrecked farm.

Not far from Bourges, a gendarme signaled Brigitte to stop. The children crowded the open window.

"Madame, I recommend you take a rural road."

"I don't know the area."

"Where are you going?"

"Le Falgoux. Then the estate of Montauloup."

"D'you have a map?"

She showed him her map. He pulled a pencil from his pocket.

"Good. I'll mark the way on it." He spread the map on the hood to trace the route. "There you are. You'll be much safer along those roads. They're unpaved so take care."

"Why do we have to detour?"

"There a lot of damage farther along. The Germans are bombing heavily and Bourges is overrun with refugees. Best to avoid it." He pointed to Julie, still prostrate. "What's the matter with her?"

Tears filled Brigitte's eyes. "Her daughter was killed on the road. Strafing."

"Oh! *Mon Dieu!*"

After a moment of grieving silence, he bent his head through the window and pointed to the gas gauge. "Do you have enough gas? It shows empty."

Brigitte's hand flew to her mouth. "Oh! I forgot. But I have two jerrycans."

"Don't move. I'll fill the tank for you."

Damien helped Sylvestre get out and the children attended to nature. The gendarme put the empty jerrycans back. "Did you hear that Italy declared war?"

"No! What have we done to the Italians?"

"Bunch of fascists!"

"We have family in Pontcharra, near Grenoble."

"I wouldn't worry too much. The Italians aren't a fanatical nation like those Nazis."

"Still. Anyway, thanks for your help."

"Good luck!" He went to advise other travelers.

Tense with concentration, Brigitte changed gears and the Mathis responded. She turned onto the side road. Although they could hear the planes and the explosions, they were finally away from immediate danger. Farther along, Brigitte realized she could no longer hear the battle noises. She relaxed and kept a steady hand on the wheel on the narrow road until a cry from Sylvestre jolted her concentration.

"Pee-pee!"

She pulled up close to an opening in a hedge bordering a field of what to her looked like tall grass but was probably a crop. "Go behind the hedge, but don't walk on the crop."

Julie sat up. "Thank you." Her strained voice barely reached her friend's ears. She climbed out and went to help the children in automaton fashion.

Brigitte picked up Christiane, changed her and breastfed her. With the gurgling baby lying on a blanket on the grass, Brigitte unwrapped the last of the stale bread and cheese. A silent Julie attempted to eat, but gave up. She let Damien have her bread to share with Lyse-May while Sylvestre grabbed a piece before Estelle could break it.

"Damien, see if you can get a can of fruit from the food box," his mother said.

He scampered to the back of the car. A moment later, he handed a can of strawberries and the can opener to his mother. When everything had been consumed and the can opener and empty can had been returned to the box, Brigitte took a big breath. "You know, Julie, I think we should camp here."

Unable to speak, she nodded.

In no time, the children were wrapped in blankets. They giggled till sleep overcame them. Brigitte lay next to them and the baby carriage. "I'll stay in the car, just in case someone came along." Julie rasping voice was barely heard.

In the early morning, once more back in the car, the children settled down. Julie slid into the front seat. "Sorry, I'm useless." Her voice scratched against her tight throat.

"Take it easy, Julie. We'll make it. If this map is correct, we're close to Le Monteil or is it Trizac? I've lost track. But if we don't reach Le Falgoux before dark, we may have to sleep out again. Hopefully, we can stop at a farm and buy some food."

The road stretched empty in front and behind them, save for the occasional cart driven by a local. They passed through a large village. "We're not far now."

The Mathis slowed down on the hill but made it to the top. A knocking sound from the engine broke the quiet. The motor sputtered, coughed, stopped and started up again. In fright, Brigitte swung toward the grass bank just as the car died.

"Out of gas," Julie said.

"Merde! I should have known. And we just passed a village." Brigitte mopped her perspiring forehead.

"I should have helped."

"I'll walk back to the village and get help."

"No. You take care of the children. I'll walk." Julie extracted her purse from the bag at her feet. "Make sure to switch off the ignition so the battery doesn't go flat." Like a ghost, she set off in the failing light. Her senses were totally numb. Her brain functioned on automatic. She advanced like a wooden doll.

She had been walking for about half an hour when the sound of a cow bell caught her attention. In the twilight, she glimpsed a building. She found the track going to the farmhouse. A thin ray of light shone to the side of a window. The blackout curtain didn't reach far enough. Two dogs, barking all their might, bounded toward her. The door opened. A man voice called out. "Who's there?"

"I'm Julie. My car ran out of gas and we have small children with us."

"Come in."

She stepped into the kitchen. Two girls in their teens and a boy of about fifteen sat at the table where a crock of soup filled the room with a delicious aroma. An older woman stood up. Julie thankfully accepted a chair and told her hosts about her and Brigitte's predicament.

"You said you heard a knocking before you ran out of gas?" The man asked.

"That's right."

"It doesn't sound good."

"Dieudonné, enough talk! Take the Renault and fetch the lady and the children. You'll see about the car in the morning." The woman turned to Julie. "Sit at the table, you must be famished. Francine, get a bowl. Lucette, let's prepare the spare bedroom."

"Thank you so much, madame," Julie said automatically.

"I'm Gertrude. This is the Dumonteil farm. We're not far from Le Falgoux."

Gertrude and her daughter disappeared upstairs. Francine, the oldest of the sisters, ladled the hot soup into Julie's bowl.

"Where in Le Falgoux?" the boy asked.

Julie was toying with the spoon. She summoned some energy. "Actually it's the estate of Montauloup."

"I know it. My Pa tells me stories when he went hunting with old Monsieur de Montregard."

She made an effort. "That would be Gontrand, my father-in-law. I'm Julie."

The boy leaned forward on the table, eagerness on his features. "That's right. He's got a metal leg. Monsieur Arnaud doesn't hunt like his brother. He and madame Huguette have been staying all the time for a few years, now."

"Robert! Forgive my brother, madame Julie. Everyone knows everything about everyone in these parts, and we all like the de Montregard family."

"Don't worry, I know. We've spent many summers at Montauloup." The headlights of a car flashed through the curtain. "I must go and help," Julie said.

Just then Gertrude and Lucette came down. "Just sit. My girls and I will carry the children in."

Soon everyone was eating the hearty soup. Then, the exhausted children were tucked in bed, Damien, Estelle and Lyse-May across the double bed, Sylvestre on a cot and baby Christiane in the cradle Gertrude brought down from the attic. Julie and Brigitte settled on thick quilts and pillows on the floor.

***

By the time the little family had washed and eaten breakfast, Dieudonné and Robert sauntered in. Lucette and Francine went to do their chores and took Damien and Estelle with them. "Madame Julie, I'll go and tow the Mathis with the tractor. It's not just gas that's the problem. Did you check the oil on your way from Paris?" Julie and Brigitte looked at each other. "No."

"Didn't think so. I'll be able to fix it, I think, but it might take me a while. We've got to do the hay first."

"Pa, I could take them to Montauloup with the horse and cart."

"Ah, that's where you're going. I know the family. Good idea, son. But it'll have to be tomorrow morning, early. It's an all-day journey by cart, and we've got to do the hay today." He addressed Julie. "Please stay here till tomorrow. Okay, Robert, hop in, you can steer the car."

They left without delay. Julie helped Gertrude clear the table. "Can I help with something?"

"Can you help with the haying?" Lucette asked.

"No, no, Lucette. It's backbreaking work for someone who's not used to it."

Francine started to wash the dishes. Julie dried them. "I need to take my mind off... I'd welcome the hard work."

Gertrude threw her a shrewd glance. "Lucette, get madame Julie a wide straw hat and some gloves. I'll prepare a lunch."

"Please, just call me Julie."

"If you tell me what to do, I can do the lunch for you," Brigitte said.

"Then it's all set. You're on."

The women had organized the work and the children by the time Dieudonné pulled into the yard. Robert helped his father push the Mathis near the old barn which was used as a workshop.

While Julie walked to the water pump in the yard, Gertrude discreetly pointed with her chin. "A death?"

"Her three-year-old daughter." Brigitte swiftly wiped tears from her eyes. "She hasn't even cried yet."

"She's so tight inside. It takes time. I notice how she hugs the little ones today."

Brigitte sniffed and swallowed more tears. "I hope staying with you is helping. You're so kind."

"We're friends with the de Montregards. I think you were guided to break down here." Gertrude made a quick sign of the cross and went out.

The exceptionally hot weather had been good for the hay. The windrows stretched across the hillside, dry and sweet smelling.

Gertrude led the horses pulling the hay wagon. "Dédé, where do you want the wagon?"

Julie turned her head but there was nobody else. Francine saw her gesture.

"We call Pa Dédé because his first name Dieudonné has two D in it and we're Dumonteil, another D."

"That's nice. So we have to rake the hay toward the wagon, is that it?"

"Not all the way. We'll make conical heaps, like little haystacks, every twenty meters and then Pa will come round with the wagon so we can pitch the hay into it."

The sun beat relentlessly on the backs of the workers. At one o'clock, Lucette and Francine left the field to go and fetch Brigitte and the lunch. Soon everyone sat in the shade of some chestnut trees. Much teasing went Brigitte's way. She took it with good grace realizing the Dumonteil were complimenting her.

Julie stared without seeing and never once smiled. The gracious family encouraged Julie to eat. Their warmth and friendliness was drawing her out of her despair.

The first load was on the wagon. Dédé and Robert lifted Damien, Lyse-May and Estelle onto the top of the hay. Brigitte, with Christiane in the sling across her chest, squeezed onto the bench between Robert, who sat Sylvestre on his lap, and Dédé. Gertrude and Julie stayed behind to rake another windrow while it was still light.

At the homestead, Brigitte gathered her children and began preparing the evening meal, while father and son pitched the hay into the hayloft.

The sky was exploding with bursts of red and gold around fluffy pink clouds. The sun was dipping below the hill when the women returned from the field.

The next morning, Julie offered to help finish bringing in the hay.

Brigitte nodded to Gertrude. The hard work was helping her friend to refocus. In the evening, they returned to a substantial meal. A golden loaf of country bread stood in the middle of the table. Brigitte had baked it with the dough Gertrude had prepared the evening before and which had risen overnight.

Dédé turned on the wireless set. A strangled cry rose from all the throats.

The German army had entered Paris that morning, Friday, June 14.

Dédé mopped his brow with the back of his hand. "They're spreading like spilled milk!"

"Our soldiers were waiting to fight on the Loire," Brigitte said. "It doesn't look like the Germans will be stopped, now."

To allay the gloom which threatened to settle, Gertrude filled their cups with coffee. "We're grateful to you for helping with the hay."

"I'll do my best with your car but I'm not sure when I can get it fixed. There's nothing I can do about the bullet holes in the body, though."

"Never mind those. Take your time, we're going to stay in Montauloup. If it is still on, Robert can take us there in the morning," Brigitte said. "Since it takes all day, he'll stay the night with us."

"We'll do that."

Chapter Nine

In the playroom. Bérangère searched the cabinet where paper and pencils were stored and pulled out an unused school notebook. "Just what I need to begin a diary." She took her find back to her writing desk.

Paris Friday, June 14, 1940

Ever since that morning in April, when we saw off our sons at the train station, a premonition of disaster has gnawed at my insides. Yes, our men are fighting on the frontline, but we women are back home trying to make sense of it all. We have to feed the children, send them to school and tell them everything will be all right, when we know it's not and won't be for a long time. Whoever thinks that a conquering army is going to go back home after a few days of sightseeing and shopping in Paris needs a new brain.

I feel the need to write all that's happening. There are historians who are already chronicling the war, the fighting, the tanks, the planes and the heroic deeds. They won't write about the women who worked in the factories to make the munitions and the machines the fighting men need. When the Great War to end all wars was over, men were awarded medals for their exploits. I don't deny them their due. They fought with bravery. I was a nurse in a field hospital during the First. I patched up many soldiers and sent them back to fight. I wrote soldiers' last letters home. And when it was all over, I was told to go and care for my house and children. That's where they thought all women belonged.

I can't talk about it with my husband. He believes in our government, since the prime minister called Maréchal Pétain to take the helm. I don't trust the old man.

This morning I was startled in my sleep. I shook Gontrand, I thought the Germans were bombing us again. He yawned and stretched. How can he be so tranquil when bombs are falling? We listened. Then a peel of thunder rolled in the sky, deepened before lessening and dying. He burst out laughing. He teased me. "Your bombs are only a thunderstorm."

I don't like thunderstorms any better than bombs but I'll take the storm over bombs anytime.

"It's only five o'clock. Go back to sleep."

I couldn't. I got up and dressed. I opened the window to let in the damp fresh air. Gontrand sighed and started to get up. "I need coffee."

"I'll go and make some."

He pulled on his prosthetic leg. "Where's the maid?"

Why did he ask? He knew very well the maids and the gardener had gone to their homes the day the Germans marched into Norway. A neutral country, indeed! The phoney war had suddenly changed. I don't think we could get our heads around that fact.

Gontrand heaved a sigh. "What's this war doing to me? I had just about forgotten. But it's not right that you should take on household chores."

"It's war. We'll do what we have to do." I worry about my husband's state of mind. I made the coffee while he listened to the T.S.F. in the dining room. When I brought in yesterday's bread and a dish of butter for breakfast, he was slumped at the table. My heart missed a beat. "What now?"

"The German planes are shooting at the refugees on the roads. And I sent our daughters-in-law and their children out on those same roads."

"No one-"

"Sshh..." The strained voice of the announcer interrupted the reporter. "...the advance guard of the German army is entering Paris as I speak."

We looked at each other. We didn't need to speak, I sensed the despair in his heart, like in mine. Gontrand stood to go to the window and pushed the shutters open. The rain had tapered off.

"Paris was never taken in the two previous wars. Why this time?" he said.

"Because we've had years of corrupt, incompetent governments. Paul Reynaud was the only one who wanted to fight on."

Gontrand sighed again. He's doing a lot of sighing these days. "Our prime minister resigned two days ago..." At that moment I heard a blaring horn outside in the street. We rushed to the window. I saw a German military vehicle with a huge loudspeaker on its roof advance at walking pace along the Bois de Boulogne.

"...Paris inhabitants will stay indoors for the next forty-eight hours. Any resistance will be crushed by the most rigorous means... The Paris police remain on duty... Looting and sabotage will not be tolerated..." The rest was lost when the vehicle continued its progression along the avenue. But I'd heard enough. My heart was tight and hurting. I tried not to cry.

Marie stood respectfully by the door. "Madame Bérangère, we heard. And we have been told to advance the clock two hours to be on the same time as Berlin."

Silent tears ran down my old soldier's cheeks and got lost in his moustache. I stared at my cup of coffee. Marie warmed up the stale bread in the oven to make it more palatable.

The hours passed. The coffee cooled. The bread hardened again. The silence full of despair weighed heavier and heavier. I didn't have the strength to do anything until Gontrand slapped the table with the palm of his hand. "I'm going to see what they're doing."

"They said to remain inside."

"Nobody will force me to stay inside if I don't want to!" He limped to the bedroom. Half an hour later he appeared dressed in his best dark suit, his military ribbon bar firmly pinned to his left breast pocket. The ribbon of his Légion d'Honneur – France's highest honor – adorned the buttonhole of his lapel. I began to fear for him.

"You look smart, but don't you think it's a bit much to wear your decorations?"

One fist on his hip, he gave a defiant shake of the head. "I dare them to say anything."

"Then, wait for me." I rushed to my dressing room and put on my black dress, the one I wear at funerals. It's a little old fashioned but it'll do for now, along with my straw hat trimmed with a black ribbon. I picked up the black gloves and black purse that matched the dress.

Good old Ernest waited, ever so polite and old fashioned. "Do madame and monsieur want me to drive them?"

I reminded him our car had taken the family to the Auvergne so we were on foot. The old fox winked and said he had borrowed our neighbor Count de la Ferrière's Hispano-Suiza automobile, because the count had asked him to look after it when he fled south or to the Americas, I can't remember which.

He drove us up Avenue Foch. No one in sight. Store and apartment windows remained shuttered. He said he'd wait while we walked a little way down the Champs Élysées. As we began to direct our steps around the Arc de Triomphe, we spotted a huge, red Nazi flag, with its extra large black swastika in the center. Gontrand nearly wrenched my arm off. He threatened the world with his cane but I became scared when he started yelling, "Look at their bloody Nazi flag under the Arch! Putain de Boches! Get that filthy rag down. Dirty swines! How dare they! I'll show them—"

I tried to shut him up. I finally got through to him but not before a man turned his head to look at Gontrand, looked at the decorations, and pointed to his own. The two men shook hands.

"We, the Poilus, never thought it'd come to this. Us, old soldiers of the Great War, to be obliged to witness this is sickening," the man said.

These two old men, who fought in the trenches of the First, suddenly bent, hid their faces. I've never seen Gontrand cry. In the distance I could hear martial music and studded boots stomping the pavé in time to the beat of the brass and drums.

I was surprised to see people crowd the sidewalks. People with morose faces showing mute despair. Here and there a white handkerchief mopped someone's silent tears.

"Strut all you want, bastards," Gontrand murmured. "You wait and see how long it'll last."

"They look tired," the old man said.

"Not surprising, they've been on the go for a whole month."

"Still, they look like a formidable machine of flesh and steel, but the horses are beautiful."

Gontrand snorted. I really wanted to drag him away and began to turn round when I saw a disgraceful sight. A German soldier was tearing down the posters from a closed newspaper kiosk and pasting on new ones. I had to squint to see better. There was a bad drawing of a German soldier carrying a child and holding two more by the hand. Populations abandonnées faites confiance au soldat allemand. I was beginning to get angry, "What do they think? What do they mean abandoned people? Trust German soldiers? They don't know the French people!" I wasn't aware that I hissed those words loud enough for those about me to hear.

Next to me, two adolescents looked up. As soon as the soldier moved on, they directed a long jet of saliva at the poster. "Germans, go to hell," the tallest of the two said.

Good boys! I told them the Fritz had it all planned, posters and all. And they don't know the language. A population can only be abandoned if it is owned by someone. Nobody has owned us since we chopped off the king's head after the 1789 Révolution. I heard several grunts of approval around me.

Eventually, those who had defied the order to remain in their homes dispersed. I managed to drag my husband back to the car. Ernest must have been watching too. His face like a granite rock was a prize to see. He turned the car round and we drove home.

We sat at the table in the dining room. Marie had been crying, her eyes were red and puffy. She apologized that she was only serving a salad with canned meat because there was no gas to cook with. I'd noticed earlier the electricity had gone off. Ernest walked up to the door, fidgeting with his cap.

"Monsieur Gontrand, I just want to let you know that I parked the Hispano-Suiza in our carriage house."

"And why?"

"The count's place being empty, the car could get stolen."

He was right. As if the morning had not been enough, my husband did it again late this afternoon. He dressed again in his best suit. He's so stubborn "At six o'clock, it's the reviving of the eternal flame over the tomb of the unknown soldier at the Arc de Triomphe. I just heard on the T.S.F. that the Kommandant in Paris had forbidden the ceremony. If there is nobody to do it, I will." I knew better than to argue. I got dressed again.

"That's your mourning outfit."

"Today, I mourn the loss of France."

Ernest had rushed out as soon as he had heard Gontrand and brought the Hispano-Suiza to the front. This time he took the Avenue Victor-Hugo and parked under the trees, close to the monument.

Many German soldiers and some officers were already under the Arch. Gontrand crossed the road, his cane rhythmically tapping the pavement. Unlike this morning, a larger number of Parisians, their faces now set in defiance, had come to attend the ceremony. The guardian of the flame is a veteran of the First World War. He seemed unsure of what to do in the face of the Germans that had gathered, along with the crowd of civilians. His orders were to extinguish the flame forever, according to the Kommandantur's orders. The flame had never gone out since it was lit to honor the unknown soldier at the end of the Great War and who symbolically represented all the soldiers who had fallen on the battlefield. Just prior to the daily ceremony the flame is always lowered. Gontrand marched past everyone and looked his old friend in the eye. "Proceed. Revive the eternal flame, soldier."

Monsieur Gauvin breathed deeply. Encircling the tomb the soldiers and officers came to attention. The old man knelt on one knee, reached into the brass mouth of what used to be a canon and turned up the gas. The flame leapt up. He stood back and saluted. The German officers and men also saluted.

Gontrand strode away. I had to wipe away the perspiration that mingled with my tears. It was terribly moving. The Germans had just been defied and yet had done nothing about it. On the contrary, they too paid their respects to the Unknown Soldier. I then saw an officer signal and soldiers began to lower the Nazi flag from under the Arc de Triomphe. At least the formidable Wehrmacht still had a sense of ethics.

Tonight, Marie had something to say as soon as we were seated.

"We heard that some people committed suicide this afternoon."

"Good Lord! What for?" Gontrand shuddered. He didn't want to show how he

was affected but I could tell. "So they don't have to look at the Germans? That's not going to throw them out."

I was a bit anxious. "Anybody we know?"

"I'm afraid so, madame. Your friend at the American Hospital, Dr. Thierry Martel."

I couldn't speak. Thierry! Thierry couldn't have done that.

"Oui, madame. I took two calls when you were out."

What does one say in the circumstances? Just "May God rest his soul." It sounds so remote. Gontrand stared at his soup bowl with his jaw clenched. He had nothing to say. His pain was too great.

***

Mireille de Montregard stood on the Place du Châtelet and fumed. "Where's my father?" A young man put his arm around her shoulders. "I don't how if he can come. No Métro, no bus service. Come back to my place."

"No. Oh! Look, a German."

An officer climbed onto a chair provided by a nearby café and began haranguing the sparse crowd about the inefficient government France had had. "We are going to change all that."

The café waiters served free drinks to the soldiers. Some old men straightened their jackets and offered to guide soldiers to view the monuments.

"That's disgusting," said the young man.

"Well, now they're here, we may as well be reasonable," Mireille said.

"Quite right, daughter."

The voice startled her. "Oh, papa. I thought you weren't going to come."

"I got a ride with one of those gentlemen."

The young man snorted, pivoted and strode away.

"Was that your boyfriend?"

"Just a student friend. I got stuck here yesterday. He has a place nearby and cooked me dinner."

"Well done, ma fille. I admire how you always manage. But really, I should punish you. Well-brought up young ladies do not spend the night with a young man."

"Oh, Philippe. I'm twenty. I'm an adult even if not legally yet."

"And since when did I become Philippe?"

"Since the day I spirited out your pocket handkerchief covered in lipstick."

"You didn't tell your mother. Why not?"

"Because you genuinely love maman. You'd been away on business. Things happen."

"You're so mature for your age."

"And you won't tell maman where I slept last night."

They both laughed.

"How are we getting back to Suresnes? Or is one of your gentlemen going there too?"

"I'll ask."

A short while later, they were comfortably seated in a Mercedes Benz, next to an officer who spoke fluent French. He was most interested in hearing about the bombing of the family factory.

"I'm really sorry the factory was damaged. Those lazy Luftwaffe pilots were supposed to target only the airfields."

"Maybe the wind pushed the bombs too far."

The officer smiled. "So, tell me about the project you were working on. We may be able to do something about the factory, that is if you think we could work together."

"Oh, absolutely, Herr— ?"

"Sturmbannführer von Hauffen."

"Philippe de Montregard. My daughter Mireille."

A look of appreciation crossed the Sturmbannführer's face. "Enchanté, mademoiselle."

The two men shook hands. The rest of the short journey passed in technical talk that bored Mireille no end. How come they all seem to speak French? She looked at the large red and white flags emblazoned with the black Nazi swastika emblem that wafted in the breeze. She pulled a face. "Decidedly ugly." But she kept that thought to herself.

The driver slammed on the brakes. The passengers were jolted from their seats and braced themselves. Up ahead, a French soldier had just shot at an armored car. The car's gunner fired back and the soldier fell to the ground. Passersby screamed. Then silence.

The Sturmbannführer got out. The driver pulled his pistol and covered his officer. A corporal had already jumped out from the armored car and was examining two bodies lying on the ground.

"Sorry, sir. This civilian was too close to the soldier. I couldn't avoid him."

"Very unfortunate. This soldier mustn't have heard that a cease-fire had been proclaimed this morning."

People peeked out of their windows. Two gendarmes arrived. The Sturmbannfürher explained the incident to them. A woman came out and spread a sheet over the soldier. Another woman crossed the street and handed a sheet to a gendarme who laid it over the civilian.

An ambulance arrived to take the bodies away. Life resumed. Mireille struggled to keep her breakfast down.

Chapter Ten

Bérangère took a moment to sit at the table and write.

Saturday, June 15, 1940

Second day of the occupation of Paris. The war continues. Could our army reverse the defeat? Then what? Will the Germans leave Paris if our army pushes them back? Or is it finished because of the cease-fire?

Marie was flustered. "I hope we can still get some beef, madame, but maybe not tournedos."

Although I told her in an assured tone, that meat can be sold on Saturdays and that surely the butcher would be open. They, the Germans, said, that shops must be open, workers back to work and utilities restored,

Marie has little education. Like less fortunate families, she had to leave school at twelve to go into service. But she has a very fine sense of right and wrong, and an uncanny understanding of human nature. "Oui, madame. The gas is back and I can cook, but I just wonder if all those soldiers are going to buy up everything. I suppose they have to eat too."

What could I say when I was thinking the same. But being pessimistic isn't helpful. Therefore, I said: "Nonsense, Marie. The military takes care of their own needs. They want everyday life to continue as usual so they won't have to worry about the Parisians."

"I hope you're right, madame. I certainly hope you're right."

The sweet smell of Gontrand's pipe preceded him. "Do you want to come with me, my dear? I see you have your mourning outfit on again today."

I made an inelegant noise with my lips and pinned my straw hat on my head without disturbing the great rolls I made around my head. Obviously, he wanted to go onto the Champs-Elysées.

Dear Ernest, he's been with us such a long time and knows what to do without being told. He had already brought the borrowed Hispano-Suiza to the front. "I'll park at the top of Avenue Victor-Hugo. There's a lot of German traffic on Avenue Foch."

The Germans were going to stage a parade again, of course, like yesterday. A rather quiet crowd had already gathered on the sidewalks of the Champs-Élysées. Some German soldiers lined the avenue along with French gendarmes to prevent anyone from rushing at the marching soldiers. That's normal whenever there's a parade. I could hear their martial music and drums in the distance. I didn't try to hold my husband back when he parted people to get to the front. A man, his beret at a jaunty angle, made room for me, the typical Frenchman, and even more the typical Parisian. He kindly stubbed out his Gauloise.

A Frenchwoman, carrying a plate of cookies, also pushed through toward the front row. She was about to offer them to the German soldiers when the man with the beret spoke. "Hey, old gal, hold off a minute. Those bastards killed our boys, you know!"

Startled at the man's harsh tone, she trembled in fear, then dropped the plate and fled. A couple of children watched her and then cleaned up the fallen biscuits in seconds.

Now that makes my blood boil. It's one thing to come and watch them strut like peacocks, but to give them cookies? She should go to Germany if she loves them so much!

After the parade passed, Gontrand wanted to know what the fracas was about. I was happy to tell him how I admired the fearless man. "It was a worker, a man used to hard work and able to hold his own. A man who adheres to his fundamental values, and who told off the woman who wanted to feed the Fritz." Gontrand laughed. "A true titi parisien."

"Yes, a man the likes of which only Montmartre can breed, with his values in the right place, still young, but too old to be conscripted and resenting the fact he had to stay behind. A man who won't put up with the occupier."

"Wow, my dear! You're militant all of a sudden."

"Are you going to sit and do nothing?"

"My dear, the war is not over just because Paris is occupied. Maréchal Pétain is in charge now. You'll see how the old fox'll reverse the situation."

Gontrand was back in dreamland. I had to rub his nose in the truth. First, Pétain is not in charge. Just part of the government. The English have fled and thousands of soldiers have been taken prisoner. Only old men and youths are left. I don't think he really saw those Krauts' display of arms and machines. What can we do against them? All he had to say was, "You know nothing of the strategy of war."

I was getting rebellious. "I can see that strategy doesn't work." I guess I pouted a bit too.

Ernest got us home in some haste. He did avoid a couple of pedestrians, fortunately. It wouldn't be good to be arrested for running spectators over.

The lunch done with, Gontrand in his study to smoke his pipe and I was about to sit at the piano in the music room when car engines and doors slamming attracted me to the open window looking onto the Boulevard du Maréchal Payolle and the Bois de Boulogne. Germans soldiers stood on the sidewalk. My husband too had heard the commotion and asked what was going on.

I didn't know how to break the news. I tried to soften that what I could see were a bunch of Germans moving in next door.

"What?" He didn't wait. In seconds he had crossed the kitchen and was out into the courtyard. He wrenched the side door open and strode limping, with his cane, to the German officer who was watching a locksmith at work on the Count's front door. I followed quickly. Gontrand can fly off the handle pretty fast.

"What the hell do you think you're doing? This is Count de la Ferrière's residence."

"Good afternoon, sir. Baron von Hauffen." He inclined his head. "Monsieur de Montregard, I presume." Now that was trite. A parody of Mr. Henry Morton Stanley's famous words when he met Dr. Livingstone in the middle of Africa didn't sound right with a Teutonic accent. Monsieur le Baron didn't need to show that he's educated.

Gontrand threw a hard look at the officer. When he has that look, people cower. Not this German, though. "You cannot force your way into someone's house, Monsieur von Hauffen."

"I have a requisition order. I would have loved to have Le Manoir but I have to be content with Count de la Ferrière's property."

"Why?"

"I deal with the development of industry and need to set up a suitable headquarters. Our Führer wants France to prosper. I hope we shall see more of each other, Monsieur de Montregard." The locksmith had finished his work. My poor husband looked stunned. He turned on his good leg and put one sluggish foot in front of the other until he reached the courtyard door. He went straight to his study and slumped into an armchair. "The bastard!" I rushed to close the window. Although his study opened on Avenue Chantemesse, I didn't

want the whole district to hear his outbursts. "They think they have won the war and are settling in, taking over empty houses. But wait, you damned Boches." Our thoughtful Marie brought in a small glass and a bottle of Chartreuse. She placed them on the desk and withdrew. Gontrand poured and downed the green liqueur in one swift motion.

After a moment, he stood. "I better go and see about our children's houses."

"Not a good idea to take out the Hispano-Suiza. Your officer next door might see it and requisition it too."

For once he didn't argue and agreed with me right away to keep it hidden. He lit his pipe and poured himself another glass of Chartreuse. A brooding mask settled over his features. I don't like to see him like this. He reminds me of the time when he was so depressed after coming back in 1919.

I wanted to drown my worries and sadness and played the piano while he got dressed.

Chapter Eleven

Montauloup, June 1940

The Dumonteil's horse-drawn cart reached the gates of the château. Robert clucked to the horse. The cart entered the drive leading to the château. The horse picked up the pace as if he knew they had arrived and there would be oats and hay when he stopped. Arnaud and Huguette rushed outside to stand at the bottom of the ornate stone stairs. They helped the children down, amid exclamations about how tall they had grown.

"Come in, come in, you must be tired," Huguette said. "But, where's Claire?"

A stony silence fell. Julie turned and walked away. Pedro, the general handyman, led the horses to the barn. In a few short words, Brigitte told of the tragedy on the road and ushered the children indoors with their great-uncle and great-aunt's help. Elissa, Pedro's wife, maid and cook, took charge of the little ones and they were soon cleaned up and sitting at the table.

Brigitte drank a long draft of cold water. "I hope Charmaine and Madeleine will get here soon. She was driving behind us but we lost sight of her. Eugene was driving Marie-Ange."

"Trust Charmaine to get through anything. And my brother is a sly old fox. He'll get through, too. We heard some awful things on the wireless and this morning all the stations shut down, except Radio-Paris." He made a fist. "An announcer with a German accent came on to say that from now on this was the only official station and that it was verboten to listen to any others."

Huguette wanted to defuse her husband's mounting anger. "Shall I go and look for Julie?"

"Give her a little more time," Brigitte replied. "We have to watch Lyse-May. She and Claire were like sisters. She's hardly spoken or laughed since it happened."

The children ate their fill and Elissa took them to the playroom. Lyse-May stayed behind and kept looking at the door.

Robert and Pedro came in with Julie. Lyse-May bounded to her aunt and hugged her. Julie lifted her into her arms. Pedro kept on talking. "...My wife and I made it over the Pyrénées but I didn't want to go to a refugee camp. So we hid and only traveled at night. We met a curé and even though I've no time for the black robes I listened and he told me to come here. Monsieur Arnaud hired us."

"What an odyssey! I'm glad you made it."

He sighed. "We can't go back to our home in Barcelona. We'd be thrown in jail." Pedro deposited the suitcases he was carrying at the foot of the staircase. "Which rooms, madame Huguette?"

Brigitte glanced at Julie. "Could we have the Blue suite? We'd like to stay together."

"Of course. All right, Pedro, the Blue Suite. It still has two beds." She looked at Brigitte. "We renovated the nursery last fall. We added bunk beds."

Between Huguette, Elissa and Brigitte, all the children were soon tucked in bed and sleeping. Their hosts retired. Brigitte and Julie dropped onto one of the beds.

"What's the story about Pedro and Elissa?" Brigitte asked.

Julie took a long breath. "They were fighting in Spain with the Republicans, so when fascist Franco won, they were being pursued. Many of them were summarily executed. Pedro and Elissa had a son who was killed while he was at school."

"Mon Dieu! Why is it children have to be..." Brigitte checked herself.

Julie sighed. "Don't treat me with kid gloves. Of course I'm torn inside. I want to crawl into a dark hole and die, but it wouldn't change anything. It should have been me, not my little Claire." She raked her fingers through her hair. "Like Pedro and his wife, I'm going to survive. Now, I'll dedicate my life to getting rid of the Germans. I'll kill as many as I can. I hate them with the deepest hatred possible."

"Do you really believe the war is over now that they are in Paris?"

"They called for a cease-fire. When warring nations do that, it's a prelude to an armistice and a peace treaty."

"Oh, Lord. Will they go everywhere, even come here?"

"Dédé doesn't think so. They'll stay in the big cities. But who knows?"

***

The morning began with a flurry of activity mostly due to the children becoming boisterous now that they had recovered from the fatigue of the journey. Lyse-May stayed near Julie to watch Robert hitch up the horse and wave goodbye.

Sometime in the late morning, an asthmatic-sounding pickup truck rolled up to the foot of the steps. Marie-Ange and her children, Paul and Micheline, jumped out, followed by Eugene. Berthe took her time. The driver from Le Falgoux saluted Arnaud and declined to stop for a drink.

The hugging and laughing was briefly interrupted when Julie told about her daughter.

"*C'est la vie.* So don't mind me if I cry. Just keep on doing what we need to do, please." The sight of her stoicism encouraged the rest of the family to act in what passed for a normal manner.

"We crossed the Loire at Sully, but we haven't seen Charmaine since then."

"So what happened to the Peugeot?"

"It took a hit near Moulins. I jury-rigged the beast and we got to

Clermont-Ferrand in leaps and bounds. There, its leaky radiator finally fell to pieces," Eugene said.

"Then we took the train. It was a micheline, like my name," the eight-year-old said with pride.

"And Monsieur Voisin drove us in his truck," Paul added.

"I hope Charmaine gets here soon," Huguette said.

Berthe shook her head. "I hope she's all right. Traveling with Madeleine mustn't be a picnic."

"Come on, the two most beautiful women on earth will always find help," Arnaud said. Giggles greeted his words. "Did you meet any Germans?"

"Yes. I didn't think we'd see any south-east of the Loire. I don't know how they got there. But they behaved correctly. They even helped some old people. What bothered me was our soldiers being taken prisoner." Berthe shuddered and let out a long breath. There was a collective gasp. She continued. "People gave them food and water. The Germans grumbled that it was slowing them down, but they didn't really bother anyone. Have we lost if our soldiers are prisoners?"

No one replied because Pedro walked in. "Arnaud, I'm going to change the ropes on the swing and check the solidity of the oak branch."

"Good idea, Pedro. Do you have new ropes? If not, go to town and get what you need."

"D'accord."

Berthe and Brigitte looked at each other, eyes wide with surprise at the familiarity of the new employee. Huguette caught their regard. "He's a Spanish independent ex-fighter who believes in everybody being equal. We are fine with that."

Chapter Twelve

Paris Saturday, June 15, 1940

"Gontrand, are you going out again?" Bérangère looked at him, a frown marring her brow. "Haven't you seen enough of them?"

"I want to see who's left. I'll go and check on the photo studio, then I'll walk to the printing shop."

"I'm going with you."

"Not in your mourning outfit."

"As long as you wear your funeral suit and your decorations, I'll match you with my dress."

A smirk crossed Gontrand's lips. "And your decorations?"

"I'm not fool enough to display my nurse's medal, even if it's an unofficial one. I remember the Boche shot nurse Edith Cavell."

Arm in arm, they strolled along the streets, now and then meeting small groups of eager German soldiers with cameras.

The steel shutters on the Bourgmestres' printing shop was intact. Cafés were reopening. On Boulevard Saint-Germain, the Lebeaus' photo studio was open. In a rage, Gontrand strode to the door. Before he could bang on the glass, Gus opened it. "Bonjour, Guvnor. When is Madame coming back?"

"Ah, Gus. I don't have any news."

"Me thinks I'll keep the business going, so those Boches don't come and steal it."

"Well, I think you did the right thing, Gus. Can you manage by yourself?"

"I ain't as good as the boss, but since monsieur Alexandre took me on, I learnt it."

"Thank you, Gus."

The two men shook hands. Gontrand guided his wife steps toward the Eiffel Tower, and halted in his tracks. A large banner defaced the monument, DEUTSCHLAND SIEGT AUF ALLEN FRONTEN and a Nazi flag fluttered at the top. He began muttering some expletive. "Germany victorious on all fronts, just wait, just wait. They're not going to be victorious on all fronts much longer." Bérangère pulled him away without consideration. In a state of shock, he didn't protest, nor did he react when he saw a gendarme saluting passing Wehrmacht officers.

"Saluting the Germans? That gendarme should be shot!" Bérangère's angry tone touched her husband.

"Gendarmes are military. In the military you salute officers." He spoke in a monotone, distracted voice.

"Pfff! Salute our officers, not theirs. We've seen enough. Let's go home."

As they passed their local bakery, Bérangère caught sight of the baker. She knocked on the glass door.

"Ah, Madame de Montregard, I'm glad to see you. I don't know whether I'm supposed to be open or not. I baked some bread, but not too much."

"I saw quite a number of stores and cafés open. If I'm right, I heard the Germans say that everybody had to go back to work."

"Then I'll open fully. People need to eat."

Bérangère bought two long loaves.

"Would you like a loaf of pain de mie? I only baked two because I don't know if there'll be customers for them."

"Yes, please. We like your lovely sweet loaf. But I think it won't be long before you get the Chleus as customers. I saw them going into stores and coming out with packages."

"Hopefully, they won't come here on Dufrenoy. We're a bit removed from the city center."

"Don't believe it. A German baron just requisitioned our neighbor's property."

The baker's eyes rounded. "You mean they took the count's house?"

Gontrand straightened. "But they'll have to give it back as soon as the army regroups and throws them out of France."

The baker waved and muttered, "I hope you're right!"

***

In the Ritz's employee bathroom, Yolande Bourgmestre brushed her dark wavy hair once more and pinned the roll securely at the back of her head. She rubbed her lips together to ensure her lipstick was evenly spread. One last look at the dress fitting her tall and slender frame and she was on her way to an interview with an Oberleutnant. She walked with her usual poise to the salon and pushed open the door after knocking.

A handsome officer in a dapper Luftwaffe uniform stood up. "I am Oberleutnant Lohse. Take a seat."

She perched on the edge of the chair in front of the desk while he resumed his seat. "Your name, mademoiselle?"

"Yolande Bourgmestre."

"Ah, yes. It is here." He checked the sheet in front of him. "What exactly do you do at the Ritz?"

"I'm the manager of the housekeeping staff."

"I see that you have one hundred and thirty staff. Is that not a lot for a hotel?" His French was flawless.

She relaxed somewhat. "No, sir. There are one hundred and fifty rooms and suites."

"This is very inefficient. It is almost one maid per room."

"Perhaps you haven't had time to inspect the hotel. Each room is more like a small apartment. The suites are more like a complete house. Then

there are ballrooms and banqueting halls. The staff has to work in shifts."
"How do you keep track of the staff?"
"By careful organization, sir."
Ernst Lohse let a half-smile lighten his features. "You are twenty-seven years old, and single. Why so?"
"I'm perfectly happy as it is."
"Normally, a woman of your age is married with a brood of children."
Yolande repressed her frown and stared back at him. "It wasn't my destiny." She mentally added and it's none of your business.
He glanced at the papers in front of him. "I see that instead of walking up the aisle you went to the École des Hautes Études de Commerce. Why not the University of Paris and the Sorbonne?"
"The Sorbonne if the faculty of the Humanities. I was eligible for the higher education in commerce and successfully passed the entrance exam. Don't confuse the word École with a children's school."
"Touché. What is your ambition?"
"To become director of the entire hotel staff."
He raised an eyebrow. "Four hundred and fifty employees. You are certainly ambitious."
"Eventually, I want to become the managing director of the hotel."
His lips pursed into a dry smile. He inclined his head. "Monsieur Claude Auzello needs to watch out or he will be out of a job."
Yolande smiled for the first time. "Not just yet."
"How do you feel about serving us?"
She held his gaze steadily. "No different from any other tourists."
He laughed. "But tourists we are not. We intend to stay."
She deliberately soothed away the angry feeling that was creeping over her. "We have some long-term residents. Mr. Auzello told me you made reservations, so you are our guests."
Lohse laughed out loud. "For a woman, you have attitude. I like that. Though I am sure many of your compatriots are wishing they had never seen us."
Yolande made no reply. He switched to German. "I see that you speak my language."
"A little. I also speak a little English and Spanish."
"Perfect German, maybe with a hint of an Austrian accent. Where did you learn?"
"I spent a year in Vienna. I love the mountains."
"I guessed right. In a hotel with an international reputation, it is no doubt a necessity to speak other languages. Are all staff members going to stay?"
"Nobody has tendered their resignation. Only a few apprentices haven't come back to work. I'm hiring to replace them."
"Good. Some employees might just prefer to leave. Are there any employees you would like to fire?"
She bristled. "No, sir. Everyone was carefully vetted before being hired. The Ritz is a luxury establishment. Only the very best work here."

His smile revealed perfect white teeth. "That includes you. Very well. I shall recommend you continue working here. I will now interview the other managers and assistant managers. I hope I can see you again."

Yolande stood at the same time as the Oberleutnant. "Tell me, Mademoiselle Bourgmestre. What happened to your fiancé?"

La vache! What a bloody cow! They know everything those pigs. "It'll be six years in the summer that he drowned."

"That is what it says in our files. But healthy, athletic young men do not just drown."

"He saved my life when I was caught in a riptide."

A silence stretched between them.

"I take it you do not want to marry out of respect for his memory?"

"I haven't found anyone interesting enough."

He smiled and held out his hand. After a slight hesitation, she took it. Warm, dry and firm, it sent a shock through her arm. She was thankful she too had dry hands. He held her hand a moment longer than a mere handshake warranted then released her and escorted her to the door.

Chapter Thirteen

The heat settled like a lead blanket over the city. Commandant de gendarmerie Jacques Werner sighed in relief when he breathed in the cooler air of the Manoir's great hall. He shed his uniform jacket.

"Ah, come in, old friend," Gontrand said. "So what's the latest news from the Préfecture de Police?"

The two men installed themselves in the petit salon. Bérangère joined them, while waiting for Marie to prepare the Sunday lunch.

"General von Stutnitz gave up trying to keep the Parisians indoors. It's too hot, for one thing, but in reality it's because half the population is already out on the streets watching the Krauts and he wouldn't be able to get them back inside without shooting at them. *Ah, quel chianlit*! Forgive my Latin, Bérangère."

They burst out laughing. "I agree it's a pain in the ass," Gontrand said. "But it's temporary. The fight's not over."

Jacques ran the fingers of both hands through his cropped hair. "My friend, nous sommes foutus."

"Of course not! We're not finished. The army is regrouping as I speak."

"You wish."

"What about you and your gendarmes? You're army too. You didn't retreat."

"We weren't at the front. Since most of the gendarmes and policemen were called up, someone had to stay in the city and keep the peace, especially after they declared Paris an open city. We kept getting contrary orders. First we were to evacuate. Then telegrams from General Weygand ordering us to stay on post. Prefect Langeron and I stayed with a small group. The others were sent away. Some on the barges."

"What barges? You don't fight with barges!"

"We piled all the files from the headquarters into two barges with enough dynamite to blow up a city block and sent them south. Not a good idea to let the Nazis have files of our delinquents. Then yesterday morning, some Geheim Staatz Polizei goons got Prefect Langeron out of bed before dawn. They wanted the files." Jacques laughed like a boy who had played a clever trick on someone.

Bérangère shook her head. "It doesn't sound like the government knows what it's doing."

"Quiet! Maréchal Pétain certainly knows what he is doing. He'll get us out of this mess and send the Germans packing."

Bérangère rolled her eyes. "You don't get it, do you?"

Jacques held up his hand. "Gontrand, my friend, have no illusions. The

Germans are not going anywhere. We need the Americans and the Brits to come and help us throw them out."

Gontrand frowned. "Who, us?"

"You don't think that all the French will sit down and wait, do you?"

Bérangère glanced at Gontrand's bellicose face. "Haven't you seen all the French prisoners removing the sandbags from the monuments? Prisoners can't fight. They can't fight with bare hands."

"I'm afraid your beautiful wife is right, Gontrand. We've got zero chance to get the Germans out right now."

"What about the English?"

"They took a serious beating at Dunkirk and I hear they left all their arms and materiel behind."

"That's not what the wireless said."

Jacques mopped his balding head with his handkerchief. "Don't tell me you believe the news. They, and we, had orders to keep quiet so the population wouldn't panic."

Bérangère spluttered. "As if that stopped people from running out from their homes to try to get to an illusion of safety in the south."

"My dear, we, too, sent our children south."

"We planned their journey to the family home in the Auvergne. That's different."

Further argument as to what was different was cut short when Marie announced that lunch was served in the dining room.

"Your T.S.F. working? Pétain's supposed to speak tomorrow."

Chapter Fourteen

Montauloup, Sunday, June 16, 1940

The quiet of the evening was shattered by screeches and groans that sent everyone scurrying to the front door to see what the noise was. To the amazement of the adults and the laughter of the youngsters, the Citroën Rosalie puffed and panted toward the foot of the front steps but zig-zagged several meters past it before stopping.

A perspiring and bewildered Madeleine clambered out of the vehicle. François got out from the other side and opened the driver's door. He gallantly offered his arm to a shaking Charmaine. Marianne and Baptiste tumbled out and ran to the adults now waiting on the lawn. François called to two people still inside as a chorus of shouts welcomed them. "What happened?"

Engulfed in warmth and smothered in hugs, the new arrivals let themselves be led to the salon. They were barely seated than Elissa was already bringing in cold homemade lemonade.

With hand raised, Charmaine asked for silence. "Jean-Pierre Levy and his little sister Ruth got a ride with us. Jean-Pierre was the first to help when bullets did something to the engine. He's got the car going every time it broke down."

"Thank you very much, young man. Have you somewhere to go?" Huguette asked him.

"No, ma'am. Mother was killed on the road." He wiped a tear and hugged his sister closer. "Ruth is three."

"Then you can stay here with us."

Marianne crouched by Ruth. "See, poppet, everything will be all right."

"Are you eaten?" Elissa's French was still far from perfect.

"We had some bread and cheese a while back," François replied.

"I make supper."

Everyone including the children sat at the dining table to partake of the savory omelets Elissa whipped up one after the other. They then trooped outside to examine the Citroën. "It's lost a couple of springs."

"That must be when I hit a bomb crater. I drove to the side of it but the asphalt collapsed. Several old men stopped to lift the car out."

Arnaud and Pedro kept poking at the damaged vehicle and lifted the hood. "Is that a piece of wood wedged against the alternator?"

"Yes, sir," Jean-Pierre replied. "It was kinda loose."

"Very clever," Arnaud said.

Pedro pulled a soaked rag from a hose. "Can't do much about the bullet holes, but I can fix things like this." He poked some more about the car and sat inside. "The brakes are shot."

Arnaud glanced at Charmaine who hovered close by. "How did you manage downhill in the mountains?"

"Jean-Pierre found a length of chain on the road and tied it underneath the car, in front of the back wheels. It worked when I zigzagged right over the grass on the side. Then he'd untie it on the flat and uphill."

"You're very resourceful, young man," Arnaud said. "I wouldn't have thought of that."

Jean-Pierre reddened with pride.

Pedro stroked his chin. "Once I get it running again, I'll take it to the village, Arnaud. I can help the mechanic fix the brakes."

"Fine. You do that. Shall we push it into the workshop?"

They pushed and heaved and steered the car through the double doors. Back in the house, everyone gathered in the grand salon, Charmaine and Madeleine had to tell the harrowing story of their journey. Julie sat on the fringe of the animated group. Lyse-May, leading a tearful Ruth came to her. The little girl held her arms out.

Without a word, Julie leaned forward and picked her up. She passed her fingers through the girl's tangled mass of red curls. "Let's go and get cleaned up." She carried the child upstairs, preceded by her niece. In the bedroom, after Ruth was bathed and her hair disciplined again, Lyse-May pulled a small suitcase from under the bed and opened it. She didn't notice Julie stiffen.

"These are Claire's clothes. She's an angel now, in heaven. She doesn't need these clothes anymore. She's wearing a beautiful dress made of sunshine and moonbeams." While she talked, Lyse-May picked out a dress.

With lips firmly compressed, Julie helped her dress Ruth, with socks and shoes too. It took an effort to curb her tears, but she smiled. "Thank you, Lyse-May. Now Ruth looks lovely." Love for the two young girls in front of her threatened to submerge her. It was the love she could no longer give her own daughter. She gathered up the dirty garments and accompanied the children back downstairs.

***

Monday, June 17, 1940

While the children played outdoors under the watchful eyes of Elissa and Berthe, the adults gathered in the grand salon to listen to the noon news. Arnaud switched on the wireless set and requested silence. The news reader's unemotional voice filled the room. "This is Radio-Paris. In a few moments, Marshal Pétain will be taking the microphone to make an important announcement." François and Jean-Pierre sneaked in behind Pedro, who had dropped his workman's overalls in the hallway.

"*...It is with a heavy heart that I am informing you today that we must cease the combat. Last night I went to speak with our adversary in this conflict to ask if he is ready to seek with us, after our soldiers on both sides have fought with honor, the means to end all hostilities...*" A roar in the room drowned out the old man's voice.

Voices wailed as one. "He's sold us out to the enemy!" It was followed by imprecations and a stream of insults. Arnaud nodded. "He's doing what's best for France. It can't have been easy for the hero of Verdun to admit defeat. He had tears in his voice when he spoke."

Huguette stood up. "Pfff... He wasn't crying! That was the bleating of an old goat, and his trembling voice is just feeble with old age. He's eighty-four and should just go and water his roses."

Arnaud's voice rose in pitch. "Enough, woman! You don't know what you're talking about."

"You think women have no brains because we don't yet have the vote, but I ask you, who kept the country going during the last war? And the same thing's going to happen now. The Chleus are here, our soldiers are prisoners. It's the women who will fight."

Berthe rang an antique school bell. They quieted. "Please, let's go to the dining room for lunch. I see the children are already in the kitchen. I forbid you to talk until we've finished."

In silence, but with long faces and slumped shoulders, they took their places at the table. The food was dispatched and polite thanks given to Elissa. Then everyone retired to the sitting room. Julie put her coffee cup down, "I'm going back to Paris."

Stupor prevented anyone from speaking. She needed to explain. "I should go to look after Bérangère and Gontrand. He can be quite volatile, as you know. The news of defeat, surrender must have made him raging mad."

Eugene sighed. "Unless it killed him."

"Bérangère would have phoned," Berthe said.

"The telephone doesn't work," Arnaud said. "And don't bother to try to buy a newspaper. There are none."

"It's going to be mighty difficult to go to Paris, Julie. It's full of Germans," Berthe said.

"You must wait a couple of days until we know the result of the armistice and know the conditions they might impose," Arnaud said. "Soldiers who aren't prisoners will be demobilized. You should wait here for Sylvain."

"He'll go home, to Paris. That's where I'm going. I'll go to the village tomorrow. Maybe the mayor or the gendarmes will have news we don't."

It was recognized that nobody could stop Julie when she made up her mind. Gloom settled once more.

***

Paris, Monday, June 17, 1940

The de Montregards, and Marie and her husband, sat in the salon, with the wireless on. They listened to Marshal Pétain deliver his address. Her face red with anger, Bérangère roared. "The man's senile. They should lock him up in an asylum!"

"Enough! Don't you realize he is winning us more time? He

understands war. Didn't he save France at Verdun in the First War? He'll reorganize and strengthen our army and, when everything is in place, he'll teach the Boche another lesson."

"Pétain's simply the head waiter who has just handed them the country on a silver platter. But you can bet the kitchen staff aren't going to take it lying down."

"You stop your subversive talk and obey the Maréchal. He's fooling the Boches into thinking that we're happy to have them."

Bérangère and the Latours exchanged long looks and gave a subtle shake of the head.

Chapter Fifteen

Montauloup, Tuesday, June 18, 1940

The morning didn't bring any joy to Montauloup despite the warm summer day. In the workshop, hunched over the damaged car, Pedro banged on metal. His vigorous blows could be heard from the house. The adolescents found ways to amuse the children. In the kitchen, Elissa, Brigitte and Huguette peeled vegetables and baked. Julie came back hot and sweaty from having bicycled to the village and back.

"No news. No one knows anything." She collapsed onto a chair and took big gulps from a glass of cold well water.

By evening, the children who, all day, had received undivided attention went to bed without protest. A gloomy silence reigned over the table where people lingered over coffee. In the salon, Jean-Pierre watched François fiddle with the wireless. "Surely, we can get England on shortwave, non?"

"Let me try. You're all thumbs. You must turn the dial very slowly..."

The wireless crackled and whined. Jean-Pierre adjusted the tuning and a voice came through loud and clear. "*...fate of the world. I, General de Gaulle, presently in London, invite all French officers and soldiers who are on British soil, or might end up here, with or without arms, to join me. For, whatever happens, the flame of the French resistance must not be extinguished and will never be extinguished. Tomorrow, as today, I will speak on the radio from London.*"

The two youths looked at each other before hurling the biggest whoop their voices were capable of. They charged into the salon talking at the same time.

"General de Gaulle said he'll continue fighting."

"The flame of the resistance will not die!"

Arnaud raised his hand. "Whoa! Steady now. One at the time."

The boys glanced at each other. "You first since you picked up the broadcast."

"General de Gaulle is asking officers and soldiers to join him in London."

"Because he wants to resist the Germans."

The family's surprised stares went from one to the other. Eugene cleared his throat. "Who's this General de Gaulle?"

"I don't know."

"Never heard of him."

"I don't care who he is," Jean-Pierre said. "He's going to fight on. So I'm going to London to join him,"

"You're too young, my boy."

"I'll be eighteen on my next birthday. That's old enough to be a soldier. Besides, I've aged ten years in the last ten days." His voice broke. He swallowed hard. "Anyway, I have to go because of my name."

"What about your name?"

"Levy. I'm Jewish."

Arnaud scratched his head. "But you're French."

Julie leaned forward. "The Germans are imprisoning and killing Jews in Germany, regardless of whether they're citizens, practicing Jews, or not. They'll start that here too."

A collective gasp greeted her words.

Jean-Pierre smiled. "See, one more reason why I shouldn't hang around. I'll go to England. There are other Frenchmen there, those who got away at Dunkirk. I'll enlist. We'll make an army and come back to fight the Huns."

"Spoken like a true French patriot," Huguette said.

"But now isn't the time. Maréchal Pétain..."

Arnaud's words were cut short by boos.

Pedro had come in unnoticed. "Would they take me? I volunteered for the French Army but they didn't want me. Wanted to put me in a detention camp."

A fruitless discussion ensued. François raised his hand.

"Speak, you're not in school," his mother said.

"I believe that being a communist refugee from the Spanish Civil War, Pedro might have serious difficulties getting into England. It's not like we could just take the ferry from Calais. But if I understand General de Gaulle's words, he'll form an army in England but everyone here in France, in our Hexagone, ought to resist. So we need to create an army too, a secret army, and Pedro would be invaluable because of his military experience."

"What has happened to our children? Sixteen going on sixty," Huguette said.

"I'd just like to ask you the biggest favor on earth."

Huguette looked at Jean-Pierre thoughtfully. "What is it?"

"Could you take care of my little sister? You understand it is my strongest desire to go and fight for my, our, country, but Ruth... she has nobody when I leave. Our father was killed in Arras. I don't really want her to go into an orphanage."

"You can count on us. No harm will come to her. Children are not responsible for the mess of the adults."

"Thank you, ma'am. I'll do my best to stay alive and come back for her."

"It might be a good idea to give Ruth another name, something more French sounding," Julie said.

A why question crossed all faces but remained unspoken until François snapped his fingers. "I get it. If the Germans were anywhere near her, they'd know straight away that Ruth is a typically Jewish name and would take her away to be killed."

Arnaud threw his arms up. "Don't be stupid. They aren't coming here."

Huguette stood up to serve more coffee. She put her hands on her hips. "Who knows? You? Why? You haven't a clue, my dear Arnaud. You still live in the 1914 war. Julie is absolutely right. The Nazis have done lots of bad things. We don't know the half of it. Why do you think we had so many Germans, Jews and others, seeking refuge in France over the last six or seven years?"

No one dared reply to her tirade.

"If you all agree, we'll call Ruth, Reine. It's close and she should adopt it without difficulties."

"Thank you, madame Huguette. While I'm here, I'll make sure she understands."

***

Now that Jean-Pierre was adept at picking up the broadcasts from London, the adults spent most of their time in the salon. Elissa enrolled Marianne and Pedro to supervise the children outside on the lawn, playing on the newly refurbished swing, while she prepared meals.

"Did you hear on Radio-Paris that Hitler is letting Marshal Pétain govern France?" Huguette asked.

"Hitler doesn't want the responsibility of a bunch of rebellious people," Berthe replied.

"What rebellion? Everyone is too down in the dumps to rebel," Charmaine said.

Eugene put a finger to his lips. "Listen!"

In the silence broken only by the announcer's voice, they looked at each other. Brigitte burped Christiane.

"You mean, they're going to sign the armistice and give Pétain half of France?" Julie asked.

"That's what it said," Eugene replied. "But this new French government will also administer the other half where the Germans are going to settle."

Arnaud puffed out his chest. "Well, it's not so bad, is it? I told you Maréchal Pétain knows what he is doing."

Moments later they learned that a demarcation line would be established, like a border. Montauloup would remain in the non-occupied zone.

Julie stood. "Then it is imperative I leave right now. Bérangère won't be able to hold Gontrand back by herself."

Arnaud shrugged. "You're a fool to return to Paris. It's crawling with German soldiers. You don't want to live cheek by jowl with them. At least here we can live normally. The government is to be in Clermont-Ferrand and everything will soon be running normally."

Julie pulled a face. "Too close. The air stinks." Guffaws greeted her words. "You heard what General de Gaulle said? Resist. I'll go and make the Germans' life in Paris as miserable as I can."

Arnaud wasn't done. "That's crazy."

"You could go to Pontcharra. The mountain air is purer," Madeleine said.

"And find the Italians ensconced there? No thanks, they're as bad as the Germans." She didn't want to offend Madeleine who had obviously missed the point of the conversation.

Arnaud took his head in his hands. "What did I do to God that he gave me women like these to look after? Don't you realize that you can't do anything against the German power?"

Brigitte and Charmaine tittered.

Julie lifted her chin. "I know the story of the lion and the mouse. The powerful lion was kept in bonds, the tiny mouse gnawed at them, and freed the lion. I'm a mouse, and I'll find other mice to help me."

Berthe sighed. "I fear for your safety."

"I'll take care of myself, don't worry. I'll leave in the morning."

"Do you have a backpack? And good hiking boots? You might have to walk," Huguette said.

Julie nodded. "After our last big holiday, we left all our outdoor gear here."

Everyone sank into their private thoughts. Julie's mind went back to the last holiday, three years ago, when they were all gathered at the old château to celebrate Claire's christening, still believing there would be no war.

In the morning Julie brought down her backpack only to find Lyse-May dressed with a bag at her feet.

Julie looked at Huguette and Elissa. "What's going on?"

Fingers pointed at Lyse-May. "Ask her."

"I'm going with you. I want to stay with pépère and mémée. Like you."

"Julie, you should take our car," Huguette suggested.

"Thanks, but the roads are still probably littered with debris. I'll take the train."

"With me."

The women stared at the child. At last, Berthe spoke. "You should stay here until your aunt finds out the situation in Paris. Then you can go with one of us."

"I'm going with tata Julie."

Huguette sighed and shrugged her shoulders. "Stubbornness is a de Montregard trait."

Julie smiled. "That's all right, Lyse-May. You always work miracles with your grandfather."

Pedro had been hovering on the threshold for a little while. "Madame Huguette, I can drive the ladies to the train station in Le Falgoux in your Packard. I need to find some parts to repair the Citroën."

Lyse-May picked up her bag. Julie nodded. "Let's go."

The goodbyes were soon over. Pedro was silent and that suited Julie. He understood. Her silence was filled with scraps of memories that streamed through her mind. Sometimes she didn't hear other people. She was absent-minded. They arrived in time to catch the micheline train from Le Falgoux to Clermont-Ferrand.

On the station platform, Pedro turned to Julie. "Madame Julie, I heard you don't accept *them* occupying France."

"That's right. *They* killed my daughter." Her tone hardened. "I don't know how yet, but I'll find a way to get rid of them. And I'm Julie for you."

"You let me know, and I'll be right by your side, Julie."

"That's a deal, Pedro." They shook hands. Pedro helped her and Lyse-May into a carriage.

In Clermont-Ferrand they changed trains. They had just found a compartment when the ticket inspector thrust his head in. "I hope we can get to Bourges, madame. Nobody knows whether the rail line has been repaired yet. This is the first train going north."

"Let's hope everything is in order."

It wasn't and at Comentry they had to disembark. "So, what shall we do, Lyse-May?"

"We can ask a car driver to give us a ride."

"I guess that's a good idea. Let's see if we can have a bite to eat first." She wasn't going to tell her niece that there didn't appear to be any cars or trucks on the road. A meal would give her time to think of a solution.

They walked to the Café de la Gare. It was packed but a jovial man signaled to Julie. "There's room here for you at my table. I'll steal another chair for the little princess."

Lyse-May beamed him a smile, and in no time they were seated. A harassed waitress offered them the plat du jour.

"You were on the train and it's going nowhere, is that it?" The man bit into his mushroom omelet. "No meat today. Too bad. But hopefully now things will be back to normal."

"I hope so. Is there another rail line we can take?"

"Going to Paris? No, I'm afraid not. But I can offer you a place in my truck. I'm going to Moulins to deliver my cheeses. I'm Les Fromageries Biquette."

Was there an unknown force that'd drawn her to this café? "If you don't mind, I'll be glad to accept."

"And I'll be glad of the company. Here come your omelets."

The young woman put two plates on the table and a glass of milk for Lyse-May. Soon afterwards they were on the road. Time passed quickly with Lyse-May wanting to learn everything about cheese-making.

As they approached the city of Moulins, they saw the destruction on all sides. At the bridge over the River Allier, they gasped in shock. At a roadblock manned by German soldiers, the guard waved them to a stop. They had to detour to the iron bridge. There another barrier blocked their way. A soldier asked where they were going.

"To deliver the cheese to the distribution center."

"And you, madame?" a soldier on the other side asked.

"I'm going home to Paris." He looked at her identity papers. "Is that your daughter?"

She held his gaze and frowned. A cramp gripped her insides. "Of course, why the question?"

"Give me her identity card."

"Children do not have one."

He turned to Lyse-May. "And who are you?"

"I'm Claire de Montregard."

"How do I know?"

Lyse-May looked puzzled for a second or two. "You asked me so now you know."

With a chuckle, the soldier returned the papers to Julie and raised the barrier. Julie couldn't get over the cleverness of her niece. Did she work out her grief by pretending to be her beloved cousin at least some of the time? Julie was aware that a young child could pick up on the mood of adults. Did Lyse-May sense her fear and by saying Claire it'd give her aunt strength?

Monsieur Biquette drove to the station in silence. "Merci, monsieur."

"De rien, madame. It's nothing but I think we just got a taste of what those B... Germans are like." He threw a glance around but there were only a few civilian passengers. "If you're ever back in these parts, look me up. Every week, like clockwork..."

"We won't forget, Monsieur Biquette."

They said goodbye. The train departed.

Julie was wondering whether the train would make it to Paris, when it stopped. She looked at the sign on the station, Saint-Amand-Montrond. The stationmaster shouted for everyone to get off.

"What are we going to do, tata?"

"Maybe you shouldn't call me tata because we don't know how much those Germans understand. We have to pretend you're my daughter."

"May I call you mama?"

She swallowed hard. "Yes, chérie, that's better."

"So what are we doing now, mama?"

Julie gave a tight smile. "I have to think. First, we should find a place to eat supper and stay the night."

The Hôtel de la Gare was their only choice.

"I don't have room, madame. These gentlemen are staying here." The owner motioned with his chin to a group of German officers seated at a table.

"Please, monsieur. I cannot sleep outside with my little girl."

"But, madame, there is no room available."

As if on cue Lyse-May burst out sobbing very loudly. If she hadn't been so tense, Julie would have laughed. Lyse-May's swift grasp of the situation amazed her. One of the Germans, a handsome, fair-haired Hauptmann, turned his head, stood up and walked over. "Why are you crying, little girl?"

"The man said there's no room for me." Lyse-May gave an inelegant sniff.

"Please forgive my... my daughter. We are tired. She easily gets upset."

"Don't worry. We will find room." He turned his head toward his table.

"Friedricht pack your bag and bunk with Helmut for tonight." He then summoned the manager. "Monsieur l'hôtelier, have your maid make up the room for these two charming ladies."

"Merci, m'sieur." Lyse-May lifted her face where a radiant smile illuminated her pixie features.

"Thank you so much, Herr Hauptmann."

"How do you know my rank?"

"My husband was.. is a captain, too." Whether he was or not, she presumed that one officer would be sympathetic to another officer.

The German pulled up a chair and sat next to Julie. A serveuse brought two bowls of steaming soup. "You said was?"

"I don't know. We've had no news. This is why I am returning to Paris."

"And the train won't be going for some days while the line is being repaired. May I offer you a ride to Paris? I'm leaving early in the morning."

Butterflies swirled in Julie's stomach. "We don't want to be an inconvenience."

"No inconvenience at all. It will be my pleasure."

German or not, she wasn't going to let pass such an opportunity. "Then, thank you again. We'll be ready."

When Julie and Lyse-May finished their meal, the hotelier took them to the now vacant room. "I must say you're lucky," he said, "but don't get too friendly with him, okay?"

"Believe me, I won't. I hate *them* with every bone in my body."

Lyse-May tugged the hotelier's jacket. "Claire was killed by the planes. I hate *them* too."

Tears sprung to Julie's eyes. She pulled Lyse-May close. "My other daughter."

"Oh, how I'm so sorry, petite madame. I'll get my wife to knock on your door in the morning to make sure you don't miss the ride. Please, don't kill the captain. It wouldn't advance us all. Actually, ils sont corrects."

She gave a half-laugh. "Ah, yes. I hear they are good and proper. Thank you, and goodnight."

The morning broke with that freshness that precedes a hot day. Comfortably installed in the official military Opel, with Lyse-May between her and the captain, Julie began to relax. "Allow me to introduce myself. I'm Hans Schneider, and as you recognized, I hold the rank of Hauptmann. My colonel is sending me to Paris on his behalf." He smiled. "The good food and the superior wine got the better of his fragile constitution."

"Sorry to hear that, Herr Hauptmann. I'm Julie de Montregard."

"And I'm Lyse-May de Montregard."

"Enchanté, mademoiselle. We have to make a detour to some little town to cross the Loire River. Your Saumur officer cadets... It is that what you call them?"

"Indeed."

"Well, they blew up the stone bridge at Orléans. There was really no need for such wanton destruction. Now we have an armistice. No need to fight. We want to get along with the French people and build the new Europe together."

She gritted her teeth but managed a polite, "That sounds good."

"We'll be organizing a reception at the German embassy, I do hope you'll come."

"I'll try my best to be there. First I have to make sure my father-in-law is all right. He can fly off the handle a bit."

He flashed a smile with fine white teeth. "I understand. My father does too."

The roads had been more or less cleared. Any abandoned cars and other discarded items had been piled up in the ditches. The sun was about to set when they arrived in Paris. "Please let me off by a Métro station, Herr Hauptmann."

"No, no. I'll take you home."

"Thank you." She gave the directions. What will the neighbors think!

The Opel purred to a stop in front of 184 Avenue Victor-Hugo. The driver took her bags from the trunk while Hans helped her and Lyse-May out of the car. "Are you sure you're all right?"

"Yes, and thank you very much."

She grabbed her backpack, Lyse-May was already holding her bag. She opened the heavy door and saw the Opel drive away. Julie crossed the lobby as fast as she could with Lyse-May. As luck would have it, the elevator was on the ground floor.

Julie fumbled with the key to the apartment, thankful that Madame Durand hadn't been standing outside her loge. Hopefully, she hadn't been behind her curtain either.

A wave of sadness engulfed Julie as she stepped into the apartment. Lyse-May ran to the bathroom. Before Julie could dwell on memories, there was a knock at the door. It was her neighbor, Madame Mahut.

"I heard noise. I'm glad to see you back. Do you need any provisions?"

"I'm glad to be back. Actually, I could do with some bread and perhaps a little bit of milk for Lyse-May."

At the puzzled look of her neighbor, Julie told her of the tragedy. Madame Mahut took Julie's hand in hers. "I know there are no words, but I feel. I feel like a mother. I'll get you some food."

Julie wiped her eyes. She'll have to get used to it, tell people, hear the words of comfort... or not.

Chapter Sixteen

The air, already hot, penetrated the apartment through the wide-open windows. Lyse-May entered the kitchen. "I'm hungry."

"Have the rest of the bread and milk. We'll shop after we go and see your grandparents. Let me have your dress. It's a bit wrinkled. I'll iron it so you can look pretty."

The little girl stepped out of her sundress and handed it to her aunt. Breakfast over and looking less crumpled, they headed to the Manoir. It didn't take long. No cars on the streets to hinder their walk. They turned onto the Avenue Chantemesse and approached the elegant stone mansion. Julie halted in fear. Lyse-May looked up, not understanding.

In front of the Manoir three German cars were parked and men in uniform milled about. At the top of the steps, Gontrand stood intractable, his puffed up chest displaying all his medals. No doubt about his attitude. He was barring the door to a soldier.

A Wehrmacht Hauptmann appeared to be arguing with Gontrand. Another officer jumped out of a Mercedes. Julie remained paralyzed by fear, but realized he was a higher ranking officer than the captain. Pushing her fear aside, she bounded across the road, followed by Lyse-May. Obviously, Gontrand didn't know they could imprison him, medals or not. She heard the senior officer addressing her father-in-law.

"Monsieur de Montregard, I am General von Trennen. I am in need of accommodation. I requested to be assigned to your residence because you are just on the other side of the Bois de Boulogne and I have a horse that I would love to have your permission to stable at Le Manoir. I only need a few rooms and will do my best not to disturb you and your family."

Gontrand crossed his arms over his chest. Then frowned. "I lost my leg in Paschendaele. I have earned the right to remain alone with my family in my home."

"Then, Monsieur de Montregard, we were neighbors in Paschendaele. I took your bullets in the shoulder."

Gontrand's lips creased imperceptibly. There was nothing he could do except take the high road. "I agree to be neighbors again, but be reassured, there won't be any bullets this time."

"You mean that there are no firearms in the house?"

"Indeed. I locked my revolver securely in the cellar. With all the grandchildren running around, it wasn't safe keeping it in my desk."

General von Trennen inclined his head. "Very wise. Of course, you must have heard that all citizens must turn in their firearms."

"I did. And I ignored it. Now if you'd like to come in." Gontrand stepped aside and held the door open.

Aghast at her father-in-law's defiance, Julie, followed by Lyse-May, went to Bérangère who was biting her lips and then exhaled a long breath when she saw that her husband was behaving in a civilized manner. She knew they couldn't object and the general was asking politely. After due introductions were made, Bérangère introduced her daughter-in-law.

"General, this is Julie de Montregard, and my granddaughter Lyse-May. Now let me show you the house."

The General told his orderly to stay outside until called and signaled to the captain. "Permit me to introduce my aide-de-camp, Hauptmann Langen."

Preceded by Bérangère, the party toured the mansion. Lyse-May slipped her hand into her grandfather's and pulled him into the petit salon to tell him all about their journey.

"This is the ballroom," Bérangère said. "The windows open onto the Bois de Boulogne. Those sliding doors at the far end lead into the music room. We open them for receptions.

Reynard von Trennen approached the Pleyel grand piano. "You play, I believe, madame."

"I do."

"I play the violin. I see you have one here."

Fear made her heart beat a little faster. "It's my grandson's."

"Would that be François?"

She paled. How did he know?

He smiled as if had guessed her thoughts. "I am an Abwehr officer. But have no fear, madame. I hope music will bring us together."

She relaxed visibly. The Abwehr, she recalled, was the counter-intelligence branch of the Wehrmacht. It didn't sound as bad. "As you can see, this is the staircase to the second floor. There's a smallish room partly under the staircase in the turret. I store a few handy things in it."

"With a window looking over to the Bois de Boulogne. This is delightful."

Bérangère continued. "Here's a W.C. The doors to the kitchens are next. On the other side of the great hall is the dining room. The double doors lead into the salons." Bérangère opened the glass doors and invited the general in. "By sliding these back, one can combine the petit salon and the grand salon if you need more space. And here, close to the entrance, is my husband's study."

They walked back into the great hall. "Would you like to see the bedrooms upstairs?"

"Yes, please."

At the top of the stairs, they stepped onto the gallery overlooking the great hall, and walked on.

"That is the end of the gallery?"

She opened the door. "Yes. There are now only seven bedrooms located above the salons and dining room." We sacrificed some rooms to have a water closet, with washbasin and bidet installed in every bedroom. There's also a cubby hole between those two bedrooms."

"You have a beautiful home, madame, but my staff and I will be content with the downstairs."

"Not practical, General. We built an addition for the servants, but since they have all gone, except for Ernest and Marie Latour, who have their own little cottage at the back, we'll move into the annex, the west wing, as we call it, if you'd be so kind as to give us enough time to move what we need."

"You do not think it is possible to share the mansion? My staff and I have to spend the majority of the day out of the house, anyway."

"I think that might prove difficult. We have a large and noisy family. No doubt, you'll need to give receptions. We'll move into the west wing."

He smiled. "I really insist, madame. I refuse to have you relegated to the servants quarters. I would need a bedroom for Hauptmann Langen and one for myself. The cubbyhole will suffice for my ordonanz." He corrected himself. "My orderly."

"Ah, we call it the monk's cell."

He laughed. "What is the story behind that?"

"Just a bit of space left after the renovations. We put in a bed and a chest of drawers. It works fine. The older grandchildren fight to sleep in it."

A laugh shook the general. "I'm sure Günter, my ordonanz will be happy with your monk's cell."

"The playroom is next."

"Very fine architecture. What is above the ballroom?"

"Since the ballroom has a high ceiling, there's only a low loft where countless generations have stacked furniture and other objects they didn't need. At the top of the stairs, more attic over the rest of the house, with small bedrooms for servants but they're not comfortable, cold in winter, hot in summer, no running water, just one W.C. That's why we built the addition."

"It is grand. I love it. Please let's share, I really don't want you to move into the annex."

"You're kind, General, but I know my decision will be approved by the whole family."

The general sighed deeply. "I do not need much of an office here, Monsieur de Montregard will keep sole use of his study."

"That's where the telephone is, General."

"Then I shall see if we can get another line installed. In fact, I think that the small room in the turret will make me a fine office. I like the window overlooking the Bois de Boulogne."

"I'll remove the bric-à-brac. Would you care to see the stables now?"

He nodded. They walked through the kitchen where Marie and Ernest waited with some anxiety.

"Ernest, would you show the stables to the officers?"

Ernest preceded them. Bérangère followed.

"General, I expect you'll need the garage," Ernest said. "You enter the courtyard from Boulevard Payolle by way of the old coach gate."

"The garage has been converted from the horse stalls, but we kept two stalls on the other side of the entrance just in case the children would want a horse," Bérangère said.

"Perfect for my horse. I see you kept the hay loft, too. I shall get it filled with hay."

"There's an apartment above the garage for the driver and a groom. At the far end of the yard you see my cottage next to the sheds and workshop," Ernest said.

"An excellent use of space."

Bérangère pointed to a gracious extension of the building. "The servant quarters are small but convenient."

General von Trennen turned to Bérangère. "Merci, madame. I will enjoy living here and I hope we can become friends."

Bérangère managed a smile. "We'll see how it goes, General."

With pinched lips, Ernest led the way back through the kitchen. Julie and Gontrand came into the great hall at the same time.

Reynard von Trennen took his leave. "I shall be back this evening, but Hauptmann Langen will supervise our moving in. He will make sure you are not disturbed and that you get all the help you need to install what you need in the annex or, rather, in the west wing," he said with a smile. "But I wish you would reconsider."

Bérangère called her distraught husband to the kitchen where Julie was waiting. They sat at the table. After they made suitable fuss of Lyse-May, Bérangère asked where was Claire.

It was time for Julie to share her tragedy. Marie served coffee. When all eyes were dry, she began preparing the noon meal. Bérangère explained how they'd be moving into the west wing.

***

When the general came back in the evening, he asked for Marie.

Marie, looking nervous, stood in front of the general.

"Madame, I would be obliged if you were to cook for me and my staff when I am home, mostly for breakfast, and dinner as well as days when I am off duty."

"Yes, sir." She didn't see how she could refuse.

"I hope you will not resent me too much."

"And you're not frightened that I'll poison you?"

He laughed. "No, because that is what I would think of doing if I were in your place."

She frowned, not sure she understood. "But you wouldn't do it. You want to protect your family."

"Exactly. I do not want to force you to work for me, especially that at times I shall need to receive colleagues." A disdainful pout passed over his face.

The faintest of smile came to her lips. "It looks like you don't much like your colleagues."

"I did not choose to make war."

"But you were in the First War."

He nodded. "And that was enough. But sometimes an individual has no choice."

"There's always a choice."

He raised an eyebrow. "Perhaps I already made it."

She stared at him for a long moment. A ghost smile hovered over her lips. There she was, a servant being familiar with a general. Well, he was just a man, a man who looked tired.

"I will pay your wages."

"That won't be necessary, sir, if you ensure there is enough food to cook with."

"Explain."

"Well, today there wasn't much left at the bakery and the charcuterie was rather empty." At his frown she added. "That's where we buy cold meats, saucisson, ham, pâté. Your soldiers had bought everything. They must like the dry garlic sausage and the various pâtés."

"I am sorry about that. Probably because the situation is so new. I do not want to cause hardship to the de Montregards. Be reassured I will ensure that the house is well-supplied. And you will be paid for your work."

"Just what is needed for you and your staff. I prefer if you let me know how many will be at your table a day ahead, if possible."

He nodded. "Certainly. My orderly will usually be here. And when I hold a reception, you will hire whatever staff you need."

"No problem, there'll always be meals ready in the kitchen for him and I suppose your driver too."

"Indeed. Can you recommend someone to do the housework?"

She thought for a moment. "I think I could ask Madame Léonie Bodénan. She is madame Julie's friend and I know she doesn't have a job at this time."

"And I can trust her?"

"Entirely, sir."

"Very well, can you ask her to come and see me?"

Marie nodded her agreement and went back to the kitchen, her head teeming with thoughts. I better talk to madame Bérangère. The general is against the war. That could be useful. You never know what we could glean in his office. Because it won't be long before Frenchmen throw the Chleus out, send them back to Prussia. If I understood what he didn't say, he's against Hitler. Good to know.

***

"But, madame Bérangère, the general said he wants you to use the kitchen."

"You will cook his meals, store his food in the ice-box, and I will cook our meals on the old stove in the west wing."

"That stove's a beast, madame. That's why you got me this big gas range and put the old stove in the annex. I can cook for the family, still."

Bérangère massaged her neck. "No. You have a job with the general. We want nothing to do with his setup. The family will use the courtyard entrance too, and the back stairs if we need to get something from the attic or the cellars. We can't avoid contact with him, but we'll keep it to the minimum."

"The facilities are not very good, madame Bérangère. It's mainly a place to sleep for the staff. Then, maybe the maids will come back."

"I doubt it." Bérangère heaved a breath. "It could be worse."

***

Sunday, June 23, 1940

The new arrangement went smoothly. What with six stalwart soldiers to carry furniture to the new sitting room and other necessary tasks, it was easy. I just ordered them about. I'll confess I enjoyed it. But be reassured, I said please and thank you, though I just used my mother's tone, "Dear when you speak to servants, you must be polite but superior." To my surprise, Gontrand took it all well. He won't use his study, though. He said that if I can write on the kitchen table, he can do the crossword puzzles on it, and smoke too. I'm glad the architect insisted on making the kitchen in the addition as big as the one in the mansion. He'd told me that's where servants would always gather after work. That's where we eat now. We made a sitting room but we easily sit in the kitchen. It's rather cozy. Lyse-May has her own room. It leaves one spare bedroom for when the grandchildren stay with us. After I said it'd be really good if we had a double set of bunks, they materialized by evening. I didn't tell Gontrand. He doesn't know whether we have beds, bunks or lounge chairs and doesn't need to know.

Gontrand is expecting Jacques as usual. He couldn't wait to get rid of me. "Are you going to church?" Gontrand looked out the window. "It's raining again."

"I won't melt."

"Pray that God of yours kicks out the damned B—"

"Shhh! Don't say that word. They get quite antsy when they hear it."

He reminded me no one can hear anything beyond the kitchen door. His impatience while waiting for his friend Jacques was growing. I told him that Jacques wouldn't know to use the coach entrance. Gontrand reddened with fury. "He will use the front door! I will use the front door! And you will use the front door!"

As his voice was rising, Lyse-May rushed out of her room. "Pépère, come see my drawing."

Unable to resist his granddaughter, he followed her. My husband has not yet used the coach entrance, but he will. He didn't make too much fuss at moving into the west wing.

A while later, Commandant Jacques Werner, climbed up the stone stairs of rue Chantemesse and pushed open the door, while, in passing, giving the buzzer a brief jab of the finger, as was his habit. In the great hall, he halted in his tracks. He was confronted by a German soldier. He immediately identified him as an orderly. He had that air about him.

In bad French, the orderly asked him where he was going and repeated the question in German. "*Wo gehst du?*"

"*Ich möchte Gontrand sehen.*"

The orderly smiled. "*Im Nebengebäude.*"

"*Danke.*"

Marie rushed from the kitchen. "This way, monsieur Jacques."

Puzzled, Jacques followed her into the kitchen and to the servants' connecting vestibule. She knocked on the sitting-room door. Gontrand stood up to greet his friend.

After a firm handshake, Jacques dropped into an armchair. "What's the meaning of the Kraut in the hall? He can't even speak French. If I wasn't Alsatian I wouldn't have known what he said, and would have flattened him."

Gontrand looked at Lyse-May. "Can you play by yourself for a while? I want to talk to my friend."

Lyse-May shrugged and left the room. She spent most of her time playing by herself. Gontrand took a key from his pocket and opened a tall cabinet. He brought out two small glasses and a bottle of Calvados. After pouring, he turned to his friend.

"We have a general living here with his aide-de-camp and Günter the orderly. A Baron von Hauffen took over Count de la Ferrière's residence."

Jacques' whole body swayed forward and back. "I knew they requisitioned lots of hotels and empty houses and apartments, but I didn't think they'd requisition your house, since you're in situ."

Gontrand lit his pipe. "They obviously think they have the right. What can we do?"

Jacques lit a Gauloise. "*Putain de Boches!* An armistice was signed yesterday."

"I heard. Damned Fritz. Can't use the word Boche anymore."

"Why not?"

"They don't like it. Any useful news?"

Before Jacques could answer, Bérangère entered the room. "There were more devout Fritz in church than French people."

"Huh, so devout! They asked us to turn over German refugees from before the war," Jacques said.

Gontrand shrugged. "Well, if they are German–"

"C'mon, my friend. It's not a question of nationality. Those German refugees were against the Nazis, and if they are caught it'll be death for them."

"I wasn't thinking straight. These days, I can't think straight."

"No, you weren't. And now that the armistice is signed, it's going to be dicey trying to get rid of that plague."

"You have to wait until the Maréchal reveals his game. He's calculating and cunning."

"My friend, Pétain is a decrepit old goat. His ministers, who are all in the Nazis' pocket, manipulate him on Hitler's orders."

Gontrand inclined his head and grumbled under his breath.

Jacques pulled a face. "Can you get England on your wireless set?"

"I expect so. It has two short waves, like most wireless sets."

"Listen to it quietly. You don't want anyone to know that you're listening to foreign broadcasts. If caught it's punishable by death."

While the men were talking, Bérangère had prepared lunch. The four of them sat at a large oak table, recuperated from the attic.

Later, Julie joined them. "Tomorrow, I'll go and find out whether my magazine is reopening."

"Don't get your hopes up. Some newspapers have been banned," Jacques said.

"It's a women's magazine. It isn't political."

"The Germans have a whole set of rules they intend to apply here."

Julie's features hardened. She raised her eyebrows. "You mean they won't tolerate dissident writing?"

There was a moment of silence before they burst out laughing. Jacques sobered first. "You're actually right."

Bérangère smiled at her daughter-in-law. "Our rebellious Julie no doubt will find a way. But I'd like to caution you all, there're now Germans on the other side of the vestibule doors. We have to speak quietly if we're going to say anything about them."

"Sure, but there's the other kitchen in between. We're safe," Jacques said.

Sceptic, Bérangère nodded. Gontrand kept muttering under his mustache.

Chapter Seventeen

Montauloup

The cool morning air announced another hot day. In the château, adults were reluctant to move but the children were already clamoring and running around. The dogs barked outside to signal the arrival of a stranger. Arnaud ran downstairs. The barking ceased and was replaced by the happy whining of recognition. Arnaud relaxed.

At the front door, a man in ragged clothes waited while petting the two Braque dogs. "Bonjour, mon oncle."

"For heavens' sake, Bernard! Come in." Arnaud engulfed his nephew in a bear hug.

He directed him to the dining room. They were barely seated than the whole household descended on them, Brigitte carrying a screaming Christiane. Paul and Micheline yelled, "Papa! Papa!"

Hugs all round and joyful exclamations contributed to the chaos. A tearful Marie-Ange kissed her husband while his children encircled his waist with their arms.

When order was restored, Elissa and Huguette brought freshly baked bread, butter and jam to the table. Once Bernard had eaten, Arnaud silenced the squabbling children.

"We're eager to hear your story, Bernard."

Bernard nodded. "You know I was a stretcher-bearer, a non-combatant. An order to retreat and regroup came to us. The company's officers objected to the retreat. General Gamelin had just sent a message, Vaincre ou Mourir. If we couldn't defeat the Germans, then were we supposed to die, was that it? We could see the enemy tanks coming at us, and planes overhead. The men didn't wait and retreated."

Arnaud leaned forward, elbows on the table. "We heard some conflicting reports about our soldiers."

"What do you expect? They fight. They're overrun. They flee. They fight again. It's a different war than holding trenches in the Great War. The Germans must have had a whole division, we barely had a company. Although I thoroughly disliked it, I grabbed a gun. A lieutenant and I decided to hold the post until the soldiers could disappear and avoid capture. A bit of shrapnel found me. Lieutenant Lamouroux carried me to the Laon hospital. I'll never know how he evaded detection. The surgeon sewed me up. At that point, I was in fact a prisoner because Laon had been taken by the Germans. I didn't see the lieutenant anywhere and decided to leave.

"As I was trying to get dressed at about five a.m., a nurse walked into the ward and told me to wait. I was fuming. I had missed my escape. She got the doctor. Instead of turning me in, he helped me dress and gave me an old civilian jacket to put over my uniform. Said he couldn't let a medic colleague become a prisoner. He showed me a rough map of the town, where to go and what places to avoid and with his help I memorized it. Then he led me outside through the morgue and up a basement stairs into a garden."

Bernard paused to take a sip of coffee. "I limped out of Laon through alleys and people's gardens until I came to a rural lane. I oriented myself and headed south. There were abandoned farms on the way, so I helped myself to water and whatever food they had."

"Did you leave a thank-you note?" Paul asked.

Bernard smiled at his son. "Actually, I did with a few coins too. I walked through the woods and along hedges. Finally I arrived at Condé-sur-Aisne, pretty exhausted, and looking for a place to spend the night. That's when an old man overtook me on his bicycle. He jumped off and said, "Bon Dieu! Soldat. Didn't you hear all men in uniform are to be prisoners?" I hadn't heard there was an armistice. He took me into his house and made me stay until I could walk properly. He couldn't get over that I walked thirty kilometers with stitches from knee to hip. That surgeon did a good job."

Bernard stopped talking, lost in memories. André Leroy had been a medic in the Great War. The two of them had talked and talked when they weren't trying to listen to the wireless.

He shook himself. "One night, André and I listened to the English radio. Did you hear that General de Gaulle wants to continue the fight and is asking for volunteers to join him?"

Eugène pointed to Jean-Pierre and François. "We did, thanks to these two rascals."

"That was it. I was determined to get to England. By then I had healed well enough. André found me civilian clothes, bread and cheese, and I walked with a cane that he made for me."

Arnaud tilted his head and made an incredulous grimace. "You've heard that all the soldiers in the northern zone are considered prisoners and cannot be demobilized?"

"That's why I kept walking and hiding until I could get here. Actually, farmers were good giving me rides on their hay wagons. It was as if they knew who in the next village would be willing to give me a ride. At Gannay-sur-Loire, a peasant told me I wasn't the first soldier they were helping south of the demarcation line."

"The gendarmerie in Le Falgoux will demobilize you. Then what? Will you stay here and help on the farm?"

Eugene shot his brother a dark look. "Bernard, don't listen to Arnaud and Gontrand. They're besotted with Pétain. They have blinkers on."

"I'll find a way to get to England," Bernard said.

Marie-Ange jumped from her seat. "Bernard! You've just come back to us. You can't leave. You've done all the fighting you could do, even though you promised you'd be fine because you were a non-combatant. And you lied about that."

"Darling, in times of war, a man has to do whatever comes his way."

Huguette discreetly ushered the children outside, except Paul and Micheline who clung to their father.

"For us, the war is over, there's an armistice."

The three men glanced at one another. "No, Marie-Ange, Hitler is continuing the war with the countries allied to us. An armistice is not the end of the war. Just a reprieve," Eugene said.

"But we aren't occupied. We are still France and we have a French government under Marshal Pétain."

Charmaine drew Brigitte into the foyer. "Marie-Ange's a Pétain supporter now?"

"Sounds like it. And her way is the only way."

"It's a wonder the children are so nice."

"Bernard used to spend a lot of time with them."

Brigitte acquiesced. "He did, and he's a man who thinks of others before himself."

"That's why he was in the medical corps." The two women went to sit outside and watch the children play on the lawn.

After supper, Huguette nudged Bernard, who had slept all day. "Are you sure you still want to go to England?"

"As soon as I get my demobilization papers, yes."

"I have a cousin, Mistral Lambert, who is a fisherman in Valras. If my geography is correct, it's in the free zone and I'm sure he could get you to Gibraltar. It doesn't look far on the map."

They consulted the map she had brought. "Do you think, it's feasible?"

"It depends on your cousin's political views. Has he accepted Pétain's surrender, like Arnaud?"

"Oh, no! Not him. Just before they cut off the phone, he called to say that he and his friends would come and hide in our mountains to continue fighting, and would I help. You can trust him."

"Thanks, Auntie Huguette."

"Don't mind me listening," interrupted Jean-Pierre. "But I'm going with you." Bernard looked him up and down.

Before he could speak, Huguette said, "Jean-Pierre really helped our friend Charmaine on the road. He's very resourceful, determined and Jewish."

A smile lit up Bernard tired features. He held his hand out to the boy. "I won't ask your age. Tomorrow, I'll get demobilized, and next day we'll leave at dawn. If we can find a couple of bicycles."

"We should talk to Pedro," Jean-Pierre said.

"Does he want to come with us?"

"He would, but a Spanish refugee might have a few problems getting to England." Huguette leaned closer. "You see, he's a communist."

"He's going to organize an army here to help throw out the Germans as soon as the Americans and British come to help crush the invaders. But he'll know how to get us to Valras because he escaped over the Pyrénées, near Perpignan, and walked all the way here."

"He's right, Bernard. Go and talk to Pedro."

Chapter Eighteen

Paris

Her arms weighted down with a bag of potatoes and two long loaves, Julie let herself into the Manoir's kitchen. She found Bérangère looking with dismay at her hand holding the knob from the gas range.

Julie took it from her. "Here, I'll fix it. The stove is old and worn." With a knife, she opened the two prongs and refitted the knob. "It should work now."

"Thank you. What did you manage to get?"

"Not much. I was early, but things disappear fast from the stores. If our baker hadn't saved those two loaves for us, we'd have no bread."

Bérangère put her hands on her hips. "So, the rationing doesn't work."

"No. And did you see all the restrictions?"

"Gontrand just about put his fist through the wall, but it doesn't make sense. I think it's because Alsace and Lorraine have been annexed to Germany that he's so angry."

A sad ghost of a smile crossed Julie's lips. "They now say that it's *verboten* to gather in groups in a public place, to travel after ten in the evening without authorization, to talk badly about Germany, to be disrespectful to German officers and soldiers, to go to the seaside, to go abroad, to write graffiti on walls, to listen to foreign broadcasts, to own a car without authorization and so on, and so on. Can you believe it?"

"I imagine that since England declared they are continuing the fight, all coastal areas are forbidden, too. Ah! Misère."

"Yes, what a wretched shame! People look downtrodden, really apathetic."

Bérangère grimaced. "Yet, some are all smiles and can't bend backward enough to help the Fritz."

Julie pursed her lips. "What are we going to do?"

"Keep on living."

"Just like that? Accept everything? The owner of the perfume store put a notice in the window that he had no more Chanel Number Five. And I saw a couple of officers walking out with packages."

Bérangère shrugged. "Of course, with one Deutschmark worth twenty francs, they can buy the whole city."

"I'm going to see if the magazine is back in publication. I have copy for it."

"May I come with you?" Lyse-May lifted her head from her drawing and waited for the reply.

"I'll be taking the 'Métro. It will be very busy."

"Not the bus?"

"No buses running yet, sweetie."

"That's all right."

The crowd in the Métro jostled and pushed and shoved. German soldiers were squeezed inside a second class carriage without ceremony. Julie picked up Lyse-May to keep her from being crushed by the throng. A soldier tapped a seated man's shoulder. The man leapt out of his seat, causing a ripple of unbalance in the carriage. Then the soldier indicated the vacant seat to Julie.

"Merci, monsieur."

He smiled proudly.

At the *Pour Elles* magazine offices, there was no one except for the editor-in-chief sitting at her desk. "Julie! You're here! Do you have some articles for me?"

Julie put her copy on the desk. "I certainly hope so."

"The only trouble is we are waiting for the authorization to publish. The Propaganda Abteilung will censor the publication. We have to conform and relay the official propaganda."

"What propaganda? We're nothing political."

"If your articles praise the new order, you'll be fine."

"I wrote about the refugees, the exodus and the strafing of civilians on the roads by the Luftwaffe planes."

"Oh là là! I don't want to disappoint you, but it doesn't sound like your articles will pass the censorship. Sorry. Can you rewrite them and concentrate on how helpful the Germans are?"

Julie stared at the editor. "I can't believe what I'm hearing."

"Well, if we don't comply, we won't have a job. That's how it is now. We need to eat. And to buy food you need money, and to have money you need a job."

Julie gritted her teeth. "I'm not writing that kind of filth! You can shove your magazine in the fire. I'm through!" She turned and took Lyse-May's hand. Downstairs, she tossed a defiant chin toward the stairs. *As if I'm going to lick their boots!*

Chapter Nineteen

Montauloup

Charmaine joined Brigitte, who was supervising the children at the swing. "I don't know about you, but I'd like to get back to Paris. I'm worried about the photo studio. It's our livelihood. My savings won't last forever."

"I'm glad you mentioned it. It's been on my mind, too, to return. We won't get any news about our husbands here." Brigitte cradled Christiane before putting her to sleep in a blanket-lined basket.

"Unless they do like Bernard."

"I wouldn't put it past Alexandre to flee to England."

"In which case, he could end up here. I don't know what Hubert would do. He retired from the Air Force three years ago, but he still has the military mind-set, and couldn't wait to join up when the war broke out. We'd probably have another argument and I'd probably end up with another baby."

The two women chuckled. Charmaine blew a ladybug off her hand. "Alexandre was supposed to follow the armies as a war artist and photographer. I wonder what happened to him."

"I think we'll get news back home. If they're prisoners, the notifications will go to our homes."

"Should we try to take the train?"

"You heard on the wireless that train service is disrupted while the tracks are being repaired," Brigitte said.

"And with five children and a baby, the logistics might get awkward if we get stuck in the middle of nowhere."

"I wonder how Julie managed."

Charmaine lifted a shoulder. "Probably all right. Lyse-May is no problem. That child can get herself out of any situation."

"How do you propose to go? Drive?"

"Pedro has repaired the Citroën. It's big enough. We travelled with my children, Madeleine and François. Then Jean-Pierre and little Reine managed to squeeze in. Those boys are as big as adults. Not comfy but not too bad."

Brigitte laughed. "It must have been a tight squeeze, though. I agree, we should go. We'll just pack a change of clothes and enough food."

Just as they stood up, Berthe and Madeleine arrived. "We'll take over if you two want to cool down inside."

Brigitte brushed the grass off her skirt. Her friend carried the basket with the baby in it. They sauntered across to the house. In the salon, Eugène and Arnaud were having words.

Pedro was leaning against a pillar in the foyer. He shrugged. "Pétain vs de Gaulle. If they weren't brothers, I'd probably be mopping blood off the floor by now."

"Oh, dear! That was bound to happen."

"But, Pedro, you're just the man we want to see," Charmaine said.

"I'm flattered."

"Can the Citroën get us to Paris?"

He stroked his chin. "It runs like a lion."

"Then let's get ready."

With bits of straw in his hair, François marched in, carrying Sylvestre. "The scamp gave the slip to mother and found his way into the cowshed."

The little boy held out his arms to his mother. Eyes shining with anticipation, François asked, "Did I hear right? You are going back to Paris?"

"Your hearing is good," Charmaine replied.

"I'm going with you."

"Life here is boring now that Jean-Pierre's gone?" Brigitte jiggled Sylvestre. "It'll be crowded, you realize."

"I don't mind, and you need a man with you."

They burst out laughing. "Aw, François, you're the sweetest man I know," Brigitte said.

They set about getting ready for the journey.

***

"Are we in the occupied zone yet?" François asked.

"Probably. We don't know what the demarcation line looks like. We're following the back roads the gendarme drew on the map," Brigitte replied. "It isn't the fastest route but we know it's clear."

"At the rate we're going, I think we'll have to camp. We must be only half-way," said Charmaine.

A while later, Charmaine turned onto a main highway. "Oh... I think I took a wrong turn."

"There's a sign coming up... Vallan. We're on the road to Auxerre. That's all right. Maybe we could find a hotel," François said.

"A gas pump would be better."

"Here!" François shouted. "Just off the road, there a sign for an auberge."

Charmaine applied the brakes carefully and pulled into the yard. The innkeeper barred the front door with his large body. A look of suspicion over his unsmiling face.

"Can you pay?"

"We need two rooms. And yes we can pay." He stepped aside. The family gasped. Broken doors and furniture were propped up against the walls in the lobby.

"What happened?"

The innkeeper heaved a long sigh. "We left when the Germans invaded. We didn't go far but when we came back, the place'd been vandalized and looted. We should never have left, but, you know, it's hard to know what to do. Whoever did that took all the food from the pantry, but they didn't find the root cellar. So we still have some food."

"We're so sorry for you," Charmaine said.

The innkeeper's wife wiped her eyes with her apron. "At least the building is solid. We can repair stuff. Fortunately, I had packed the silver and our most precious possessions in the root cellar. I'll make you some dîner."

They negotiated the price and settled for the night after the innkeeper's wife served them vegetable soup, goat cheese and bread.

The next day dawned as hot as the previous one. Sometime in the early afternoon, they had a picnic of stale bread and Camenbert cheese.

For a while, Charmaine had heard a noise in the engine. "What do you think this knocking noise is?"

"We checked the oil. It's good." The clanging got louder. "I hope we can make it to Fontainebleau and a garage," Brigitte said.

Even Sylvestre sitting on François' lap stopped chattering. Another bang, a screeching sound and Charmaine had just enough time to drive to the side of the road before she lost control of the steering. "Now, what?"

They spilled out and, with long faces, contemplated the Citroën. François bent down and looked underneath. "There's a broken piece dragging on the ground."

Helpless, the two women turned toward the road. Except for useless junk left from the Exode, the road was empty. Always practical, Brigitte took the children behind the hedge to attend to nature. François held Christiane. In the distance, he caught sight of a vehicle. It was traveling fast but slowed down when it came in sight of the children lined up along the ditch between the two women. It halted in front of them. It was a German car. The driver got out. "*Was ist passiert?*"

"We broke down."

The driver shook his head. His passenger got out. Older, and with various stripes and insignias on his uniform. "*Was ist das?*"

For a moment François regretted having neglected his German lessons at school. He tried. "*Auto ist kaputt.*"

"*Ja, das kann ich sehen.*" The officer said a few words to his driver, who went and took a bag from the Mercedes car.

"He said he sees we're stuck," François said.

The driver handed the bag to the officer who then gave chocolate and candies to the children. Led by François they all said "*Danke.*" The driver bent down to look under the car. "Das Kreuzegelenk ist gebrochen." The Germans exchanged a few words, which François didn't make out.

"We'll give you a ride to the town. There's another car following us. Ah, yes, I see it coming now."

François struggled to understand. In halting German he asked, "You are going to give us a ride?"

"*Ja*. I think we can fit all of you in two cars."

François racked his brain. "*Zwei Wagen*. Two cars?" A broad smile spread on the officer's face. "*Jawohl. Zwei Autos*." Another vehicle approached at speed. A second Mercedes stopped smoothly and an officer got out. François told the two officers they were going to Paris. They understood and replied they were going there too. They asked for an address, or that's what François guessed it was. He gave them Gontrand's address. The older officer took a map of Paris from his driver and showed it to François. He pointed to Avenue Chantemesse.

They thanked him and the two officers talked for a minute. François, who thought the older officer must be at least a colonel, interpreted what he thought they said. "I think they said to split the children and the ladies."

"Are we going to be safe?"

"The innkeeper said they are correct. It's the armistice. They won't shoot us," François said.

Brigitte and Charmaine quickly sorted out the children. Brigitte climbed in the older officer's Mercedes with Damien, Estelle, and the baby, while Charmaine took Sylvestre, Marianne and Baptiste and was joined by François in the younger officer's car.

The journey didn't take long and they soon came to a halt in front of the Manoir. The Germans expressed their admiration for the grand house. François desperately tried to remember the right words and tried. "*Kommen, bitte*." The officers smiled and nodded their appreciation at his efforts. Charmaine led the way up the steps. Brigitte with the drivers' help followed with the children. They had been seen. Charmaine halted in surprise on the perron as a German officer opened the door. "Entrez, madame." Unsure of what to do, she hesitated and looked back.

"I expect you to be Monsieur de Montregard's daughter." He looked past her. "He will be happy to see you all safe and sound. Please, come in."

They walked in. General von Trennen came out of his office and approached. He talked with the two officers. Everyone entered the great hall. The drivers went back and carried in the travelers' bags. They were sent to the kitchen for refreshments. Ernest went to fetch Gontrand and Bérangère.

"What will the neighbors think when they see all those uniforms," Bérangère muttered.

"My dear, they'll get used to it. They'll know it wasn't our choice.

Marie brought lemonade and coffee to the salon, and asked General von Trennen if everyone was having dinner.

"If you can manage it on such short notice, madame Marie, I would like to invite the officers to stay to thank them for helping Gontrand's family."

"I'll manage, sir. Will seven o'clock be all right?"

"Perfect."

Reynard translated the conversation. François promised himself to hit the books and learn German as soon as the guests would depart. Without having to consult each other, Charmaine and Brigitte gathered the children and stepped toward the kitchen, followed by Bérangère.

"Let me show you the new arrangement. The General and his aide-de-camp Hauptmann Langen have the house. We've moved into the west wing." She opened the back door. "We made a sitting room in one of the bedrooms. So we have one spare bedroom and Lyse-May's room beside ours. We eat in the kitchen." Brigitte looked round. "Why are you obliged to stay here?"

"Actually, the General wanted us to share the house, still use the salon and for Gontrand to stay in his study. But I didn't think it would work out. Gontrand is bound to say something to annoy them. Probably not the General and the Captain. Marie got the feeling General von Trennen is anti-Nazi. But if they have receptions, which they no doubt will, that's when it might be difficult if not dangerous."

"Don't you want to go to Montauloup? It'd be better for papa-Gontrand," Charmaine said.

"Don't even suggest that to my husband, Charmaine. He's a powder keg ready to explode, even though he's been very civil with our guests."

"Guests, eh?" Brigitte shook her head. "If you don't mind keeping an eye on the children, I'd like to run to the apartment and check it out. I won't be long, it's only a house away."

"Sure, but you should stay here until tomorrow when you can get food and what else you need. It'll be a bit cramped but we could work something out."

Brigitte laughed. "Don't worry, maman-Bérangère, we've been sleeping out in the open and on inn floors. We'll manage one more night."

"Hauptmann Langen had soldiers help with the move. I told him we needed a couple more bunk beds and by evening we had them. Not as spacious as before but in case we need to look after the children, it's enough."

They nodded. Brigitte was allocated the spare bedroom. Lyse-May was happy to share with Charmaine, Marianne and Estelle. François, Baptiste and Damien elected to sleep on the sitting room floor. Baptiste grinned from ear to ear. "That means I can stay up late."

François ruffled his cousin's hair. "Wake up call at six to do chores." They all laughed.

Brigitte resettled Christiane on her shoulder. "We didn't have room for the baby carriage. I've an old one at the apartment."

"Before I go and make dinner for us, we better get to the attic and find a cradle. I confess I forgot to ask the captain." Bérangère said. François and his grandmother went up the backstairs to the main attic. "All that stuff, grand-maman. We could furnish a couple of houses!"

"That's what happens when several generations of one's family live in the same house. Here, take this cradle. It was my favorite."

They dusted off the cradle before installing it in the spare room. Marianne took the children outside to the courtyard.

Bérangère and the two young women set about preparing the evening meal. "Julie might come for dinner."

"How's she doing?"

"Like we all do during catastrophic events, she survives."

"I can't imagine what, papa-Gontrand feels," Charmaine said.

"General von Trennen is a veteran of the First. Both he and Gontrand were wounded at Paschendaele. That fact smoothed over the requisitioning and occupation of our house. The General and the Hauptmann are tout à fait corrects."

"That's we hear everywhere, that they are so well-behaved. Well, they gave us a ride," Charmaine said.

"A Hauptmann Schneider, gave a ride to Julie and Lyse-May."

"Oh! How did she bring herself to accept?" Brigitte asked.

"Graciously. In time of need you put your feelings in your pocket. Enough talk, let's cook. I'm making progress in that department."

***

In the morning, Charmaine and Brigitte went shopping. "Germans or not, I'll be glad to be in my own home again," Brigitte said.

"Me too. Papa-Gontrand told me Gus has kept the studio open."

"Where has the animated Paris gone? No cars, almost no people."

"Bérangère did say private cars are not allowed, except for doctors." Charmaine's shoulders sagged. "We have to memorize the list of all the things that are no longer allowed. This armistice and Occupation is beginning to sap my strength."

"No, we've got to show them. Stand tall and proud, don't look at them. It's a give and take game. We were rescued on the road by a couple of German officers. So was Julie. Yet she must absolutely detest the sight of them. I just hope the French people will react soon. I think, right now we're still in shock."

"You're right. It's just that seeing that odious banner on the Eiffel Tower and the one on the Palais Bourbon got to me," Charmaine said. "Not to mention all those direction signs in German! They're ugly as sin."

"Did you notice how white papa-Gontrand's knuckles were when he told us the armistice had been signed in the Rethondes clearing, in the forest of Compiègne, in the very same railroad car in which they signed the 1918 Armistice?"

"I didn't but I heard how strained his voice was."

The chatting continued while they went from store to store. "Good Lord! Look at that!" Brigitte pointed to a sign in a store window. "*Juden verboten.* No Jews allowed. What's going on?"

"Is this what Julie talked about what they did in Germany?"

"*Mon Dieu*, what's happening to France?"

Finally, they had enough provisions to replenish their pantries and made their way back to the Manoir in a somber mood.

Thursday, June 27, 1940

I haven't had too much time to write. This afternoon, the grandchildren and their mothers went home. They had fun, but I'm sure they'll be happy to have their own place again. It's amazing how resilien children are. We haven't heard from Philippe so François is staying with us for the moment. He's hinted at staying here. All his books were here and I saw him studying. All this upheaval must have matured him. I've never seen him so keen about his studies.

The people I meet when shopping - an activity that's fast becoming difficult - are somber. I think the armistice killed off all hope. Before it, we hoped that we could keep fighting and push the Germans back into their own country. And peace would be restored.

What I find difficult to understand is the attitude of some of the neighbors. They are happy that the Germans are here. They talk about prosperity in a unified Europe. I think that's a load of rubbish.

In the meantime, the Fritz are settling down. I wonder whether the stores will be able to meet the demand. I saw soldiers going into the lingerie boutique and come out with big packages. They must be sending gifts to their womenfolk in Germany.

Yesterday, a military band gave a concert in the public garden of Place Lamartine. There was no way I was going to go, but Lyse-May escaped and went to listen. Fortunately, Marie saw her and told me. I caught up with her but didn't let her know that I was watching her. She loved the music. I admit, it was very good. Lyse-May was dancing with a wonderful sense of rhythm. I think I'll start teaching her piano. Poor child loved to tinkle with the piano, but now she's deprived of playing. Since the general invited me to use the piano - I can't help snorting here, it's still MY piano ¬I'll take Lyse-May and teach her.

Yesterday, we all had a fright. German planes flew very low over Paris, but we didn't know what they were up to. It's not so long ago that they were dropping bombs. Some railroad stations have finally reopened.

Chapter Twenty

Pontcharra

"Thank you so much for the mountain boots, tante Camille," Pierrette said. "I could walk all the way to Paris, if necessary. I just heard that the baccalauréat exams will be held on the seventh and eighth of August. I'm not going to miss them. I fully intend to go to university in October, German occupation or not."

Hughes slapped her on the back. "And I'm going with you."

"No, you are not," his mother said. "Otherwise I have to go with you, and I can't walk on crutches. The trains are not working, except on some short routes or parts of routes. And there is no way I will drive on those awful roads again."

"Well, Lorraine, you cannot drive with a broken leg anyway," Camille said.

Pierrette lit up. "I can drive. I drove all the way from Roanne, after you broke your leg and tante Camille was so sick."

"You don't have a license. It's one thing to do it in an emergency but not to set out deliberately without a license. So no, you are not driving anywhere, my dear."

"Maman, we need to go! I can keep the print shop open. It's important to be there to show that it's not abandoned."

Camille put a soothing hand on her sister-in-law's arm. "Yes, Lorraine, your son's right. You need to have a presence in your store."

Hilaire scratched his head. "The German army that found themselves south of their demarcation line are going back to the north of it. They're probably repairing the rail lines as fast as they can. I could drive you to Lyon, since the Germans left already, and you could try the train from there. It being a major city, it probably got priority on the repairs."

"Maybe the train is running, then?" Lorraine couldn't hide her anxiety. "With all the upheaval of people fleeing and all the mess on the roads, I just don't want to see you children walk anywhere."

"Maman, I'm fifteen, not a child anymore."

Lorraine's voice wavered. "We don't even know where the demarcation line is."

"Then we'll find out," Pierrette said.

"You're both minors."

Hughes stood and went to hug his mother. "You know, mother, dodging bullets, picking up dead bodies, bandaging wounded people, feeding little children, killing an injured cow and whatever, all that has made us age many years in a few days. You don't need to come to Paris with us. You get better first. I'll keep the store and start studying for next year."

"Auntie Lorraine, I'll stay in the apartment with Hughes. I can cook, well, all right just simple stuff, and I can help him in the store."

"Maybe our printer and our typesetter will have come back. They said they were too old to run away. But if you're going to make your way to Paris, can you stay with your grandparents, and just go to work in the store every day?"

"Brilliant!" Pierrette said.

Hilaire got to his feet. "Then we can leave in the morning. My sergeant can keep the fort at the gendarmerie till I get back in the afternoon."

***

In Lyon, Pierrette and Hughes thanked their aunt and uncle and once more reassured Lorraine, who insisted on seeing them off, despite lurching unsteadily on her crutches. Tickets for Paris in hand, they boarded the late afternoon train.

Pierrette shoved their backpacks onto the luggage rack. "We've got enough food for a week!"

"Better than not enough."

The train got under way and they were still the only occupants in the compartment. They lifted the armrests on each side and stretched out, soon falling asleep. It was becoming dark when a jolt woke them up. Hughes yawned. "Where are we?"

"A place called Saint-Rémy. Someone yelled everybody out."

They gathered their backpacks and followed the few passengers onto the platform. Hughes approached the stationmaster. "Is the train leaving later?"

"Where to?"

"Paris."

"No. This is how far we go. Beyond Saint-Rémy is the demarcation line. The train stays in the south." He looked at their feet. "You've got good boots. Are you scouts?"

"Yes, sir."

"You should walk. The B... Germans are all right if you walk."

"Thank you, sir. How far up to the line?"

"Just over half an hour's walk. Take a left on the road. But you won't get there before curfew on their side. You can sleep here in the waiting room or go to the hotel."

Hughes and Pierrette looked at each other. "Let's save our money. We might need it."

"Very wise. There's only a woman and her two young children in the waiting room. I'll lock up the station now."

They shared some food with the children and made themselves comfortable for the night. Dawn was breaking when the stationmaster showed up and told them they should be on their way. They thanked him and set out on the road.

Half an hour later they reached an obstruction. Several Wehrmacht soldiers were erecting a barricade across the road. Others were building a hut a few paces away.

A soldier pointed to them. "*Halt! Papieren bitte.*"

"What did he say?" Pierrette asked.

"I don't know."

The German nodded and repeated. "*Papieren bitte.*" Then in French. "*Papiers.*"

Pierrette batted her eyelids. "Sorry, sir. I'm only learning German. I'm not too good yet."

"C'est bon."

The two cousins handed their identity cards to the soldier.

"And the Ausweis?"

"What's an Ausweis?"

"Permission d'aller. *Fous poufez pas passer zans permission.*"

"We can't go without the permission. What do we do?"

Pierrette smiled. "Where can we get a permission Ausweis, sir, *bitte.*"

The soldier showed them a table sheltered by an obviously temporary structure. "Go."

They walked up to it. From the worksite, a young Unterfeldwebel strode up to them. "Do you hafe trafeling papers?"

Pierrette used her charm smile again. "You speak very good French, sir. We were told we need an Ausweis, but we didn't know where to get one."

François bit the inside of his cheek to stop himself laughing, very good French, indeed. They must have learnt French out of a book and transformed all the V as F, like in German, same with the S which they pronounced Z.

"No, of course. It's just being implemented. Just a moment. You're scouts? Where are you going?"

"Home to Paris."

"Gut." He leaned over the table to fill a couple of forms. He took their identity cards and entered their names. He examined a couple of rubber stamps and shook his head. "*Nein. Das ist ein Ausweis für den kleinen Grenzverkehr.* I need to get them stamped by the Oberleutnant. Those stamps are for people living here near the *Ubesetztes Gebiet*. Just a minute, please." He went to a parked car some distance away from the road block.

Pierrette looked around and swifter than lightning grabbed a handful of blank Ausweis forms which disappeared inside her blouse in a split second. Just as fast, a stupefied but quick thinker, Hughes had moved between her and the soldiers at work.

The young officer returned and handed them their papers. "You must keep them with you at all times. Bon voyage!"

Hughes wanted to ask if there was a train going to Paris but Pierrette gave him a shove and they walked toward the center of town. "Let's walk far away. I saw a sign for Chalon. There must be a station there."

"What exactly went on back there?"

"If I understand right, the officer has two sorts of Ausweis stamps, one for people living close to the demarcation line and one for people like us wanting to go home."

"So you took some forms but you don't have stamps."

Pierrette bumped her cousin. "Sometimes I think your brain is full of printing ink. Stamps can be made."

Hughes grimaced. "Crafty you! How come everyone seem to recognized us as scouts?"

Pierrette sputtered. "Could it be you have a straight spine, are wearing shorts and hiking boots and the badges on your backpack?"

Hughes laughed. "I forgot the badges. You've got a Girl Guides of France badge on your pack."

"That's why I put my hair into two braids, to look young and innocent. For once my small size serves me well." They giggled and kept ambling forward.

"Look at those swastika flags on the town hall."

"Nazi flags. Get used to it."

"You took a risk stealing those Ausweis forms. Mind they don't fall out."

"Women have stuffed secrets between their breasts throughout the ages. The forms are secure enough."

Hughes blushed and directed his eyes ahead.

They walked on, not too fast, not too slow so they wouldn't attract anyone's attention. Stores were opening. Wehrmacht soldiers strolled by taking photographs of quaint, white cob houses with flower pots on ledges outside the windows.

"We could walk to Paris," Hughes said.

"You're kidding. It's at least three hundred kilometers. Here, we're arriving in Chalon-sur-Saône."

They asked for directions several times and eventually reached the station. They went to the ticket office and showed their tickets and their Ausweis to Paris. "Are our tickets still good?"

The attendant glanced at the German official at the back of the office. With a negative shake of the head, he put their tickets in the drawer beneath the counter and pulled out two new tickets for Paris. Pierrette thanked him with a smile.

"Make sure you keep them together with your identity cards and Ausweis. Just in case."

Hughes led his cousin to the right platform where a train was waiting. They found two seats in a compartment. After many stops and starts, and being shunted onto other lines, the train entered Paris' Gare de Lyon close to midnight. "I guess we'll be sleeping in a waiting room again," Pierrette said.

Wehrmacht soldiers checked the passengers' papers at the exit to the concourse. The cousins went to a waiting room, which by now was crowded, and found a corner to sleep for the remainder of the night.

They were the first to leave the stuffy waiting room after checking that the curfew was over for the day. Outside the station, they stopped. "Darn flags, again!"

Pierrette kept looking around her. "There's nobody. It's as if Paris is deserted."

"People have been replaced by German soldiers."

"There aren't any cars."

"Hey, what's that?" Hughes pointed to a bicycle pulling a trailer with a person sitting in it.

"It says Vitesse-Confort-Sécurité Vélo-Taxi."

At that moment a tandem vélo-taxi pulled up next to them.

"Speed-Comfort-Security, that's us. We can take both of you wherever you want. Reasonable rates."

Pierrette and Hughes stared at the two men on the tandem bicycle.

"You two have just come back from the south?"

"That's right."

"How is it over there?"

"Well, there are no Germans soldiers for a start," Pierrette said.

"And no Nazi flags," Hughes said.

"How much to go to Chantemesse Avenue?"

"For you, nine francs. Plus five francs to take on passengers, payable in advance."

"That's a lot."

"Oui, mademoiselle, but we'll get you there faster than the Métro."

Hughes put his backpack into the trailer. "Let's go." He climbed in.

Pierrette followed and handed the money to the first cyclist. It truly was faster than the Métro. She remarked that the only cars on the streets were German and that there were other vélo-taxis. Although the ride wasn't uncomfortable, Hughes and Pierrette were glad to arrive at the Manoir. They bounded up the steps, pressed the buzzer and barged in.

"*Salut tout le monde!*" Hughes shouted the greeting to everybody.

Pierrette's modulated voice rang out. "*Bonjour, bonjour!* Where are you all?"

The door of the salon opened and General von Trennen stepped out. Pierrette and Hughes' forward motion came to an abrupt end. They stood transfixed and speechless.

"Come in, come in. I am General von Trennen. I guess you must be two of the grandchildren."

"Pierrette de Montregard."

"Hughes Bourgmestre."

"Your grandparents insisted on moving into the west wing after I had been assigned accommodation at Le Manoir. Please, come through the kitchen."

The general went ahead. In the kitchen, he saluted Marie. "Madame Marie, would you please make an extra cake to celebrate the safe return of Hughes and Pierrette?"

"Certainly, monsieur."

Still dumbfounded, the two youngsters followed the general through the connecting vestibule. He knocked on the door. François opened it. Whoops of joy resonated and attracted Bérangère. The arrivals were engulfed in hugs. A smile on his lips, General von Trennen closed the door and went back to his work.

Pierrette recovered first and jerked her thumb at the closed door. "What's the meaning of all that? A German general in the house and you in the west wing?"

François launched into an explanation and related their experiences since they had left Paris. Then it was Hughes' turn to give an account of their adventures.

Gontrand and Lyse-May came back from their walk. More hugs and retelling of their life away from Paris was demanded. Pierrette fished the blank Ausweis from her blouse.

"What are those?" Gontrand asked.

"The documents you need to travel anywhere now."

"How did you get them?"

"When the officer went to get our papers stamped, I sort of just reached onto the shelf. No door or anything."

"You stupid goose! You could have been shot stealing them!" There was no doubt what Gontrand thought about his granddaughter.

Bérangère smacked the salt shaker on the table. "She's a very smart girl. You never know, they may come in handy when we're ready to boot the Germans out of France, or before."

After Gontrand's vehement outburst, a silence settled over the group. Bérangère set about preparing lunch. Pierrette carefully smoothed out the five Ausweis forms on the corner of the table.

"François has the spare bedroom. Hughes you can bunk with him. Pierrette can share with Lyse-May."

"With me, Pierrette. With me."

"All right, poppet, I'll bunk with you."

"I'm going to open the print shop and see what I can do," Hughes said.

"Not on your own."

"Grand-maman, you have the same concerns as my mother. But Pierrette and I made it back here, didn't we? Doesn't that show we are as capable as any adults?"

Bérangère stood for a moment, spoon in hand. "Oui, indeed. You're very capable. But you will accept help from all of us."

Without warning, Lyse-May scrambled to her feet and ran into the corridor to the entrance. "Mama, Julie!" She dragged her aunt into the kitchen and took the half loaf from her aunt's hands. "Here, mémée, more food."

More hugs, and retelling of their respective journeys, and Julie was able to sit down. Pierrette and Hughes cried openly on hearing the death of their lovely little cousin.

Julie put the magazine *Pour Elles* on the table. "First one allowed by the censor."

While Bérangère finished the cooking, with Pierrette's help, Julie opened the very slim magazine to her column, though didn't expect to see her articles after the way she parted from her editor. It was actually the only content beside a glowing editorial about German correctness and helpfulness. "What? What's that rubbish?"

Gontrand grabbed the magazine. "What's the problem?"

"They've completely changed the articles I had previously submitted. They didn't publish the one about the refugees. They made the Exode sounds like a scout outing. No mention of the planes strafing people. By the way, those planes are called Stukas. And see how Germans soldiers helping refugees is front and foremost. It makes me sick. The editor rewrote all that."

"That's all propaganda. You can't write for that type of magazine."

"The editor wanted me to alter the articles and I told her I wasn't going to. I don't know why she published it."

François slid the magazine toward him and flipped through the four pages. "Because there was nothing else. Just yours and Violette Leduc's article on the back."

"Let me see. More neutral, not lavishly praising like the editor's rewrite of my article. Well, she needs the money. Me too, but I can't do it. I can't write that rubbish."

Hughes stretched his neck to see. "I, for one, am glad we don't print that rag. Father would have a fit if he saw that."

A hand seized the offending magazine and all eyes followed its trajectory toward the garbage can.

Chapter Twenty-One

Paris, Saturday, June 29, 1940

It is a warm but pleasant day. The children, no, Pierrette and François are no longer children. The young people came in with leaflets that they said had been dropped by the English. I didn't hear any planes but these days with all there's to do, and the curfew, we don't pay too much attention to unusual noises in the night.

Anyway, they were quite excited and vehement that thanks to that General de Gaulle the résistance had begun. I can't see what the résistance can be about, the Bo Germans are here and behave like masters. When they tell the shopkeeper they want all the cakes, no one can refuse because you'd get shot. But even Hughes said that there are now graffiti on walls saying "down with the Vichy traitors" and others more osés, like "Vive le Général de Gaulle". I presume that young people are taking the risk of writing on public billboards things like long live the general and things like "Français. Understand. Resist." Not too much to understand, but resist? I wonder...

I met a neighbor at the bakery and she told me that if her aging husband wants to keep his car he has to get a special permit from the Kommandantur, which is always refused unless you're a doctor.

The worst really is that buying and stocking more food than needed for the family is an offence. See how much the soldiers buy and take away! Up to now it was that any hostile act was reprimanded. It's been changed to hostile act will be punished by death.

Misère! What a shame!

***

The waiting line wasn't too long and Julie entered the cool grocery store. The storekeeper glanced at the women waiting and weighed tomatoes for the customer he was serving.

"But I asked for one kilo."

"Sorry, madame. But I didn't get much at the Halles this morning. The German supervisors were very strict in allocating groceries to store owners. I have to share with all my customers now."

The woman went out grumbling.

"And it's worse for the fishmongers and the butchers," the grocer said. "She should go rue Boissière and pay the inflated price my competitor is charging. *Ah! Mon Dieu*! What is happening to good honest people?"

Groans of sympathy were heard. Without complaint, each woman took what the storekeeper gave her. When Julie's turn came, she handed over her filet and the grocer put a small amount of potatoes and tomatoes in it. "My father used to be a coach driver for a grand family. He has just managed to get a small carriage and a horse. He thinks he can earn a little money, since there are no taxis."

"A good idea. There'll probably be more to think like him."

"Still, they will have to feed the horses. But the Fr... Germans have horses too, so hay's got to be available somewhere."

"Let's hope for the best."

On the way home, Julie reflected on the fact she was non-committal when talking to the merchant. It was part of that insidious fear that you never knew who you were speaking to.

At the crossroads, Germans work trucks were busy with ladders against a building. She looked up to see men installing machine guns on the flat roof of a three storied Art-Déco house. She stopped at Brigitte's. "Did you see that? Guns on the roof of a house."

"They have done that on other buildings. Lots of people were unhappy to say the least. The Chleus are stupid. It won't gain them the people's trust if they continue to threaten to shoot anyone who as much as squints at them. Somebody said their neighbor refused to work in a German-controlled factory and was arrested."

Julie sighed. "I heard they've requisitioned private cars."

"Houses, cars, what else, now?"

"I think they're building resentment and rebellion in the French people."

Brigitte tossed her head. "I'll join the rebellion. Let me know when it starts."

"It has started. I saw small stickers with a V on them, and the Germans' large posters not only have Vs but also two vertical lines."

"What for?"

"A stick or fishing rod is a *gaule*. Two makes *deux gaules*," Julie said.

"I get it! de Gaulle, same pronunciation. I wonder who's the witty mind that started it."

"Now it's all over walls and Vespasiennes."

They burst out laughing. Brigitte scoffed. "Men can piss and put more sticks on the urinals at the same time."

"We women have to be content with drawing on walls."

"Are you going to church tomorrow?" Brigitte asked.

"No. Do you want me to stay with the children? Then we'll go to the Manoir."

"I'll take Damien and Estelle with me. A bit of religion can't do any harm. I noticed so many more people are attending now. I'll feed

Christiane before leaving, so she'll be all right."

Julie chuckled. "Sylvestre and I will push the baby carriage to the Manoir and wait for you there."

***

Bérangère and Brigitte arrived from mass and greeted Jacques Werner, in his gendarme uniform. "No day off?"

"Alas no, Bérangère, someone has to be at HQ at all times. How were the halls of divine goodness?"

Sarcastic laughter burst behind her back. She shrugged. "I had to go all the way to the Invalides to Saint-François-Xavier church because Saint-Honoré was closed. And guess what I heard."

"The Fritz have had enough and are going home."

The general laughter resonated freely.

"Monseigneur Chevrot was in the pulpit. He didn't beat around the bush. He was scandalized that the new rag La France au Travail, supposed to be from our Vichy government, is promoting passive acceptance. Not for the Monseigneur. He said Pétain has set France on the road of shame."

Gontrand's voice thundered in the room. "How dare he be disrespectful to the Maréchal!"

Jacques raised a hand. "Keep calm, my friend. Keep calm. Nice to hear that a bishop, at least, sees the situation clearly. Cardinal Suhard is all for Pétain and the defeat. He wants us to believe it's because of our sins."

"Our sins? What sins?"

"Brigitte's calling. Lunch's ready. Come on you two."

As they sat down at the table, Brigitte asked about François.

"He and Pierrette are helping Hughes fill in a whole lot of forms to get an allocation of paper to continue printing what is now allowed," Julie said. "I've helped too, and Guillaume is really directing the shop."

"Who's Guillaume?" Jacques asked.

"The old typesetter. He was making noises about retiring before the war. But after Jean-Luc was conscripted, he stayed on," Julie said.

Jacques tapped his forehead. "Ah, yes. I remember now."

Lyse-May knelt on the chair and sat back on her heels. "How come the church bells didn't ring?"

The adults looked in awe at the child. Bérangère recovered first. "That's very observant of you to notice the bells didn't ring. Actually, to think of it, the bells have not been ringing since the Germans entered Paris." The adults pulled their bottom jaw down in an appreciative grimace at the child's perspicacity.

"The Germans don't like bells," Brigitte said.

"They like bells. They've got little ones in the parade band." Lyse-May forked mashed potatoes into her mouth. "I know. The bells are sad because the Germans are here. So they don't ring."

"Right. You're right," Julie said.

Chapter Twenty-Two

Wednesday, July 3, 1940

Philippe contemplated the unassuming façade of his newly requisitioned factory in Suresnes.

"Do you like it?" Baron von Hauffen's affable tone made Philippe shiver.

"You made a wise choice, Sturmbannführer von Hauffen."

"I shall let you organize the premises. I have other business to attend to."

As soon as the officer had departed, Philippe took a step toward the door, keys in hand. Inside the entrance hall, a man was leaning against the wall.

"I hope you're happy taking away my livelihood and that of ten family men."

"I didn't choose your factory."

"So why are you working for the sales Boches?"

"The bloody Boches won the war, so we may as well work with them."

"They haven't won the war. Not yet. The English are still fighting. There'll come a day of reckoning."

"I can employ your workers."

The older man spat on the ground. "They don't want to work for Judas." He pushed himself off the wall and left, slamming the door behind him.

Dumbfounded, Philippe stood for a moment before going into the manager's office to prepare for the team of specialists due to arrive that afternoon.

***

The day was warming up. Bérangère crossed the courtyard and was saluted by a young man grooming a beautiful chestnut mare. She returned the greeting before entering the kitchen. She dropped her filet on the table.

"Did you see the General's horse? Such a beauty!"

"Grandfather was out there giving advice to the young man on how to currycomb a horse. But the groom doesn't understand a word of French," Pierrette said.

"Nothing like a hands-on demonstration to learn. Where's my husband?"

"He was feeling a little tired and went to lie down. I'd like to ask something."

"Well, go ahead."

"Would it be possible to clean up one of the servants' bedroom in the big attic?"

"You want more privacy, I suppose."

"Lyse-May is the most adorable little girl, but she's a very light sleeper. I make sure I don't make any noise but she wakes up the minute I open the door."

"I see the problem. Then when you want to sleep she's ready to have a conversation." She laughed and Pierrette joined in. "There's no heat up there and it must be hot right now. It's the lead roof. It carries the sun's heat through the roof."

"I inspected the rooms up there. It isn't too bad. I only want to sleep there."

"Why don't we clean all the rooms after the déjeuner. You pick yours. I bet François will also want to have a room away from us."

"We did talk about it."

Bérangère sighed. "You're all growing up. Here, peel the potatoes and make the peels very thin. There aren't many potatoes."

"If I scrubbed them thoroughly, we could eat them with the skin on."

"You can't purée potatoes with the skin on."

"Don't be so scandalized, grand-maman. I can cut thin slices and fry them. It's good."

"Is that how you do it in the Girl Guides over a campfire?"

"It works, believe me. Did you hear the government has settled in Vichy?"

"The spa won't do any good for the arthritis in their brains."

Pierrette doubled up with laughter. "You're so funny, grand-maman. But truly, they're a bunch of incompetent weaklings."

Gontrand pushed the kitchen door open. "Who you're talking about?"

"Just that the baccalauréat exams are to take place in August."

"Good. Then go and study instead of idly gossiping."

Spoon in hand, Bérangère faced her husband. "We're cooking lunch. If you want to eat, leave the women alone."

Gontrand grumbled but left the kitchen.

***

The silence in the empty apartment unnerved Julie. She resisted the impulse to leave her half-cooked dîner and go to the Manoir. "I must get used to it." The sound of her own voice scared her. There was a tap on the door. In the hope it was a neighbor ready to spend a few minutes with her, she hurried to the door and opened it with a flourish. Her lips forming a welcome greeting. She stood frozen on the spot. "Sylvain!"

He lifted her in his arms and slammed the door shut behind him with his foot. They kissed and hugged each other swaying. Their hands reconnecting feverishly with familiar contours. They were still standing in the vestibule when Sylvain pulled back and looked towards the hallway.

Julie buried her head in his neck and for the first time let her tears fall.

He carried her to the salon and cradled her on the sofa. Between sobs and cries of pain, Julie told him about the Exode, the strafing and the death of their beloved Claire. For a long time they held each other, crying all the tears a body can produce.

Sylvain blew his nose. "Ma chérie, I'm so sorry you were alone with your grief."

She kneaded her handkerchief between nervous fingers. "Our baby is buried at the edge of the road, in the trees of the Sologne forest. Brigitte told me the good doctor dug a deep hole so our child wouldn't be disturbed."

"Should we try to have her reburied in a proper cemetery?"

Julie laid her head on his shoulder. After a while, she looked at him. "Doesn't it say somewhere that we were made of dust and the mortal remains will return to dust?"

"Something like that, yes."

"Then, I think we should let nature take care of our baby. Her spirit is with us, or in heaven, but she's still in my heart."

"And in my heart, too." They remained silent for a long while. "Maybe after the war, we'll take her to the family plot so she won't be lost forever."

***

The next morning, in a mood of grim acceptance, they walked hand in hand to the Manoir. The courtyard gate was open and they saw that Reynard von Trennen had just come back from riding in the Bois de Boulogne. The groom took the horse to the stable while Julie made the introductions. The general put his hand forward. Sylvain took one step back. "I don't shake hands with the barbarians who killed my baby daughter."

Dumbstruck, Reynard von Trennen directed an inquiring gaze to Julie who related the event. The general paled. His blue eyes welled up. "I cannot say how so very sorry I am. I had hoped so much to know my..." He stopped in mid-sentence.

Surprised, Julie frowned and addressed her husband. "General von Trennen has been the most courteous and helpful person to our family."

"I'm glad to hear that." Politely, Sylvain nodded and took his wife's hand and headed to the west wing.

"He looked moved, really upset," Julie whispered. "Like if he was about to say he'd hoped to know her." A vision of her child's blue eyes passed in her mind. She shook it off.

Reynard's eyes followed them. He raked his fingers through his hair, then walked into the west wing vestibule and opened the connecting door to the main house. Nobody heard the sorrowful melody flowing from his violin.

In the sitting room, Sylvain disengaged himself from his parents' long hugs. "What now you're a civilian, son?"

"Not yet a civilian. I have to get demobilized first."

"How come you're wearing a suit if you're still in the army?"

"There's no more army. We surrendered."

Disdainful in the extreme, Gontrand turned his head towards the window. "Bunch of cowards. In the First, we fought to the death."

"Obviously not, since you're still here!" Bérangère's glacial tone hit her husband squarely.

Sylvain's anger mounted. "We fought till the last minute. It's your stupid government led by a cowardly senile marshal that gave the order to surrender!"

Gontrand's roar echoed as far as the street. "You'll be respectful to the hero of Verdun!"

Startled, Lyse-May abandoned her book and burst out crying. She took refuge against Julie who put an arm around her thin shoulders. Sylvain remained calm. "Verdun was twenty years ago."

Elbow on his knee, the old man leaned his head into his hand. "Why aren't you a prisoner, then?"

"Because it is the duty of every soldier to escape and return to fight another day. It was the same in your day, father. England is still in the war."

"How come the battle was over in six weeks, if you fought so well?"

Sylvain gritted his teeth. "They came at us with five-hundred and eighty planes. We had thirty-two. My company ran out of ammunition. Because the old colonels and generals hadn't moved on since 1918, they were stuck with the belief that trenches and fortifications like the useless Maginot line would hold. The Boche drove Panzers, that's tanks if you don't know, right over our lines. Our forward outposts gave the alarm at three in the morning, but the aged colonel said it was a false alarm and went back to sleep."

"That can't be."

"Father, don't defend that bunch of weaklings. The Germans were equipped with Stukas, dive bombers. They flew very low to try to get us in our foxholes. Many of those same foxholes became graves."

Subdued, Gontrand looked up. "Before the Germans put a boot on French soil, why didn't the regiments go over? Like in Forbach, why didn't you continue advancing into Germany and wipe out all the Boches?"

"I was there. It was my unit. We were only a scouting patrol. We had orders not to shoot."

"Wimps!"

"You were a soldier, father, you know soldiers have to obey orders. I was a soldier and I obeyed orders. That is until the Germans, who didn't know we were there, entered the house we used as an observation post. Then we exchanged fire."

"And then went back to your hiding holes."

Red in the face, Sylvain clenched his fists.

Bérangère raised both hands. "Didn't you read the news during the phoney war? The first one to shoot was going to be the aggressor so the other one could retaliate in good conscience. At that time everyone on our side still believed we could have peace. It took the tenth of May to wake us up to the fact that Hitler was hiding behind that façade."

"Did you get that on the gossip mill?"

"Sure! We went to enough receptions where people in the know would talk to people like me, all keen to educate us poor idiotic women, who dare say aloud that propagandist Mr. Giraudoux's elegant, but totally empty prose was trash. There were so many warnings but the top brass was too busy drinking Champagne to listen."

Sylvain stood up.

"No, stay," his mother said. "We're having déjeuner."

"I didn't bring anything, belle-maman," Julie said.

"I have enough. Bring something tonight when the family comes for dîner."

After a mostly silent lunch, where Lyse-May was encouraged to tell the stories she had read, Julie and Sylvain went home. They stopped at the post office to place a phone call to Charmaine. They filled a form, paid the money, and after a short delay while the German official looked over the request, Julie was allowed to phone.

When Julie and Sylvain made their way back to the Manoir in the evening, Charmaine and Brigitte had arrived. Bérangère had the children eat first.

"This kitchen isn't big enough for all of us. What we miss is a playroom."

Brigitte nodded. "We'll manage. Look, Lyse-May is reading a book to Sylvestre in the sitting room. Nothing keeps him more quiet than listening to stories."

"Marianne is supervising Damien and Estelle in the spare room," Charmaine said.

"What's Baptiste doing?" Julie asked.

"I got him a stack of paper and a new sketch book. He won't budge until bedtime," Charmaine replied.

"How is Hughes managing the printing shop?" Sylvain asked.

Bérangère stopped stirring the contents of a pan on the stove. "Guillaume, remember him?"

"The typesetter, of course. He's been with Jean-Luc and Lorraine forever."

"He's working with Hughes and François. They just got a contract to print posters... for the Germans."

A disbelieving cry came from all the throats. Pierrette came in at that moment.

"It was either accept that or close the shop. How are Lorraine and Hughes going to eat without the business?"

Gontrand had joined the women in the kitchen and let his weight drop on a chair. "Unbelievable! Lorraine won't accept that. As soon as she's back, she'll throw them into the garbage."

"You don't know your sister, dear. She'll do what she has to do until better days come." Bérangère returned to her saucepan. "Take a seat. It's ready."

A stampede on the back stairs announced François and Hughes' arrival. Charmaine laughed, "Just in time. Do you have a clock in your stomach?"

"My sister trained us to be punctual. Her lunches cannot wait."

The laughter relieved the tension that seemed to pervade everywhere.

"We've finished arranging the attic bedrooms," Hughes said.

Bérangère and Julie served the vegetable soup. Silence reigned until the last piece of cheese had been eaten.

Charmaine looked at Sylvain. "How did you get here?"

"I walked."

"I mean, you were at the front. So what happened?"

Sylvain looked at his father.

Gontrand took a deep breath. "Let's have it from the beginning."

"When we got the orders to retreat, I and a few of my men decided to go and reinforce Fort de Longchamp. I'd received a field promotion to the rank of captain but hadn't yet got the official papers. I put my men under the command of Lieutenant Henri Martin and told him I'd abide by his command. Together, we held the fort for four days. We could see Fort de Dogneville from our post. I think we were surrounded by then. We were under heavy fire. All telephone lines had been cut. We lost two men."

Sylvain passed his hand over his face. "Then Friday twenty-first of June, we saw a red flag being raised on Dogneville. At first we thought they were asking for help. We'd also lost radio communications. Then we saw the swastika. The fort had fallen. The Germans sent Lieutenant Charvet, and chef Lutz to translate–he's Alsatian– carrying a white flag and a message. The Germans firepower was enough to reduce the fort to rubble and since an armistice had been negotiated, they asked that the fort surrender without further bloodshed."

Eyes closed for a moment, Sylvain took a deep breath.

"Lieutenant Henri Martin discussed the surrender terms with the German major. Martin wanted military honors and to distribute the last of the food to his men. Both commanders had fought in the First and respected each other. It was agreed that the French garrison would walk out at eleven o'clock next day. We sang the Marseillaise. In the morning, Martin pointed to the forest behind the fort, and said I was no longer under his command." Sylvain stopped and rubbed his neck.

"So what did you do?" Hughes asked.

"We marched out and lined up at the edge of the forest. We had heard that the Chleus mowed down prisoners of war and expected the worst, despite the agreement between our commanders. But the German commandant saluted us and congratulated our commander for a heroic defense of the fort. It was the last fort to fall. I'd slipped to the back of the men, against the trees. I had no intention of being sent to a POW camp in Germany. A corporal sidled up to me and together we quietly slipped into the woods and up the mountain behind. We kept going most of the afternoon. When we were far enough away, we sat and introduced ourselves. Robert Leguénec is a seasoned mountain climber and decided we should go high up and travel along the Jura ridges. It made sense. The

Germans would be on the roads and in the towns."

When Sylvain paused to take a breath, Brigitte handed him a glass of water. He nodded his thanks.

"We moved on a little more and found an old hut, a charcoal burner's hut, and waited until nightfall. We had the food given to us the day before and a canteen of water each in our light pack. Robert had had the same idea. We'd packed our shaving kit, two pairs of socks and a sweater, but our uniforms were just too conspicuous. We took turns to reconnoiter the route up to a small village. On the edge, we saw a woman taking her laundry off a line. I approached and called to her quietly. In fright, she dropped her basket. "I'm a French soldier," I said. She looked relieved and I said there were two of us. She invited us inside. One day when this is all over, I'll go and thank her and her husband. They were an older couple and hadn't wanted to evacuate."

A happy memory fleeted across Sylvain's face. He shook himself. "They sheltered us overnight. Early in the morning, Monsieur Villers went out and came back with a bag of civilian clothes. Neighbors who had evacuated had left them behind. He wanted us to have them before the Germans arrived in the village because any man in uniform would be automatically made prisoner. He knew the region well and drew us a map. Then I turned west towards Paris through the forests, mountains and fields. Robert continued towards the Alps. Along the way I met farm people who gave me food and lodging." He stopped talking.

There was a silence while everyone reflected on his odyssey.

François spoke first. "You're fantastic, mon oncle."

Gontrand removed his pipe from his mouth. "How are you going to be demobilized? Jacques could help."

"I don't want to involve him. He's too close to our family and could get into trouble. I intend to go to Montauloup. Our gendarmes there won't ask questions and will stamp the right date on the papers. Then I'll join de Gaulle in England."

Charmaine lifted her arms in the air and dropped them back on her lap. "Why's everybody wanting to go to England?"

"To continue fighting, ma tante. I'd go too if I could," François said.

Sylvain smiled and ruffled his nephew's hair. "That's the spirit! In the meantime you can find useful work to do here."

"Like drawing Vs on walls?"

"Exactly! To remind people that we'll be coming back to boot the Chleus out of France."

Gontrand brought his fist down on the table. "This is subversive talk!"

"Aw, father, you want the Germans out of here as much as I do."

"But we have to listen to Maréchal Pétain. He knows what he's doing. He's fooling the Boche."

Bérangère stood up and planted herself in front of her husband. "You're just as feebleminded as your hero is! You speak again like that and I'll get you a one-way ticket to Vichy."

"Bernard's already gone to England," Charmaine said.

Giggles were heard, interrupted by a gesture from Sylvain. "News time."

Instant silence. "...the French fleet in Mers el-Kébir. Admiral Somerville issued an ultimatum to Vice-Admiral Marcel Gensoul to sail his ships to Britain. The Vice-Admiral refused. Admiral Somerville ordered his ships to open fire."

"And you want to join the English salauds! Those bastards! They're shooting us in the back."

"Father, I think I understand that the English, who are the only ones left to fight, do not want the Germans to get hold of our powerful navy and use it against them."

"It's treason! They were our allies."

"It's very regrettable that they should sink our fleet, but necessary because that old Vice-Admiral lives in the past. Another one of those First World War veterans whose mind hasn't moved beyond 1914."

Gontrand's abrupt standing up sent his chair crashing backward. "Apologize! Apologize right now to all who fought in the First!"

"I admire and respect all those who fought during the wars. What I have no respect for are the old men at the helm."

Red in the face, Gontrand searched for his cane. Bérangère beat him to it and held it behind her back. "Enough!"

In silence, Lyse-May, who had crept in without anyone noticing, encircled Gontrand's waist. He sat and pulled the child onto his lap. Brigitte poured a cup of coffee and placed it in front of Gontrand. A small glass of Chartreuse in hand, Sylvain walked around the table and put it down in front of his father, who took a sip.

Quietly, Brigitte, Charmaine and Marie-Ange gathered their children and made their way to their respective homes. Sylvain kissed his mother's cheek. His father kept his head down, sipping his liqueur. The adolescents stood in the kitchen for a moment and slipped upstairs to the attic bedrooms. Tomorrow would be time enough to tell their grandparents that early in the afternoon, when everyone was out, beds complete with bedding, had been delivered and installed in three rooms in the attic thanks to General von Trennen. Or maybe they'd only tell their grandmother.

***

In the morning, Julie was awakened by a knock on the door. She donned a robe, tied back her hair and hurried to the door wondering who it was going to be this time.

"Pierrette." She opened the door wide and pulled her niece in. "You're all wet."

"Bonjour, tante Julie. It's raining. I have something that would be useful for uncle Sylvain when he wants to get to the non-occupied zone."

Sylvain approached, his hair dripping from the bath he'd just taken. "What's this?"

"An Ausweis. At the printing shop, we worked on making the rubber stamps. They are good. Baptiste came and he drew the best ones. For a little child he's so good, it's amazing. Like Uncle Alexandre."

A beaming Sylvain hugged Pierrette. "Clever girl. Julie told me how you got those."

"You'll need a photo, but Gus is really quite an expert now. You should see..."

"We should see what?

"Er... The studio gets lots of Germans wanting their picture to send home."

"Then let's go."

"Problem. You need demobilization or an exemption certificate. Do you want me to steal Phillippe's?"

"Oh! No."

Pierrette shrugged. "I'm sure you can talk your way out of producing one if you're stopped. But I'll get my father's. He doesn't need one now that he works for the Fritz."

Stunned, Julie watched the two of them. Her niece suddenly a woman. Her husband treating her like an equal.

"We're having breakfast." Julie put bread and coffee on the table. "That's the last of the butter. I'll shop later."

Julie poured the coffee. "There's Monsieur Biquette, of the Fromageries Biquette. He does business in Moulins but lives in the non-occupied zone. If you could make contact with him when he makes a delivery at the distribution center. I'm sure he'd help."

"Any idea how often he goes there?"

"Once a week, I think. That's what he said to Lyse-May who bombarded him with questions."

"That's fine. I can wait for him. I've learned to be invisible. Are you ready so we can go and take my photo?"

***

In the evening, the family sat around the table once more. Pierrette was chewing her lip, letting her soup get cold. "Uncle Sylvain, you could hitch a ride with a German official going toward a garrison near the non-occupied zone."

The spoon half-way to his mouth, François stopped to look at his sister. "That's crazy! How could he do that?"

"He's got an Ausweis and, since the trains are not reliable, he could say he missed the train."

"Sister, dear, your imagination will get you into trouble one of these days."

Sylvain smiled. "Actually, it isn't such a bad idea. I'll consider it as I go along."

Pierrette wasn't to be deterred. "If you go to some small place outside Paris, I think the Germans would be quite agreeable to give you a ride, because of train problems. Every little place has a street called Victor-Hugo so it'd fit with your papers. They don't look at them too closely, especially when they don't speak French."

"You're a smart girl, Pierrette. And after I've gone, remember about being careful."

"I promise."

"What's all that about?" Charmaine asked.

Marianne put her spoon down. "It's all right, maman. We promised oncle Sylvain not to do anything stupid against the Germans."

"I'm relieved." A slight sarcasm entered her tone.

The goodbyes were brief. Gontrand shook his son's hand. "Since the English are still fighting, you may as well go and help."

Chapter Twenty-Three

The cool dawn air filtered into the kitchen through the half-open window. Julie rested her head against her husband's chest.

"Why do you need to go to England and join the fight? Risk your life again? Is it because your brother has already gone there?"

He sighed. "I can't really answer why. It's an anger deep inside me that wants to destroy every single German. I want them out of our country. I don't care who has done wrong to whom. War is a senseless destruction. The sooner the occupier is sent home, the sooner we can begin to live again."

"Why do I fear this is only the beginning?"

"You heard de Gaulle last night when he said we have lost a battle, we haven't lost the war. There's evil out there. This isn't just a war between two armies."

"When will I see you again? Will I get a telegram?"

The passion in his kiss denied his fears. "I'm being careful. I'll get my rightful promotion to the rank of captain over there. It gives me more control over my particular fight."

"Soldiers don't get promoted unless they do some heroic deeds. You took risks."

Sylvain laughed. "Ma chérie, in a battle everybody does heroic deeds, everybody takes risks."

"Are you sure you can't stay here and do something? I'd like to do something. I just don't know what. I'm keeping calm but I hate the Boches with all my being."

He was thoughtful for a long moment. "I think there'll be other people like you. You'll find each other and then you'll know what to do." The clatter of horses' hooves sounded below the window.

"My transport."

A last kiss and Sylvain grabbed his knapsack. He closed the door softly after him. Unlike his previous departure, he didn't turn to look back. From the window, Julie watched him climb into a hackney carriage. The pain in her chest intensified. Her eyes burned. "Noooo.... no..." She crumpled to the floor and sobbed, unable to stop.

She cried for Sylvain.

She cried for Claire.

She cried for all the orphans of war.

She cried until she had no tears left.

Until her chest was so tight it cut her breath.

Until a void enveloped her, pulling her toward a bright light where she could see her little girl laughing in the middle of a field of wildflowers, her blond curls dancing around her head.

A knocking on the door penetrated the fog in Julie's head, but she didn't move until a hand touched her shoulder.

"I saw Sylvain leave."

"Oh, Léonie. Thanks for coming down. I'll be all right now."

"Can I make you a cup of coffee?"

"If there's any left. The grocer had run out before my turn came yesterday."

"I brought some and a piece of cold ham. We could have lunch." Léonie Bodénan busied herself in the kitchen while Julie went to wash her face.

"Thank you. I was a wreck, but it's over. I won't let myself get depressed. It serves no purpose. How's the job at General von Trennen's?" The effort Julie was making took all her strength and left her trembling.

"Easy. When you meet him, you get the impression of a tidy and efficient person, but his office isn't. He leaves papers on the desk and on the coffee table. I stack them neatly for him. If we meet, he never fails to say thank you."

"Next he'll hire you as a secretary."

The two friends laughed. "I don't think that's likely. If I didn't know any better, I'd say he deliberately makes no effort to put his papers away."

"What did you learn?"

"I only have basic German but saw nothing of importance. But if I did, how can we use it?"

"I'm sure there'll be a way. We just have to keep looking."

"I'm trying to improve my German."

"I'll help you."

***

Pierrette walked across the courtyard, where the general's driver was polishing the Mercedes.

He looked up and smiled. "*Bonjour!*"

She turned toward the voice and muttered "*Bonjour*."

"Il fait chaud aujourd'hui."

She shrugged. "Go practice your French on somebody else."

"I've no need, My mother is Alsatian."

Her voice rose a notch. "So what the devil are you doing in the German army?"

He straightened with pride. "I believe in the new order. We can teach everyone greater freedom, better living for workers."

"That's called democracy."

"Democracy has been ruined by the Jews and the communists. They control everything."

She frowned and lifted her chin. "Is that what your parents taught you?"

He made a face. "My father's German. An invalid of the First. My mother is totally devoted to him. She has no thoughts of her own."

"How come an Alsatian woman married a German? I thought there was no love lost between Alsatians and the Chleus."

"She was his nurse."

"Classic story. So you went to Germany?"

He brightened. "Three years ago I went to stay with my uncle for the summer holidays. He wanted me to stay and go to school to improve my German. I did and joined the Hitlerjugend. It was great. I realized what I was missing. Being with the boys, camping and hiking. It was exciting. We had classes and I learned about Hitler's magnificent ideology."

"Phooey! I'm crying. Poor misguided boy."

"I'm not a boy, I'm nineteen."

"War and savagery, that's Hitler's ideology!" She tried to keep her temper in check.

"No it isn't."

"Oh, no? Why did Germany start the war, then?"

"We didn't, you did."

Disdain dripped from her words. "First of September 1939, Hitler's army invades Poland. And no, don't you dare say the Poles did it. They were just surprised at the way that clown in Berlin did it."

He hung his head. "That's what my mother said."

"What did your father say when you enlisted in the army?"

"He hoped I'd get killed on the first day, but nobody was fighting."

Pierrette put her hands on her hips. "What about your mother?"

A cloud passed over his face. "She told me never forget that I'd be shooting my own family."

"She's got the right attitude. How come you're the general's driver if you're so keen on warring?"

"Well, the Hitler youth was good, but I didn't fit in like the other boys. In the army I didn't take orders quite like I should have."

"Like what?"

"First time I was opposite French soldiers, I couldn't shoot."

Pierrette's interest was piqued. "They must have court-martialed you for that."

"No court for treason. It was straight to the firing squad. When my sergeant reported me to the unit major for the execution, the major said he understood and sent me to General von Trennen's who needed a driver."

"So you didn't shoot because your French half couldn't do it, is that it?"

He lifted a shoulder and dropped it back in place. "I had no trouble shooting the black soldiers. They're not Aryans."

"You're a disgusting racist."

"Would you like to go for a walk in the Bois de Boulogne?"

"No thanks, I'm busy. You're a disgrace to your side of the French nation."

"Aw, come on! French, German, what does it matter? Don't you see it's a new future for us?"

She pursed her lips. "I'm not part of us." She spun round regretting having spent so much time talking to the young soldier.

***

On the pedestrian path along the Bois de Boulogne, Brigitte held the baby carriage with one hand while she turned to watch Sylvestre trotting behind. "Come'n, mon chou. We're going home." Her darling looked at her and dropped his behind on the grass. At that moment a young man ran past, slammed her shoulder and stuck a handful of papers into her shoulder bag, which fell to the ground and spilled. She lost her grip on the carriage. The youth disappeared.

"What a rude idiot!" She bent to pick up her bag. The carriage moved forward and stopped with a jolt before she could grab it. She looked up. A German soldier had a hand on the handlebar and a broad smile on his face.

Shocked, Brigitte managed to articulate, "I'm so sorry, sir." He was familiar. Where had she seen him before? At the Manoir.

"I saw that impolite man."

To her horror she saw the papers the impolite man had thrust into her bag were leaflets depicting V and ||. She bent and desperately tried to gather the four sheets. He crouched to help. Damien and Estelle approached but stayed a good distance away.

"Thank you. Danke. I can do it." His hands covered hers. They looked at each other. A moment of awareness passed. "Please, let me go. I've got to get the children home."

The two older children came closer.

Calmly, the soldier glanced at the leaflets, gathered them and tucked them into her bag. "I am Hauptmann Langen. I lodge at Le Manoir. We met in passing."

Brigitte's heart slowly return to a normal beat. She remembered now. "I'm Madame Brigitte Marchand."

"Brigitte." He rolled her name on his tongue. "Come and have lunch with me."

Panic set in. She didn't think she could refuse. It was quite clear that as long as the Germans weren't antagonized, they behaved well. "Thank you. It'd be very nice, but I have to get the children home and feed them. Damien, Estelle, come say good morning to Hauptmann Langen."

Barely shy, they came to stand in front of the Captain. "*Guten Tag*," Damien said. Estelle repeated the words.

"Very good, Damien, Estelle. Are you learning my language?"

"We went in the big black car with another German. He had more stripes on his shoulders than you. He taught me to say bonjour, in German."

Captain Langen smiled to the boy. "Very good." He then looked at Brigitte. "It would be my pleasure to take you to lunch."

Still uneasy, she took a long breath. "I'm flattered. It's very nice of you, but—"

"Because of the children. I understand. Will you be able to come tonight, for dinner?"

Her heart raced again. What am I getting embroiled in? What would happen if I refused? "I can make arrangements with my friend."

He nodded. Brigitte turned to Sylvestre who was busy pulling blades of grass and stuffing them in his mouth. "All right, we're going home, little man. Stop that. Come on. I'm going."

The captain scooped up the toddler who offered him a fistful of grass. Her face heating up, Brigitte pushed the carriage toward home.

Her escort saw her to her door. "What time shall I come for you?"

"Seven?"

"*Dix-neuf heures.* Perfect."

"Very well, I'll be ready."

Flustered, she got lunch for the children and hoped that Julie would call in. By the middle of the afternoon, Brigitte sent Damien to the Manoir, which was only two houses away. "Go around the back and ask your grand-maman if Julie can come to see me. I hope she's there." Always eager, Damien ran off. He was soon back with an alarmed Julie in tow. "What's going on? You have to go to dîner with Hauptmann Langen?"

"Afraid so!"

Julie smiled. "He's a sweetheart. He must have taken a shine to you."

"Can you imagine me going to a restaurant with a German? What will people think and say?

"People are getting used to them. They haven't been here a whole month and you already see them everywhere with French girls on their arms."

"I'm not a French girl!"

"No, not that sort of girl. Let's make the best of it since you can't refuse."

"You mean it's a case of they command and we obey?"

"Yes, at least in outward appearances."

Brigitte paused, then smiled. "Compris!"

"Glad you understand. What are you going to wear?"

"A black dress?"

They burst out laughing.

"Where's he taking you?"

"I don't know. Officers seem to congregate on the Champs-Élysées."

They pushed hangers along the rail in the wardrobe. Julie pulled out a delicate sundress. "This is lovely." She held out the dress.

"I'm not wearing anything with bare shoulders. Anyway, I couldn't get in that now. Babies and breastfeeding do alter the body."

"Right." She rummaged some more. "I remember you wearing this ivory silk, embroidered dress. The boat neck is high enough. Try it on."

Brigitte did. "Still showing too much flesh."

Julie put her hands on her hips. "You can't go dressed as a nun. It's summer."

"If I wear a silk blouse underneath, it'll be modest enough. This dress was always a bit too big for me."

"How about this barely pink voile blouse with the minimal collar? Long sleeves with pearl buttons to give it chic. It makes you look very Victorian and modest."

Brigitte clasped her head in her hands. "If he wasn't lodging at the Manoir and could cause trouble for my substitute parents, I'd refuse to go." Brigitte put on the blouse and put on the dress. "What a rigmarole! Imagine me, mother of four, parading in high heels with a German officer." She selected her beige pumps, with a small heel. "I haven't worn heels since before I was last pregnant. Those are low enough to prevent me from falling on my backside in the restaurant."

Julie giggled and handed her a small light-colored beaded purse. "Now for the hat."

"I do have to wear a hat. The girls we mentioned don't wear hats."

"Nothing big." Julie took out the round boxes and spread half a dozen hats on the bed. "This one is small, sits slightly forward on the head." She placed it on a resigned Brigitte's head. "The flowers are unobtrusive."

"Can we remove the feathers?"

"No problem." Julie examined the decorations and gave a tug. The feathers came off. "And now you have a really chic little bibi."

Brigitte laughed. "What a silly word for a hat.

Brigitte occupied the ground floor of a three-story mansion that had been converted into three apartments. Hauptmann Langen pulled up in front of the building in the general's black Mercedes. A shout from Damien, whose forehead was glued to the windowpane, announced to his mother that it was time to go. Julie checked her friend's appearance, from hat and matching gloves, one last time, and closed the door behind her.

A smile on his lips, Gerhardt held the car door open. "You're absolutely beautiful."

"Thank you."

"I thought maybe you would have had a change of heart."

She refrained from shrugging. After her long discussion with Julie, she understood that humoring the Fritz was the first step toward the day they could free themselves of them. After all, he had seen the subversive pamphlets in her bag, and although he also had seen the man put them in, the captain could easily assume she was complicit. "It did cross my mind, but I also believe that being friends is the best way to get along."

"I am glad to hear that."

He navigated the streets and stopped in front of the Brasserie Lipp, Boulevard Saint-Germain. Not only was Brigitte's heart beating fast but dread insinuated itself through her whole being. Why had he chosen the Saint-Germain des Prés district, probably the busiest area, after Montmartre, to have dinner?

The patrons of the Brasserie appeared to be mostly Germans officers along with a few ordinary soldiers. Several women, obviously French, were draped against them. From behind the bar, the owner gave Brigitte a malevolent look. She blushed. A couple of officers greeted Hauptmann Langen and gave him a good ribbing. He made some replies and they all burst out laughing.

A stone-faced old waiter showed them to a table and handed them a menu. For the next few minutes, Brigitte explained the offerings. The captain picked huîtres for a first entrée and insisted on a second hors-d'oeuvre *terrine de foie gras maison.* A brief smile flitted over the waiter's mouth on hearing the order of a crock of homemade goose liver pâté. When the sommelier presented him with the wine list, Captain Langen handed it to Brigitte. "I know nothing about wines."

She racked her brain for which wine to order with the hors d'oeuvres and chose a white wine Baron «L» Pouilly Fumé. The sommelier nodded his approval and left with her order.

While they waited for the oysters, the captain told her to drop the Hauptmann and that he was Gerhardt. She nodded. Gerhardt tentatively asked her about her interests. By the time the *escalope de veau viennoise* course was put on the table, they'd discovered a common interest in and knowledge of architecture. Again, she received the sommelier's approbation when she selected the best red wine of the house, the Nuits Saint Georges Les Porrets «First cru » to accompany the meat course.

"I'd really like to have been able to study architecture in order to restore old buildings, but that's not an avenue open to women."

"More the pity. I think you would have been very good."

"Women are supposed to be mothers. Then I was introduced to Hubert and now I have four children." She smiled. "But I love children."

Brigitte carefully avoided drinking more than one glass of wine. She declined the cheese course but agreed to a dessert. The head waiter, more relaxed now, took it upon himself to serve a *crème brûlée à la vanille*, with a pinch of roasted almonds on top.

"Has your husband been demobilized?"

"I haven't had any news since last April. He was in the air force."

"It is early days. News will soon arrive."

The waiter brought coffee. They sipped it in silence. Finally, still feeling slightly uncomfortable, Brigitte stood up and thanked Hauptmann Langen for a delicious meal. The waiter collected the money and the bill from the table.

Gerhardt lifted an eyebrow. "Does one tip the garçon?" He pulled out a bunch of marks from his wallet.

"Yes." She knew she was breaking etiquette. Anyway, she took them from him and turned to the waiter. "Is that enough?"

A strange smile hovered on his lips. "More than enough."

She handed him the deutschmarks and, tears welling up, murmured, "It isn't my choice."

He winked at her and while taking the money, slipped a small piece of paper in her hand. She closed her fist, swallowed hard and headed toward the door. She didn't know why she needed to justify herself to the waiter. As nonchalantly as she could, she stuffed the paper into her purse.

Chapter Twenty-Four

Dressed in his gendarme uniform, Jacques Werner pushed his bicycle across the courtyard, grousing all the way, and leaned it against the wall of the annex. He burst into the kitchen. "It's so damned hot out!"

"Still on duty?" Bérangère asked.

He dropped onto the chair next to Gontrand. "Those damned Boches. You know what they've done now?" He didn't wait for an answer. "They demolished the bas-relief of the Jeu de Paume museum and then, they demolished the statue of Edith Cavell. As if it wasn't enough that they'd executed her!"

Lyse-May tugged on Bérangère's skirt. "Why they execute her?"

"Sweetie, I thought you were playing outside on the swing. All right, Edith Cavell was a nurse in the First World War. She cared for wounded soldiers, whether they were German or English or French, as well as helping them escape from being taken prisoner. The Germans said it was treason."

"*Sales Boches.*"

"Sshh! Remember what I told you?"

The child gave a theatrical sigh. "Bad dirty Germans!"

Gontrand pulled his granddaughter onto his knee and handed her paper and coloring pencils. He turned to Jacques. "So, my friend, why are you on duty on a Sunday?"

"We don't have enough gendarmes. And policemen are civil servants, so they don't work on Sundays. Anyway, they don't do traffic and peace keeping."

"No, really?"

Jacques sighed. "Not quite, but we're short of supervisors. Since I'm single, I always get picked. We're supposed to chase the youths that paste bits of paper with *mort aux Boches* on walls everywhere."

"Monsieur Jacques, you can't say death to the Boches. You're supposed to say death to the Germans."

The adults repressed their laughter.

"You're right, mademoiselle Lyse-May. I'll watch my language."

"You're staying for lunch, aren't you? The family's coming over at about one o'clock," Bérangère said.

The noisy arrival of Damien and Estelle, cut short Jacques' reply. Brigitte followed, carrying Christiane, then Julie with Sylvestre. Soon after, Charmaine and her children made an entrance. Pierrette, her brother and cousin clattered down the backstairs. In the crowded kitchen, Pierrette and Marianne rounded up the children and led them into the courtyard to play. François and Hughes were charged with taking a picnic to the small fry. Julie and Charmaine helped with the food preparation. They had all brought a contribution for the lunch.

Charmaine grumbled. "Yesterday's bread. That's the new edict. Did you see the posters? Cut thin slices."

"Croissants and brioche are banned," Julie said.

"Except at Ruc. That restaurant is a second headquarters for the German brass and the Brasserie Lipp still has incredible desserts."

"Right, Brigitte. How was that dinner last night?"

She groaned. "I have never felt so embarrassed in my life. Hauptmann Langen is a perfect gentleman, but the looks the owner threw could have killed me. Same for the head waiter, a distinguished old man, but at the end, he mellowed. When I tipped him with Gerhardt's money, he slipped a paper in my hand."

"Hey, so it's Gerhardt now!"

"He insisted. The fact he lives here makes it a little more acceptable."

"What was on the paper?" Charmaine asked.

"V and ||."

Jacques stretched out on the chair. "He ought to be careful. Even though the Germans don't have a clue what it means. They don't understand the subtlety of two sticks meaning de Gaulle."

"It's all a matter of pronunciation, and of course, knowing that a long stick is a *gaule,* and two are *deux* close enough to *de*," Bérangère said.

"It's good to know other people think like us," Julie said.

Agitated, Gontrand slammed his fist on the table. "Don't you dare do or pass papers around. Maréchal Pétain wants us to obey. He knows what he is doing!"

Julie diverted the conversation. "The Tour d'Argent has posted a bilingual menu."

Jacques griped. "The Nazis have taken over the restaurant." He brightened. "But do you know that young Claude Terrail, yes the owner's son, has walled off the back of the wine cellar with five-hundred thousand bottles of rare wine?"

"If the Chleus discover it, they'll hang him."

"He's gone abroad."

"How do you know all that?" Bérangère asked.

"It's the job of the gendarmerie to know what's going on in Paris. I can already tell you that all celebrations of Bastille Day have been banned."

"The bastards!" They looked at her with astonishment. They'd never heard the matriarch swear. "All right. Food is ready."

Chapter Twenty-Five

Sunday, July 14, 1940

Jacques won't be coming today. The Fritz have forbidden all demonstrations and celebrations of our National Bastille Day because they fear Parisians will go out and revolt like in 1789. Right now people are just beginning to recover from the shock of being defeated. If our men were here, it might be different. After all, when the Revolution happened, it was against the internal enemy, the aristocracy. Now I, being an aristocrat, can write that with the wisdom of hindsight. I wonder whether my ancestors, many of whom lost their heads, saw it in the same light. I have seen some awful anti-Semitic posters. I still don't see what's the problem, but won't talk about it with my husband! He so touchy these days. All the news we'd heard that sounded so far away about Jewish stores being vandalized in Austria and Germany are not so far away now. I saw notices proclaiming Juden Verboten. Interdit aux Juifs. Bilingual just in case someone didn't understand. I'm getting worried about our young people. They keep muttering about doing something. So did the old man at the bakery. Anyway, I should go and see how Madame Ducharme manages now that she has tenants. It must be hard for her to have other people living in her house, but it was the best way to avoid having Germans in residence in her mansion. She'd have committed murder. Monseigneur Chevrot isn't going to preach today, so church can wait next week. The family is coming for dîner tonight.

Brigitte and Julie were first to arrive with the children. Bérangère fed the children right away. Damien and Estelle went to play in the courtyard where Günter was smoking a Gauloise. He had taken it upon himself to watch out for the children every time he wasn't required by the general.

"What's keeping the boys and Pierrette?" Bérangère asked.

Julie glanced at her father-in-law. "They're preparing tomorrow's printing."

Brigitte burped Christiane. "They're getting better but not very fast."

The women looked at each other, eyebrows raised. They didn't like to think that the eagerness of the young people went a little further than learning a trade. They weren't going to share their suspicions, though.

"Good. Keeps them out of trouble on this Sunday!" Gontrand said. He put his pipe back in his mouth and struck a match.

"I told you not to smoke in here when the family's here. It's too small and too hot."

Chastened, Gontrand put his pipe away. The outside door opened and a brouhaha of voices invaded the passageway and the kitchen. Pierrette came in ahead of the boys who soon followed, carrying three bags of produce.

"Guess who's here?"

Moments later, Madeleine and Marie-Ange accompanied by her children came in, dragging along a tall wiry man. Brigitte and Julie jumped up and hugged him. "Dieudonné Dumonteil's here."

Gontrand slapped his old friend on the back. Then, Eugène, wearing dungarees, and Berthe, wearing a peasant skirt and a long apron, squeezed into the kitchen. There was no end to the shrieks of joy. Marie poked her head into the kitchen to welcome the new arrivals and slipped two fresh long-loaves into Julie's hand. Finally Bérangère ordered everyone to sit down. Marianne collected her four youngest cousins and with her brother took them into the courtyard to play.

Gontrand came up from the cellar with a bottle of wine. "Now, tell us how you've got here."

Julie finished making sandwiches and, with Brigitte carrying tin cups and a pail of water, took them to the children. She offered a sandwich to Günter who accepted with a childish delight.

Eugene took a sip of wine. "Dédé successfully obtained a contract with the German Supply Corps—"

"You're not working for the B..."

"Quiet, Gontrand!" Bérangère threatened him with a wag of her finger.

"My dear brother, there's working and there's working."

"I don't see the difference."

"I'll explain later, grand-papa. Please continue, Uncle Eugène," Pierrette said.

"The contract gave him the right to go to Paris to deliver his products to the Supply Corps."

Julie frowned. "What type of products?"

Dédé passed his hand in his hair. He tried to find the right words. "I made myself into a transport and brokerage company. The Germans have imposed a quota for everything, so I find what they need. It's good for my farm and the neighbors' farms. It's very useful in other ways."

"Ah!" Julie smiled. "Good for you, Dédé. Please, Eugène, continue."

"We knew all about the demarcation line, and decided to try to cross it in a small locality rather than at Orléans where there would be tighter control as we didn't have that damned Ausweis. A good soul told us to go to Chaussin. Not the most direct route but we had no choice. Rather than hide in the truck behind the bales of wool, Dédé sent Madeleine and Marie-Ange ahead with the children. The line was guarded by a single soldier, and the control barrier was just a pitchfork on two chairs across the road."

Marie-Ange continued. "I asked him politely to let us go home. He didn't speak too much French." Laughter greeted that statement. "He said, you afe to afe permizione from Kommandant. You go und zee Kommandant. So we walked back to the truck. Since it was near noon, we had a picnic by the river and came back. Dédé told me to say that we had seen the Kommandant and that he said it was all right."

Madeleine laughed. "You should have seen her school teacher's authority when she told him. The poor guy didn't realize that his Kommandant was on his side and we couldn't have gone to see him."

"He was probably more at ease with the pitchfork in a field than with a uniform and guard duties," Berthe said.

"Besides, he couldn't take his eyes off Madeleine, our beauty queen," Eugene said.

Dédé took over. "When I saw they were through, I didn't give him time to think. I handed him my Ausweis and said Eugene and Berthe in the truck were my employees. He barely looked at them. He was still looking at Madeleine."

Laughter erupted.

"It could also be because you handed him a loaf of fresh bread with homemade saucisson that smelled so terribly good," Eugene said.

"I'm glad everyone is back home, but I'll remind you of the curfew. Dédé, we'll have a bed for you. Marie-Ange did you go home?" Bérangère said.

"Yes, Dédé dropped me at home. Everything is in order."

Eugene stood. "We'll catch the bus to Suresnes."

"No, you won't. No buses running as yet, if ever. They're still all on the battlefield, what's left of them, anyway," Bérangère said. "I suggest you take the spare room, Lyse-May can sleep in our room and Dédé can have her room."

"Mémée, can I go with tata Brigitte to sleep?"

"That's fine with me," Brigitte said.

"Madeleine is coming with me," Julie said. I have room."

"We need to get in touch with Philippe to tell him his wife's back," Bérangère said.

"That won't be too difficult," Pierrette said. "Just watch the new neighbor. The baron and my father are close friends. He visits often."

A stupefied silence followed her announcement. Julie broke it by saying. "There's no rush. Madeleine can stay with me for a while."

Madeleine's voice wobbled. "Then I'll get an apartment."

The chaos got sorted out and everyone went on their way.

Pierrette and François whispered with Dédé for a while before climbing up to their attic rooms with smiles on their faces.

***

The next day, Brigitte was awakened by a pounding on the front door of the apartment building at six o'clock in the morning. The children were already in the kitchen. She dressed quickly and just then there was a loud knock on her apartment door. Dread filled her as she heard booted feet clambering the stairs. She thrust her feet into her mules and opened the door a crack to find a knot of soldiers crowding the foyer.

"Requisition order, ma'am. You're to vacate the building by eighteen hundred hours tonight." A soldier thrust a sheet of paper into her hand. "You must leave the furniture and..."

Christiane chose that moment to let out a piercing scream. The other children, including Lyse-May peering from behind the door, came out in full view. The soldier looked taken aback. Brigitte noticed he was wearing slightly different German uniform. "Surely, you won't need the babies' beds."

His face registered his confusion and he growled, "Eighteen hundred hours. Six o'clock!"

Brigitte closed the door and grabbed her baby daughter. "All right. Let's organize. Lyse-May and Damien you run up to grandmother's. Use the garden side door. Tell her we have to move out by six o'clock. We need Julie."

"Got it." Damien spun on his heel and, with Lyse-May close behind, dashed out.

The upstairs tenants were moaning loudly and began dragging packages down the stairs to the basement storage.

"Where are we to go?"

"So unjust! *Putain de Boches!*"

Brigitte was too anxious and too busy to help. Before closing her door, she threw a word of caution. "You won't be able to retrieve your possessions if you put them in the basement. Better pack a couple of suitcases with your most precious items." She didn't wait to hear their replies. "Estelle, ma chérie, collect the toys in the middle of the living room. Bring pillow cases from the closet and put the toys in them."

By the time Christiane had been fed and changed, Bérangère arrived, along with Günter. Not long afterwards, the adolescents were lending a hand.

Bérangère folded clothes swiftly. "Let's pile everything in one of our sheds for the moment. Too bad Dédé has already left. The truck would have been handy. He drove Berthe and Eugène to Suresnes."

To everyone's surprise, the general's Mercedes came to a halt in front of the building. Hauptmann Langen stepped out and told the boys to load the car. He stood still for a moment to watch Brigitte order her helpers about before greeting her.

"I'm so grateful for your help, Herr Hauptmann."

"Gerhardt."

She smiled. "Gerhardt. How did you know?"

"Günter phoned General von Trennen who ordered me to come and help."

"That's so good of all of you. Who's the soldier with the lightning bolt symbols on his collar?"

Gerhardt pursed his lips. "Those! They are the SS. That's the Schutzstaffel Polizei. They're detested by the Wehrmacht and everybody else. I am afraid I should not tell you that, but you will keep it to yourself."

"You know, I will."

"The man taking over the building is SS-Obersturmbannführer Meinhard. The nastiest of all."

"Is he of high rank?"

"Yes. They rise quickly in the SS. Let us keep going. You do not want to leave your personal effects in your apartment."

"Thank you."

Julie, seeing Brigitte well-taken care of, told the other tenants to stack what they didn't want to fall into the hands of the Germans on the sidewalk and she'd help them take it to her storage basement.

By mid-afternoon, Brigitte's apartment contained only basic furniture and household items. The boys and Pierrette were helping the other two tenants remove their personal possessions, ferrying them to Avenue Victor-Hugo. By six o'clock that evening, the street was quiet. Around the dinner table, Julie and Brigitte made plans.

"Ernest told me he knows someone with an empty apartment. Shall we go and see it tomorrow?"

"Absolutely. Do you think I should go and thank the general for sending Ge... help?"

With a teasing smile, Julie said, "You mean for sending Gerhardt?"

Brigitte reddened. "Don't make me more embarrassed than I already am."

"Just kidding. I'll bicycle here in the morning and we'll walk to rue Mignard. Hopefully, Ernest has got it right. It's quite a long walk!"

"Hauptmann Langen told me the Fritz moving into my building is a high ranking SS, an Obsturm... something or other. They wear a uniform I've not seen before."

"You mean SS-Obersturmbannführer?"

"That's sounds like what he said. I didn't study languages like you."

"When your father's been an ambassador to Germany, it's easy to learn. Does he have a name?"

"I'll try to pronounce it like he did: mine hat."

Julie froze. Then her hand shook and her cup of coffee spilt over as she hastily replaced it on the table. "Did he say Kurt Meinhard?"

"Yes, just like that except for Kurt. You've gone pale. What's wrong?"

Bérangère was watching too. "The coffee's rather weak. We don't seem to be able to get any from the store. I put half the quantity to make it last."

Her diversion helped Julie recover. "He and I were... friends when we were at university together in Heidelberg in '32. But I broke it off. He made me sick with his Nazi ambitions and ideology."

Two hands covered Julie's hand. Silent comfort. She couldn't tell anyone how he'd charmed her. How in her inexperienced youth, she'd almost believed his theories when he murmured them in her ear and her agitated senses were battling with her upbringing. Shame burned her face, but a rebellious flame sprung into her breast. She'd have nothing to do with him anyway and she'd fight in whatever way she could to get rid of his sort.

Chapter Twenty-Six

Julie parked her bicycle in the courtyard and joined her in-laws at the breakfast table, but first depositing a bag of potatoes and a day-old long loaf on the kitchen counter. Brigitte had just finished feeding the children.

"Do you think the government is going to sort out the food distribution problem? I was at the grocer's store when it opened and his wife said he was still at the Halles wholesale market. It takes hours for storekeepers to get anything."

Gontrand nodded. "Transport is still disrupted, but Maréchal Pétain is looking into it. He'll soon get it back to normal."

Bérangère exploded. "You old fool! He has no power on this side of the demarcation line."

"Of course he does! The B... Chleus have asked him to keep the administration running."

Bérangère rolled her eyes. "Providing he, and the administration, do exactly as they're told."

The discussion was heading from bad to worse. Julie and Brigitte nodded to each other. Their chairs scraped the floor as they stood up. They called to the children and in the ensuing ruckus, Gontrand gave up talking. They winked at Bérangère, who handed them sandwiches and a bottle of water. Brigitte tucked them into the basket under the bed of the baby carriage.

"Wait. I have a larger English carriage with big wheels and good springs in the attic. Would you like it for the long walk?"

"Please."

Moments later, Günter, who'd just entered the vestibule, carried the carriage downstairs and helped to dust it off. There was a stiff bag at the front on which Sylvestre could sit, and a sun shade.

"What a luxury!"

They happily set out.

"I can't get over how empty the streets feel," Julie said.

"It's the absence of noise."

"That's right! There're quite a few vélo-taxis, but they make no noise and pedestrians never did make much noise. It's the din of car engines and hooting horns that's missing."

"And the few horses' hooves on the pavement are rhythmical but not really noisy."

The different form of silence was broken when they turned the corner and encountered a squad of German soldiers singing as they marched past.

Damien and Estelle slowed down and took Julie's hands.

"Are you sure the apartment is empty?" Brigitte asked.

"Ernest told me that when he went to see his friend, the building was half empty. It isn't a luxury building."

"But perhaps people will come back."

"Ernest seems to know. Just like my concierge, she knows everything and everybody. I don't know how they do it! She was able to tell the other tenants where to find empty accommodations." They laughed. Sylvestre also laughed and let go of the handlebar. "Walk! Walk!"

"In a moment, mon chou. We have to cross Avenue Henri-Martin."

"No! No! Walk! Walk!"

"Let me carry him over. Estelle, Damien, take hold of the handle."

The children scooted on either side of the carriage. The toddler leaned forward and Julie plucked him up from his seat. His warm squirming body open the memory gates of another small warm body. She clenched her jaw until the wave of pain passed, then forced herself to relax and kiss the child's rosy cheek. Finally, they reached rue Mignard. "Almost there."

They passed several stores and found number thirteen Mignard street. Brigitte exhaled a satisfied breath. "I hope it works out. This is very convenient for the grocer and the Amiot dairy."

The ornate façade had seen better days. On an enamel plaque near the door, the traditional inscription read, *eau, gaz, électricité à tous les étages*.

"Well, that's reassuring. At least I'll have water, cooking gas and electricity, since they're available on all the floors."

"Some people want to rewrite it as water, cooking gas, electricity and Jews on all floors."

"Why?"

"That's the current bad joke, nobody should make fun of those poor people, not when the Germans are after getting rid of them."

"Surely they don't get rid of them as in kill them?"

"You're kidding? Before I left Germany, six years ago, he was boasting that his father was in charge of building a camp for the 'trash of humanity'."

"He, I suppose, being the one taking over my apartment."

"Meinhard himself."

"So Jews were the trash?"

"And gypsies, homosexuals, intellectuals and dissidents."

Brigitte shivered. "How awful."

They pushed open the heavy door and maneuvered the carriage inside the hallway. They knocked on the loge de concierge. No response.

"The curtains are drawn and the outside shutters closed. Nobody home. Let's go to the second floor, left door."

They ascended without noise. On the landing, there was a doormat on the right, nothing on the left. Julie tried the door. It opened. They looked at each other with apprehension.

"All right, let's see," Brigitte said.

A slightly musty smell rose to their nostrils. Beyond the small vestibule, a large kitchen, with a dining table, lay to the right. The window overlooked a small inner courtyard. There were still pots and pans in the cupboards. Opposite the kitchen, the living room still had a couch and armchairs, as well as table lamps. The two windows overlooked the street. Three bedrooms, two of them partly furnished, opened onto a hallway. The last door was a Water Closet, with a sink, a bath and the ubiquitous bidet.

"This will do, so long as the owners don't come back. I'll only need to bring a few things and the children's stuff and my own cooking utensils. Once freshened up, it will be cozy. A bedroom for the boys and one for the girls."

"We'll bring what you need for the empty bed—" A noise made them jump.

A woman stood framed in the entrance way, a scowl on her face. "What are you people doing here?"

"We need an apartment and M. Loiseau told Ernest there were empty ones in the building," Julie said with calm.

"Who's Ernest?"

"My father-in-law's factotum. His wife Marie is the cook and cleaner. The Loiseaus are their friends, sort of country cousins."

"Ah, the small man with a béret. I've seen him. Who's your father-in-law?"

"Gontrand de Montregard."

"Don't know him."

"He lives near the Bois de Boulogne."

"Posh! So why do you want an apartment here?"

"Because a Nazi officer just threw me out of mine." Brigitte's tone reflected the anger she'd been keeping in check since the day before.

"Why didn't you say so in the first place? In that case, you're welcome. I live across the landing. I'm Amélie Bergeron."

They introduced themselves.

"And I'm Damien. This is my sister Estelle. She's five. I'm seven. Sylvestre is two. And my new sister. She's got no number of years."

Amélie Bergeron leaned toward the little boy. "You're smart, Damien. My big boy Marc's thirteen, Sylvie's eleven, Sophie's nine and Angeline five. They've gone to the market to see if a fisherman would give them some fish." She turned back to the adults. "I already know my husband's a prisoner. It's a great shame. I know he fought hard. He's good Frenchman. And you?"

They all sat down at the kitchen table.

Brigitte resettled the baby against her shoulder and unabashedly began breastfeeding her. "I've had no news of my husband. Nothing, not whether he's a prisoner, dead or an escapee. But it's early days. They haven't finished processing everybody."

"That's too bad. You need a certificate to get your allocation. When the Fritz arrived, I was going to go to my brother in Clermont-Ferrand. He works at the Michelin rubber factory. I didn't want anybody to take our apartment so I stayed. Already there's two Fritz on the ground floor. The concierge left in May, too frightened to stay."

Julie cuddled Sylvestre. "So who had this apartment?"

"Monsieur and Madame Hartmann. They left in 1939. The keys are on the hook. Here." Amélie got to her feet. Julie followed her to the entrance door. Against the wall, a small panel held some keys. "This is the key for the door, this one for the downstairs entry, and this one for the cellar."

"But they left a lot of stuff. They might be back," Brigitte said.

"Unlikely. They're in their late seventies and went to their daughter in Valence. They came from Alsace after the Great War. With their name, they're dead scared of the Boches."

"Can't blame them," Julie said.

Madame Bergeron sighed. "It doesn't look too good, you know. Did you see how the Fritz scoops up everything in the stores?"

Brigitte nodded. "Even milk is hard to get."

"I tell you, the Fritz take everything. Everything, and they send it to Germany. What a shame!"

Estelle interrupted. "Can I pee in the W.C.?"

"Yes, sweetheart, go. Then we'll need to come and start moving here. Christiane is almost finished."

"Can you get enough milk for the baby?"

"I'm only breastfeeding her so it's fine for the moment."

"Bless you. I'll make sure no one takes the apartment until you're back."

"Thank you, madame," Julie said.

"Upstairs, above you, there's the Loiseaus, friends of your Ernest. On the other side it's Monsieur and Madame Danton, with their sons Laurent and Raphaël and daughter Sarah. They keep to themselves... I better tell you, it's not their real name but if you hear their accent you might wonder."

"Be assured of our discretion, madame Amélie," Brigitte said.

"Just call me Amélie."

"In these troubled times, we ask no question, we see nothing and we don't hear anything unless it's where food can be had," Julie said.

Madame Bergeron sighed with relief. "I'm glad you'll be moving in. It's enough having two Boches downstairs. Don't want more of them. But they're no trouble those two. The fourth and fifth floors are empty. Have been for a long time. I suppose people don't want to live in a building that doesn't have an elevator. And the water is only on the fourth landing. It used to be on the fifth floor but doesn't now. After you've moved in you can tuck the baby carriage under the stairs. There used to be a closet but the doors have gone. Still, it'll be safe there."

"What about the rent?"

"The concierge being gone, there's no one to collect it. So we didn't pay in June and the next one should be due in December. Who knows where the owner is? Never saw him in my life."

"So much disruption! I'll save the money anyway. Now I think we'll feed the children before going back."

Amélie retreated to her quarters. Brigitte and Julie fed the children the sandwiches they'd brought. Then they left the apartment and walked along the seemingly endless rue La Tour. Julie carried Sylvestre who soon fell asleep on her shoulder.

Brigitte was enumerating a list of the things she would want in the apartment. "But how am I going to get all this if we have to walk all this way?"

"Oh, I'd think a certain captain might just borrow a vehicle to help."

"No! What will the neighbors think?"

"That it's a practical way to move when all other cars are banned."

"No good. I'll manage."

"Of, course, silly, I'll help too. In fact, we'll get the boys and Pierrette. There's a handcart we can use to move the children's beds. If everyone carries one or two bags, it won't take long. It isn't as far as I feared it'd be."

They made a stop by the Lamartine park and the artesian well to refresh the children and refill the water bottle. Julie leaned against the bench backrest and stretched her legs in front of her. "Do you ever wonder what life would have been like if Philippe had continued courting you and married you?"

"No, not really. I grew up with the de Montregard's boys. Philippe was older by about eight years, so he was kind of the boss. Bérangère and Gontrand made me part of the family when my mother died and that's what they became, brothers. Charmaine was my best friend. The teacher sat us at the same desk on the first day of school because Charmaine didn't have a mother, either. So, we were both sort of adopted by the de Montregards."

"They are both genuinely good-hearted."

"Agnès didn't like being the only girl and pretended to be a boy. I used to like playing with dolls but I wasn't going to miss anything, so I was a boy too. Charmaine was more refined, she stayed with maman-Bérangère and loved helping. We were in paradise with our warm-hearted, ready-made family. And that's how I saw every one of them, like brothers. I didn't know how to take Philippe's attention when we grew older. I hate hurting people's feelings."

"Belle-maman told me Philippe was rather sweet on you and planned to marry you."

Brigitte laughed. "Until Madeleine appeared in our midst. There was no competition. She's too beautiful for words. I was relieved, really."

"She's gentle and has a calming influence on her husband."

"She's not going to be happy when she learns he works so closely with..." Brigitte glanced around. "the Fritz."

"Wasn't Charmaine hoping to marry one of the boys? Bernard maybe?"

Brigitte chuckled. "She was just ten when she became smitten with Bernard's best friend. They could barely wait to be married."

"Alexandre is an ideal husband."

"Sure is."

They left the bench and resumed their walk. Damien and Estelle squabbled as to who was going to push the carriage.

***

The dubious look on Bérangère's face disappeared when Lyse-May, standing on a chair by the table, clamored, "Look, mémée, I stirred it all smooth."

"You did! You're so much better than I at making batter."

Before the two cooks could proceed with the next step of the recipe, the outside door was thrown open and the vestibule filled with noise.

"Lorraine!" Bérangère hugged her sister-in-law. "When did you get back?"

"An hour ago. I went to the printing shop and then I was dragged here by our young people. They said it was closing time."

"The Germans decreed that stores would be open from nine to six. Lyse-May and I were just making dinner. How's the leg?"

"All good again, or rather a little weak, but no lasting damage."

Pierrette and the boys scooted up to their attic bedrooms.

"It'll soon get strong. Since we have no buses and the Métro is overcrowded, we're all bicycling or walking."

"Do you have any idea how Hughes and his cousins managed to get the contract to print the newspaper *La France au Travail?* It's an absolute rag, full of propaganda and sententious maxims. I don't want to be printing that garbage."

"We've seen it. Yes, you do want to print it. If you don't, you'll be closed down. I believe Pierrette is the smart businesswoman who negotiated the contract."

"And Hughes signed it. Mon Dieu, he doesn't even shave yet but he takes on responsibilities like a man."

"They've all lost years of their childhood in the last few months."

"Mémée, the pan's going to boil over!"

With a shriek, Bérangère grabbed the offending saucepan. "You'll need a bicycle. Ernest has been renovating some old ones he found at the Marché aux Puces."

"Of course, the Parisian bazaar, and he's got a knack for resourcefulness."

After the dîner, Lorraine tried out the bicycle Ernest was proud to offer her. After a few wobbling moments, and the family's encouragements, she found the right balance. Hughes borrowed François' bicycle to ride home alongside his mother.

Chapter Twenty-Seven

Thursday, July 18, 1940

Pierrette and François were excited because my sister-in-law paid them for helping keep the printing shop going. Those two, and sometimes Hughes, hold confabs like plenipotentiaries. I hope they're not going round pasting those stickers. They ought to be studying. Pierrette has to take part two of the baccalauréat, and François ought to prepare for the forthcoming school year. Though I must say he's making an effort to learn German. The scamp said it wasn't because the salauds de Boches are here – I didn't have the heart to reprimand the swearing - but to better understand how to throw them out. Maybe he's right. Fortunately, now that Lorraine is back, Hughes won't be following François around like a puppy. I do suspect my grandson of, shall I say, illegal activities?

My husband has been quiet lately. He takes Lyse-May for walks and teaches her the history of France. I don't suppose it does any harm. She's not yet four, we don't even know her birthday, but she talks like a grown-up. He was furious because the letter he sent his brother Arnaud in Montauloup came back with a stamp stating Inadmissible in Non-occupied Zone. In short, no one can correspond with the other zone. At least, Eugène's return brought news and that soothed him a little. Arnaud, like Gontrand, worships that old fool Pétain.

I hear the Germans are making plans to bring back all those who fled south, starting tomorrow, so that normal life can resume. I suppose they've repaired the railroads. The weather is rather cool for July. I hear a knock...

"Belle-maman, I brought a guest." Julie entered the kitchen with a young man. He limped to the chair she pulled out for him.

Bérangère noticed Julie's red eyes. "I got a little coffee at the grocer's this morning. I'll make a pot."

Gontrand took his unlit pipe from his mouth. "Who do we have here?"

Julie finished setting the cups on the table. "Xavier Despins. He was in the same unit as Florent."

Bérangère's hand stopped half way to the cupboard. Gontrand sat up straighter. There are times when words are unnecessary, when hope becomes brittle and dies.

Xavier spoke with effort, "It was June 17. Florent and I defended a position at Orchies. No one had heard about a cease-fire. A shell exploded in front of our foxhole and buried us in earth. By the time I dug myself out, it was dark. Florent had taken a hit straight to the heart. He didn't have a chance. I buried him in the foxhole." Xavier dropped his head in his hands.

A long silence settled. Julie poured the boiling water into the cafetière. The coffee dripped into the pot below.

No one had heard Lyse-May enter. She climbed on Gontrand's lap. "Uncle Florent is an angel like Claire all dressed in gold light. They're going to pick flowers in the beautiful light and make daisy chains in Heaven."

Julie's mouth fell open. Her eyes widened. Was it possible that the child had the same dream, or was it a vision, than she did? Was there something real in what people whisper about a dearly beloved reaching out from the beyond?

Gontrand kissed her. Handkerchiefs held by trembling hands wiped away tears. After a long silence and quiet sobs, Bérangère swallowed. "I saw you limp. Are you hurt?"

"I was taken prisoner before I could hide. There must have been thousands of us herded into a camp. I didn't want to be a POW in Germany, but didn't get a chance to escape until we were put on a train. It was going through Belgium. I jumped off somewhere before the border with Germany but fell badly and twisted my knee. I rolled down the embankment to the bottom of the slope. After the train vanished, a couple of Belgian women came to my rescue and took me to their house. When I could walk again, they gave me the identity papers of a Belgian who hadn't made it, a Roland Dupuis. He had a certificate of exemption, unfit for service, but he'd joined and served anyway. It fitted my condition. I walked, sometimes got rides in farmers' hay wagons. Florent and I had an agreement should only one of us survive. If I were the survivor, I was to go to Madame Sylvain de Montregard. So I did."

His voice rasping in his throat, Gontrand said, "We are very grateful to you, Xavier."

"You'll stay here, won't you?" Bérangère asked.

"I have nowhere to go at the moment. My mother's in Toulouse."

"You'll need proper papers to travel," Julie said. "There are other ways but not right now, not until your knee is fully repaired."

"You mean Dédé could help?" Bérangère asked.

Julie nodded then gave Bérangère a hand with the dîner. Her heart was torn anew as she thought of the pain her in-laws were suffering. The silence, heavy and somber, was barely broken by inconsequential words, until Pierrette and François arrived. On learning the news, they sobbed without restraint. Finally, calm of acceptance settled over the household. Xavier picked up his bag and pulled out Florent's army pack. He handed it reverently to Bérangère who pressed it against her chest.

Julie motioned with her head, the small movement swiftly understood by her nephew and niece. They tiptoed up to the attic. She showed Xavier to the spare room. He nodded his thanks. Still silent, she bicycled home. On the stairs she bumped into Léonie and told her the sad news.

"If I could get a job at the town hall..."

"That'd be good. You could steal some useful papers."

"Léonie!" They burst out laughing. A hollow laugh, but it was good to relieve the tension brought on by death and pain and grief. "Xavier can't use his Belgian identity. If there's a control, he'd be sent back to Belgium and they have a gauleiter there. Probably trying to germanize the country. For his own, he needs a demobilization certificate."

"Is it at all possible to get a job at the town hall?"

"I've been thinking about it. If Pierrette could pilfer blank Ausweis, so could I pilfer what we might need. Tomorrow I'll go to the Préfecture for Xavier's real papers."

***

Early in the morning, Julie called at the Manoir and asked Xavier for his papers. On Quai des Orfèvres, she parked her bicycle and went into the Préfecture de Police. She asked to see Commandant Jacques Werner and blatantly lied that he was expecting her. A worried look on his face, he rushed out of his office, dismissed a secretary and closed the door.

"What?"

"We need demobilization papers for a friend." She spoke in a low voice.

He raked his thinning hair. "I see. Who's he?"

Tears welled up in her eyes. "Florent... was killed. Xavier was his friend."

"Florent, my godchild." Jacques grabbed his head in both hands. After a long silence, he shook himself. "Did you bring Xavier's papers?"

She handed them to him.

"I'll get them done and will take them to the Manoir. Thanks Julie."

Back at the Manoir, she explained what she'd done.

Xavier thanked her. "You're wonderful. I'll be able to get back to my apartment."

"No rush. You need to regain your strength and make sure your knee is completely healed," Bérangère said.

"Thanks, madame Bérangère."

Julie took her leave. She was fighting the door to her building to get her bicycle inside when Madame Durand ran from her loge.

"Ah, madame Julie, let me give you a hand." She helped Julie store the bicycle. "My sister wants to get to her daughter in Le Lavandou, but it's in the free zone. Any idea how she can get that paper thing to travel?"

"You mean the Ausweis. She needs to go to the Kommandantur and apply, saying that her daughter is about to give birth and already has three small children and needs help."

"It'll work? Because it isn't true, you know."

"I don't know, madame. But it seems it's everybody's excuse, or funerals or severe illness. It seems that everybody lies about something these days. There are long lines of people waiting for Ausweis too."

"I see. By the way, Monsieur and Madame Bloch have left. They paid the rent and gave me the keys. A doctor's car picked them up. They had a lot of luggage."

"I hope they make it to their daughter's without incident."

"This afternoon, a soldier came to say that I had to let him know who lived here and which apartments were empty. He gave me a sheet to fill in."

Julie blew air in disgust. "They want to find billets for their soldiers."

"Oh, no, mon Dieu. The Bloch's apartment's empty now. Then the two apartments on the fifth floor. The tenants have been gone for a year now."

"Too bad I didn't know. My friend needed a place."

"Madame Marchand? No, those apartments are too small for four children. And they share the toilet on the landing. And the elevator only goes to the fourth floor. No good. I hope the soldiers don't like them."

"Let's hope. Goodnight, madame."

Julie hastened up to her apartment. She was just opening the door when she sensed a presence. Noiselessly, Léonie Bodénan slipped in behind her.

"I thought the *pipelette* would never stop," Léonie said.

"Yes, she's the queen of chatterboxes. What's new?"

"I have copied two documents from the general's desk. They were marked secret. They're in German but I think they may be of interest to the English, from what I understood with my high-school German."

"Let me see." A moment later, Julie looked up in surprise. "My, my! If we could get this to the American embassy, they could send it to the English."

"Sure, but how to convince the ambassador it's important? Do you know him?"

"Me, no, but he knows my father. I'll go there tomorrow and see what I can do."

"If only I'd understood the importance of languages when I was in school, I'd have studied harder and be so much better now."

"But when we're young, we do just the minimum to pass the exams."

"True." Léonie handed her two sheets of paper in her neat handwriting.

The next day, Julie took a vélo-taxi to the embassy. After some discussion at the reception desk, a Mr. Edmund O'Reilly was summoned and he showed her into his office.

"I'm William Bullitt's secretary. He's on the phone to our displeased President Roosevelt right now. You could confide what your business is and I could speed up the process when he's through."

Julie stared at his intelligent eyes and open face. If she had to pass on messages, it'd be easier to do so with the help of the secretary. "Indeed. Let's say that if I came across some German information, which could be important to the English, I could possibly drop by for a visit in case you wouldn't mind sending my letter to the right person."

He smiled. "But you realize that the United Sates is not at war with anyone."

"This wouldn't involve the United States. Just sending mail when we cannot."

"Cloak and dagger stuff, eh? I don't know about that."

"No, seriously. A friend works for a Wehrmacht general and things happen. So I thought things could also happen at the embassy."

He gave an exaggerated sigh. "I suppose I could personally take the documents and, with the ambassador's approval, put them in a diplomatic pouch. But you can't come here too often to post your letters to your, hmm, parents."

She smiled, knowing she'd won him over. "There must be a way? Don't you need someone to clean the office?"

He laughed. "If you weren't the daughter of a respected ambassador, a friend of my boss, I'd have thrown you out by now. I'll talk to William. Let me see... We could use an office helper three days a week, either morning or afternoon."

Julie considered him for a moment. "I have someone in mind. Totally reliable. My own niece Pierrette de Montregard."

"William knows her grandparents well. They're regularly invited to our receptions. I'm sure it'll work out. That is providing President Roosevelt stopped being mad at William for staying in Paris instead of going to Vichy, as ordered."

"I hope he stays, but if you go to Vichy, I'll find a way."

"I know why my boss loves Paris and the French. You people are more cunning than a fox."

"Well, thank you." There was a little sauciness in her tone in the way she drew out her words. With a light heart, Julie left the embassy and headed to the nearest Métro station. She went straight to the Manoir hoping to catch Pierrette.

"Glad to see you're studying, Pierrette."

"Just doing some revision for the bac exams, now that Lorraine is home and dealing with the printing shop, I'm not needed."

"Would you have some time to work three half-days a week?"

Pierrette straightened eagerly. "Yes, yes. Where?"

"The American embassy."

"Super!"

"You would need to carry some letters... discreetly."

A brief moment of silence while Pierrette stared at her aunt. Then she stood. "When do I start?"

"I'll take you to meet Monsieur Edmund O'Reilly tomorrow morning."

That evening, Léonie knocked on Julie's door. "How did it go?"

"Smoothly. The U.S. are not at war, but I can write letters to my... er.... parents from time to time and the nice secretary will send them along."

"I suppose the diplomatic pouch will first go to Madrid, right?"

"I believe so."

"I wish I could squeeze inside a pouch and go to England," Léonie said.

"My dear, if everybody goes to England, there won't be anybody left to work here."

"It just seems that getting a bit of intelligence from time to time isn't advancing the English fast enough."

"You heard General de Gaulle's broadcast. Every little bit helps and that it's only a matter of time till the Nazis are thrown out."

"Patience isn't my strong suit."

Chapter Twenty-Eight

Julie gnawed the top of her pencil. She again added up the figures in front of her. I have to find work or I won't be able to buy groceries for more than two weeks. Not that there's much in the stores. Her musings were interrupted by a knock on her door.

She opened and her jaw dropped in surprise. "Bernard!"

They hugged.

"How did you come back? I thought you were in England."

"I was. I'm back. I'm an experiment."

"That's sound interesting. I guess you called home first?"

"I did. The children were overjoyed. Marie-Ange is relieved that I'm all in one piece. I met Sylvain in London. And here is some money for you." He reached inside the back of his pants. "Don't mind me." He pulled out a cloth envelop. "We know it isn't wise to travel with a lot of money in a bag or wallet."

"Thanks. I don't mind where it comes from."

They chuckled.

"It's Sylvain's pay."

"All right, tell me who's we? And what about the experiment?"

"I didn't tell my wife but my brother assured me you'd understand. I've met with General de Gaulle but I'm not keen on joining his army. I'm afraid he only wants to rebuild an army. He only sees military goals. But some Brits have ideas about gathering intelligence directly in France with the aim of disrupting the Nazis' hold on Europe. I volunteered."

"Right, when do I join?"

He laughed heartily. "My brother knows you well. The war isn't over for France and the other occupied countries. We need people inside and outside to help."

"Fine. Give me a gun and I'll kill as many Boches as I can."

"You'd soon be dead and a dead body can't help boot the Krauts out. So let's do our best to stay alive. It starts by keeping total secrecy."

"I'm good. Just explain. I'll make some coffee, weak, I'm afraid. None was available at the grocer's so I'm reusing the dregs a couple of times."

"Just fine for me."

While she busied herself making the watery coffee, Bernard continued talking. "There's a delicate job to do. There are thousands of children who have been separated from their families during the Exode. The Red Cross and other organizations are attempting to reunite them. Would you be willing to escort children? If it's too painful for you..."

"I love children." She burst out crying. "I lost my sunshine."

Bernard put his hand on hers. After a short pause, they wiped away their tears.

"How can escorting children help mount a resistance movement? Because that's what we hear being whispered about. Resistance. I don't want a desk job."

"First, we need to gather as much intelligence as we can. Traveling with children for a legitimate cause would be invaluable."

"I see."

"Any chance of you claiming an American passport? They can travel without restraint."

"I'm a French citizen, born right here in Paris and since the French don't accept dual nationality, my father registered me as French since my mother's French."

"Too bad. So tomorrow morning nine o'clock you go to the Red Cross HQ. You'll get the job. You're expected. Then go to Café de Flore on Boulevard—"

"I know it."

"There, you'll meet a friend of mine from Sweden, Lars Gunnarsson."

"You were pretty confident of my response, weren't you? I'll be there. Will he know me?"

"He will." Bernard grinned. "Now, I must return home and get a few things ready for my new job."

"Which is?"

The grin became a smirk. "I'm a sales representative for champagne and wines from Maison Vander-Veken."

"Quite a change from your work at the Musée de l'Homme."

"I'm still an archaeologist for the museum, though I might not be there all the time. They're all right with that and I'm totally legitimate living a normal life with my wife and children."

"Marie-Ange must be happy."

"That's not so sure. But that's her. Anyway, if you see Brigitte before I do, you can tell her Hubert is well and training with the RAF."

"Any money for her?"

He rolled his eyes. "Hubert isn't as considerate as your hubby."

"I'll help her."

***

It was only nine o'clock but the Red Cross offices were already crowded. Dismay threatened to dampen Julie's enthusiasm. If she had to wait until all those people were served, she'd never get to her late morning appointment with Lars Gunnarsson. She approached the reception and gave her name. Instead of being given a number, she was ushered to an office. She glanced at the name Jean-Guy Barrand on the door. The receptionist pushed the door open after a brief knock. A middle-aged man stood up and offered Julie his hand.

"I'm glad you've accepted to escort the children. Many parents are still in the non-occupied zone and others are here but their children are in zone nono. It's imperative we reunite the children with them as fast as possible. You'll have to travel by train or by coach depending where you need to go. You'll be met by Red Cross representatives when we can communicate. The Germans are pretty good at letting the Red Cross phone or cable our people in the south. But it could be that at times you'll have to inquire in the town where to find the parents."

"That won't be a problem."

"Good. I'm told you are very resourceful."

"I also speak German and English and some Italian."

He nodded. "Excellent. Here is the Red Cross hat you'll need to wear and a jacket with the Red Cross badge. You can wear any dark skirt. Do you have a leather belt? We ran out."

"I have something suitable, yes."

A broad smile spread on Jean-Guy's face. "I'm so glad you'll be working with us. You know it won't be every day of course."

"Due to traveling time, n'est-ce-pas?"

"You understand perfectly. We'll call you for your first... mission. Now I believe you have another appointment?"

"I do. Thank you, Monsieur Barrand." She put her jacket and hat into a string bag. Women carried a filet or two in their purses, just in case they came across some food.

Julie sensed a thrill run through her as she left the office and walked to the nearest Métro. At the Saint-Germain-des-Prés station, she got out and walked to the nearby café de Flore. As she approached the terrasse, a tall, skinny man stood and invited her to share his table.

"Monsieur Lars Gunnarsson?"

"Enchanté, Madame de Montregard."

The garçon approached and bowed. "What will it be for madame?"

She flashed a smile. "If you have coffee, I'd love a cup."

"For special clients, we do." He turned and left.

Lars nodded. "You're beautiful and you certainly charmed our garçon. I didn't get proper coffee, just a watered-down version."

They talked quietly for a while. "So you won't mind having a couple of extra children among your Red Cross charges?"

"I think I can act, as do children, so that the guards won't look too closely at our papers."

"You don't have the telephone?"

"My concierge does."

"Like all concierges. Even if she can be trusted, I'll avoid calling her. I can send a youth with as message, as if he was a telegraph boy."

She laughed. "That will arouse Madame Durand's suspicions. But if you phone her and say that I have to report to work, she won't think anything of it."

"Very well. The unfortunate part is that you need to go to the Oberfeldkommandantur to get an Ausweis – a real one. With a Red Cross uniform and those official papers, you should get to the head of the lineup. You have a photo?"

He pulled an envelope from inside his summer jacket and handed it to her.

"I do."

She examined the various forms, all duly stamped, and put them in her purse. "I'm glad they're both in French and German. It helps with the fussy administration."

"Go to the Kommandantur before the afternoon rush. Your first trip is Monday."

"Then, I better be off."

They shook hands, and she went straight to the Métro, direction Opéra. The station had been re-opened. Her stomach rumbled with hunger. Place de l'Opéra, she scrunched her nose at the large sign over the building. She pushed through the door of the Kommandantur, and looked around. She strode toward a desk manned by an army private. He was about to ask her name and was pulling a numbered card from a stack when she said sweetly in German that she was on official Red Cross business and couldn't wait. Surprised, he smiled and told her to follow him. In a large corridor, he pointed to a door.

"Knock on this door. Oberstleutnant Freider will take care of you."

"Danke." With some apprehension, Julie raised her hand to knock when the next door opened. Shock froze her on the spot.

If Kurt Meinhard was surprised, he didn't show it. "Julie."

She nodded, incapable of speaking.

"What are you doing here?"

Adrenaline pumped into her veins. Julie straightened. "I am on official Red Cross business to obtain an Ausweis, for work."

Kurt pushed open the Oberstleuntant's door. "Oberstleutnant Freider, give an Ausweis to Madame Julie de Montregard."

"Yes, Obersturmbannführer Meinhard. Right away. What dates, madame?"

"Monday twenty-second of July."

"And return?"

She bit her lip. "I don't know, sir. It depends if trains are on time or delayed."

"Make it open for two months," Kurt Meinhard said.

"Yes, Obersturmbannführer Meinhard. I have to write the reason."

Kurt Meinhard looked at her. "What exactly is Red Cross business?"

"I'll be escorting children to reunite them with their parents." She handed him her photo.

Kurt pointed to the form. "On the reason line, write escorting children."

Julie pocketed her precious Ausweis and thanked the Oberstleutnant and Kurt Meinhard.

"I shall accompany you home."

Most uncomfortable, Julie followed him out. "It's not necessary for you to take time off your work."

"It is my pleasure."

"I was going to walk home." There was no way she wanted to be squashed against him in a Métro car.

"I would enjoy that."

Julie wasn't going to talk first. She noticed, however, the looks that young women directed toward her escort. He seemed taller and more handsome even than when they were students together. His muscular physique and well-defined features were bound to attract attention of women. Julie wondered why all these German soldiers had to be so good-looking.

"I always questioned why you had to marry that husband of yours."

"Because I love him."

"You used to love me too."

A wave of disgust ran through her. Yes, she had loved him until her love drowned in the sea of Nazi ideology. He had forgotten the intense arguments that pushed them apart shortly before their breakup. "I admit I loved you for a time. We were students away from home, young and silly. It was a time when everybody had a crush on someone. Just that, a crush. Infatuation."

"I loved you with all my heart. I believed you loved me."

"A mistake. Mistaken youth."

"For me, it wasn't a mistake. I never forgot. Fate has reunited us. I did not know that I would be appointed liaison to General von Trennen. Like this, I shall see you more often."

She swallowed. "The general who lodges at my father-in-law's?"

"Exactly. I know you visit your in-laws often and I will make a point of seeing the general frequently. I want us to start over."

"Impossible. I'm married."

"Your husband is dead."

"No!" The violence of her denial surprised herself.

"He did not come back. There is no demobilization file in his name."

The bastard! He had the means to find out everything. Actually, not everything. She breathed easier. "Could he be prisoner?"

"No, I obtained that information, too. He is not."

"As long as I don't have proof, I'll believe my husband is alive."

He took her elbow. She promptly freed her arm.

"Do I inspire disgust in you?"

She sighed. She mustn't antagonize such powerful enemy. "A lady quickly loses her reputation these days. I don't want to lose mine."

"I shall never understand the French."

She didn't reply. Just as well that he didn't understand French people, because if he, and the likes of him did, the French would never be able to throw them out.

They had arrived in front of her building. "Thank you, and good afternoon." She spun on her heel and raced inside before he could react, but she heard him call after her, "Will be seeing you again, Julie."

***

Head down, François strode along the street. He ruminated why his Uncle Bernard shook his head when he was about to ask him about

England. Maybe because he didn't want grand-papa Gontrand to hear. François was determined to learn more. He was brought up short by a couple of women and a boy struggling with suitcases in front of a hôtel particulier, on Square Lamartine. He stopped.

"*Bonjour.*" A boy about François' age came and stood in front of him.

"Oh... er..."

"My mother is moving in that mansion."

"I see."

"Do you live close by?"

"Yes."

"Where do you go to school?" The boy's French was precisely correct.

"Uh... I go to Lycée Janson de Sailly, close by on rue de la Pompe."

"Then, I suppose that is where I will be going too. I am Helmut Sauter. I am sixteen."

"And I'm François de Montregard. Sixteen too. Why are you moving here if you're German?"

Helmut shrugged. "I did not want to move and leave all my friends, but when my father... Mutter decided to escape to France. Can we be friends?"

"Sorry. You're German and I'm French."

"I do not see a problem."

"Your lot invaded my country and are now preventing me from being what I want to be."

Helmut shook his blond head. "Stupid adults. What do you want to be?"

"A professional violinist."

"I want to be a scientist. Why cannot you be a violin player?"

"Because your lot tossed out my music teacher."

"I hate it when you say your lot."

"Well, what should I say? I've got other words but they're not as nice."

"It is not my lot. It is what befell me. I am sorry about your teacher. He must have been a Jew."

"And you're anti-Semitic as well!"

Helmut looked skyward. "I do not care what people are as long as they leave me alone, do their jobs and pay their taxes. I want to be a scientist and now I cannot."

François frowned. "Why can't you?"

"Because after the Gymnasium, that is like the lycée here. My father..."

"What about your father?"

"He threatened to kill me because I refused to join the Hitlerjugend and other stuff. He had my older brother killed because he was in the *die Weisse Rose.* Mutter and I fled."

"*Die Weisse Rose?* What's the White Rose?"

"A student group opposed to Nazism. Mother and I have been hiding in Paris since before the war started but the landlord told us to move out now that Paris is occupied."

"Shit! So you're being hunted? By the Germans?"

"My father is such a rigid, high-up SS man. Mother refused to have anything to do with him. It would be such a dishonor for him if anyone in the Party learned that his wife and sons were dissidents. So the Gestapo is after us. The French do not like us. I am trying to look French. My mother too."

"That was her moving the suitcases into that mansion?"

"Yes, Madame Ducharme sounds like a nice lady. I mean really ladylike. Maybe my Mutter will be safe."

"You too. Do you have another first name?"

"Daniel is my middle name."

"That's totally French. So you should register for school under that name. Your family name is spelt S.A.U.T.E.R?"

"Yes. You know German?"

"Just the bit we learn in school, but I'm learning as fast as I can. I'm good at English too. So you need to pronounce your name like the French verb to jump – *sauter*. Or better *sauterelle*."

"A grasshopper. You mean change names?"

"Yes, and you'll get papers with that name."

"How can you get papers?"

"There's a way. You should say you came from Alsace. They have blond people there and they have a funny accent. You could say you came from Natzwiller. Alsatians have been evacuated or expelled, so it's not odd to have a refugee here, especially those with a French sounding name."

Daniel's sad smile mirrored François'. "Natzwiller. I shall go to the library and learn all I can about the town and Alsace."

"We can meet every day to practice your French."

"You would do that for me?"

"D'you know something? We're both victims."

"Could I get a job somewhere? Our savings are getting very low. I can lie about my age."

"Not a good idea. What can your mother do?"

"She never had a job. She knits a lot."

"I'll tell my grandmother to come and see her."

"Danke."

"No. From now on, only merci."

"You are right. Merci."

"I had a German friend once, Wilhelm Fischer. We used to correspond." He fell silent for a few moments. "I'm thinking, if you passed both parts of the baccalauréat, you can take the exam for Écoles des Mines or the École Polytechnique. It's tougher and higher than the university but you can become a scientist, an engineer or whatever you want."

"Merci, François. I will try my best."

"Repeat, I'll try my best."

"I'll try my best. Is that the way to speak?"

"It is."

François continued on to rue de la Faisanderie where his uncle and aunt lived. England. Surely, his uncle didn't just go there for a holiday, not in war time, and if he was back, there was something afoot that he was going to find out.

Chapter Twenty-Nine

Sunday, July 21, 1940

I thought my heart would tear completely and stop beating when I learned my youngest son would never come home again. But I'm still cooking and cleaning, and trying to keep the family together. Nobody notices a father's shoulders drooping in sorrow. Nobody sees the pain of a mother. Nobody sees the pain of a grandmother when an innocent child is killed by man's savagery.

It's still rather cool for July. Everybody has now been counted in the census. When I say everybody, that isn't entirely correct. François' new friend and his mother didn't go and register and Julie tried to dissuade her friend Rebecca from going. I'm not sure what's behind all that. What I'm sure of is that some German high-ups are the bosses at Renault and, according to Philippe, at our factory too, or what's left of it. I met my son in the street since Gontrand won't let him come into the house. So I didn't get much detail. I'm really saddened that he and his daughter are so friendly with Baron von Hauffen. Pierrette is in a real dither that her sister is sleeping with the baron. Mon Dieu, what is the world coming to? Such a nicely brought up young woman, too!

And now we have the Propaganda Abeitlung installed in Paris. Civil servants have been busy getting Pétain propaganda material distributed everywhere including in the schools. Marie-Ange was furious she had to go to her school, despite being on holiday, to help store blotting paper printed with Pétain's face, his framed portraits and other knick-knacks, to be ready for the start of the school year in October. The Marshal has to be made known to children. Even the alphabet primer which used to start with A for apple now has A for Amour du Maréchal — what a stupid, egotistical man! Love is earned not imposed by law. I've got to go to the attic to find old coloring books for the little ones. Maybe our bookstore man has hidden the traditional ones. I'll go and talk to him, or rather his wife and daughter. He hasn't come back yet.

I also have to go and talk to Rose Sauterelle. I think Madame Ducharme *must have enough tenants now. The poor soul would die if she had to have Germans in her home. Yet I'm quite suspicious that François was going to say the Sauterelles were German refugees.*

The Germans have organized the return of the refugees from the non-occupied zone. I'd have thought our neighbor had some class, but no, as we queued for bread, she went on a rant about them being caught up in the Exode and shot at, while I stayed home. Somehow illogical, but I'm told many espouse that view. They reproach those who stayed to admire the Boches. Idiots! Can't judge everyone by the women who are profiteering from the occupier.

I'm told Pierrette will be working at the American embassy. What's going on?

Time to go and cook. My cooking is improving. Jacques is coming.

"What's the latest news?" Gontrand asked.

Jacques pulled a chair to the table. "The Bo... Germans have asked the prefects of all the regions to compile lists of hostages to be shot in case of an attack against the occupier."

"Surely they wouldn't do that?"

"The prefects refused, so the Germans made the lists themselves."

Bérangère turned round, waving her cooking spoon. "Like all those threats they have on posters and billboards. Don't they have a code of behavior? I read about it in that new rag, *La France au Travail.*"

"Sure, a long list of instructions to soldiers. "Do not carry French women in the *Dienstwagen.* Or *Abstand von der Französischen zivilbevölkerung.*"

"You've lost me."

"Avoid all contact with the French civilian population."

Bérangère snorted. "If only it was true! Then they wouldn't buy up everything in the stores and wouldn't strut along the streets singing or taking photographs – while, if we take photographs, they confiscate our camera. Verboten!"

Gontrand helped himself to stew. "I don't like all those threats. Maréchal Pétain asked the French people to respect and be courteous toward the occupier. So nobody's going to attack the Chleus."

Jacques shook his head. "You're in denial, my friend. I saw some croix de Lorraine painted on walls. General de Gaulle has taken the cross of Lorraine as his symbol."

Bérangère set down a plate of bread cut into thin slices. "I think the occupier is not feeling secure, because they started a propaganda campaign on that Radio-Paris station, which is German run, and they confiscated the T.S.F. sets from the Jews. Then we had to surrender the sets that have shortwave."

"You didn't I hope?"

"Of course not. I went with Julie to the Marché aux Puces. We got a couple of old sets which we turned in so we could get the legal T.S.F. permit."

Jacques chortled. "Women! You'll always amaze me."

Pierrette and François arrived at that moment. Bérangère motioned to the pot. "Help yourselves, I need to go and see a friend."

"Monsieur Jacques, there was a bunch of young thugs that were preventing people from entering a store that had a *Juden* label on," François said.

"I hope you had the sense to cross to the other side of the street. Those stupid little whippersnappers! But that's where it starts. Youths that try to make themselves important in the eyes of the Boches. Already indoctrinated and wearing brown shirts."

Pierrette bit into a slice of bread. "Then they join the Wehrmacht, like the general's idiot driver did. Stupidity personified."

"I hope I'll have the opportunity to arrest them and let them cool their heels in my hotel." Jacques helped himself to another portion of stew.

***

"Madame de Montregard! Please come in."

Bernadette Ducharme waved Bérangère into the salon.

"What's the situation with your tenants?"

"I'm very pleased. Older persons, very stable with just enough money to pay a little rent, though that's not important. My last tenant is an Alsatian refugee with her son, a very quiet, polite boy. They have no money but Madame Sauterelle is trying to find work."

"Yes, my grandson is friends with her son and told me she can knit."

"Is there work for someone who can knit?"

Bérangère nodded. "I'm sure we can find a company that'd buy hand knitting. There's one in Amiens."

"If she does good work, I'd think she could find customers closer to home. Let's go and see her. She lives on the top floor."

The introductions were quickly made, and Rose Sauterelle showed Bérangère several beautiful sweaters and skirts she had knitted.

"I had a machine in Germ..." She breathed and recovered quickly. "Alsace. But I can knit by hand if I could sell it."

Bernadette Ducharme paled. "You mean you came from Germany?"

In her halting accent, Rose tried to speak without emotion. "Forgive me, madame. I fled my country my husband..."

"What did he do?"

"He... killed my first son..." Emotion choked her words. "He tried to kill Daniel... and me too. I must protect my son."

Bérangère took a deep breath. "Forgive me for asking. What did your oldest son do that his father'd kill him?"

"He was part of the *Weisse Rose*, the White Rose organization. Students who resisted Nazism."

"Where's your husband now?"

"I do not know. Berlin I guess. He is a senior SS officer in the government."

Madame Ducharme looked at Bérangère. "What do you think?"

"That my grandson probably suggested the small deceit about being from Alsace. He's right. Not all Germans are Nazis."

"Then it's all right by me, Madame Sauterelle."

Emotion thickened her accent. "I do not know how to dank you. De Gestapo might be hunting us."

Madame Ducharme glanced at her friend, "Gestapo?"

"Secret police."

"But here?"

"My daughter-in-law, the one who studied in Germany, said they must have been right on the heels of the Wehrmacht. So far, we don't hear much about them. But you saw those posters forbidding the population to listen to foreign radio broadcasts, with a death penalty for those who defy the order, and threat of shooting to anyone who tampers with their installations. That must be the Gestapo's doing."

"I would not be surprised," Rose Sauterelle said.

Bernadette Ducharme let out a long breath. "I hope they go back where they came from as soon as possible. In the meantime, madame, you can stay here. You'll be safe."

"Let's talk business," Bérangère said. "There's something with needles sticking upright in our attic. It may be a knitting machine. I have no idea where it came from. There's still something knitted hanging from it. We should go and see what you can make of it."

Rose Sauterelle put away the sweaters and brought out hat and gloves. Bérangère explained about her unwanted tenant, adding he was correct. It didn't take much to time to get home. To Bérangère's surprise, the attic was well-ordered.

"I wonder if my grandchildren tidied it up. It was a bit of a mess last time I came up here."

"Not much dust either."

"The little rascals, or rather big rascals, have taken over a couple of the maids' rooms. They don't want to live with their father."

"What about their mother?"

"She's a sweetie, but a faithful wife who obeys her husband. I'm afraid my son had his friends requisition an apartment in Neuilly. Not far, but the youths won't go."

"Ah. He works for a *deutsche firma*."

"Our factory was bombed and he wormed his way into some German company or vice-versa, I don't know. They're working together on our unfinished project, which was really promising, but I'm not an engineer, so again I don't know. Here, is this round thing a knitting machine?"

"What a beauty! It is a sock-making machine."

"But will it work?"

"Absolutely."

Rose pulled the machine into the center of the floor to examine it. "Everything is here." She laid the length of yarn on top and turned the handle. Needles moved up and down. She wound it the other way. It worked smoothly. "It has not been used very much. I can clean it and it will run beautifully."

"Then it's all yours. I'll get Ernest to take it down and deliver it to your place."

"When I work with it, it will be quite noisy. It will disturb the other tenants at Madame Ducharme's."

Bérangère thought for a minute. "Did you see if the old coach house is still standing in the courtyard?"

"Yes, she gave me a tour. It is a beautiful mansion, quite secluded."

"I'll ask her if we can arrange for you to work there. I'd be happy to have you come and work here but since we're always at the mercy of an over-zealous gendarme wanting to check our papers, I think it best that you go out in the street as little as possible."

"*Ja*, until I get papers. I am so thankful to you." Rose pointed to a large box. "The label says wool. Could we look in it?"

"Of course." Bérangère pulled out the heavy box and opened it. Cones of yarn were stacked in the box. "There, we're in business now."

Rose bent down to examine the yarn. "Pure wool. What a treasure trove! I can make socks, stockings, mittens."

"I know lots of people who will be happy to buy your work, especially now that the stores are being emptied by the occupiers. There's nothing left for us, and shopkeepers raise the prices every day."

"As long I make enough money to pay the rent and buy food, I do not need anything else."

"But your Daniel will need books and supplies for school."

Rose was taken aback. "Oh. Yes, I was not thinking."

"Don't worry, we'll survive. I'll get him a bicycle, and one for you too. Ernest is a whiz at rebuilding bicycles."

They walked back to Madame Ducharme's.

"Bernadette, we need your help. Can we rent the coach house to install our knitting business?"

"I wouldn't rent it. You can have it for free. It isn't in the best of state."

The three women went out to the courtyard. The door of the coach house was jammed but it finally opened.

"Given a little cleaning, this will be a suitable space," Rose said.

"Can we bring in electricity?" Bérangère asked.

"Monsieur Renoux is a good handyman. He fixed the plumbing. I think he could install a light."

They went to knock on Monsieur Renoux's door.

After the women explained their plans, the old man said, "I'd be pleased to help, Madame Ducharme. Can we go down and you show me what is required?"

He took a notepad and a pencil and followed the women to the coach house. He drew a diagram of the interior. Outside, he looked at how the electricity wires arrived at the house and finally to the meter. He made some calculations and told Madame Ducharme what he would need.

"I'd prefer if someone else than me bought those items."

Bérangère promptly said, "But of course, Monsieur Renoux. I'll ask Ernest to do the purchasing. If the ironmonger is surprised, he can say it is for the general who lives in our house."

Gilbert Renoux nodded his thanks and handed Bérangère the list.

By evening, the machine and the wool had been settled in the refurbished coach house with the help of the enthusiastic adolescents. Thanks to the Ducharme and the de Montregard's attics, the coach house was furnished with tables, chairs and some old-fashioned lamps. It was agreed that socks were the first items to be produced.

By the end of the next morning, Ernest came in with a large carton of electrical supplies.

"Monsieur Renoux, check if this is what you need."

"No formality, please. I'm Gilbert. Yes, everything seems to be here. Was it difficult to obtain?"

Ernest shrugged. "You just need to know where to ask."

They chuckled.

"I know some places too, but I'd rather not be seen in my old neighborhood."

Ernest nodded his understanding. "I'll help."

While the men worked, Rose set up the machine to make the first pair of socks.

Chapter Thirty

A few minutes after six in the morning, and carrying a small overnight bag, Julie took the Métro to the Sainte-Marie orphanage where she was to collect her charges. The sister supervising the children shepherded a toddler and a four-year-old boy, explaining to him that the nice lady was going to take them to their maman. She then addressed Julie.

"The aunt of the two older children, Guy and Ghislaine, came for them. You'll only have these two young ones."

"Merci, ma soeur," Julie said.

The sister murmured a quick blessing and Julie signaled to the vélo-taxi that had been hovering nearby. There had been expense money and train tickets in her Red Cross envelope. She paid the young driver at the Gare de Lyon. Children under seven years didn't pay for the train. She went to the ticket office and got a refund for the two tickets the older children would have used, then found the platform for her train. There was plenty of time. She settled the children and relaxed.

The train stopped at Chalon-sur-Saône. Two German soldiers boarded the train just as Julie gathered her bags.

"Papieren bitte."

She handed them to one of the soldiers. He barely looked at them before returning them. Julie hoisted her bags on her shoulder and picked up the toddler. "This is my stop. I'm not staying on the train." She brushed past the soldiers and grabbed the little boy's hand. The boy looked up at one soldier, who smiled at him and followed the little group. He helped the boy down the steep train steps. She thanked the soldier and took the little one's hand, shoving her bags higher on her shoulder. Before she could reach in the pocket of her uniform jacket for the papers, the guard controlling passengers as they exited the station platform simply waved her through.

After a ten-minute walk, she arrived at the control post on the demarcation line and joined the queue. She craned her neck to determine the cause of the bottleneck. A man and his wife were being questioned and pulled aside. Two children next to them started to walk on past the line. A shout from a guard.

"Are those your children?" he said to the couple.

"No, sir. Never saw them before."

Turning to the impassive children, the guard asked, "Are those people your parents?"

"No, sir. We don't know them," the boy replied. He took a step away from the guard post.

In a lightning moment of awareness, Julie realized the children had been instructed to walk on no matter what happened. With excuses right and left, she pushed people aside and, brandishing her Red Cross papers, called out.

"Guy! Ghislaine! Wait up. Excuse me, these children are with me." She switched to German. "Always getting into trouble when I'm busy with the little ones." She waved her Ausweis along with the Red Cross forms showing a ten-year-old boy and an eight-year-old girl. "I'm taking them to their parents in Messey-sur-Grosne."

The immobile children glanced at her, then looked straight ahead. The surprised guard glanced at her papers, then at the children, and nodded. Julie thanked him and stepped forward. In the corner of her eye, she saw the woman throw a covert look toward her and the children while she and her husband were shoved into a small building by one of the other guards. Julie caught up with the children.

She whispered, "Follow me. Don't talk." With a very natural gesture, the young girl took the hand of four-year-old Marius and the little group moved on.

The French border guards looked at her curiously but with a shake of the head motioned her forward.

Julie found the way to the station of the micheline train that would take her to their destination. In the carriage, she instructed the children in a low voice that for the time being their names were Guy and Ghislaine Bouchard, until they were with someone safe. Stoic and silent, the children nodded.

At their stop, Guy took Julie's bag and gave her a sad smile. Ghislaine took the little boy's hand again while Julie carried toddler Juliette and her purse. Outside the station, they were met by an unmistakable Red Cross official. The woman wiped perspiration from her forehead even though it wasn't really hot.

"These are the children?"

"Only Marius and Juliette. Guy and Ghislaine Bouchard were collected by their aunt in Paris. But these two children's parents were arrested at the line. The guards were about to take the children too, so I brought them along."

"That is highly irregular!" The woman voice rose in pitch. "They needed to stay with their parents."

"Madame. you don't realize that people of Jewish origin are arrested and disappear. I couldn't let that happen to those children."

The woman screeched. "You don't know that! You can't go around taking away children just because their parents have to answer a few questions. This is highly irregular. I will report you."

The heated discussion was attracting attention. A gendarme ambled toward them.

"You take them back." The woman's arms flailed in the air.

"No kidding. You don't have a clue about what's going on in the occupied zone. You're so comfy on your traitorous Vichy side!"

The woman signaled to the gendarme. "Monsieur, as *gardien de la paix*, you must send this woman and those two children back. They are not the children I was expecting. She kidnapped them! We've got enough work with all those displaced people without a... someone taking the law into their own hands."

Although still angry, Julie repressed a laugh. The guardian of the peace had that look on his face which she interpreted as "not that woman again!" But she couldn't help the barb that sprung to her lips. "I'll let your superiors know about your attitude which is totally unworthy of the Red Cross mission."

"Mesdames! Ladies! Let's move into the police station."

Little Juliette began to cry.

The Red Cross official plucked the toddler from Julie's arms. "I'm taking these two children as planned. Their parents are waiting. You can arrest her."

Juliette bawled her heart out and held her little arms out to Julie while Marius clutched her skirt. Julie crouched and spoke soothing words. At that moment a frazzled woman rushed forward calling to her children.

Marius shrieked, "Maman!"

"Madame! You stay in the house until I bring the children to you," the official yelled.

"You think I'm going to wait until you finish harassing people? You've got something else coming to you."

"You must sign—"

"I'll sign, but first I'm taking my children to my assigned lodging."

Julie and the gendarme watched the two women go, still arguing. "Come with me." His quiet voice was reassuring. She followed the officer to the nearby gendarmerie, two anxious children clinging to her hands. Inside, the gendarme showed them to his office and told them to sit.

"I'm the captain for Messey-sur-Grosne."

Julie gave her name. Then she told what happened at the demarcation line.

"Brave woman. You did well, but you know you put your life at risk."

She shrugged. "So be it. I couldn't not do something."

"Now, children, what are your real names? Don't worry, I'm not sending you back."

They looked at her. She nodded.

"I'm Samuel Lewinski and this is my sister Abby. My father is Fahim and my mother's Sachi. Mother told me we left Poland when I was just little and Abby got born in Paris."

"We'll take care of you. I'm going to drive you to my mother's house. You'll be safe there. Then we'll find you new names." He sighed and turned to Julie. "We don't have Germans breathing down our necks here, but since we're army, most of the gendarmes are loyal to Vichy. Pétain is busy trying to remove anyone with a Jewish name from society. They can't teach. They can't bank. It's a crazy time we're living in and it's going to get worse, I think, but there're people who won't let children be maltreated."

Julie brushed off the moisture from her eyes. "Thank you."

"We'll ride in the police wagon and the busybodies will think I'm taking you back to the train station."

Five minutes later, they stepped into an elegant house on the edge of town. Geranium planters and window boxes of petunias brightened the façade. A matronly Paulette Curie welcomed them on the doorstep.

"Ah! Michel, who are you bringing me, this time?"

"Little lambs and a shepherd," the gendarme replied.

Once they were inside, Julie introduced herself and retold the story.

"Then Samuel, how about we call you Martin? And Abby, would you like to become Jeanne Clément?"

"Oui, madame. Mother told us we were going to have to change our names, all of us, as soon as we got to safety." His voice trembled.

Michel put his arm around the boy's shoulders and at the same time Abby burst into tears. Paulette drew her into her arms.

They cried for a while. Then Samuel, now Martin, sniffed. "How will our parents find us?"

Michel glanced at Julie with eyebrows raised. Her face reflected the helplessness that gripped them all.

"The police'll hear what happened to your parents at the demarcation line after you left."

"Mother told us to keep walking, not to look back, because we're Jews, but someone would help us."

"Yes, and now you have three people to help you."

"My parents won't come back, will they? They'll be put in prison. But they didn't do anything wrong."

In awe, the adults looked at the child imbued with a maturity beyond his years.

"No, they didn't do anything wrong. We don't know what will happen now, Samuel, rather, Martin. We don't know. There are evil people in this world. We'll make sure you and your sister are kept safe. When this war is finally over, we'll do our very best to find your parents."

"Thank you, sir."

Paulette sent her son back to work while she and Julie prepared two bedrooms.

"You'll stay here tonight, madame?"

"If it isn't too much trouble."

"Not at all. If you don't mind sharing with... Jeanne."

"Since the Germans planted their boots on French soil, our family's done a lot of sharing..." A shadow passed over her eyes. "...everything from food to beds, to a spot on the bare earth."

"Were you on the roads when the Germans invaded?"

She nodded, tears pearling in the corners of her eyes. "My little girl..." She bit her lip.

The children were watching intently. Jeanne encircled Julie's waist and laid her head on her stomach.

Paulette Curie shook her bent head. "I'm so sorry. Let's go down and make dinner."

They went downstairs. Julie pushed the grief away and pondered on her second mission, gathering intelligence, even though she didn't see how people's opinions in the south could help the English. Unless finding out that there were people against Vichy as well as the Germans was valuable. Of course, it was. She could see it now. Since Paulette was more than willing to talk, Julie kept asking questions. After supper, they played name games with the children until they could tell their names and their story flawlessly. The children went to bed exhausted but with a new confidence about their future.

Whether Paulette guessed that Julie wanted as much information as possible, or not, she provided plenty, particularly on the divided loyalties of the gendarmes.

"They won't let anyone know what they really believe, but Michel says that within the force it's easy to recognize the ardent Pétainists. Others just keep their mouths shut. And now we have General de la Porte du Theil who's organizing the adolescents. They're going to call it *Chantiers de la jeunesse.* The idea is that they are going to learn discipline and help farmers whose workers haven't returned."

"These youth work-camps sound like a scout movement."

"It does. Of course, since the general is totally devoted to Pétain, the youths are going to become devoted too and will fit into the marshal's motto of Travail, Famille, Patrie, and return to the land."

"Work, Family, Country. What's wrong with our traditional *Liberté, Égalité, Fraternité?*"

"The old man wants to put his mark on the nation. He ordered all the busts of Marianne removed. She's the symbol of the republic and he wants to be king."

"Next thing will be his bust with a crown."

The two women laughed. Laughter was good. It kept depression at bay.

"If the Chantiers are directed by a general, they might become militaristic, won't they?"

"It's possible. Time will tell. Let's go to bed. Will you be going back to Chalon in the morning?"

"I'm thinking to avoid it. It might be better to cross the line at Montceau-les-Mines."

"Very wise. You don't want to be recognized. Who knows what can happen these days?"

Chapter Thirty-One

Gontrand grumbled as he sat at the table. "So the Renault car and truck factory is now controlled by German bosses. So is ours. I don't like Philippe using somebody else's factory. Even if they wouldn't be able to continue making toy cars and lead soldiers."

"We can't do anything about that. Did you read the paper?"

"I don't read that unadulterated shit."

Bérangère pulled a face but didn't reprimand him for his language in front of young Lyse-May. "British citizens living in France have been interned."

"I suppose that since the English are still fighting, they are the Germans' enemies."

Bérangère pushed the newspaper away. "Did I tell you? Pierrette got herself a part-time employment at the American embassy."

"Good. But why is the embassy still here in Paris?"

"What do you mean?"

"The government is in Vichy. Embassies are always in the same location as the government. Maybe they haven't yet got a place in Vichy. Jacques said the town is overcrowded and that civil servants have to share rooms."

"For the moment they're here and, in any case, Pierrette will be back in school in October so it can't be a long term-employment."

Despite himself, Gontrand glanced at the newspaper. "The Alsatians have all been expelled?"

"And their possessions confiscated. But only those that weren't Aryan enough."

"What's this stupidity about being Aryan?"

"Blond and blue-eyed and speaking German."

"They all speak German in Alsace."

Bérangère raised her hand in an air of resignation. "They speak French first, then they speak the Alsatian dialect which is very close to German. Some families have French names. They're the ones that have been thrown out."

Gontrand muttered as he rolled the newspaper into a ball and was about to garbage it when his wife stopped him. He pulled it back. "You don't want to keep that darn thing."

"We decided not to throw anything away as you don't know what might become useful later."

"You and your squirrel mentality."

"Go and take your granddaughter for a walk."
Still muttering, Gontrand took Lyse-May's hand and left.

***

Julie debated whether to bicycle or take the Métro to visit her friend Rébecca. After sitting in a train for the last two days, she needed to move and opted for the bicycle. Because only German cars, and not many of them, circulated in the streets, bicycling had never been so easy. As she was about to cross the Champs-Élysées at avenue Montaigne, the daily Wehrmacht parade marched up toward the Arc de Triomphe. She dismounted. As the marching men approached the crossing, she bent her head to avoid looking at them. Several pedestrians nearby also kept their heads down. Others looked somewhere else. After the parade passed, Julie pedaled on her way with renewed vigor, chanting in her head "boot them out, boot them out!"

To her surprise, Rébecca wasn't at home. On her way back, she stopped by Brigitte's new apartment. As he was going out, one of the soldiers occupying the ground floor helped her carry her bicycle into the lobby. She thanked him politely and mounted the stairs in haste. She knocked on the door. Brigitte opened.

"Good to see you, Julie. Come join us."

Crouched on the floor of the sitting room, Yolande was playing with Sylvestre.

"Great to see you, Yolande. Did you abandon the Ritz today?"

"I had a few days off and took that opportunity to go to my little cabin in the country. There's always vegetables to be had from my friends' gardens, and it's the strawberry season."

"Hmm, did you bring any?"

"Actually, no. I got there and then came back this morning at all speed. My backside's sore."

"Explain."

"I'm looking for... food and clothing."

"Yolande, I don't understand. What's up?"

"I need more food... for a charity."

Julie rolled her eyes. "Are you feeding an elephant?"

Brigitte burst out laughing. "I, too, would like to know."

"We're waiting," Julie said.

Yolande looked at the children. "Someone has squatted at the cabin."

Brigitte understood. "Let's go to the park."

Half-an-hour later they sat on a bench, while the children played in the sandbox.

"Don't tell anyone, not even anyone in the family."

"You can count on us, that's why you called in at Brigitte's, right?"

"Yes. It's an English soldier. He escaped from a prisoner convoy in Belgium. A farm woman gave him food and civilian clothes but didn't want him to stay. So he walked and hid. Sometimes a woman or a youth at the farm he was hiding in found him. The women would feed him and sometimes let him rest for the day. At some farms the woman would tell him to run before her husband found him. He's in a bit of a rough shape, but he said he was a boy scout in an earlier life and was able to navigate by the sun and his watch."

"He must have walked over two hundred and fifty kilometers. I guess he kept to the woods," Julie said.

"He did and tried to stay close to rivers and streams till he got into the Froidmont forest. He eyed the country houses near Neuville, but it's summer and they were all occupied. Anyway, it's too close to the village. He stumbled onto the pond and followed the brook that drains it. The ru de la Garde has such lovely bubbling water he could drink its water without fear of getting sick."

"You could hide for a million years in that forest. It's so thick."

"And devoid of habitation. He got near the ruins of the old convent in his search for shelter. He explored around to make sure it was isolated, but it's too far from the ru. He followed it, then spotted my cabin. He crept closer. It was empty, so he broke in. I have only a couple of neighbors, about two kilometers away. He ate all the canned goods cold since there's no electricity or cooking gas."

"Don't you have an alcohol burner?"

"You mean the tin cans that Ernest brilliantly concocted into a mini-stove? I was bringing fuel for it. Anyway, he sneaked into the neighbors' gardens. They became suspicious because the lettuce and the strawberries were disappearing rather fast."

Brigitte shrugged. "Between birds and rabbits, that's not uncommon."

"The problem is the ravages were mostly in the same area... between my cabin and theirs."

They nodded. It was a bit too obvious.

"I left him a dish of potatoes and the bread and cheese I had brought for myself. I promised to come back tomorrow with food and clothes."

Julie shook her head. "He can't stay. We have to get him here. If your neighbors discover him, wagging tongues will soon alert German ears."

"Only the wives and the children are there, but children are curious."

Brigitte resettled Christiane in the carriage. "We can't go to get him and walk from your cabin."

"He's tall, quite visible even with a haircut and a better shave."

They pondered a moment.

Julie gestured with her hands. "We should rent a vélo-taxi, a tandem preferably."

"You couldn't trust a driver, even less two of them," Brigitte said.

Julie agreed. "We could rent one without driver or we could buy one."

Yolande brightened up. "I have money. Let's go and see what we can find."

They walked Brigitte and the children back to the rue Mignard and continued on to avenue Victor-Hugo.

Yolande and Julie greeted Madame Durand and stored their bicycles at the back of the lobby. Behind the closed door of her apartment, Julie heaved a sigh of relief.

"Madame Durand is a good woman but she sees too much, hears too much, knows too much, and I'm still not sure how to interpret her, for or against the Fritz or sitting on the fence. Anyway, do you think Sylvain's clothes will fit your soldier?"

"They will. He's as tall as Sylvain but not as good looking."

They laughed.

"Shoes and underwear too, so he can become completely French," Yolande said.

"Let's go and see Monsieur Fidèle Outterick. He's the one who makes those vélo-taxis. If I'm not mistaken, my father-in-law knows him."

They bicycled to the Outterick workshop and introduced themselves. The wiry middle-aged man greeted them with big smiles after they told him who they were.

"Let me finish sanding the paint on this beauty... There, all done."

"It's a cab for a bicycle trailer," Yolande said.

"That's right. When the bad weather comes, everybody will want one."

"We do, right now. Can we buy this one?" Julie said.

"Madame de Montregard, I'd be honored to sell it to you, but surely, you don't want to go into the taxi business?"

Julie laughed. "No, but we need transport for a few days to go to the country with some of the children."

He stroked his chin. "Let me see. You don't need to buy it. I'll rent it to you."

"You're the best friend of all," Julie said.

"Can you ask madame Charmaine to take a really good photo?"

"Of course. Then you can use it to advertise."

The deal was soon concluded. The two women left their bicycles at the workshop and after a few minor mishaps found their rhythm. They arrived at the studio. Gus and Charmaine admired the contraption and took several photos. When Charmaine asked what all this was for, Julie replied with a little flippancy that they were getting vegetables from the country.

Charmaine watched them leave. "You know, Gus, I think my friends are up to something."

"Of course they are, but they wasn't going to tell you nothin' when there's ears all around."

The tandem vélo-taxi disappeared from view.

"Can we stop by a park?" Yolande asked.

"Just a moment."

They stopped and dismounted. "We need a plan," Yolande said.

"How long would it take us to get to the Froidmont forest?"

"I did it in six hours this morning starting before dawn but it was a suicide mission. We'll be caught by the curfew if we left now."

"Let's go to the Manoir. There's room in the yard for this contraption. We can stay there and leave as soon as curfew is lifted."

"Great. I wasn't looking forward to doing more pedaling tonight."

"First let's go and pick up the bag of clothes from my place and some food. We make a point of bringing our food so Bérangère doesn't deplete her reserves to feed us. And we need some for the journey."

"Let me know when food is needed. I eat at least one meal at the Ritz on workdays. I stash my rations."

"That's useful!"

"A small perk for having to work for those…er, guests."

At the Manoir, Julie and Yolande were bombarded with questions but skillfully deflected most of them.

Early next morning, they crept out of the room they shared with Lyse-May. The girl cheekily waved them goodbye. By sunrise they were clear of Paris. They stopped once to drink from the water bottle clipped onto the tandem frame, then Yolande took the lead. The climb to the plateau of Froidmont drained a lot of their energy.

The noon sun was beginning to beat down on them when they finally entered the shade of the beech and oak forest and rested a moment.

"I'm glad it'll be downhill with our cargo." Julie mopped her face.

The cab-trailer bounced over the rough path between the trees. They pulled into the yard of Yolande's cabin in the afternoon. They purposely talked in loud voices while unloading the trailer.

"Psst... psst."

Yolande spun toward the brook. "It's all right. You can come in," she whispered.

The soldier crawled toward the two women who stood between the door and the path, not that anybody was around but they had the urge to keep everything hidden and secret. Once inside, Yolande made brief introductions.

"Sergeant Kevin Atkins, meet Julie."

They all sat down to a dinner of bread and cheese with the tomatoes and plums Julie had managed to buy. Kevin produced strips of rabbit he had snared in the night.

"It's the duty of a soldier to know how to survive in the wild."

They burst out laughing. He had skinned and cleaned the rabbit in the woods dispersing the unwanted guts and skin.

"You were a boy-scout?" Julie asked.

"I was and absolutely hated it, but my father made me. I'll never thank the old man enough."

"Did you have enough alcohol in the stove to cook it?" Yolande asked.

"Just enough to boil those pieces. The rest is wrapped in a dish towel and tied in the brook. It's cold enough to keep it from going rotten."

"Clever man," Julie said. "We brought more fuel. I'll go and get the rest of the beast."

"The nosy children don't come out as soon as the sun begins to dip, so it's quite safe for me."

"Yolande and I'll still go. You stay put and change into those new civilian clothes."

When the women re-entered the cabin, Julie put her hand over her mouth at seeing the soldier in her husband's clothes. A pang of sadness tugged at her heart. With effort, she dismissed it.

When the last of the rabbit was cooked, they feasted.

"Such a nice change from spinach leaves and strawberries. I ate wild gooseberries in the woods and watercress from the brook."

Yolande smiled. "I hope we won't have too much trouble tomorrow trying to buy some vegetables from my neighbors. What time should we go?"

"The children are out playing by eight o'clock."

"Good. we'll call in at half-past eight so we can be on the road soon after that."

The two women shared the bunk and Kevin slept on the floor. Bird songs woke them up in the morning. After a breakfast identical to the evening meal, Yolande and Julie went to see Madame Lormont. The greetings over, Madame Lormont launched into a tirade about squirrels, rabbits and birds.

"They are a pest, but actually I wouldn't mind taking a rabbit or two to Paris," Yolande said with a straight face.

"I'm sure Madame Rousseau's boy will have one or two. He sells them at the market in Clermont. The more he snares the better for the garden. Let's go before he leaves."

They hurried along the path to Madame Rousseau's. She happily sold two gutted and skinned rabbits and wrapped them tightly in the dishtowels Yolande had brought. She parted with green beans and peas she had gathered the day before, and added a couple of leafy lettuce. They went back to Madame Lormont's cabin.

"The children picked cherries yesterday. You can have them all, the tree is loaded. You can also have some spinach before the darned rabbits get it all. Fortunately, it's growing well. Is it true that it's difficult to find food in Paris?"

"It is. The Germans get served first, and there are a lot of them to serve," Julie said.

Madame Lormont made a face. "I hope they don't come to the country. We saw them pass in Clermont but they didn't stay. The market's same as usual. I think I'll take cherries back home at the end of the week and preserve them."

"A good idea, madame, to make preserves."

"Did you want some early potatoes? There's a good crop coming up. The rabbits don't touch potatoes."

Julie extracted a tightly crocheted filet from her purse to put the cherries in. They went to the garden and cut some juicy spinach leaves. They dug up a couple of potato plants and a handful of radishes and added the produce to their bounty, along with some fat tomatoes.

"Thank you so much, madame."

"I bring my children and a couple of their friends for a few days every week throughout the summer if you want to buy some more. There'll be zuchinis, pumpkins and cucumbers later."

Yolande nodded. "Thank you. We'll come again later."

"If I'm not here, help yourself."

"That's nice of you. I'll leave money under the water crock."

The goodbyes were brief. Loaded with their purchases, they lengthened their stride on the path. As soon as they were out of sight, they put on speed. Kevin greeted them with a smile and showed them a heap of watercress he had picked while they were at the neighbors. The wet cress was spread on top of the rabbits to keep them cool. Yolande found a cloth bag into which she folded the dirty clothes Kevin had worn on his long journey..

"You mean I have to sit in that box?"

"It's the latest fashion in vélo-taxi, sir. It will get you to my house in Paris in comfort and speed." Julie's deadpan face made Yolande laugh.

"I'll pedal, Miss Yolande. You can sit in the cab."

"Kevin, you cannot be seen. Get in and pray we don't get stopped at a checkpoint coming into Paris. We're taking a back road but gendarmes can spring up out of nowhere. Not that they usually bother women. But a man? They'll ask for a demobilization certificate. Now, when we're out of the forest, you'll keep the bags of produce on your lap. If someone glanced through the window they should only see vegetables."

"Yes, ma'am."

He twisted himself through the narrow door and folded his length onto the seat. The women handed him the bags of vegetables. He put the bag with the rabbits on the floor next to his old clothes. "It isn't too bad," Kevin said with a smile. He arranged the produce so that the tiny windows in front and in the door showed the vegetable greenery, while Julie made paper cones and filled them with cherries.

At Yolande inquiring look, she said, "Bribes."

Then she checked their tires and the cab-trailer all around. "Not too bad a disguise, as long as we don't get stopped."

"I'll lead now and you'll take over when we get to Paris."

Going down from the plateau was relatively easy. Thanks to Kevin's weight the cab-trailer didn't bounce and they made good time. They paused in the forest near the ancient Abbaye de Royaumont to attend to nature and eat the last of the bread and cheese.

"Poor Kevin's sweating," Yolande said.

"He's probably seen worse than a ride in a cab-trailer."

Kevin laughed. "But I never had the view of a cute behind to comfort me."

They booed him. Julie tapped Yolande on the shoulder. "We'll take a dirt road through fields until we get to the Carnelle forest. That'll be rough but we can stop for a few minutes now and then. Then Saint-Denis where I hope we can take a side street with no checkpoint. The Germans seem to avoid the less bespoke areas of Paris."

By the late afternoon, they could see the city in the distance. More houses lined the road, but the journey continued without incident until they had to cross the railroad bridge at Porte Saint-Denis. A sentry-box stood at the edge of the street. Julie began braking while still a long way from the lone guard. She half-turned her head. "Let's stop and look at our tires." Her heart beat faster. For the second time, or was it third, she experienced visceral fear. She read the same apprehension in Yolande's eyes.

They dismounted and knocked on the cab-trailer as pre-arranged. Julie grabbed the small bag she had prepared. Kevin re-arranged the leafy vegetables to shield him from the two windows.

Julie and Yolande applied lipstick and retied their headscarves in a jaunty fashion, knowing instinctively that looking attractive served as a kind of passport. As Julie pointed out, elegance always impresses men, and an impressed German soldier is less likely to ask awkward questions. As they approached, Julie watched the guard push himself off the wall of the sentry-box and throw his cigarette away. A quick glance at his shoulder flashes confirmed he was a simple soldier. He must be bored and tired and hoping to be relieved soon. She put her best smile on and addressed him in German."

"*Guten Tag*. It's a hot day, no?"

"It is indeed, *Fräulein*."

Yolande smiled at him. "It's hot pedaling too," she said in German.

"You both speak very well, *Damen*."

"We've been to our aunt's in the country," Julie said. She plunged her hand into the small bag hanging on her handlebars and brought out a paper cone, made with the German newspaper Signal, full of cherries. "Would you like some cherries?"

The soldier's eyes brightened. "*Gut! Danke, Damen*."

"*Auf Wiedersehen!*" Yolande and Julie said in unison.

They waved to the soldier who waved back. Without speaking they pedaled hard. Once out of sight, they adopted a more conventional speed and paused in the street. They opened the door of the cab-trailer so Kevin could cool off a little without getting out.

"See? No need for paper check when you have a bored soldier and a bribe from two pretty girls," Julie said. Yolande shook with laughter. Kevin wanted to know the details.

"How come you had a German newspaper in your bag?" Yolande asked.

"And a French one too. When I traveled on the train, that's what was in the toilet. It's a good idea to be prepared."

Yolande and Kevin chuckled. He settled himself on his seat once more among the greenery, and they set off. They finally arrived in front of Julie's building. Without needing to consult each other, they stopped a few steps before the door. Julie took her bribe bag while Yolande let Kevin out. He carried as many vegetables as he could in his arms and successfully hid his face. Yolande guided him past Julie who was handing cherries in another paper cone to Madame Durand. The latter glanced over her shoulder at Yolande and the man. She was about to speak but Julie cut her off.

"I hope you like the cherries. Now, I better get the rest of the produce out of the cab-trailer."

Madame Durand went back inside her loge while Julie hurried upstairs with their remaining purchases. Kevin hugged the two women.

"Now what?"

"Don't be impatient. First Yolande, you'll take the vélo-taxi to the Manoir for safe-keeping in the courtyard. We'll take it back to Monsieur Outterick in the morning. Take some vegetables to Bérangère. You can stay at the Manoir."

"Fine with me. Next?"

"By morning our brains will have hatched a plan."

***

The cool morning promised a hot day. Julie stood by the window ready to go.

"No matter what, you do not open the door. Pull the door curtain closed behind me. It deadens sounds. Make absolutely no noise, even though Madame Durand saw you and must assume you're here."

"I'll read in the bedroom and no one'll hear me turn the pages."

Julie looked through the window between the half-closed shutters and saw Yolande pedaling the vélo-taxi. She blew a kiss to Kevin and let herself out. She ran down the stairs rather than wait for the elevator.

Without a word, Julie climbed on the tandem. They reached Fidèle Outterick's workshop. Julie handed him cherries wrapped in the Paris-Soir newspaper.

"How did it go? Was it difficult to pull with the cab?"

"Not at all, monsieur. The whole trailer is well-balanced. You're a genius," Julie said.

Fidèle grinned, pleased by the compliment. The two women retrieved their bicycles and left the shop. They stopped by the park.

"Getting to the zone nono isn't too difficult."

"What did you call the free zone?" Yolande asked.

"Nono for non-occupied."

"All right, go on."

"We have a friend who crosses the demarcation line on business. He knows more tricks than he lets on. I suggest we go and see Bernard, who's another one with tricks in his bag."

"Is he home?"

"I don't know. He has this job for champagne and wines, a salesman of sort, for Vander-Veken, and a job at the Musée de l'Homme, but he seems to be around a lot." She wasn't going to tell what she knew about her brother-in-law.

"He went through the line without an Ausweis?"

"He did. So did Sylvain and Hubert. But, unless the Fritz don't care, it won't last. They'll put more checkpoints."

They rode to his apartment rue de la Faisanderie. After struggling to park their bicycles in the lobby, helped by a matronly concierge, they automatically took the stairs to the third floor. Bernard himself opened the door.

"Come in, beautiful ladies. You're in luck, Marie-Ange took the children shopping with the promise to go to the swimming pool afterwards."

"Swimming is good on a hot day," Yolande said.

"Why are we lucky?"

Bernard chuckled. "Because you didn't come here just to talk about the weather, especially since it isn't hot at all, and my wife's rather uptight."

"You're right, Bernard," Julie said. "We have an escaped British soldier who wants to get back home."

"Where is he?"

"In my apartment."

"Safe?"

"We think so."

"Tell me the story from the beginning."

They did and got a few laughs from Bernard.

Head tilted, Bernard stroked his chin and frowned. "It'd be better if he had identification papers, but we don't have anybody who can make really good ones."

Julie and Yolande glanced at each other, a gleam in their eyes.

"Dédé's coming in the first week of August to deliver some wine to the Supply Corps and going back with empty barrels," Bernard continued. "Who else knows about your sergeant?"

"Brigitte knows Yolande rescued him but nothing of our jaunt to bring him to my apartment."

"I didn't tell anyone at the Manoir. Of course, Bérangère notices everything. She said nothing, though."

"Mother won't say a word until she can get you on your own. You know she's the soul of discretion. When are you going south again, Julie?"

"Tomorrow. There was a note in my letter box. I'm picking three youngsters from the orphanage at five to take the night train to Chatellerault." She didn't need to tell anyone that Lars Gurnnarsson would meet her at the station with two more children.

"Good." Bernard glanced at Yolande. "What do you hear from those top Luftwaffe people?"

She pressed her her lips together, her eyes shining with amusement. "What do you want to hear about? Their sexual exploits or their strategic secrets?"

Bernard swatted her hand.

"They're complacent and happy to be in Paris. Less happy about the crews that are going over the Channel to bomb England, but since they don't have to fly over themselves, I think they're not really concerned. Strategic planning and other military stuff happens at their HQ at the Palais du Luxembourg."

"They're digging near the palace, right in the gardens," Julie said.

Bernard nodded. "To build a bunker, I suppose. They're building one in the Bois de Boulogne and on Place de la Concorde. Are you ever likely to work at the HQ?"

"Not me. A chambermaid or a cook could be seconded there, but it's unlikely."

"A waiter would be ideal." He made a throaty noise. "What did you learn during your trip south, Julie?"

She recounted her trip in detail, including people's talk and Paulette Curie's opinion. "It's all trivial, really."

"Not at all. How long are you staying in Chatellerault?"

"Two or three days, depending on the connections. I'm taking a twelve-year-old boy back to Besançon. Then hopefully I can get a train straight to Paris."

Yolande tilted her head. "That's some travel. You'll have to change trains a dozen times."

"Not quite, but, indeed, it isn't straightforward. Especially if a line is under repair."

"You can stroll about, stop at cafés and listen?" Bernard asked.

"Absolutely. I'll have the whole afternoon and evening and next day till late afternoon to myself when I meet the boy off the train."

Bernard stood, went to his desk in the corner of the salon, unlocked a drawer and took out some money before relocking the drawer. "That's for the better restaurants."

"Officers hang out in chic but pricey restaurants. I'll lunch in the bistros with the Red Cross funds. Ordinary soldiers patronize the café-tabacs."

Yolande leaned back on the chair. "Tell us, Bernard, you suddenly have time on your hands and lots of money. You ask us to spy on people. What is this all about?"

A thoughtful air about him, he took his time to answer. "I certainly wasn't going to involve you, or anyone else in the family, but it looks like fate brought you an escapee and you're in whether you chose to or not."

"Am I right thinking that you're are recruiting us to help throw the Boches out?"

"I've already signed on," Julie said.

Bernard explained his mission to Yolande.

"Count on me. Although the Luftwaffe is installed at the Ritz, with an entrance on Place Vendôme, the part on rue Cambon still functions as a hotel. All the upper echelons of society want to be seen there. The top brass already had a conference in the Luftwaffe's part, and I work in both."

"Heard anything?"

"It was all about Paris nightlife and how Mr. Göbbels thought Paris was presently looking sad and that the carefree Paris of old had to resume pronto. One of them complained about the Waffen-SS quietly getting into Paris, along with the Gestapo. But they felt it didn't concern them. The Luftwaffe is above all 'that bunch of ragtag misfits'. Their words, not mine. The entrances on rue Cambon see many different types of people, beside officers. Frank hates the Germans but he's all smiles to them."

"Who's Frank?" Bernard asked.

"Frank Meier is the cocktail barman. His reputation transcends borders.

We talk sometimes. Blanche Auzello suggested I spend more time on the floor than in the office. She too likes to know what the officers are saying."

"Blanche, the director's wife. Hmm... That's interesting. Well done, Yolande. Make sure you visit the Manoir more frequently. You can always leave a note with my mother."

Julie raised her hand. "I hear the elevator."

They stopped talking. Seconds later, the door opened and Marie-Ange followed by the children came in.

"Are we having a conference?" Marie-Ange smiled.

Julie picked up the bag at her feet. "Yolande and I went to the country yesterday and we have a few cherries and watercress to share." She handed the bag to her sister-in-law.

"Wonderful! Thanks."

After a few minutes of small talk, Yolande and Julie left. They munched on stale bread and cheese for lunch while sitting on their bicycles by the curb.

Julie signaled to stop as they came to a bakery. "I need bread."

"I'll buy my ration and you can have it for your friend."

They laughed. There were a few people waiting inside the shop when two German junior officers came in and everybody stepped back to let them be served. They beamed, proud of the attention.

In an approximate French, the taller of the two complimented the baker. "Madame, your Paris is beautiful."

"*Ben oui*, but you should've seen it before you were here." The Germans beamed wider and left with a loaf of sweet bread.

Laughter erupted in the shop.

"Should I have kept my mouth shut?"

Julie shook her head. "Not at all, madame."

The baker's chin jutted forward. "They didn't get the meaning."

A just as well thought sprung in Julie's mind.

"They don't get lots of things," someone said.

"Except our food and clothes and perfume," another voice said.

Discontent rumbled through the small crowd of customers. Yolande and Julie hurried out with their bread ration and parted company, after Yolande handed her bread to Julie.

An agitated concierge greeted Julie. "They moved in!"

"Sorry, who moved in?"

"The Germans. The ones with lightning bolts on their collar."

Julie shook her head. "Take your time and tell me what happened."

"You know I had to make a list of the empty apartments. This morning two of them came and took the Blochs' apartment. What can I do? What if monsieur and madame Bloch come back?"

"Don't worry, please. They went to live with their daughter. They're not coming back while the Germans are still in France." She had the feeling they might even try to go to America, but she wasn't going to share that with the concierge.

"But are the Fritz going to go away?"

"Absolutely, but it may take a while before they do."

"Are they going to pay rent?"

Julie grimaced. "I don't think so. The Wehrmacht general and his entourage at my in-laws are polite and very correct but they didn't offer to pay rent."

"I'll ask them anyway."

"It's best to keep quiet."

"Is your friend still here?"

Taken aback, Julie thought quickly. "You mean my husband's cousin? Yes, he'll be here a few days while he's writing. He needs to concentrate. I'm going to be away for a few days for my job with the Red Cross. Madame Bodénan will come to cook and clean for him."

"That's all right, then."

We're at war and the concierge worries about my reputation! Julie muttered as she hurried upstairs, hoping that Léonie would have the idea to come to see her. Her wish came true, just as she was fitting her key in the lock.

"Don't creep up on me like that, Léonie," Julie whispered.

They walked inside and closed the door and pulled the heavy curtain. "I'm practicing my spying skills."

Julie laughed. "All right, come and meet Kevin."

She knocked on the guest bedroom door. Julie explained about Madame Durand's nosiness. Léonie agreed to take care of Kevin.

"Don't worry about a thing. Marie feeds me at noon on orders from our boss. I've extra food I can bring down for Sergeant Atkins."

He smiled at her. "Where did you learn English? You have an accent."

"I studied for two years in Canada, got married, came back to Paris, divorced and worked at the Crédit Foncier, until the Boches arrived and some of us were let go."

Chapter Thirty-Two

Sunday, August 4, 1940

Paris must be in mourning. I see unsmiling people everywhere. Of course, no one, except for the occasional woman, is going to smile at an enemy soldier. I noticed how pedestrians look straight ahead, avoiding eye contact with the Fritz. They're here, and there're still the enemy despite what Pétain might say. My husband gets in a rage when we scoff at the Head of State. It isn't good for Gontrand's health. Dear little Lyse-May always turns up at the right moment. He simply adores her and meekly obeys her.

Today the whole family... not Philippe or Mireille. Why couldn't he have gone to war and be made prisoner? At least we wouldn't feel this shame when we see him working so enthusiastically for the Boches.

Why couldn't it have been Rodolphe to have been killed? No, a mother shouldn't ever say something so awful. Rodolphe is such a disappointment, so full of hate. I must put it in the past, hide it in that corner of my heart where I keep all the hurts.

I must go and start cooking. I'm making progress there. It's a tight squeeze in the kitchen. Pierrette, dear girl, has made friends with Xavier and they will take the children across the boulevard to the Bois de Boulogne for a picnic and games. François and Hughes promised to help too. We've been blessed with beautiful grandchildren.

I hear Charmaine in the entrance.

"May I go to the Bois, right now?"

"Baptiste, you have to wait until everybody's here for the picnic."

"I'll be back. I just want to see the horses."

"All right. Ten minutes, no more."

The boy ran off. Charmaine greeted her in-laws and put two bags on the table.

"I made some chicken sandwiches and a rice pudding for the children's picnic. I roasted a chicken for us too."

"Merci. Can we just cut it up and make a salad? It might get warm in here to reheat in the oven."

"That was the idea."

"Where did you get the chickens?"

She blushed. "From a customer."

Her mother-in-law gave a half-smile. The majority of the photographic studio's customers were now Germans. In short order everyone arrived, including an excited Baptiste, and Bérangère dropped the questioning.

"I saw the horses. The officers were so smart." Everyone stopped talking and turned toward him. "The gate to the Bois was closed so I ran to open it and they said Danke."

Charmaine's chest rose. Her hand flew in the air and landed with a resounding smack on her ten-year-old son's cheek. A stunned silenced settled.

"You will never, ever collaborate again. Understand?"

He held his flaming cheek. "How could I refuse to open the gate?"

"Did they ask you?"

"No. But they were going to, and if I refused they could've shot me."

"There's a difference between volunteering to open the gate and being ordered to do so. To do it voluntarily is helping the Germans, and we are not, I repeat, we are not ever going to help them."

Baptiste pondered her words for a moment. "I get it. I think."

Marianne encircled her brother's shoulders. "Maman takes photos of the Germans who come to the studio because they give the orders and we have to obey, but she doesn't volunteer to take their photos when they only come to buy postcards. Now let's go with Pierrette."

Baptiste looked at his mother and rushed into her arms. "I'm sorry." He followed their leader. François, Hughes and Xavier carried the picnic basket.

Jacques Werner had entered quietly. "You were right, Charmaine. I wish I could do that to some of my gendarmes." He sat himself between Bernard and Gontrand.

Brigitte set Christiane in the crib near the window and squeezed herself between Lorraine and Julie at the table. "We went to the town hall when they posted the list of soldiers who are prisoners and... dead. Officially, Hubert and Sylvain are among the dead, so we can apply for the pension."

A chuckle greeted her words. By now, the secret was out. They all knew that both of them were alive and well in England.

"Jean-Luc was prisoner but apparently he's on his way back. He was deemed an essential worker," Lorraine said.

"Printing, an essential job?"

"Of, course, Jacques. All that Pétain and German propaganda comes out every day. Not enough small printing shops to keep up with the demand. They can't do it on the big presses, that's for the daily newspapers," Lorraine said.

"We're all glad he'll soon be here," Bérangère said.

Charmaine sighed. "There was nothing about Alexandre. I enquired at the desk and they told me that some prisoners might be wounded and still in hospital. They might not get put on the list until they're sent to POW camps. Another official came and said that Alexandre Lebeau was missing in action. That really means he's presumed dead."

Gontrand turned toward Jacques. "Anything you can do to find out?"

"Alas, no, my friend. Not when the damned Boches dared blow up the First World War memorial in Vincennes. What's next?"

Gontrand exploded in a rage, throwing vile imprecations at the enemy. "How dare they? A memorial is sacred."

Yolande went and brought a bottle of wine to the table. "Aunt Agnès sent this rosé Floc de Gascogne. It's your favorite, uncle."

Red in the face, Gontrand grumbled. "My only daughter! And she's always too busy to join us."

Julie looked pointedly at Bérangère. "How's Lyse-May doing with her piano lessons?" She said in a loud voice.

Bérangère's voice was equally loud. "She's very gifted. You should come and hear her sometime. General von Trennen insists that we practice every day but I only go when he isn't at home."

On hearing the achievement of his favorite granddaughter, Gontrand made a visible effort to calm down and smile. He was proud of the child. The danger of him blowing his head off again had passed and the conversation resumed normally. Julie stood up to go.

***

Julie collected her charges from the Bon-Secours orphanage and settled the giggling youngsters in the tandem vélo-taxi. In front of the station she was met by Lars Gurnnasson and two thin girls about eight and six. Lars handed a Red Cross envelope to Julie, kissed the girls' heads and melted into the gathering crowd. While the girls amused the two youngsters, Julie, holding the toddler, examined the papers she knew were false and didn't see a flaw. There was an address in Chatellerault where she was to take the girls after the youngsters were delivered to the Red Cross and their mother.

She saw no problem, and there wasn't. In fact, she enjoyed hanging out in cafés-tabac, and having a home-cooked meal in a café-restaurant where most of the tables were occupied by German soldiers. There she overheard their conversations, sometimes from one table to another, about what they'd do when they invaded England. They agreed they weren't in any hurry to leave such a beautiful place as France, English food wasn't going to be as good as the French.

She had booked a room at the Gourmandine Hotel. The manager told her she could go stay in a small auberge nearby where there were no Germans. She thanked him but declined. It must her Red Cross uniform that suggested she'd be better off in cheaper accommodation.

When she appeared for dîner wearing a turquoise dress trimmed with navy blue braid designed with a high front and a low back, a delightful small hat perched jauntily on her head, the beaming manager himself escorted her to a choice table by the tall windows. Julie repressed her amusement. Her transformation from the dowdy Red Cross worker to the chic Parisienne had obviously bowled him over.

The dining room soon filled with German officers. They passed by her table and greeted her in good French. Aristocratic to the tip of her painted finger nails, she thanked them and looked blank when one of them addressed her in German. He corrected himself back to French. She smiled gracefully.

It wasn't long before they started talking about what was obviously their most pressing concern – the imminent invasion of England. They weren't as optimistic as the soldiers in the café. They deplored the Luftwaffe losses and wondered why their news bulletins claimed they were already in England.

Next day, dressed in a well-tailored suit, she met the boy at the station and she arranged for their journey to Besançon. She'd had enough of the Red Cross uniform.

On the way back to Paris, the train's motion lulled her into a half-sleep. A hand on her shoulder jolted her fully awake. She gathered her suitcase and purse and stumbled after the middle-aged woman who'd awakened her.

"It's late with the train being stopped when the engineers had to check a bridge. It's almost curfew time," the woman said.

"Oh, no. Maybe I can get the last Métro?"

"I doubt. Papers ready? We have to hurry."

They reached the exit waved their papers at the control. Both made a dash toward the outside but pulled up short when passing the clock.

"Five to eleven! We can't go anywhere." Julie mournful face didn't deter her new friend.

The woman grabbed her by the hand. "Let's run across to my cousin's hotel. He'll let us in." Without waiting for Julie to reply she started running, dragging her along. Julie mentally shook herself as she followed.

The woman hammered on the door. "It's Simone, let me in!"

The door opened and the two women pushed their way inside, knocking their legs against their suitcases, just as a German patrol was marching toward them.

The hotelier hurriedly locked and bolted the door and pointed to another on the side. The two women had already anticipated the move and taken their shoes off. They ran noiselessly toward the room. Loud knocking resounded on the outside door.

"Coming! Coming!" the hotelier yelled.

He made a show of unlocking the door. Two Germans pushed it fully open and looked inside.

They spoke in approximate French. "*Fous afez pris clients après coufre-feu.*"

He repeated, "*Vous avez pris clients après couvre-feu.* No sir, I didn't take any client after the curfew."

"Vhere are the two vomen?"

"I'll complain to your superior that you're not patrolling the streets and that you want to have women. My hotel is respectable and doesn't have women for soldiers."

The two soldiers looked at him, then to each other and high-tailed it.

With a grimace, the hotelier relocked the door and joined the women in his own suite. He hugged Simone and nodded to Julie. The introductions were quickly made.

"Glad to meet you, Julie. You can count on Gustave anytime you need it."

"Merci, Gustave. I have to travel a lot for my job and trains being late, this could happen again." Julie chuckled. "You sure put fear in those two!"

"Those Fritz think they can do whatever they please, but we won't let them. Threatening them with report to their superiors always works."

The vehemence in his voice told Julie all she needed to know.

Simone yawned. "Gustave, we're beat. Do you have a spare room?"

They went back into the small lobby. Gustave took a key off the panel behind the counter and handed it to his cousin. "Sweet dreams."

Chapter Thirty-Three

In the morning, Julie headed to the Manoir, full of hope that Bernard would call in. She didn't want to risk meeting Madame Durand without knowing what the developments at her apartment, if any, were. He might have found a way to get Sergeant Atkins out. Back in her Red Cross uniform, she stopped at the office to hand over the papers confirming the children had been reunited with their families. On Sunday, for her next assignment, she'd be taking two children and an infant to their aunt in Montpellier. She put the envelope in her bag. On her way to the Manoir, she queued for a short time at the bakery and drew stares. She was debating going to the grocer's when an acquaintance greeted her and motioned her over. A consignment of cauliflowers had arrived at their grocery store.

Loaded with her provisions in a filet and weighed down by her suitcase, Julie let herself into the courtyard. Lyse-May jumped off the swing and rushed to greet her. Julie put her luggage down and hugged her niece. Together they walked into the kitchen.

"Mémée! Mama Julie's back."

Julie kissed her in-laws and took two cauliflowers out of her filet for Bérangère.

Bernard winked at her, stood and gave her his chair. "How was the trip?"

"Successful and uneventful. I'm off again Sunday."

"Where to?"

"Montpellier."

Bernard's eyes lit up for a fraction second. "That'll be nice. Can I help you carry your suitcase and groceries home?"

Bérangère turned from the stove. "The poor girl just arrived. We're having lunch and you stay too, since you brought a ham."

"Thank you. Can I help with anything?" Julie asked.

Bérangère switched off the stove and transferred the contents of the saucepan to a serving bowl. "All done. Carrots and the last of the new potatoes you brought us are ready to serve."

The conversation was about to resume when Madeleine entered. She put a bag of groceries onto the counter and sat at the table. "Do you have enough for me? I have a two-hour lunch break."

"Of course. Help yourself to the stew and the ham. How's the job at Neuilly town hall going?" Bérangère asked.

"I classify and file the new ration cards. I'm in charge of checking the carte d'identité of the people who apply for them. I enter the number of the identity card and then I can issue the ration cards."

Bernard smiled at her. "That's a good and important job. Well done, Madeleine."

Julie imperceptibly raised an eyebrow. By now she had discovered a side to her brother-in-law that she'd never have suspected before. She was pretty sure that the next thing he was going to do would be to ask Madeleine to put a couple of blanks in her pocket. That would solve the problem of Sergeant Kevin Atkins and who knows? Maybe others. And Madeleine's good but not-too-bright nature would oblige him.

Madeleine glanced around. "Are Pierrette and François coming for lunch?"

"Today they were studying," Bérangère said. "I expected them to be down already. Lyse-May, *mon chou*, run upstairs and ask them to come down."

The little girl was about to lick her plate while no one was looking. She put it down and scampered up the backstairs.

The adolescents were soon seated and tucking into the food.

Madeleine addressed them both. "Won't you come and live with us now that we have that nice apartment in Neuilly?"

Pierrette shuddered. "Mother, we love you, but we've made a nice place for ourselves in the garret. It's very quiet and an ideal place to study. I'm revising for the bac exams next week."

"And I'm catching up too. I want to start school well-prepared," François said.

"Your father isn't happy. He said you're underage and you have to be home. It's an order."

Pierrette gave a defiant shrug. "When he stops working for the Germans, we might consider it."

Gontrand, who had been somewhat withdrawn since learning the death of his youngest son, straightened and slapped the table with the palm of his hand. "Tell Philippe that I'm quite capable of keeping two youngsters on the straight and narrow. Ask him if he remembers the spankings he got. Not that's doing him any good right now. But those two are under my roof now and they obey me."

Some repressed titters were heard. Madeleine blushed.

"Beau-papa, I know you'll take good care of my children."

Bérangère poured some weak coffee into the cups. "Since you have long lunch breaks, Madeleine, you can come here any time to talk to them."

"Thank you, belle-maman."

Julie stood and kissed her in-laws. "Thank you for lunch. I've got to get home and do some laundry."

Bernard hugged his parents. "I'll help Julie and I've got to get back to work." He hadn't told them about his champagne brokering job.

As she'd expected, Bernard walked with her and carried her suitcase. "Kevin's still in your apartment. Léonie's taken care of him. You're leaving for Montpellier Sunday. He'll follow you. I've papers for him. How are the controls at the line?"

"It depends. The trains don't go back and forth between the two zones. So we'll have to get out at Chalon and walk through the checkpoint and board a train on the other side. It'll only be a German or two checking Ausweis and a couple of gendarmes in the zone nono. However, Kevin doesn't speak French."

"He'll have to act as if he had laryngitis and learn the appropriate words. What do you say when there's a control?"

"Actually, no one speaks. We hand over the papers. If they ask for the destination, we just say the name."

"We? Meaning all the people?"

"That's right, nobody gets chatty with the Germans."

"So it could work."

"I've a suggestion. What if we act as we're a family? The children I'm taking are four, almost three and nine months. He could hold them while I handle the papers."

"It'd put you all at too much risk."

"My prim Red Cross uniform garners a lot of respect." Julie laughed. "And I'm not shy about charming the Germans, if need be."

Bernard joined lightly in the laughter. "Rather than act as a family, have him act as if he just happened to offer help to a lady with three young children."

"That's perfect. Especially I'll have a baby carriage too. I actually would need help."

They arrived at avenue Victor-Hugo and casually greeted the concierge who hurried out of her loge but they kept going after a brief greeting. Julie unlocked her door. Not a sound, not a smell, not a trace of occupancy. She closed the door and curtain.

"It's me Julie and my brother-in-law, Bernard."

After a long moment, Kevin appeared in the kitchen. The two men shook hands.

"Did it work?" Kevin asked.

"Perfect," Bernard replied.

Julie's eyes widened. "You two know each other?"

"I came by while you were away"

"You got past the concierge?"

"Like a charm. Being Sylvain's brother, Kevin is also my cousin. The concierge was keen on filling me in before I could speak."

They chuckled.

"Did you know there's a hidden space inside the servants' spiral staircase?" Kevin said.

Intrigued, Julie followed him out of the kitchen to look at the backstairs. He demonstrated how he could slip inside the central column that supported the stairs.

"I never knew that! I don't think anybody uses those stairs anyway. Not since demand for servants has fallen to zero."

"Léonie told me she discovered it when her little nephew disappeared and they couldn't find him until he cried."

Bernard examined the space. "Fantastic! Must be slim to get inside, though."

Julie scoffed. "Everyone's getting slimmer by the day."

Bernard sat down with Kevin and explained how he was to appear to help Julie. "Once in Montpellier, you'll be relatively safe as long as you avoid the uniforms. You'll make your way to Valras where you'll meet my Aunt Huguette's cousin. He's a fisherman. He got me out. You'll tell him you come from us."

"I'll need a map."

"No map. You can't carry a map. It's *verboten.* You'll memorize the way right here and you'll make yourself invisible."

"My specialty."

They laughed. A series of taps of the bronze door knocker silenced the laughter.

"It's Léonie," Kevin said. "We have a code."

Madame Bodénan brought in supplies. While Bernard and Julie rehearsed with Kevin, she sorted clothes and folded them in a small, pressed cardboard suitcase with metal corners.

"There, you have what a traveler going to visit a relative would carry. I checked that there's no name on any of the clothes."

"Léonie, you're ahead of us!" Julie exclaimed.

"We all know he'll have to travel, so I got a few things ready. I've a note for you, Bernard. Nothing extraordinary but could be useful."

"Where did you get the men's clothes?" Julie asked.

"When I showed the door to my ex-husband, he left everything behind. I'd put them in moth balls. But I aired them."

Bernard asked Julie if she had any cartes Michelin.

"I've one at 1:750,000 scale."

"It's a day's walk from Montpellier," Bernard said.

"How about if after I deliver the children, I walk with Kevin to Valras?"

Kevin shook his head. "You've done a lot for me. I don't want you to take more risks."

"No Germans there. Only the gendarmes but they can be avoided," Julie replied.

Bernard detailed how he made his escape. "It's possible the custom officers patrol the coast more closely now, but I don't see why. Now, tell me how you got from Belgium to Paris and who helped you along the way."

"I'll never forget the people who helped me."

He pointed out his route on the map and where people had helped him. Bernard was taking notes. When they were done, it was agreed Kevin would leave the apartment building with Julie on Sunday. He'd be carrying his suitcase and Julie a backpack to make it easier for her to handle the children.

Julie frowned and leaned forward. "Let's do it in reverse. I use the suitcase and Kevin the backpack. I can leave the suitcase in a locker at the station. It will look more natural, and more practical, if he has the backpack and we go for a picnic."

Léonie nodded. "Smart!"

Bernard agreed.

"What about his papers?" Julie asked.

Bernard winked. "He's Roland Dupuis, has an Ausweis and a doctor's certificate for broncho-laryngitis and suspected tuberculosis."

"I heard that name before." With a chuckle, Julie craned her neck to look at the identity card photo. "Good resemblance."

"Baptiste is very talented for a ten-year-old."

"Takes after his father, the war artist. I hope we hear about him soon. It's the wait and not knowing that is hard to take," Julie said.

Chapter Thirty-Four

Sunday, August 11, 1940

Now we have little tickets to buy food with. We still need money to pay for it. The tickets only give the bearer the right to buy the appropriate rations. And we have to register with each merchant.

Gontrand is just mad that to write to Arnaud he has to use those silly yellow cards where you have to check the word that applies: good health___ tired___ slightly, seriously ill___ wounded___ killed___ prisoner___ dead___ no news from___ family is well___ need food___ need money___ luggage___ news___ back at___ work___ go to school___ passed exams___ is going to___ thinking of you___ love___ signature___

That's how we learned that our nephew Matthieu had been killed. Twenty-five years of age and such a promising young man. Poor Arnaud and Huguette alone with their grief. Their first son. They'd tried for so long to have a baby. Gontrand's devastated.

Isn't it just so crazy? All we could do was to tick "Thinking of you" and "Love"

Sugar is rationed too. Marie had disobeyed and hid three big bags for us. We'll have to be careful.

What an awful August! It's raining. I heard that the Germans requisitioned the entire wheat harvest. No doubt we'll have bread shortages. I can't help sighing these days. But what can we do?

The newspapers and that magazine Julie used to write for are full of announcements for lost children. How can one lose a child as if it was an old sock! I suppose that in the confusion when everybody was fleeing the German army children got separated and were taken in by some good souls. Still, I'm sure I wouldn't have lost my children.

I'm beginning to fear for my grandchildren. The older ones are not taking the Occupation very well. Foolish youth! They'll get into trouble, but what can I say. It's this stupid war. All that people want is a peaceful existence, work, have fun and take care of their families. Nothing complicated about that.

Instead there's so much suffering. I'm glad François made friends with Rose's son. Still, her situation is worrying. At least now she can survive. I sold the lovely woman's sweater she made, and several pairs of socks. She's knitting more. She now has enough money to keep her going for a while. Bernadette, good soul, doesn't charge her rent.

Bernard made a request for a dozen "absolutely", that's his word, plain dark socks, men's size. I guess he can afford it and needs lots of socks. Though, he isn't going to dig for old bones now the Germans are here. I wonder... yes I wonder if he and my grandsons are cooking up something. Maybe they're planning to go to England too.

As usual, it's time to get the cooking started. There's a disgusting looking vegetable on the market. A rutabaga. The grocer told me that's what farmers feed to cattle. The Fritz said they would make Parisians eat grass. It's coming!

The family and Jacques won't be long now. I'll blot the ink and will lift the marble top of the mantlepiece to hide my journal under. Not even Gontrand knows that those tops are held in place by gravity. Heavy, but I can manage.

Marianne and Baptiste arrived first to hug their grandparents then straightaway ran upstairs with Lyse-May to play in a room in the attic that Pierrette and her brother had arranged as a playroom, soon joined by Micheline, and Paul. The adults sat around the table while Julie and Yolande helped with the food.

Julie transferred the vegetables into a serving bowl.

"I'll wash the pan." Yolande elbowed her cousin. "Did you see Marie-Ange's hat?"

"I saw her straight back and disapproving air."

"Where's Brigitte?"

"I told her I'd help with the children but she said it was all planned and she'd be a little late."

Hands in dishwater, Yolande glanced out the window. "Talk of the devil..."

Julie craned her neck to see Brigitte and Hauptmann Langen helping the children out of the general's Mercedes.

Yolande's eyes opened wide. "What?"

"He's been very nice to her. Actually, to the whole family. It's raining so he went to fetch her."

Yolande tilted her head with an amused smile. "They forecasted the weather and made an appointment?"

They giggled, keeping their head down to avoid attracting attention. Jacques entered, boisterous as usual.

"The Opéra has re-opened. They are performing Carmen. We have to deal with all the demobilized soldiers at the Préfecture. At least they can get back to work."

"Why do they go to the police headquarters?" Madeleine asked. "They should come and work at the factory, Philippe complained he's so short-handed."

A silence settled. Madeleine looked bewildered. Bernard, who sat next to her, patted her hand but wasn't going to enlighten her why demobilized workers had to sign in at police stations. "Men are going back to their previous jobs. It takes time. The Renault car factory doesn't have enough workers either."

Madeleine smiled at the explanation. When the meal was over and everyone'd helped with the dishes, they found seats in the sitting room. The older children were happy on the floor. Marianne read a story to the younger ones in the spare bedroom.

Cigarettes appeared in Yolande's and Lorraine's hands but a withering look from Bérangère made them disappear again. During a lull in the conversation, Baptiste spoke. "Do you know why you should never touch a Wehrmacht uniform?"

Heads turned toward him.

"Because there's always a piece of shit inside."

Baptiste caught his mother's look and prudently moved away. Pierrette, her brother and their cousin burst out laughing. Adults clucked to repress their laughter.

The stern voice of his mother made him jump. "Baptiste, go and play with the other children."

Gontrand cleared his throat. "You will keep your bathroom jokes out of this house. *Compris?*"

"Understood, grand-papa," Subdued, Baptiste bent his head and left the room.

Coffee cup in hand, Jacques stretched out his legs. "We forget children have ears. There're plenty of jokes on the streets. What is not a joke is the new edict we'll have to enforce come the twelfth of August. Every person of Jewish faith who hasn't done so already has to turn in any T.S.F. sets in their possession to the police."

"We all had to turn in the sets with shortwave but why the regular sets?"

"It's only the beginning, my dear Bérangère. We have to prepare another census, exclusively for the Jews next month."

"Why on earth?"

"By order of the German high command, so they can find them quickly."

Gontrand snorted. "And you're going along with that?"

"My friend, if you want a short life, protest. If you want to live long enough to see the Boches out of France, you shut up."

"That's what everybody does," Charmaine said.

Julie stood up. "I have to go." She blew kisses all round.

"It's raining. Do you have an umbrella?" Bernard asked.

"I don't. I'll run between the drops."

He stood. "I'll see you to your door with father's large umbrella." To the rest of the family, "I'll be back."

With a sneer, Marie-Ange tilted her chin upward. "How gallant!"

Bernard shrugged and followed Julie out.

"You didn't have to do this. It's not raining hard."

"I know. I just thought that if I came out with you and Kevin, Madame Durand was less likely to try to grill you."

"Maybe add Léonie to the mix."

"Good idea." They both laughed.

***

François and Daniel were strolling in the Luxembourg gardens.

"Isn't it forbidden to come here? With all the Germans?"

François gave a tap on Daniel's shoulder. "Get used to it. They're here for a while."

His friend chuckled. "*Ja*, I'm getting used to it."

"Let's go and see my aunt at the photo studio. She can take your photograph."

"What for?"

"Your identity card. You'll need it to register at the lycée."

"I knew it wasn't going to work."

"Of course, it'll work. Just give me your papers and your mother's."

"We burned them when we fled. It was better to be without."

"I'll ask my uncle. He'll get you what you need. Grand-papa's best friend is a commandant of gendarmerie. He'll help."

"In Germany that would be extremely dangerous."

"This is still France. We don't act like they do over there. We'll arrange with my aunt for your mother's photograph."

Chapter Thirty-Five

The passengers had vacated Julie's compartment when she had to change the baby's diaper, except Kevin who kept his head buried in a newspaper and pretended to have nodded off. Still, they didn't talk until the train stopped.

"Chalon! Tout le monde descend!"

"What's the shouting about?" Kevin whispered.

"We've reached the demarcation line. Everyone has to get out. We go through the checkpoint. You know your part?"

"Let's pray it works."

They descended the train steps. The luggage attendant wheeled the baby carriage with one squealing wheel. The baby didn't want to be put down and began screaming. The toddler, bewildered by all the people, began bawling louder than a cow. The older child, only four, cried as loud as her little brother, clutching Julie's skirt, who almost tripped over her suitcase. She couldn't have engineered a better scenario. Kevin approached, picked up the suitcase and put it in the carriage. Julie dropped the dirty diaper in it. He then scooped up the toddler and the little girl, his papers crumpled in his hand. Julie thanked him profusely and as loud as she could over the bedlam made by her charges. People parted and pushed her and Kevin through to the front.

The German soldiers grimaced at the noise and the smell of the dirty diaper at the foot of the carriage. Julie pushed the carriage with one hand and carried the wailing baby on the other arm, holding her papers, Ausweis in evidence. "*Rotes Kreuze.*" Then, she apologized in German.

They nodded to her. "*Gehen Sie Weiter.*" They threw a glance at Kevin's crumpled papers and the two screaming children. They waved him through less politely, "*Weitergehen!*"

The night was chilly. Kevin was making soothing noises to his charges who screamed even more. Two minutes later they were at the French customs post. The douaniers waved her and Kevin over the line without as much as a glance at their papers. They were in the non-occupied zone and were relieved everything had gone so smoothly.

Once more on the train, they looked at each other and smiled. "That uniform sure gets you a lot of respect."

"It makes up for its ugliness."

The rest of the journey was uneventful and the children fell asleep. Two officials met Julie at the station in Montpellier. Dutifully, Kevin handed the little girl to one of the officials and deposited Julie' suitcase at her feet. She gave him a brief thank you for helping her and dealt with the forms as he stepped away. The officials left with the children. She went to the ticket office and bought her return ticket for the following night before casually renting a locker for her suitcase. She didn't take a change of clothes and hoped she'd be back next day.

Outside the station, they were trying to orient themselves to take the shortest route when a fishmonger's truck stopped.

"Are you lost?"

"Trying to find the best way to go to the beach."

"Ah, city folks. Hop in, I'm going to Sète to collect a load. Lots of lovely beaches there."

"Thank you! It's nice of you."

They squeezed into the cab, Julie next to the fishmonger. For the next hour, he praised Marshal Pétain and his national revolution so close to the German new order, but it was what France needed. While seething inside, she made all the appropriate responses after explaining that her fiancé, Roland, had laryngitis and the doctor had recommended to go to the seaside for a day or two. The fishmonger then switched to the benefits of living by the sea and they arrived in Sète.

She and Kevin went down to the beach, followed it for half an hour, while eating their stale sandwiches before getting back on the road. They reached the Cap d'Agde and Valras by the afternoon. They had no trouble finding Mistral Lambert's house.

***

"Maman, my socks have holes and my shoes hurt."

Brigitte sighed. "I know, Damien. I can't darn the socks again. There's more darning than sock. Let's go to grand-maman, she might have some shoes."

"Can you ask Hauptmann Gerhardt to get me shoes?"

"Absolutely not! The captain has been nice and helpful, but we're not asking anything from him. He's German."

"But he likes you."

"I can't help that."

"You don't argue with him like you do with papa."

Brigitte closed her eyes for a few seconds. How observant her child was. What went on in his head? How did he interpret the Saturday visits Gerhardt had been making since their first meeting? She had to find a way to explain to her seven-year-old that there were the evil Nazis and a few good soldiers who didn't agree with that philosophy.

"When he comes to visit, he's a guest and I don't argue with guests."

"He brings milk and chocolate. Is that why you don't argue with him?"

She exhaled a breath of relief. "Yes, yes. That's why. You, and Estelle and Sylvestre need to drink milk. The store is always short. Then, soon, Christiane will also need milk."

"Can you cut the toe of my shoes so it doesn't hurt while we walk to grand-maman?"

"Good idea. Let's make a sandal out of it."

She laid a sheet of newspaper on the table and took a kitchen knife. "It's tough!"

There was a knock on the door. Damien opened it. "Bonjour, madame Amélie."

"Bonjour, young man. What is your mother trying to do? Cut her hand off?"

"Just trying to make a sandal. Damien's shoes are too small."

"It won't work. You should save the shoes for Estelle."

"But he can't go barefoot. Nothing fits anymore. Money is short and there're no shoes in the stores."

"Let's go and look if a pair that's too small for my Sophie would fit Damien."

"But you'll need them when little Angéline grows a bit more."

Amélie laughed. "By that time, Damien will have outgrown them."

They walked across the landing and soon, a beaming Damien was equipped with a pair of shoes that fitted.

***

As soon as Julie was out of the train station, she removed her Red Cross hat and pushed it inside her jacket to protect it from the light rain. She suddenly realized that the fear that had been her intimate companion since she left with Kevin and the children had disappeared, leaving her exhausted. The evening was already dark. She counted her money and hailed a vélo-taxi. In no time she arrived home and groaned when Madame Durand rushed out and called her back before she could run upstairs. With a sigh, she turned round.

"There's a man on crutches asking to see you. I let him sit inside when he said he's your brother-in-law. Come in."

Surprised, Julie perked up and followed her concierge. "Alexandre!" She spotted the crutches as he attempted to stand. "No, don't get up. What happened?"

"I lost a foot."

"Can I help you upstairs?"

Madame Durand spoke first. "Monsieur Lebeau can stay in the loge until he goes home. He shouldn't be walking too much."

"Thank you, madame. I just would like Julie to go and prepare my wife for my return. I was reported missing, presumed dead. But it's getting late."

Julie frowned. Suspicious thoughts coursed through her brain. "I think you better come with me and stay in my apartment until we figure something out." She smiled at Madame Durand. "There is no elevator in Alexandre's building."

The two women helped Alexandre with his crutches into the elevator. Julie reassured her concierge that they could manage on her floor. She grabbed her suitcase and shoved it in the elevator.

In the apartment, Alexandre collapsed on the couch.

"Clever of you to say you were my brother-in-law."

"I thought it'd pass better with your concierge."

Julie snorted. "She's already worried about the men that come to my apartment."

"Men?"

"Foreign men, friends of your bosom buddy Bernard. We're going to have canned food. I was away for several days."

Alexandre shook with laughter. "Fine by me."

"If you must know, I have a job escorting children to be reunited with their parents after they'd been separated during the Exode."

"I was wondering about the un-elegant jacket."

"Wait till you see the hat." She pulled it out of her jacket and stuck it on her head. "It's a bit crumpled, but I can't let it get wet or it'll shrink."

Alexandre laughed heartily. "I haven't laughed for a long time."

Julie set about preparing dinner. While the beans were heating, she asked what had happened to him.

"I got blown up near Dunkirk. Never made it there. Some medics loaded me and other wounded into a truck. I woke up in a hospital basement. The surgeon confirmed that it was the morgue."

"How gruesome!"

"But safe. He asked me if I wanted to go with the prisoners' convoy. Obviously not. He promised to arrange to get me home as soon as the leg was healed. It's amputated a little below the knee. The doctor and a couple of nurses found me civilian clothes and transport. They also gave me a new set of identity papers. Those of a dead Frenchman. Also the demobilization papers from someone else. The good doctor said it was better to have some identification in case my helpers got stopped at a checkpoint." He produced the papers from his pocket.

She examined them. "All in good order. That's even a good resemblance."

"I touched it up a bit. I like to do portraits, and I altered the name on the demobilization certificate."

Julie clapped her hands. "You'll soon get your wish."

"How's that?"

"Bernard needs an artist. Anyway, how did you get here?"

"I think the good surgeon and the nurses have friends dedicated to helping the likes of me. There were others who came and went in that morgue room." He chuckled. "I traveled in cars, delivery vans and, this evening, in a horse-drawn wagon delivering cauliflowers and lettuce to the Halles market. From there I got a hackney carriage. Your concierge was impressed by the fiacre. I didn't tell her how I came to be here. I didn't think it was wise."

"You're right. She'll probably think you're demobilized, so that's fine. Now we have to get you the papers in your name to be legal. Tomorrow, I'll go and get Bernard and tell Charmaine."

"How's she?"

"Doing as well as we all do. She's kept the studio running with Gus. In fact, he kept it open when we all went to Montauloup." Pain etched itself on her face. She bit her lip.

"What happened?"

"Claire..."

He didn't need any other explanation. He reached out and put his arm around her shoulders until she recomposed herself. His hardened features and gritted teeth showed both his anguish and his resolve.

"What can I do without a leg?"

"Plenty. You realize that the customers are Germans or high society women who give their portraits to their dear uniformed friends. Here, lean on me and sit at the table. It's amazing what opportunities arise."

"You're talking in riddles."

"I'll fetch Bernard tomorrow morning and he'll explain."

"And my Charmaine? I'm surprised she didn't close the studio."

"It's booming. Of course her movie star looks do attract the vert-de-gris."

"Is that the latest word for the Germans?"

"It is. Their uniforms are neither green nor gray, just in between." She served the beans along with the stale bread she had carried all the way from the south. Then added a runny Camembert to their meal. "You'll have to curb any jealousy you may have. Those athletic, blond and blue-eyed officers are just captivated by Charmaine's black hair and dark eyes. The ideal petite Parisian."

"As long as they admire only with their eyes..."

"They are. They're absolutely correct and gentlemanly. This is probably why women are happy to go out with them." Her lip curled in scorn.

***

Determined to get to Bernard's before he left for whatever work he was doing that day, Julie left home before seven o'clock. She was just turning the corner of rue de la Faisanderie when she bumped into him. Without speaking, they turned back toward her building. The concierge greeted them on her way out with her shopping bag. Julie opened her apartment door.

"Now, who do we have? Another British escapee?"

"Salut, Bernard!"

"Mon Dieu! Alexandre!"

"Sorry I can't get up."

Bernard saw the empty pant leg and sat next to his friend to clasp him in his arms. "Like my father. Two wars, two wounds. We'll have to get you a leg like his."

"Won't that be difficult with the vert-de-gris poking their noses into everything?"

"There are ways."

Julie excused herself and ran upstairs to Léonie's.

"I want to go to England," Alexandre said, "but what can I do there with only one leg?"

Bernard shook his head. "No need to go all the way to England. There's work to be done right here." He told him briefly about his mission. "You're an artist and that's where you come in. We need identity cards, demobilization certificates, Ausweis. Just name it, we need it."

"I see."

Julie and Léonie came back with bread, a little butter and a pot of jam. They all sat down to breakfast.

Between two mouthfuls, Bernard told him how young Baptiste was already very capable. "But I don't want to involve him. My niece Pierrette pretended it was a game, a sort of practice for when he'd be older and going to art school."

"I'm relieved. Dieu, he's only ten. How do you go about making those false papers?"

"We've been lucky to get blanks. When François and Pierrette with Hughes opened the print shop, they soon learned how to make rubber stamps. They were very good, but you can probably do them better."

"I'm in. Let's get those vert-de-gris out of France! Damn the Huns! Here, have the papers I got from that good doctor. Perfectly legitimate. The man didn't make it."

"I'll take them, they'll be useful. Do you have your own?"

"The lovely nurse with the blue eyes sewed them inside my shorts on the account that anyone taken prisoner keeps their underwear and they'd be safe. It's in the bathroom."

Julie went and fetched the garment. "Just as well I didn't put it in the wash."

They laughed. Léonie left to go to work.

Alexandre motioned with his chin after she departed. "Is she part of your conspiracy?"

"Gathering intelligence from a German general."

Alexandre whistled. "I get the feeling I better not ask questions, right?"

Julie patted his arm. "You got it."

"The good doctor and the nurses didn't want to give their names. And I didn't ask. They told me there were quite a number of trusted people who are helping soldiers like me escape all the way to the Pyrénées and through Spain and Portugal to get to England."

"Great. Show me on the map where your helpers were."

Bernard took notes. "I'll go now and tell Charmaine. But you have to stay here until I get the unadulterated demobilization papers. Jacques, no doubt, will help."

Alexandre handed him his real identity card and soldier's service and pay book.

Bernard sighed. "A word of caution. If you meet Philippe, do not trust him. Never tell him anything."

"What's the problem?"

"He's in thick with the Germans."

Alexandre pulled a face. "He's not the only one, I guess. On my travels here, some of my helpers told me not to trust a certain person in the village or in the next street."

Julie gathered her purse. "I'll go with you, Bernard, to tell Charmaine and we'll come back with her here for lunch."

"Who will look after the studio?"

"Gus is good with the customers. Anyway, business is slow over lunch time. The occupiers like to fill their bellies." Julie's face showed her disgust.

***

Alexandre and Charmaine and the children had a loving and tearful reunion while Julie prepared the meal. Bernard had already left. After lunch, the two women made Alexandre comfortable.

Once the dishes were done, Julie suggested they to go to the Manoir. "We ought to tell Gontrand that your husband's safe. The children can stay here."

"Let's go, then I've to go back to the studio. You'd think there was no other studio in Paris. The Fritz keep coming."

"Good for business."

"I hadn't realized how well Baptiste can use the enlarger and retouch photos. The women with the Fritz don't want any flaws on their complexions."

Julie gave a knowing smile. "He's terribly talented."

As they got their bicycles out of the lobby, Julie hesitated about telling Charmaine about the role her husband was asked to play and decided it was his duty to inform her.

Gontrand and Bérangère shared Charmaine's joy. Gontrand disappeared into the cellar. He wasn't long coming back with a bottle of Meursault Les Criots. "Here take this wine home and celebrate with Alexandre."

"Thank you, papa-Gontrand. It's kind of a miracle."

In haste Julie asked, "Belle-maman, how's the knitting venture going?" She feared Charmaine might inadvertently say too much.

"Thanks to that big box of wool, Rose has made countless socks, leggings, mittens and a couple of sweaters."

Charmaine's eyes popped out of her head. "What is that?"

"A friend with a little knitting machine," Julie replied.

"Who's buying?"

Bérangère clasped her hands. "At the moment, we do and some of our acquaintances."

Charmaine swung her head right and left in amazement. "You need a shop."

A mischievous smile came to Julie's lips. "There's room in the photo studio to display those beautiful things. They'll last just seconds once the Fritz sees them."

Charmaine was taken aback, but quickly recovered. "You're right. I can push the display case of old cameras out of the way. Better, in fact, I could just store the antiquities and use the case for the sock business. Now that Alexandre will be able to do some work, Gus and I can share selling the knitting. Tell me Rose's story."

They did. Bérangère added that socks also go to people who are in need. "And on Sunday, I'll be going to the Marché aux Puces to see if I can find an antique flatbed knitting machine like the one Rose described to me. Anyone free to come with me?"

Charmaine blew some air. "I'd love to, but I'd prefer to stay with my husband."

"Of course."

"I'll go with you," Julie said.

The two young women took their leave. In the courtyard, Charmaine placed the wine bottle in the pannier and asked, "How come Alexandre ended up at your place? I understand him not coming straight home. He could have come to the Manoir, no? We always end up there."

"Maybe it has something to do with the staff cars bearing the Nazi pennants parked in front of Brigitte's apartment, well, former apartment building."

"Ouch! I hadn't realized."

***

At the Marché aux Puces de Saint-Ouen, Bérangère and Julie couldn't avoid rubbing shoulders with the many German soldiers browsing the stalls. The Fritz laughed and sometimes mocked the vendors, who had a gift for repartee and succeeded in selling them their wares at inflated prices. The women came to a stand full of Victorian-era sewing machines, butter churns, and to their happiness, several objects looking like the drawing Bérangère held in her hand. The vendor was playing a Gypsy melody on a violin and stopped.

"Which one works?" Bérangère asked.

"Don't know, ma'am."

Julie pulled out all the pieces that looked like Rose's drawing. "We'll take all of them." While Bérangère paid, Julie found a colorful length of material. "I'll take this too. We'll wrap those bits and pieces in it."

The obliging vendor produced a ball of string and skillfully made a bag of sorts from the fabric. The two women thanked him but he'd already returned to playing his music. It took the two of them to carry away their purchases.

"We're not lugging this through the Métro," Julie declared. "Let's walk around the corner to avenue Michelet. There's sure to be a vélo-taxi."

"I think we'll take a fiacre. This is too heavy for us."

"Much easier. Shall we go straight to Madame Ducharme."

"Definitely."

Chapter Thirty-Six

Exhausted after another trip to zone nono, Julie dragged her feet to the door of her building. With a quick prayer that Madame Durand would be somewhere else, she dashed up the stairs and reached her apartment unscathed. A grinning Alexandre welcomed her.

"Just in time for supper."

"Did Charmaine come and cook?"

"Today was Léonie's turn. Pierrette brought Marianne and Baptiste."

"I'm glad you had company. How did Pierrette do on her exams?"

"She's confident of success. The soup is warming up. I've managed to do a few things."

While they ate, she recounted her trip. "It's such a shock to arrive in the zone nono and not see a German uniform. Here, I bought some Biscuits Gondolo while I was there. Can't find any here."

***

Sunday, September 1, 1940

Jacques Werner let himself into the west wing. He shook Gontrand's hand. "What an anniversary today is!"

He kissed Bérangère. "One year and no end in sight to this war."

"I don't know what's coming next now that we had to collect all the T.S.F. sets from anyone of Jewish origin, and we also had to collect transmitter radio sets from anybody who owned one."

"Then you'll collect all the other sets," Gontrand said. "It won't matter because we can't listen to London."

"I guess it's difficult. The *cons de Boches* are jamming the air waves, but you could make a frame with copper wire to extend reception."

"Monsieur Jacques," Lyse-May said, "you just said the forbidden word again, and bastard is a swear word."

"I'm sorry my little princess. I'm trying very hard. Tell me what you do all day?"

"Sometimes I go with tonton Bernard when he sells the champagne."

"Ah, yes. Do you like going with your uncle?"

"Oui. When we go and see the Germans, they give me candies and chocolate. But I can't eat them because they're poisoned."

Jacques raised his eyebrows toward Bérangère. She pursed her lips and tilted her head.

He guessed. "Maybe they're not very good."

"I saw mémée put the candies in the rice pudding."

Jacques cleared his throat. "Right. When they're cooked they're not poisonous."

Lyse-May shrugged, slipped off her chair and ran outside. Her acute ear had detected the arrival of the rest of the family to celebrate the safe return of Jean-Luc from a POW camp.

Jacques turned to Xavier. "You're quiet."

"I'm a guest. I'd injured my knee and madame Bérangère wouldn't let me out. I don't know whether my apartment is all right or if I have a job."

"Call in at the préfecture, tomorrow. I might be able to help."

Philippe had driven Alexandre in his brand new Citroën Rosalie. He came in behind the Lebeau family and kissed his mother.

"Will you stay for the déjeuner?" She took the bag he carried.

"Thanks, mother." He entered the kitchen.

"Have you finished working for the Boche?" Gontrand's voice was laced with scorn.

"Everybody needs to work. Like it or not, the only employer is the Reich."

"It's the Reich now! Get out! When your hands are clean, you can come back." The thunder in his tone created a chill in the kitchen.

Philippe raised his hands in surrender and walked out with a brief hug from his mother. Madeleine sighed. Her father-in-law motioned for her to sit next to him. His tone friendly, he enquired about her job. The rest of the family arrived.

Bérangère had the children eat first. They dispatched the food in no time, eyes shining when the rice pudding was put on the table. The older cousins, with Damien in tow, went to the sand box and the swing. Lyse-May pulled Estelle into her room. Sylvestre toddled in behind them. Quiet resumed in the kitchen. The adults and the adolescents squeezed around the table.

"The English are taking a real pounding," François exclaimed.

Brigitte glanced in Madeleine's direction, "They're fighting back like lions."

By a tacit agreement, Madeleine and Marie-Ange were not told of what the family learned from the London broadcast of Les Français parlent aux Français. Julie caught Jacques' attention. "Why did you have to do another census? We were counted already in July."

"This one is only for Jews. That damned government we've got in Vichy is doing all it can to hand over foreign Jews to the Nazis."

Gontrand's fist hit the table. "There's a good reason why the Maréchal is calling for a census!"

Jacques remained undeterred by his old friend's intransigence. "The old man's absolutely disgusting. Persecuted people have sought asylum in France because of our reputation for liberty and tolerance. Pétain is betraying them, and all of us."

Gontrand's rage billowed. "You'll be respectful of our hero. He's cunning and fooling the Boche."

Seeing the discussion turning unpleasant, Pierrette announced above the noise, "By the way, I have passed the bac *with mention très bien*."

François and Hughes lifted their water glasses and whooped their congratulations. The two belligerents abandoned their dispute to congratulate Pierrette on passing with honors. The tension subsided.

After eating a tiny portion of rice pudding, Brigitte pulled Julie's sleeve. "Come shopping with me while the children are busy? My grocer told me to come by at two o'clock. He said he'll have a load of potatoes. No ration tickets required."

"Sure, let's go."

They bicycled to the store. Half a dozen women were already inside. Julie and her friend took their place at the end of the line. Just then, the door opened and two German soldiers came in. They dutifully placed themselves behind Julie.

Brigitte smiled at them, and led them to the counter. "Please, serve these gentlemen first. England is waiting to welcome them."

His face rigid to curb his amusement, the grocer promptly pulled out a box of peaches, weighed and wrapped four of them and handed the package to the soldiers. Still wearing an air of surprise, they paid and headed to the exit. Julie heard one of them repeat, *attendus en Angleterre* and asking the other what it meant. She wasn't going to enlighten them. As soon as the door closed behind the soldiers, the grocer and customers let out their hilarity.

Brigitte deposited her bag of potatoes at her apartment. Julie took hers to the Manoir to share with the others. She relayed the story of the two soldiers in the store. Laughter resonated through the west wing.

When it was time to leave, Julie caught Bernard's eye. She'd learned to read a look, an attitude or an innocuous gesture from him. How could he pass on a message with Marie-Ange, children and family around, baffled her. In a loud voice, she announced she was helping Brigitte walk the children home.

"I'll help too," Bernard said. "You, Paul?"

"Yes, yes, papa, I'm coming too."

While putting shoes back on little feet, Julie admired how Bernard managed to steer the situation to his advantage. When out on the street, Bernard carried Sylvestre, who promptly fell asleep on his shoulder. Damien and Paul ran up ahead, then back in a big airplane game. Estelle took Julie's hand.

"I know you two are plotting something," Brigitte said. She looked away as she maneuvered the baby carriage over the curb to cross the street. "Go ahead, don't mind me."

Bernard laughed. "My darling friend, you're sharp. Though the less you know, the better for the safety of your children. It's bad enough you're distributing my nephews' leaflets."

"I'm not going to sit and do nothing."

Julie put a hand on Brigitte's shoulder. "Dealing with those subversive leaflets is dangerous enough but so absolutely necessary. People need to wake up to the reality of the Occupation."

They arrived at rue Mignard and were negotiating the door when one of the Wehrmacht soldiers ran out and helped store the baby carriage. Duly thanked, he returned to the ground-floor apartment he lodged in.

For the next few moments, Brigitte attended to her children's needs.

With a wink, Bernard brought out an envelope from his jacket pocket. He gave it to Julie. "Rose and her son's new identity."

"What's their new name?"

"Rose and Daniel Sauterel. It's an Alsatian name that sounds sufficiently French to have been expulsed when the Boche annexed Alsace and Lorraine. François had spelt it like the grasshopper, but it's better like this."

"Good, now she can go out and shop."

"How about her French?"

"Making huge progress under Madame Ducharme and your mother's tutelage. Daniel's almost totally French in speech and manner, not to mention slang, thanks to François and Hughes."

"Can you be at Square Lamartine, eight o'clock tonight?"

"I can," Julie replied.

"He'll follow you closely. He's English, decent French, fighter pilot. He chased a Junkers too far over the Channel and landed in France."

"I suppose he was given civilian clothes and helped all the way to Paris."

"The line is being consolidated."

"From safe house to safe house to the south and freedom, despite all the dire consequences the Bekannmachung promises us."

"So he can join the fight for freedom. Those threatening posters only make us want to do more."

***

At eight o'clock, Julie drank water at the artesian well, while nonchalantly looking around. She noticed a doctor's car stop and a young man climb out and walk to where she stood at the fountain. Without speaking, Julie offered him her bottle. He drank. She refilled it and stepped away. He followed, head tilted toward hers, looking as if he was chatting her up.

They passed the concierge who, for once, didn't try to engage Julie in conversation. While Julie prepared a casse-croûte of stale bread and cheese, there came a discreet knocking on the door.

Julie smiled. "It's Léonie's code."

Léonie registered no surprise. "I have some religieuses to share." She placed a box from an exclusive pâtisserie on the table.

"Oh, my! Where did you get those scrumptious pastries? Real butter cream and juicy chocolate! Makes my snack of bread and cheese pale in comparison."

"One of the perks of my job."

***

A few days later Bernard, accompanied by a young man, knocked on

Julie's door. She didn't bat an eyelid when she saw the stranger. They spoke English.

"Here are the American passports for your guest and our newcomer, Julie. No Ausweis though."

"How come?"

"We used up all the blanks and were unable to reproduce a false one satisfactorily. Our artist is working on it. Therefore, the two airmen are going to be American tourists wanting to get home."

"And I'm to be the travel agency manager, is that it? There're no boats going to the States, but they can cross the Mediterranean to Oran and Algiers."

"Right, and sometimes passengers get off before reaching port. Cousin Mistral will help."

"Are you going?"

"Dédé will be leaving Paris Monday and we'll hitch a ride with him."

The two airmen sat listening to the exchange. "You mean we have to jump ship in the middle of the sea?"

Bernard shook his head and laughed. "We'll be on a large fishing vessel transferring to a dinghy."

"I knew we should have joined the Navy," one of the pilots said.

They all laughed. Julie frowned and stretched her neck. "How can you arrange all this when communications are impossible?"

"I made certain friends a couple of months ago. Messages do get passed to their recipients."

She nodded, "I see." Obviously, he'd established the contacts when he'd taken off for England himself. "Can I go with you?"

"You don't mean to England?"

"That's exactly what I mean. That's where the action is."

"I need you here. You're important to get escapees or airmen over into the free zone. And Alexandre knows about legal papers."

She let out a puff of air at the word legal. Illegal or legal, who cared as long as they withstood scrutiny.

***

Later, her pilots left with Bernard. Julie went shopping. She was leaving the bakery when she heard her name. That voice! She froze on the spot. Kurt Meinhard fell into step beside her. He held a neatly wrapped box from the pâtissier on the corner. "Come with me?"

"*Parle français.*" She'd instinctively reverted to the familiar tu-form of their past to tell him to speak French..

"Why?"

"That's my choice." Currents of unease flashed through her body.

He snorted and continued in French. "*Viens prendre un café.*"

She clenched her jaw. His "let us go for coffee" had all the tone of an order that anyone'd be a fool to disobey. She noticed women making a detour to pass near the good looking Kurt. Why did he have to be so handsome? He'd filled out since their youth, his athletic physique enhanced by the perfectly tailored uniform. Michelangelo would have wanted to sculpt him in the finest marble. "I've got to get home. I'm working tomorrow. And I don't want to go to a café right around here."

"Then, I'll call on you later."

"Fine." She turned.

He put his hand on her arm. "I want to prove to you that I have deep feelings for you."

Rather than burst out laughing, she smiled politely. "We can talk some other time."

Every time she went out, Julie stayed on her guard. She made a mental list of unlocked gateways and stores she could disappear into in the event of seeing her nemesis before he saw her.

One evening, there was a knock on her door. She opened it to find her sister-in-law Marie-Ange.

"Come in. Nice of you to visit."

Marie-Ange didn't return the greeting. Her features set in distrust matched her hard voice. "Where's my husband?"

Julie opened her mouth in utter surprise, while her brain worked double speed. "Sorry, Marie-Ange, how would I know?"

"He spends all his time here." Her tone mounted toward the hysterical.

With a slow calm, Julie spoke, "I haven't seen him more than a couple of times when he brought a refugee that needed a place to stay."

"Why would he come to you?"

"Because you don't have room and I have two empty bedrooms."

Marie-Ange stared at her. Before she could speak, there was a knock on the door. Julie went to open it and closed her eyes, her heart beating fast. Despite the intense fear, she'd take children or airmen across the line any day rather than have to face her sister-in-law. She prayed it wasn't Bernard.

"Pierrette! Come in." She put a finger to her lips. Then, she saw the young man with her niece. "Come in, come in."

With a familiar gesture, Pierrette slipped her hand in the young man's and pulled him toward the sofa. Marie-Ange's eyes followed them. She then looked at her sister-in-law.

"I was telling you, Marie-Ange, that I sometimes have a guest who needs a room for a night or two."

"What's Bernard's role in all that?"

"In his job representing the Maison Vander-Vecken champagne and wine, he meets a lot of people. I'm sure he'd take them to the Manoir but you know as well as I do that isn't possible. I'm the next best, especially that I'm not here half the time."

Still with a suspicious expression on her face, Marie-Ange took her leave.

Julie dropped in the nearest armchair. "Phooew! That woman!"

"Is she jealous?" Pierrette asked in English.

"You bet she is."

Pierrette laughed. "She's so uptight and sour, I don't know how Uncle Bernard puts up with her. Anyway, Steve Thompson, meet your host, Julie."

"Please to meet you, ma'am."
"You're welcome. I presume you're here to stay a little while."
"I'm indeed, if it's not too much trouble."
"My aunt loves having company," Pierrette's cheeky smile drew a chuckle from Julie. "Here, I have a ration card for bread and one for sugar. If you go to rue Mouffetard, you're pretty sure to get some in that district."
"Quartier Latin! Will do. Thanks. How's the job at the embassy? Your English is really good,"
"Thanks to your tutoring. Too bad the English written and oral tests at the baccalauréat were withdrawn by order of the government, under Krauts' order I'd say. But the job is in limbo right now. Mr. Bullitt's gone and the staff are unsure whether the States will appoint an ambassador to the occupied zone or not. It's not France anymore."
"It's still France! Just temporarily under a different government."
"Of course, but that's not how the Americans see it."

***

Julie was coming back with a meager load of groceries and a precious bag of sugar, when Madame Durand stopped her.
"Say, have you finished bringing men to your apartment? I don't want that sort of business in my building."
"Madame, it isn't what you think!"
"But all those men that go up to your apartment?"
Julie did a quick thinking while giving a stupefied look to her concierge. "They're the members of my father-in-law's board of directors."
"Why can't they go to Monsieur de Montregard's Manoir?"
Julie pretended to be shocked. "Madame! Don't you know that a German general has taken up residence at the Manoir, complete with his aide-de-camp, his orderly, driver and groom?"
"I know. But why do they have to come here? You're a woman alone without your husband."
Thanks, I know that. "You may not understand that to run a factory takes more than workers, it needs directors and supervisors even architects. We're making plans to reconstruct the factory and to move most of the production into the free zone. My brother-in-law and I are passing instructions from my father-in-law."
"Why can't they just all come at the same time for a meeting?"
Julie laid it on thick with her scandalized air. "My dear Madame Durand, you've seen the posters that gatherings of more than three people are not allowed."
"How will they get to the free zone? My sister couldn't get an oosss... paper."
Now contrite, Julie toned down her voice. "I'm sorry, it's so difficult nowadays."
The concierge took a Red Cross envelope from her apron pocket. "This came for you. Is that your work?"
"Yes, it is."

"I saw you with the SS man."

"Ah, the general's liaison officer, whatever they do. Unfortunately, he's always crossing my path. I do have to talk to him. It isn't a good idea to annoy the occupier."

"He's not going to go up to your apartment, you know."

Julie didn't know whether she should be amused or angry at the nosiness of the concierge. "Of course not."

"'cause I could well plant a knife between his shoulder blades."

"We have to show tolerance until we can throw them out. And never lift a finger against a German. You'd be shot on the spot."

"Where are our youth? If everybody killed one Boche each on the same day, we'd soon rid the country of them."

Julie was getting impatient but knew better than to antagonize a concierge. Concierges had a way of making life miserable for a tenant if they took a dislike to them. "I can promise you many people will rise in due time." Madame Durand opened her mouth to speak, but Julie rushed in. "How are you getting along with your two new German tenants?"

The concierge shrugged. "They don't bother me, but, say—"

Julie cut her off. "Do you need anything?"

"Milk, butter and sugar. I'm too old now to do something. I've known the First, you know."

"Rationed. I can give you two beetroot from the Manoir's garden."

"Well, thank you."

Julie hurried upstairs. Everyone had to be so careful about what they said nowadays. Amazing what the offer of a little food does to people.

Chapter Thirty-Seven

"Come in, Yolande."

"Ah, ma tante. The Boche supervisor has invited me to a reception at the German embassy, and I've nothing to wear."

"And of course, you cannot refuse."

"I'd lose my job." She opened her carryall. "This is the only dress I have and... you can see. Not suitable."

Bérangère shook the long night-blue moiré-silk dress. "It's lovely material, a bit plain in style. Let's go to the bedroom."

Yolande changed into the dress.

"You've lost weight. It doesn't fit. Are you eating enough?"

"I bicycle every day and I walk all day. Madame Blanche made me the floor supervisor to ensure all those gentlemen are well-cared for."

"Let me guess, you only sit down to write your report."

Yolande nodded while her aunt pinned the extra material.

"I think I'll restyle it by opening the seam on one side and lining it with the silvery silk I took out of a ruined dress, and lower the neckline."

"Do I dare show more flesh?" At Bérangère's raised eyebrows, Yolande added, "Fine with me."

The two women set to work on the dress. Two hours later Yolande paraded in front of her aunt and the long mirror.

"Stunning! It's unrecognizable. Thank you, ma tante."

"I'll see you at the embassy. Gontrand is fuming, but we have to go. Julie was invited by an officer of some rank and since the de Montregards are on the Bottin of the Tout-Paris, or rather used to, we better go. I really don't want anything to do with all those actresses, writers and aristocrats who're fawning over the Germans."

"Who keeps that registry, the Bottin? It's ridiculous, isn't it?"

"Oh, I agree. It's quite funny though to see all those people trying to claim a baron or a count in their ancestry. Anyway, you're all set."

"You're a fairy godmother."

"This has given me an idea," Bérangère said. "There're old dresses in a trunk in the attic. I could restyle them."

"And sell them along with the socks and sweaters."

"Not a bad idea. But we'll need them."

"Do you think it'll get worse?"

"Have you looked in the stores lately?"

Yolande heaved a breath. "You're right."

"I wonder whether Robi would consider my designs again."

"That's the children store you worked for?"

"It is. I know Gontrand isn't talking about money, but we no longer have an income. I can't imagine our savings will stretch for very long. I must do something."

"Do you believe the Fritz are going to be here for a long time?"

"It took four years to throw back the Boches in the last war."

A somber silence settled between them until Yolande took her leave.

***

Julie jumped on her bicycle and cursed her skirt that billowed in the wind. She snatched the offending material and tucked it in as best as she could. She deftly avoided the main thoroughfares that crawled with the occupiers, and reached Rébecca's apartment.

"Will you be able to keep your job?" Julie asked.

"My boss entered me on the payroll and the list of professors by calling me Becca. He dropped the R of Rosen and said that Osen sounded Alsatian. The École Polytechnique is above politics."

"It might help for a while. However, life and institutions' status have changed. The Germans command and our puppet government obeys."

"The Germans respect higher learning. I'm a mathematician and I'm working with Yannick, my boss, on a special project."

Julie sighed loudly to show her incredulity at her friend's naivety. "Not convinced. But you're not going to go to be counted in that new census?"

"Well, I'm Jewish. If we obey the law nothing will happen to us."

"Don't you believe it. In time, new identity cards'll be issued with a big J stamped on it in red."

"How do you know?"

"A rumor that our friend Jacques mentioned."

"Only a rumor."

"The government in Vichy has been making new laws. Please listen to reason."

"Scientists like me deal in facts, not rumors."

Julie shook her head. "What's the point of hiding your name if you then claim your Jewish heritage. Becca Osen won't last long. Those goons will soon put two and two together if you register."

Julie ended the conversation that went nowhere. She bicycled back, her heart laden with apprehension.

***

Thursday, October 3, 1940

"What on earth was all that racket last night?" Bérangère asked.

Julie deposited a cabbage on the counter. "Those Boches! They blew up synagogues last night."

"*Mon Dieu!* What's next?"

"It's time we get organized and blow them out of France!"

The vehemence of her tone scared her mother-in-law. "Don't go and do something stupid."

"Sorry, belle-maman. No, I won't do anything stupid. It'd only put all of you in danger. Trust me." She grabbed a kitchen knife and forcefully shredded the cabbage.

***

A few days later, von Trennen knocked on the west wing door on his return from his horseback ride in the Bois de Boulogne.

"Madame de Montregard, I would like to ask a favor of you. I have to give a reception next month and I am expected to play the violin. It would give me such great pleasure, and help me through this ordeal, if you would be so kind as to accompany me?"

Bérangère laughed. "What ordeal are you referring to?"

"I have no time for this sort of thing. I noticed how uninterested you were at Otto Abetz's reception."

"I wonder what my husband'll say about that."

"Can we believe he has taken the first step toward... let's say... a reconciliation?"

Bérangère gave a slight shake of the head. "I wouldn't say reconciliation. That'll come only after the war is over and you Germans are back home. But perhaps the recognition that you're not a Nazi."

"You are insightful, madame. I heard François play the violin. He is extremely talented but I understand he no longer has a teacher and might not get into the Conservatory."

"That's correct."

Reynard nodded. "I would like to invite him to play along with me and perform a piece on his own. Do you think he will accept?"

Eyebrows raised in doubt, Bérangère pursed her lips. "I can ask him. Sometimes it's difficult to predict adolescents."

The front door slamming announced François' arrival. "They make us sing in honor of the marshal... oh, excuse me!"

"François, we were just talking about you. General von Trennen would like to ask you a question."

The boy looked the general straight in the eye and waited.

"Would you be kind enough to play the violin at the reception I have to host next month?"

"No!"

"François, think again," Bérangère said.

"Well, I hate the Germans, except you, monsieur, because you are a decent man. A very decent man. But I am also totally out of practice."

"Thank you for your kind words. You know that I too play the violin. I would be happy to offer you some tuition."

A flicker of interest sparkled in François' eyes, but was quickly extinguished. "That would be collaboration and I am not going to be a collaborator."

Bérangère motioned him to sit down. "Aren't we all collaborating? It's a matter of degree. Music doesn't have borders. Music doesn't collaborate."

François frowned. "You're right, grand-maman." He looked at Reynard.

"Will you really tutor me? I'm not that good."

"I heard you play. If I did not think you were good, I would not have asked you."

The youth smiled. "Merci. When you were young, did you want to be a professional violinist?"

"Yes, I did. My parents did not. My father was an army officer. I had to follow his wishes."

"Do you hate it?"

"Since the Great War, all the time." His voice had a tired tone to it.

"Why don't you resign?"

The general chuckled. "Typical youth, are you not? When the Nazis took power, it was not possible. Being a mature man I saw that by staying I could possibly do something to curb the madness of the new era."

"By being in the Abwehr?"

A far-away smile on his lips, Reynard replied, "Counter-Intelligence gets all sorts of useful... how should I say, insights?"

The youth nodded. "Do you have contacts?"

"François! This goes beyond personal. Stop asking the general such questions."

"Grand-maman, the general is a mature man. He can tell me to shove off if he doesn't want to answer."

A hint of pride passed on Reynard's features. "True."

"When do we start violin lessons?" A smiled hovered on the adolescent's lips.

"Today. And I'll introduce you to Manfred Fashingbauer. He's the conductor of the Wehrmacht orchestra. He'll help to further your musical studies."

***

Bérangère read out a notice in the newspaper. "Will exchange an almost new suit for a quarter of a hog. And here is Monsieur le député Scapini telling young men to volunteer to go to work in Germany. He calls it La Relève. Three men to "take over" working for Hitler, and in exchange, one POW will be freed."

"Those members of parliament are all corrupt. Deputy Scapini! Bet he's Italian. What does he thinks? Hein? Three for one! What's wrong with his arithmetic? It ought to be one for one," Gontrand said. His voice thundered across the kitchen.

Two bags in hand, Julie let herself into the kitchen. "Prices have gone up again."

Gontrand called Lyse-May to go for a walk in the Bois. "The ladies are going to gossip about prices and shopping. Let's go and feed the ducks."

Alone, the two women dove into the shopping bags. "You've got lots of that rutabaga vegetable."

"No ration ticket required. It's food, belle-maman."

"Not very nutritious, I imagine."

"Not so. Farmers feed it to cattle."

Bérangère sighed deeply. "How can you cook it without just boiling it?"

"I've tried and I think I've made progress."

At that moment, the outside door opened. Bernard waltzed in with a song.

The greetings were brief. "Marie-Ange was asking for you."

"I know, I've seen her. She's more than furious that the department of education put her on special availability. Married women are not allowed to hold a public function. She'll convince them that I don't earn enough to raise two children. I gave her a couple of pay slips from the Musée de l'Homme. Since the part-time pay is low and they really don't have enough teachers, they'll let her back in."

The noisy arrival of François and Hughes interrupted the conversation.

"I got a demerit because I didn't sing Maréchal nous voilà," François lamented.

"Nincompoop," Hughes said. "You should sing it the way I do. The proper version goes, Marshal, Here we are. The sacred flame, Rises from the native soil, France now energized... no problem with those verses, right?"

François agreed.

"Now replace the chorus, Salute you Marshal, by Shit on you, Marshal, and the repeat Fuck you, Marshal."

François burst out laughing. "That's gross."

"Well, he's gross too. His picture is everywhere, his words everywhere, you saw those maxims, a new one on the blackboard every day. Learn them by heart, said the teacher. Then he erased the blackboard to continue with the maths class. I think my teacher doesn't like those sententious maxims."

"All very well, young men, but don't neglect your studies," Bérangère said.

"Don't get caught," Bernard said.

"How come you're back so early? You're not playing hooky, are you?" Bérangère asked.

"No, grand-maman, we don't have to be in school until we have class and it's lunch time, anyway."

"Of course, you wouldn't miss that," Julie said.

The youths laughed and bolted upstairs. Bernard took a wad of money from his pocket and handed it to Bérangère. She made it disappear into her apron pocket, just before her husband's return.

"Tonton Bernard! When can we go to sell the champagne?"

He hugged his little niece. "Soon, poppet."

After lunch Bernard said, "I'll walk Julie home. She's looking for a job and I may have an opening."

"Careful son, your wife isn't happy," Gontrand said.

"She'll have to get used to it."

"But Julie's got a job with the Red Cross," Bérangère said.

Julie shook her head. "I don't know for how long, belle-maman. I'm told that all the children have been reunited with their parents."

"So, what work can you get her?"

"I need someone who can type invoices and promotional material."

Julie served lunch and the conversation drifted to food.

***

As they walked toward Julie's building, Bernard repeated the need for secrecy.

"I knew that right from the beginning."

He lowered his voice. "I have money for you from Sylvain."

"Is he all right?"

"He's in training and doing fine."

"How did you get over there and back so fast?"

He didn't reply. They arrived at the apartment building, greeted Madame Durand and sped up the stairs. Once securely inside, they relaxed.

"What's that job you mentioned?"

"We've printed some tracts and are planning on a newspaper."

"Underground, I assume."

"Of course. We need to inform the population. All what the Vichy government and the Germans do is tell lies. I'd like you to write articles directed to women."

"Articles to help with daily life, recipes, and how to detect lies, to be on guard in the queue at the stores, and so on. Is that what you have in mind?"

"I couldn't have explained it better. Also typing a tract or two with as many carbon copies as you can make."

"Maximum six. You'll supply paper? And typewriter ribbon?"

"We should be able to get some."

"When will you get the newspaper up and running?"

"We've got difficulties getting another roneotype machine. We need a part for the one we have. It hadn't been used for a long time."

Julie knew better than ask too many questions. "I'll start composing an article. Did you talk to Lorraine? Jean-Luc?"

"That's on the agenda."

"Good. You better go if you're done."

He chuckled and left. Julie was intensely relieved to have some money and the prospect to earn a little with her articles. She'd figured that the "we" her brother-in-law talked about must be at the Musée de l'Homme. It didn't surprise her that a museum of mankind would endeavor to inform the people of the reality of life under the German jackboot.

She jotted down some notes for her article and then bicycled to Brigitte's. Charmaine was there. After kissing Sylvestre and a gurgling Christiane, Julie plopped into an armchair.

"Nice to see you Charmaine."

Brigitte in her direct way said, "What would you do, Julie, if a SS officer had been admiring you and then asked you out, knowing you're married?"

"Is it a hypothetical question or are you referring to my situation with that Obersturmbannführer Meinhard, first name Kurt?"

"Diable, no."

"Don't call up the devil."

"Sorry. I hadn't thought about it. Actually, it's Charmaine. Tell her."

Charmaine hooked a curl behind her ear. Bicycling didn't lend itself to impeccable hairdos. "Since I came back to the studio, there's been one of those SS officers who keeps coming in every day. He has extremely good manners and brings his friends. The studio is flourishing. He's started bringing me flowers. Today, a white carnation."

"White carnations mean friendship, strong and pure feelings," Julie said. "What does Alexandre say?"

"The officer," Charmaine sighed. "I can't remember his name or his rank. Well, this morning he asked me to go and have supper with him. His French is flawless. I told him I was married, which of course he knew, since Alexandre has taken two or three portraits of him. So he asked my husband. Alexandre said he saw no problem. I could have killed him. After the officer had left, I punched my husband." She stopped talking.

"Continue, please," Julie said.

"He told me I could refuse to go but that would endanger not only our children but the whole family. I know we're not blood related with the de Montregards but we've been like family since I was a little girl."

"Along with me," Brigitte said.

"One day, when Alexandre was altering the photo on several identity cards, the SS officer walked right in the back before Alexandre could get his crutches. I was out shopping and Gus hadn't arrived."

A stunned silence settled. Finally, Julie stood and paced. "He's blackmailing you but in a friendly way, if that's not a contradiction."

"Alexandre said if I don't want to go out with him, we'll escape to the free zone. But we don't have much money, and Alexandre can't just go and get work."

"Perhaps he just wants to have a beautiful companion to go out with. It doesn't mean you have to sleep with him. Gerhardt took me out a couple of times. He doesn't ask for anything, just company."

"Brigitte's right. He might be a perfect gentleman."

"He heard me singing *Ave Maria* one day when I thought there was no one in the shop and told me he was a pianist and would love to accompany my songs."

"You do have a beautiful voice. Tss, this is becoming interesting," Julie said. "The meeting of two musical souls."

"What should I do?"

"Protect your family, my friend. Go with him and hope for the best," Brigitte said.

Charmaine chewed her bottom lip. "What will the neighbors say?"

Julie shrugged. "Everybody is asking what will the neighbors say because, suddenly, the norm has shifted. We're all becoming a bit paranoid."

Brigitte reached for her friend's hand. "Tell Gus about the blackmail before he does away with the man."

"Yes, do tell him everything. Because if he did do harm to the officer, the retaliation would be swift and terrible for you and your children."

Charmaine nodded and with a sad smile on her lips returned to the studio.

Julie accepted a glass of water. "How's your captain?"

Brigitte reddened. "He's sweet. He brings treats for the children. They like him. He's taken me out a couple of times and I must say, he was very nice. My neighbor Amélie sits with the children. We have an arrangement. She goes out with one of the soldiers downstairs."

"He's in love with you?"

"No, it's rather lonely for him when work is finished."

Sylvestre came in blowing raspberries, a sheet of paper crumpled in his little hand. Brigitte jumped up and removed the paper from him. "Do not touch the papers on my table."

Julie craned her neck. "Ah, one of Bernard's tracts."

"I'm taking a few to a bookstore on Boulevard Saint-Michel tomorrow."

"I'll help. Did you ask Gerhardt what he thought about the new status for the Jews?"

"Come on Julie, I don't ask that sort of questions."

"You should. We know he's anti-Nazi. He won't mind."

"What's going on? Bernard asked me what Gerhardt talks about beside architecture."

"Think, Brigitte, think."

"You and he are spying?"

"Not spying, but gathering people's ideas, reactions, willingness to do something to help get the Fritz out of France."

"I see. It's more than helping a stray airman out of the occupied zone. But Bernard doesn't want me to do more than carry the tracts to the bookstore."

"You have children and a baby. You can't take the risks I'm prepared to take. I must go now."

***

Bérangère and Julie left the Métro and walked toward the shops lining the Halles market, which was closed for the day.

"Do you think some of those grocers and butchers manage to hide some things from the German control?" Bérangère asked.

"I'd be surprised if they didn't. Everyone is managing all sorts of tricks."

Bérangère laughed. "The système D for débrouillardise or the ingenuity system of the people. But it'll be black market, won't it?"

"As long as we've got some money, the black market makes all the difference between starving and surviving."

"Better not tell that to my husband."

While they waited in the queue, they heard a noise overhead.

Everybody looked up. Five planes roared across the sky.
"Look at that!"
"They're writing something."
"Confiance."
"No it says RAF. Oh! Both."
"They're Spitfires."
"What are they?"
"English planes. And look, they're dropping papers."
Women rushed forward to pick up the leaflets. At that moment a car screeched to a halt. The tracts disappeared into shopping bags and the women kept their heads down. Only Germans had cars and it wouldn't pay to look defiant. The black Citroën sped off down the street. It slowed and a soldier with a megaphone announced that anyone who picked up the fallen leaflets would be shot.
An hour later, pleased with their purchases, and still chuckling about the English telling the population they were not forgotten and to keep their chins up, the two women took a vélo-taxi to Madame Ducharme's mansion to share some of their bounty with Rose.
"Thank you so much, madame."
Julie examined pairs of long black socks. "Beautiful. Do you have enough wool?"
"There was a lot in that box. And the ladies come and bring me more." At Julie's questioning look, Rose continued. "On Monday evening, Madame Charmaine and Madame Brigitte come and we knit together. Madame Marie-Ange came once but she doesn't like knitting, so Monsieur Bernard brought Marianne. She's a sweet girl and very interested and learning fast."
Julie turned a sweater in her hands. She barely noticed when Bérangère declared she was leaving to pay Bernadette a brief visit.
"Tell me, Rose, all those purl stitches what do they represent? It's an odd pattern."
Embarrassment spread a pink flush on Rose's cheeks. "It's an experiment."
"Ah! Yes. I heard the word experiment before. Would that be another of Bernard's experiments?"
"I'm not at liberty to discuss it."
"Relax, Rose. I also work for Bernard. Now let me guess, this looks like Morse code. Three purls, one slip stitch, Di di di, two purls dah, space di di space dah di dah di that's V I C. Are you spelling victory?"
"You're smart, madame Julie."
"I told you, I'm just Julie."
A smile hovered on Rose's lips. "Yes, Julie, it's Morse code. Do you know it?"
"Vaguely, I remember the few letters I learned when I was a child. Someone wearing a sweater could carry a message on his back. Might be a bit slow, though."
"I made a really good knitting machine with all the parts you brought

me. Knitting takes no time, can be unraveled and re-knitted. And I'm learning the code."

"I'm beginning to see a use for it. A name, or a place to bomb next. But it could take weeks before the wearer reached England."

A smile hovered over Rose's lips. "Monsieur Bernard must know what to do."

The return of Bérangère put an end to the conversation. On the walk home, Bérangère grumbled about Lanvin, Maggy Rouff and Nina Ricci's salons de couture that had re-opened.

"Their fashions are so sumptuous, with yards of material and all those turbans! Don't they realize we can't buy fabric? You need three months of tickets for a simple short dress!"

"They must be directed at the German market."

"And the horse races are back on."

"Well, you'll have to make an appearance, belle-maman. The Tout-Paris is bound to be there."

"I'll have nothing to do with the Arletty and Coco Chanels of this world. I'd have something to say when they flaunt their Nazi lovers, while other people are forced to rummage around the Halles' garbage to find food!"

"Can't blame you." Julie helped her mother-in-law unload the groceries. "I'll come early tomorrow to help prepare lunch." She stashed her own purchases into her bicycle panniers and returned home.

Madame Durand signaled to Julie to enter the loge. "You know, the SS man that was with you. He came. So when I asked him what he was looking for, he kept walking and said 'none of your business.' What should I do?"

"Nothing, I'm afraid, Madame Durand. It'd be best if you just said good morning or afternoon and nothing else."

"But I told him you weren't home."

"He probably visited the other SS officers on the fourth floor. Here, I got a bunch of carrots. You can have half."

"Oh, thank you."

Julies escaped to her apartment, unsettled that Kurt Meinhard had found a pretext to come into her building.

In the morning, she scanned the street to make sure that her nemesis wasn't anywhere near, and hurried downstairs. Madame Durand was already in the vestibule, broom in hand.

"Good morning, madame. I was wondering whether you had a key to the coach door. I think it would be better to put my bicycle away rather than keep dragging it through the front door and dirty your beautifully clean lobby."

Madame Durand straightened at the compliment. "That's very considerate of you. Maybe Madame Bodénan could use it too. You're the only ones with bicycles. You can put them in the shed, It's not used, but I only have one key."

"Would you entrust me with it? I'll ask Ernest to get a duplicate. He knows where to go."

"Well, all right." She stepped inside the loge and handed Julie a thick key. "Here. How long will it take?"

"I'll tell Ernest it is urgent." She pedaled hard, elated that now she could come in without having to pass under Madame Durand's gaze. Any guests could also now come in without being seen. The unused servants' staircase just found a new life. At the Manoir, Bernard had already arrived with Micheline and Paul .

"Marie-Ange went to church."

His head in his hands, elbows on the table, Paul was grousing. "I'm fed-up with stupid school."

Julie hugged the boy. "Tell me what's wrong."

"We have to listen to the Vichy Radio."

"You mean Radio-Paris."

"Yes. The teacher calls it Vichy. We have the words Work, Family, Country written at the top of the blackboard. Then we have to write a paragraph about something Pétain said."

Gontrand hit the floor with his cane. "That's Maréchal Pétain to you."

"All right, grand-papa. It's: Being disloyal in class is a sin and I want it to stop."

Julie finished scrubbing the carrots. "It really applies to greater things than the school classroom. For example, the class could be a country. One must be loyal to the country but if the country turns against another country, it's all right to be disloyal."

"But Auntie Julie, Pét... the marshal said it is a sin to be disloyal."

Bernard chuckled. "Just write like Julie said."

"I'll get a zero."

"I won't mind."

"But maman will. She's always spouting good stuff about the marshal."

"You keep putting on that bored air and she'll give up."

François had been standing for a while. "It's not as bad as the assignment we got to glorify Hitler in German class."

The Bourgmestres arrived and Hughes punched François' shoulder.

"Are Daniel and his mother coming?"

"Yes, why?"

"I found something and gave it to him for the assignment."

As if he had heard his name, Daniel walked into the kitchen, followed by Rose carrying a bundle of knitting.

"The assignment? Here, François. I've got it."

The youths leaned over the table. Daniel laid two pieces of paper on top. He pushed them together "Now, here we have the glorification of that jerk Hitler, now pull it apart and read."

"The first column glorifies the English and the second bashes Hitler."

"And together it glorifies Hitler. Smart!"

Love and admire | Hitler the Chancellor
eternal England | is unworthy of living
curse and crush | those resisting people
the Nazi on earth | only will survive.
be the support of | the German führer
that nation of sailors | will be the cursed race
to them only belongs | this just punishment.
the laurels of victory | rightly granted to him.

"Great, let's make copies and distribute them around."

Bernard craned his neck to read the two papers. "Where did you find this clever little poem?"

Hughes shrugged. "Just lying around in the print shop."

Before Bernard could reply, Bérangère shooed everyone out so she could set the table. With Brigitte and the children's arrival, the youths escaped to the sitting room with Marianne.

Pierrette, red and out of breath, threw herself onto a chair. "There was a fight on the Boulevard Saint-Michel at the café d'Harcourt."

Suspicion in his voice, Bernard asked, "Who was fighting?"

"Some students and German soldiers."

There was a gasp of apprehension.

Gontrand's tone was stern. "And where were you?"

"Close enough to watch, but far enough not to be involved."

"I should hope so!"

"I had just met our friend Xavier and he pulled me away."

"I'll give a medal to that young man," Gontrand said. He was serious.

Chapter Thirty-Eight

Sunday, November 10, 1940

Raining again. I'm worried about all those tracts that circulate. And those Advice to the Occupied will get someone into trouble. Though I like this one: "Show total indifference but keep your anger simmering, it will come in useful".

I see our young people writing away. I thought they were deep into the schoolwork, but then I saw they were writing on small pieces of paper. I asked François the subject of his dissertation that he needed so many notes for. He said it was the new teaching method. I clipped him over the ear and we went to rehearse with the general. But it's not good. I'm sure it's some subversive effort and therefore dangerous. I can't say anything. It's always the youth leading riots and revolutions. Older people become fearful, not the youth. They're the ones who are sent to war.

At least, I have work from Robi Children's Clothes. They took my first design for a stylish coat. Now I have a heap of coats to inspect and remove the basting thread. I didn't have to take on this additional work, but it's paid extra. Lyse-May, bless her sweet heart, helps pull out the basting threads and roll them up on pieces of paper. Gontrand prepared the paper saying the thread might become useful. Funny how now he doesn't jibe at my squirrel mentality.

The Occupation isn't going to remain peaceful. They sent their goons to inspect cellars. Just an excuse. Why would they need to inspect cellars? No need for passive defense since they're here. It puts the fear into the residents. When they came here, my husband threw them out before they'd gone one step into the courtyard. They had a different uniform. Must ask Jacques about it.

I think I hear our friend. Julie is already cooking.

The family had all arrived when Jacques appeared in civilian clothes.

"You're off duty today?" Bérangère said.

A thunderous look on his face, Jacques exploded. "The damned Boches took all our uniforms and weapons away! Even from me a senior officer!"

An instant silence settled. Gontrand frowned. "Why?"

"Because the Kommandant has forbidden any demonstration, any marches, the laying of flowers at the Arc de Triomphe, as Parisians have done for the last twenty years. As if that was going to stop anyone placing flowers on the Tomb of the Unknown Soldier. The stupid Krauts fear an uprising. So we gendarmes and policemen are supposed to keep order. How can we do that without uniforms and not even a baton, eh? Students are already planning to defy the asinine order. And the insane government we have in the other zone is going along with it. No marching, no flowers in the zone nono, either. And now that puppet Pétain sold what remains of our dignity in Montoire by shaking that bastard Hitler's hand. I could kill him, feebleminded marshal he is."

Exhausted after his vehement tirade, Jacques mopped his brow. To their surprise, Gontrand kept his head down and remained silent. A brouhaha of voices arose. Bérangère imperiously commanded everyone to sit at the table and forbid any talk of politics or of the Occupation. Interest in the food took over.

Charmaine and Julie sat together and conversed in low tones.

"So tell me what's happening with your suitor?" Julie asked.

Her friend reddened. "He's SS-Hauptsturmführer Ziegler. We went out to dine at the Tour d'Argent the first time. I was mortified but he kept encouraging me. Friday, we went to the Ritz. He didn't know that I had seen Yolande and she'd spotted me. Fortunately, she acted as if I was a stranger."

"Trust Yolande. Except for her boss and German supervisor, they don't know she speaks German. She listens to the guests while ostensibly checking on the staff. She could see her own mother there and would totally ignore her."

"I have to call him Wolfang, or *chéri*, especially when we're near other German officers. It feels like I'm performing all the time. He said the next time we'd rehearse together."

"How do you feel about that?"

Her eyes misted. "I'll do whatever is necessary to save Alexandre and my children."

"There're many women who do just that to get enough food for their children."

"It worries me that my Alexandre still continues to do photos for false identity cards. Bernard said not to worry. Then Ernest and one of his friend, a Monsieur Renoux, came and made some amendments to the dark room and to the back door. My husband said that now he won't be surprised by someone, and his work can disappear in half a second. Still, I wish he wouldn't do that kind of work."

"Think of the people he helps save."

The meal over, some family members went to the sitting room, others stayed in the kitchen. Madeleine took a chair by Julie and Charmaine.

"I saw Mireille in the street, but she said she was too busy to chat."

Julie patted her arm. "She's a grown woman now. Time to let her do as she pleases. At least, she's working with Philippe."

"Yes, that's my consolation." She pulled a bunch of blank ration cards from her purse. "Those were extra after I had finished my workday. Do you want them?"

With effort, Julie restrained herself from snatching them. She took them gently. "Thank you so much, Madeleine. Anyone with children needs additional cards."

"And now there're categories, J1 for the little children."

"Right, and J2 for children like mine," Charmaine said.

"Yes, and my children, being older, are J3."

"German efficiency," Julie said. "Everyone in a slot. Let's go with the others."

***

Monday, November 11, 1940

Julie and Léonie left the cellar once the seven o'clock air-raid alert was over.

"It's pouring rain! Is that why they sounded the alarm?"

Léonie laughed. "You have something to show me?"

In Julie's kitchen, they examined a newssheet, a two-page production.

"First one," Julie said. "I've got my article, well just a few lines."

Friends,

Like me, you were puzzled by that vegetable that appeared on the grocer's shelves. The Rutabaga, A root vegetable used to feed cattle. But we don't need a ration ticket for it, so let's make the best of it for the sake of the children.

1. Wash your root thoroughly, peel it thinly but don't throw away the peel, put it in the soup - unless you need to feed the rabbit you're maybe raising in the bedroom.

2. The root is hard, so sharpen your knife and cut it into as thin slices as you can so they don't take too long to cook. Cover the slices with water and add a pinch of salt.

3. When cooked, put it through the vegetable mill. What doesn't pass through put it in the soup – or give it to the rabbit.

4. Add pepper and salt, and any spices you have on hand, to the puréed rutabaga. If you have a potato add it to the mix. If you have enough oil, you can fry small patties of the purée. It's quite palatable.

5. Another way is to roast the thin slices sprinkled with a pinch of salt.

More recipes to come. We, women, will not despair. We'll show the occupier that we're resourceful. We'll show them we're not going to take it lying down.

Léonie sputtered. "Lying down. Hint, hint! That's good!"

"This is the least we can do to tell the truth to the people," Julie said. "And maybe give some encouragement."

In the afternoon, Julie called on her in-laws just in case Bérangère had received a message for her. She had no message but kept turning a piece of hand-written paper in her hand. *Rendez-vous at five o'clock at the foot of Clémenceau's statue.* "Where are François and his cousins?"

"Probably on their way to the five o'clock rendez-vous, belle-maman."

At that moment Gontrand came out of the bedroom, crossed the kitchen to the door and slammed it behind him.

"What can I do? He's more stubborn than a mule. And with all his medals on display."

"He's been brooding for a while. I'll go after him."

Julie ran outside and kept her father-in-law in her sights at a safe distance. By the time they reached the roundabout of the Étoile, there was already a large crowd of young and not so young people, many carrying two long poles. Of course, *deux gaules*, de Gaulle. She bit her lips to stop smiling, and expected them to sing the Marseillaise, but everyone was quiet. Then, farther down the Champ-Élysées, a swirling movement displaced the human mass. Shouts and cries reverberated from the buildings, then the Marseillaise erupted from young throats, then gunfire. People fled. Others joined the column of people still walking toward the Arc de Triomphe. In the crush, Julie lost sight of her father-in-law. From a side street, a black Mercedes pushed its way onto the Champs-Élysées just when Julie caught a glimpse of Gontrand. She ran to him to attempt to drag him away. Suddenly, he was whisked away from her. She only had time to see the general and the captain manhandling him into the car and speeding off.

Relieved, she tried to return home. She bumped into three young girls, arm in arm, wearing blue, white and red shifts. She applauded the crazy girls but she couldn't tell them that wearing the colors of the banned French flag was dangerous. The youths all around her were determined. Her words would have no effect.

In the morning, Julie wrote a short article of encouragement to women readers, and a tip on how to grow dandelions indoors to use instead of lettuce and to make a coffee substitute with the root. Then she shopped for bread and made her way to the Manoir. An air of consternation reigned.

"What's going on?"

Bérangère sighed. "Daniel came by to say that François and Hughes had been arrested yesterday by men in civilian clothes. Must be our gendarmes since the Fritz confiscated their uniforms."

"Do you want me to go to the Préfecture and talk to Jacques?"

"He probably knows, but it'll be up to the Kommandant to say if and when they can be released. Pierrette didn't come home yesterday."

"I saw her with Xavier. He's got his head on his shoulders, he won't have let her go near the fracas," Julie said.

"I hope you're right. Gontrand's fuming. I sent him to the Bois with Lyse-May."

The scrape of shoes on the doormat attracted their attention.

"Come in, Pierrette. We were worried about you."

"Sorry, grand-maman. I was safe but couldn't get back before curfew. I went to class this morning, but the Krauts have closed the university. Dirty pigs!"

With a strange clatter from her feet, she started toward the backstairs and all eyes focused on her feet.

"What's that noise?" Bérangère asked.

"My new shoes. The cobbler couldn't repair my shoes' leather soles. This is the new style. Wooden soles, canvas uppers. Mine are half leather because the tops of my old shoes were still pretty good. The cobbler used what he could."

"Are they comfortable?" Julie asked.

"I'm getting used to them." She turned and climbed the stairs.

Bérangère pinned a loose curl back in place. "Shall we go to the attic and see what there is besides old dresses? It's getting so cold, maybe we'll find some warm garments we could alter for the children. Maybe some shoes."

"There might be some high button-boots from the last century."

They chuckled on their way to the attic. When they came down with their booty, Jacques was talking to Gontrand.

"You got your uniform back."

"The Chleus realized that taking them away was a stupid idea. So, I was saying that François and Hughes are in a holding cell with some others, and we have to detain them till tomorrow. I came to let you know. I've got to go back."

The news brought some relief to the de Montregards, together with the realization that no matter what advice they gave, the young people were going to do it their own way and learn the hard way.

Julie helped her mother-in-law sort through the clothes and shoes and store them on a shelf for the time being, before pedaling to Brigitte's apartment.

"Damien, you're not in school?"

"They closed the school... the Germans did."

Brigitte shrugged. "I heard it on Radio-Paris this morning. By order of the Kommandanture. Too bad, the school had heat. We don't in this building."

"Anything Gerhardt could do?"

A flush came to Brigitte's cheek. "He already brings milk and bread. I wouldn't ask him for anything, and, no, he isn't asking for... sex in return."

"He's a very decent fellow. Did you apply to the *Secours National*?"

"Yes, even though I hate what comes from that clown in Vichy with the grand name of National Aid. It's so humiliating to go there. Last time, I played the grand dame copying some of maman-Bérangère's airs. It worked. They didn't ask any of their stupid questions, which I've already answered on the form."

"Good for you. You should be a Shakespearian actress... On the other hand, maybe not. Shakespeare has been banned and his books burnt."

"How come the Shakespeare & Company bookstore is still open?"

"Madame Sylvia Beach is American. The United States of America is not at war. So the Germans can't touch her."

"Until the Americans enter the war."

"They don't want to. But maybe they'll help with weapons and food. Not us, of course, but England. Though, they have to get through the German blockade. Won't be easy."

"Fortunately I have my widow's pension now," Brigitte said.

This was met with a roar of laughter.

"I've applied for mine. Let's just hope we never need it for real."

"Right. Anyway, I must run now. Oh, I came to say Bérangère has taken some clothing and boots down from the attic. Next time you go, take a look."

"Will do."

While Julie mulled over what kind of work she could try to do beside the little she did for Bernard, and her widow's pension whenever she got it. The red tape was horrendous, and some women had to re-apply more than once. She coasted on her bicycle down the street. Near a bakery, she spotted Lyse-May pick something off the ground. Julie got off her bicycle and followed her niece into the store. There was a customer standing by the cash register.

"Bonjour madame," Lyse-May said to the baker. "I found a card of bread ration tickets outside."

The two women, without noticing Julie by the empty bread rack, stared at the child. Then the customer snatched the sheet of tickets from Lyse-May's hand. "They're mine."

Julie was about to say something when Lyse-May straightened her spine even more and displayed a royal haughty look. With the innocence of childhood, she knew in that instant the woman was lying. Julie seized her niece's hand and threw a murderous look at the baker and customer before leaving the store.

Outside, Lyse-May heaved a big sigh. "She's a liar."

"You're right, sweetie. But bad things happens to bad people. She'll choke on the bread. What are you doing here?" She wheeled the bicycle along the sidewalk.

Lyse-May blushed. "I went to listen to the music."

"You like the German band?"

"I don't think about them being German. Mémée said music has no natio..."

"Nationality, it's true. Did you tell anyone you were going to the open air concert?"

Lyse-May's head tilted toward her aunt. "You won't tell, will you?"

"Only if you promise to always let someone know where you're going."

Relief in her voice, the child said, "I promise."

Julie knew Lyse-May well enough. She'd keep that promise.

***

François' release was welcomed with joy.

"Now, I hope you've learnt your lesson," Gontrand said.

A defiant expression on his tired face, the adolescent replied, "Yes, grand-papa, I learned one lesson." He strode to the bathroom.

Julie and Bérangère shook their heads at the same time. "Not the lesson beau-papa hoped he'd learn."

"If only my husband would shed his Pétain adoration!"

Pierrette clattered downstairs and put clean clothes inside the bathroom door. "Keep him here. I've got work to do. Please remind him he has to check in at the police station every day."

"We will."

"Since university is closed, what work is she talking about?" Bérangère asked.

"Maybe at the soup kitchen that just opened in Belleville?"

"She could have said so. I'd think it's more like distributing tracts."

"Tracts inform people about things they don't hear from Radio-Paris or read in those poor excuses for newspapers we're allowed to buy. I must go, belle-maman."

***

Julie parked her bicycle in the courtyard and hoped to slip inside without Madame Durand noticing. Luck wasn't with her. The concierge was waiting for her.

"Madame Julie, a man came to see you but didn't leave a note when I told him you were out."

"Did you ask for his name?"

"A funny name he has. Lasss Gunsson. It hisses like a snake. Do you know him? He wasn't German"

"Lars Gunnarsson. Did he say he'd come back?"

"He did. Who is he?"

"He heads an organization for children. I work there sometimes."

"That's good then. Do you have any tip about where to get extra food?"

"Alas, non, madame. I'll let you know if I hear something."

The concierge went back into her loge. Julie had barely closed her apartment door than there came a knock. She opened the door and Lars stepped inside.

"Julie, dear. I thought that woman would never stop talking."

"A common trait among concierges. You're here on business, I guess."

"We have five children that we want to send to Switzerland. Two sisters five and eight, and three boys eight and nine."

"How do we get there?"

"We have a passeur with a horse and cart who will meet you at the Pontarlier train station and take you through the forest to the Swiss border. You'll know he's the right person. Watch his béret. The children will have to dash across the thirty-meter exclusion zone. They know that and have practiced running where they are at the moment. One of the Swiss border guards will take the children to a safe home."

"Easy as pie, right? What about the Germans guarding this side of the border?"

"The passeur has timed the patrols."

A tremor of excitement ran through Julie. If she could get those Jewish children across to safety she'd feel as good as if she had punched a German soldier on the nose before sticking a dagger in his heart. "When do we leave?"

"Tomorrow, by the night train. You'll be followed. Don't try to make contact."

"Followed to report if something goes wrong, right?"

"I hope everything goes well. There may be a little snow already there."

"We'll manage."

He handed her one-way train tickets and a few bills. "For any incidentals and to book your return ticket from wherever you're going to be."

Next day, Julie wore her hiking boots and shopped as usual. With the cold weather setting in, boots wouldn't attract undue attention. She told Léonie she'd be away for a couple of days. At the Manoir she sought out Pierrette to ask her to let Bernard know, even though he might already be aware.

At the end of the afternoon, wearing her warmest clothes, Julie took the Métro. She carried a large handbag, as most women now did. At Reuilly, she got off and walked to the given address on Boulevard Diderot. The concierge's loge door opened before she needed to knock. She greeted each child with a kiss and memorized their faces. Without words, they followed her through the inner courtyard, into another courtyard, through an apartment building lobby, and out onto rue Hector-Malo. Bless the architects who connected buildings in that way. A short walk took them to the station. No incident disturbed their journey.

As Julie and her charges emerged from the Pontarlier station, a wiry man took off his béret. He stepped closer to Julie and put his béret back on. Julie could have laughed. Frenchmen never take off their bérets. She nodded in acknowledgement. They shook hands and he helped her shepherd the children into a waiting horse-drawn wagon. When they were out of the town on a country road, the passeur told Julie there was a basket of food under the front bench.

"We'll arrive late afternoon, when they're changing the guard. We'll stop at noon for a rest."

They soon entered the dense mountainous forest. The going was slow on the steep trail and the children were nervous. Julie taught them a silent game played on hands and fingers. Now and them a giggle broke the silence.

They reached a plateau and the passeur stopped the horse. A smattering of snow covered the ground. The children climbed down. He turned the wagon around.

"From here we go on foot. If I don't make it back tonight Anna, that's my horse, she'll go home. We have to be very quiet now."

Julie recognized the unspoken acceptance that such a mission could mean death. Anxiety and exhilaration threatened to submerge her. She swallowed, then checked the children's shoes, retied laces and buttoned up coats. They followed the man in the béret, who said he had no name. He took the five-year-old's hand and from time to time swung her up into his arms. After an hour's walk, he gestured to stop and crouch. The children were tired enough and lay down in the new snow. Next to the passeur, Julie glanced at her watch.

He brought his mouth to her ear. "No noise now. We'll see the patrol come up, turn round, and go back. It's their last round, they'll hurry back. That gives us exactly five minutes, not a second more, to send the children across."

Another nerve wracking moment passed. Snowflakes drifted down.

"Now!"

The layer of snow reflected the last light of the day. The children sprang to their feet and ran straight ahead. In the middle of the exclusion zone, the five-year-old stumbled and fell. Her sister pulled her up and they resumed running, just as the German guards appeared round the corner.

"*Halt!*"

The children kept running. The two guards raised their rifles and took aim.

From the Swiss side, the border guards shouted in German, "Don't shoot! The children are in the exclusion zone. We will return fire!"

The Germans hesitated. Then lowered their weapons. Ready to explode, Julie's heartbeat began to slow down. She could barely distinguished the children's silhouettes in the increasing curtain of falling snow. The Swiss and the German guards exchanged insults. The passeur pulled her back. They slithered on the uneven snowy ground, making a faint noise that sounded like drums and trumpets to Julie's ears. When they no longer could hear yelling, they stood up and, as silently as possible, hurried toward the plateau. The Germans were bound to start searching the woods. She sent a silent prayer of thanks to mother nature who had sent the snow, now falling heavily enough to erase their tracks.

By the time they reached the wagon, the snow had thickened and visibility was low. With one swift movement, the passeur almost threw Julie up onto the wagon seat. The good horse, Anna, lurched forward just as the passeur gained his seat. The snow muffled the noise of the horse's hooves. The mare knew the way and didn't slow down until they reached the valley. There was no snow there.

Julie looked around her. "Is this the road we took on the way up? Maybe I don't recognize it. It's getting dark."

Her companion chuckled. "Good observation. I'm going to take you to the Cluse. The guards might have alerted Pontarlier. Probably not as they'd have to explain why some children got away, but we don't know. We'll spend the night at this charcoal burner's hut you can see ahead."

"The curfew?"

"We can't get to the Cluse in time. By the way, I'm known as Émile, aka Mimile."

"I'm just Julie."

She helped her new friend unharness the horse and, while she fed her the small amount of hay and oats stored under the benches in the wagon, Mimile fetched a bucket of water from the rain barrel. From under the bench seat, Julie pulled out the box containing the last of the food. Conversation didn't last long. They wrapped themselves in blankets and lay down on the rude bunks in the hut and fell asleep.

***

Once Julie was seated in the train in Lons-le-Saulnier, the adrenaline that had kept her going left her system, leaving her thirsty and exhausted. But it wasn't until she closed her apartment door behind her that she felt utterly drained. Mental fatigue rather than physical. She picked up Claire's photo off the mantelpiece and clutched it to her chest. *My darling angel, your spirit was with me to save five children this time.*

The first thing Julie did was to take a bath despite the lack of hot water. She rubbed herself vigorously and donned a robe. Stale bread wasn't so appetizing but she munched on it. She'd hardly made a dent in it when there was a knock on the door. Tempted to ignore it, she put her bread down and opened the door.

"Oh, Charmaine. Come in."

The young woman dropped onto a chair and leaned on the table. Julie poured a cup of ersatz coffee.

"Drink this absolutely awful stuff that is now replacing coffee."

"Thanks. I just don't know, just don't know..."

Julie waited but Charmaine didn't speak. "What is it?"

"Wolfang took me out to supper last night, then we went to his suite at the Hôtel du Louvre to rehearse. That part was very good. He's really talented. I expected him to undress me when we finished. I didn't know what to do. Was I supposed to undress myself? But he simply told me it was time to go home and took me back. Is he for real?"

"The theory for companionship holds."

"He said he'll throw a reception for some of the brass and we'll perform."

"He wants to impress colleagues and superiors by showing off a beautiful woman who has great talent."

"I don't know what to think."

"Do you like him?"

"He's so nice. I don't dislike him. Though I resent the blackmail."

"It'd be dangerous not to comply, so go ahead, let feelings for liking him come to the surface. It'll be more natural, easier when..."

Charmaine put her hands on her face. "I love Alexandre. I gave up my dream to be an opera singer for him."

"That's why you'll do whatever is necessary for him."

Charmaine took both Julie's hands in hers. "You're always such comfort for everyone. I'm going to remember your words and relax. I'll need an evening gown."

"Come and take a look in my closet."

A shimmering emerald green dress with spaghetti straps suited Charmaine best.

"But it's a shade too long for you. Let's go to see Bérangère. She'll alter it."

"You sure you want to give it to me? What if I spill soup on it?"

They laughed, stopped and laughed some more till they were out of breath.

"I needed that," Julie said. "Take this shawl. It goes with the dress."

Soon afterward, Bérangère worked her magic on the dress. "I'll restyle a couple of those antiquated dresses for you."

"Thank you, maman-Bérangère. Even though he wants to buy me dresses, I've refused."

"I should hope so."

The three women giggled and kissed one another goodnight.

It was close to curfew time. Deep in thought, Julie ambled toward her apartment building. Hurried, staccato steps resonated behind her. From farther away came the unmistakable clatter of heavy boots. Before she could think, she was grabbed at the waist and pulled into a coach gate entrance.

An out-of-breath man wrapped her in an intimate embrace and murmured, "Help me." Her back was to the street. Instinctively, she gave in to the kiss just as a German patrol happened upon them.

The man buried his face in her neck as she turned toward the soldiers, her lipstick sufficiently mussed up. "*Guten Nacht*."

A flow of German followed her greeting.

"Sorry, I don't speak your language." Her heart was pounding and she could feel the man's heart knocking in his chest.

"Did you see a man run this way?" One of the soldiers said in passable French.

"No, sir."

"Go home." They resumed running along Dufrenoy.

Cautiously, she eased herself out of the man's arms.

"Thank you. You saved my life," he said.

"You better come with me. My apartment is close by."

Like a pair of lovers, they hurried along avenue Victor-Hugo. Once inside her apartment, Julie leaned against the closed door and let out a long breath. "That was scary."

"I'm sorry I put you in such danger."

"Danger is my daily companion. Anyway, you'll stay in the guest room. The bathroom is at the end of the corridor."

"I ought to leave."

She looked him up and down. He was a handsome, well-built man. "Of course not. You'd get caught. That patrol must have alerted others, and it's curfew now."

"Why would you risk your life for a stranger?"

"A stranger who did something to displease the Germans is a stranger worth helping."

The man burst out laughing. “Merci. I’m Armand.”

“I’m Julie. Goodnight.”

Armand took a step forward and folded her in his arms. Awareness passed between them. He took her lips. She responded. It was a satisfying kiss. With a smile, they parted and went to their respective bedrooms.

After breakfast, Armand and Julie left the apartment together. The streets were calm. With a brief kiss, they parted at the corner of Victor-Hugo and rue de la Faisanderie. She watched him walk toward Boulevard Henri-Martin and she retraced her steps toward the Manoir. Her lips still tingled from this light kiss.

***

Two days later, Charmaine visited Julie.

“I want to hear everything.”

“The day before his party he came to pick me up just after lunch in his Duesenberg.”

“Wow, sporty and chic. I wonder who used to own it before it was requisitioned.”

“I know, it really makes me sick. We went to the café Capoulade on Boulevard Saint-Michel. Three senior officers – I’m beginning to recognize some ranks now – were there. Wolfgang and the other officers did a lot of talking and laughing and I had to sit with them.”

“You definitely were on show.”

“And most uncomfortable, believe me. But I put on a good face, spoke nicely when they spoke in French. Then I excused myself on the pretext I had to fetch my children from school. He offered to drive me to their schools. It was hard to decline but I think I convinced the other officers that the children and I walk home together to talk about school.” Charmaine took a deep breath.

“Now the reception.”

“I gave a good performance. When everyone left, Wolfang took me home. Do you think he doesn’t like women?”

“He takes you home, never kisses you. Simple, he’s attracted to men, not women.”

“We did a couple of pseudo kisses for the benefit of the audience. I initiated those because I thought that’s what lovers would do.”

“You were perfect.”

“Why did he pick me to go out with him, though?”

“He stumbled on Alexandre forging papers and seized the opportunity to blackmail you. Homosexuality is not well-regarded in the SS. They see it as a social disease.”

“So I’m just a shield for him. At least my virtue will remain intact. I really hate all of it. The neighbors were being unpleasant but Gus went to talk to them, in his own way. Now they ignore me. That’s fine.”

“Courage, they won’t be here forever.”

“You’re right. I’ll go now.”

***

Sunday morning, Julie, bundled up in her coat and scarf, headed to Brigitte's to help with the children in weather that had turned bitterly cold. She turned the corner of rue Mignard in time to see a black Mercedes move away. A half-smile lit up her chilled face. She turned and hurried to the Manoir, where she was the last one to arrive.

Bérangère greeted her. "Come in, you're frozen. Did you bicycle here?"

Julie glanced around the kitchen. "No, I took a nice healthy walk."

Laughter erupted. Brigitte blushed and was about to speak, but Julie sat next to her and kicked her under the table.

Jacques rubbed his arms. "Let's make more balls of paper for the stove and wet them. They'll burn slower."

Everyone including the adolescents grabbed pages of the newspaper and set to work.

"There's no relief in sight from this freezing. It must be a hundred-year record for the season. It doesn't stop the résistance activities though," Jacques said.

All eyes were trained on him.

Gontrand's loud voice cut short François' attempted reply. "Résistance? What resistance?"

"Would that be the tracts that we find in the letterboxes or find in a pocket when we leave the Métro, or all that graffiti on German posters?" Bérangère asked in a casual voice.

Jacques confirmed what she said.

"Nobody is going to do résistance under my roof!" Thunder was mild compared to Gontrand's booming voice. "Maréchal Pétain wants citizens to be obedient--"

He was booed by the adolescents. "You mean collaborate, grand-papa. How can you still defend him after he shook Hitler's hand?" Pierrette spoke in a calm voice.

Gontrand lowered his head and mumbled under his breath. Lyse-May climbed onto his lap. He kissed his granddaughter and the conversation resumed. It was agreed to hold Christmas at the Manoir, as usual, but only the children should receive gifts.

That evening, General von Trennen's reception was in full swing. Bérangère and François stepped into the ballroom. Officers representing all the branches of the German military lounged on chairs and armchairs. François gritted his teeth. Reynard announced they would play Vittorio Monti's Czardas that he had arranged for two violins, with piano accompaniment. François inhaled deeply and kept his eyes glued to his mentor. The music did its magic. He forgot about the enemy audience.

In the low attic above the ballroom, Julie, Pierrette and Lyse-May sprawled on their bellies next to a vent listened to the music.

***

On Tuesday, December 24, François and Pierrette met their cousins and friends in front of a red poster announcing that Jacques Bonsergent had been executed for having fought against German soldiers. They each deposited a bouquet. They heard the slap of leather soles against the pavement. Soldiers had now been issued boots without hobnails. They ran back to the Manoir to help prepare the traditional Christmas réveillon. The anticipation of a larger than usual meal gave them wings. Though this year the family decided to skip the midnight mass which would be held early to enable parishioners to get home before the special midnight curfew.

Philippe had driven Madeleine and Alexandre, and his family, in his new Citroën. He unloaded a large bag and a grocery bag.

Gontrand stood to face him. "How dare you come to flaunt your car and your food?"

"Cool it, father. Madeleine bought it all with our ration tickets. *Joyeux Noël.* Thank you but I won't stay." He kissed his wife and children before leaving.

Bérangère sighed and hugged Madeleine. At that moment, Jacques arrived in civilian clothes and shared the general sadness.

"The first man shot in Paris," Bernard said.

"The Boches are showing their true colors," Alexandre said. "Do you know why he was in a fight?"

Jacques nodded. "He was an engineer, appreciated by all who knew him. He was accompanying a friend who had just got married. His friend came to see me and told me that the drunken soldiers had grabbed his wife. To free her he'd punched one of the Germans. Bonsergent separated them and they all ran, but some Germans caught up with him, or rather recognized him because he was tall. Such an unnecessary death. His friend wanted to turn himself in, but there's no point. The Germans wanted to set an example. There was no trial, nothing. Arrest and death."

A silence fell. Bérangère broke it by saying, "Children, take your seats at the table."

The adults stood up and helped the children sit.

"Who will say the *bénédicité?*" Bérangère asked.

No one moved. Lyse-May kneeled on Gontrand's chair at the head of the table. "I will."

Everyone bowed their heads.

"*Monsieur le Bon Dieu*, we thank you for the food we have today and please take care of our family and our friends. And, Mister God, tell our angels, Claire, Uncle Florent and the man Bonsergent that we love them. Amen."

Eyes misted over. Innocently, Sylvestre broke the spell by banging his spoon on his empty plate. When they finished eating, the children played games in the spare room and in the sitting room, while their parents ate. The older children sent an emissary to inquire when they would get their presents. The response was the same every time: "Midnight." But midnight being the special curfew for this festive day, presents were going to be distributed earlier. The younger children didn't know the difference. It was past their bedtime and they did their best to stay awake.

Finally, with the meal over and dishes done, they adjourned to the sitting room. Cries of *Joyeux Noël* resonated through the house and the youngsters tore off the brown paper to reveal presents of shoes and other useful items. The knock on the door was barely heard. Marie, who carried a pot of strawberry jam, and Ernest let themselves in.

"There're guests for you, madame," Marie said. She stepped aside to let in Reynard von Trennen and Gerhardt Langen, bearing a box of packages, also wrapped in brown paper.

"Allow me, madame Bérangère, to give a few trinkets to the children," Reynard said in the surprised silence.

Rose and Daniel moved toward the door. Reynard lifted his hand and spoke in German. "You have nothing to fear from me."

François nudged his friend's shoulder. "I told you he's good."

The 'trinkets' were books for the adolescents, wooden toys from the toy factory in Seiffen for the little ones, and wool sweaters for each member of the family, including Xavier, who had been invited by Pierrette.

Brigitte elbowed Julie. "How did he know about Rose and the knitting business?"

"He's in the business of knowing everybody's business. Just kidding. He went to the studio to have his portrait done. Charmaine has a display. At his request, she organized the sweaters with Rose."

Marie re-entered the sitting room, carrying a large traditional bûche de Noël cake. Half asleep children woke up suddenly at the sight of the log-shaped cake with real chocolate butter cream, sugar mushrooms and elves.

"Monsieur le général provided all the ingredients to the baker and paid him too," Marie said to Bérangère and Julie. "In real francs. He's a fair man."

Suddenly Julie remembered they hadn't celebrated Lyse-May's fourth birthday. She sidled up to Bérangère. "Lyse-May's been with us over a year and we never celebrated a birthday."

"Mon Dieu! I don't even know the exact date. Is she only four?"

"She could be five. She's so advanced."

"I'm pretty sure she was born in summer."

"Shall we make it today?"

Von Trennen turned round. "There is an extra gift in the box. Would you give it to her? It's for a little girl."

Stupefied, Julie stood while her mind tried to process his words. There was no time for that. Shrieks of delight and a chorus of happy birthday wishes were showered on a radiant Lyse-May. She carefully unwrapped a delicate wooden doll, with moving arms and legs, and dressed like a princess.

Amid the happy noises, Julie approached Reynard and looked into his kind eyes.

"I don't know how to thank you, Herr von Trennen. You've been so kind to us."

"I want people to know that not all the Germans are rabid Nazis."

Troubled by the blue eyes that looked at her, she shook his hand. Blue eyes, slightly almond-shaped with long, light-brown eyelashes, like Claire's. The only one in the whole family on Sylvain's side, or her own, to have blond hair and blue eyes. Reynard obviously knew exactly who the children were in the family. She was pretty sure that he had ordered the famous Seiffen wooden toys long before Christmas. Long before he knew that Claire was no longer with them. That doll was to go to Claire.

François had fetched his violin a while ago. He handed Julie a flute. "It's an old flute, Rudell something Rose I think, but grand-maman says it works."

"I haven't practiced for a long time."

"You never forget music. It's always inside you."

"Thanks, I'll try." She was thankful to be drawn away from her troubling thoughts.

Reynard asked, "Shall we go to the ballroom and make music?"

Heads turned toward Bérangère.

Gontrand replied, "In the spirit of Christmas, we'll go."

The children's shrieks of delight at the tall Christmas tree in the ballroom brought smiles all round. Gerhardt lit a few candles on the tree to a chorus of oohs and aahs.

"Do we have somebody under twenty years old?"

A chorus of "me, me", answered him. He gestured to the brightly colored bags under the tree. Sylvestre was already crawling toward the treats. The other children kneeled carefully. The adolescents waited patiently.

Music and songs echoed from the Manoir's venerable stone walls.

Then it was time to part and get home before the curfew. Gerhardt drove Alexandre and his family as well as Brigitte in the Mercedes, with the laughing sleepy children all piled up on one another.

Lyse-May trotted up to Julie. "You're bunking with me? I want you to stay, mama Julie."

***

Paris, Tuesday, December 31, 1940

This dreadful year comes to an end. The next doesn't look any better. I don't remember when it has been this cold. There're fifteen centimeters of snow in Paris, and more in the country. I listened to the BBC and heard de Gaulle asking the French to stay indoors between three and four o'clock tomorrow. This will be easy to adhere to. It's so cold I don't think anybody wants to be out, anyway.

Nothing to eat, no bread in the stores. I am perpetually worried about the children. They need nutritious food. Rutabaga is all fiber, no food value for people. Dédé made a trip and brought a large bag of lentils. Bless his soul. I shared it with the family. I took some to my dear friend Bernadette for her to share with her tenants. She was looking at a rutabaga and crying. I gave her Julie's recipe in the newssheet Résistance and asked Rose to help her.

All day long the wind howled, getting everywhere inside the house. Life in

Paris is getting very difficult. We have ration tickets for food but the stores are empty. I must stop complaining. The theaters and the cinemas are doing good business. People go because there they have heat. Can't let the German audience freeze their behinds! For a treat with my earnings from Robi, I took my daughters-in-law, and of course that included Brigitte and Charmaine, to the cinema. Gontrand was roped in to watch Brigitte's children. What a lark!

At the cinema, we were subjected to the Newsreel. A farce that is, all concocted by the propaganda bureau. We, along with most of the audience, booed. Some German came on the loudspeaker to say if we continue to boo they would leave the lights on. We quieted because we wanted to see the film, La fille du puisatier. You can count on the writer Marcel Pagnol to be funny about the daughter of a well digger man. It was good to laugh again.

We won't have a new year's réveillon, not enough food for a big meal. Marie brought a box of canned food to the kitchen. Said it was surplus. I know where it comes from. The gentleman doesn't want to hurt our feelings.

Our adolescents are very involved with their scout movement. As long as the scouting is under the control of a church, the Germans are allowing it. I should be happy because scouting is a healthy activity, but those youths have other ideas about the occupiers.

I'm so sad François gave up the idea of going to the Conservatory of Music. He said he's making huge progress with Reynard – that's what we're beginning to call him – and the other musician, can't recall his name, conductor of the Wehrmacht orchestra.

Time to hide my rambling prose.

Chapter Thirty-Nine

New Year's Eve 1940

Wolfang Ziegler parked his Duesenberg in front of the photo studio and waited. A minute later, Charmaine came out from the side door, wearing high boots and carrying her shoes in a bag. He jumped out to help her into the car. She tightened her coat around herself and took careful steps in the thick snow.

"You need a better coat, Charmaine. I can get you one."

"No, thank you. I have accepted milk for my children and that's enough."

"You are doing me a great favor by entertaining my friends and colleagues tonight. I would like to reward you."

"Wolfang, you're protecting my family. I'm very grateful. Besides, you're such a talented pianist and I genuinely enjoy singing for you... and your guests."

At the Hôtel du Louvre, Wolfang got out, while a hotel porter rushed to open the car door for Charmaine. One of the guards drove the car away. Wolfang cupped Charmaine's elbow and guided her to his suite. She didn't know what he was doing in the SS and preferred not to know. Julie had passed on what she learned from Jacques. The Hôtel du Louvre was the headquarters for the Sonderkommando unit, which dealt with workers throughout the Reich. She didn't want to know more than that.

In the suite, Wolfang took her coat and boots. She smoothed her dress and went to the bathroom to fix her hair.

When she emerged, he said, "You look beautiful."

"Thank you."

"The maids have prepared a luncheon. Would you please make sure that it fits the occasion?"

Charmaine mentally thanked Bérangère for being so strict on manners and ways to conduct a household. It now came naturally to her. Poised and regal, she inspected the buffet. The maids, visibly ill at ease, and a butler stood pressed against the wall.

A smile stretched her lips. "This is very nicely presented. Thank you all. Did you ensure the kitchens have plenty in reserve?"

The maids relaxed. "Yes ma'am. We remembered your recommendations."

Charmaine then addressed the butler. "I see no wine from Alsace but I think the guests would appreciate a couple of bottles. Add an Alsace Grand Cru Attenberg de Bergheim Gewurztraminer to the buffet, please."

"Right away, ma'am."

Wolfang sat at the piano. “Let’s warm up my fingers and your voice.”

They did their warm-up exercises until the first guests arrived.

It was almost two in the morning when Wolfang drove Charmaine home. He stood by her door until she was inside and had locked it.

Alexandre was still up. “How was the concert?”

“It went very well, but I thought those guests would never leave. We were running out of encores.”

“Did he...?”

“No. I told you. He’s very respectful and only interested in music.”

Alexandre raked fingers through his hair. “I don’t understand how a handsome man cannot want more from a beautiful woman.”

Charmaine bit her lip. She couldn’t tell her husband Julie’s theory about Wolfang. “It’s the same as your friendship with Madame Vaillant. If you weren’t at home, I could always find you at the Jeu de Paume with Madame Vaillant engrossed in discussing old paintings.”

“I think I’m jealous.”

She kissed him to make him forget his jealousy.

***

January, 1941

Madeleine and Julie bumped into each other at the courtyard entrance.

“I’ve brought a leg of mutton,” Madeleine said.

“Very, nice. Make sure to tell our father-in-law that you saved your meat tickets or he might throw you out.”

“Do you think so? I paid for it with my own money.”

“I know, Madeleine, but Gontrand is ready to explode over the smallest thing. And you must have got it on the black-market.”

“I’ll just say nothing and put it on the counter.”

They slipped into the kitchen. Marie poked her head in to announce that Bérangère wasn’t back from shopping.

They sat in the kitchen. Madeleine extracted a folded sheet of paper from her purse. “This was in my pigeonhole at work. It’s not the things I deal with. Do you know what it means? There’re names of people we know. What should I do? I wanted to give it back to the supervisor, but he’d already left.”

Julie examined the list of names. Her brain went into overdrive. A couple names she recognized as acquaintances she knew were communists, while others were unmistakably Jewish. That list must have been made by someone who took collaboration to heart and was about to turn it in to the Germans. The word Gestapo was being whispered in the queues. She knew what that meant for the people on the list. She memorized the names of the acquaintances.

“You understand that nowadays it is dangerous to be in possession of a list, any list? It could lend you in deep trouble with the police.”

“Philippe wouldn’t let anything happen to me. He has friends in high places.”

“I know. Good for him.” She choked on her words. “But sometimes it’s best to avoid trouble altogether. I suggest we burn this list so no one knows you've seen it."

"But the person who made the list will know it's missing."

"He won't. He doesn't know he put it in the wrong pigeonhole."

"He can always make it again."

Julie swallowed hard. "That's right."

"You're so smart."

Julie crumpled the sheet of paper and cautiously placed it in the stone sink. With shaky hands, she struck a match and they watched the flames devour the offending list.

"What if I get another list?"

"Just bring it to me, I'll deal with it."

Madeleine worried her bottom lip. "Tell me, why is Bernard so mad at Philippe?"

Julie stiffened. How could she tell her sister-in-law, a woman who was a shallow thinker and who saw no harm in benefitting from her husband's Nazi connections, that her apartment in the exclusive Neuilly district belonged to a Jewish family who had been told to move out? They might even be in prison right now, or maybe dispatched to a camp like the ones she'd heard about. "They have different political views and you know what men are like when they talk politics. Each thinks his is the only right one."

"That's true."

"They'll patch up in time."

"I see. Though I wish the in-laws would accept the food I bring them."

Julie was struck by an inspiration. "Maybe instead of food you could bring a ration card from time to time."

Madeleine brightened up. "I can do that. I often have more than what matches the identity cards."

"Good. That'll help."

"Philippe's really busy. He's buying stores that the Jews owners have abandoned and setting a manager in them. He said he buys them for a song. Such a wonderful opportunity!"

Julie gritted her teeth and wished Bérangère would hurry up and arrive. "I'll start cooking some pasta and prepare your leg of lamb. So no one will question where it came from." She cut thin strips of the meat and put them in a skillet.

"You're so kind and smart, Julie. Not like me."

"Don't speak like that. Being smart is different for everyone. You're a good mother and a generous person. Plus, you're beautiful."

"Thank you. I always feel good after talking to you."

Bérangère caught the last of the conversation and contented herself with greetings. François arrived with his friend Daniel. Julie grabbed a piece of the lamb, cut a length of the long bread and placed the meat inside. "À plus tard!"

"See you later." Bérangère's frown told Julie she'd be waiting for an explanation.

Julie trudged through the snow while she ate her sandwich. She remembered where Monsieur Raymond Leblanc lived on rue Sainte-Apoline. She hoped his wife, Denise, would be home. Her sandwich finished, she went down the entrance to the closest Métro station. She got off at the Strasbourg-Saint-Denis station, and soon found the apartment building.

"Bonjour Madame Leblanc."

"How nice of you to call. In these troubled times, no one visits anymore."

"Being blunt, people are frightened to be associated with someone with different political affiliations."

"Because communists are being arrested by the French police, right? Because the USSR has a pact with Hitler, right?"

"Correct. I came to warn you. Your and your husband's names were on a list I came across. So were two of your friends. I destroyed the list, but someone could remake it."

She scratched her forehead. "So, we have a day or two to disappear?"

"I think that would be a good idea."

"Merci. I'll warn our friends and organize a trip to the countryside. Give my regards to Madame Montregard."

With a smile, Julie nodded, aware that, as a communist, the woman deliberately omitted the noble *de* from the de Montregard family name. She admired people who lived by their strong convictions, though she didn't extend that admiration to Kurt or any of his Nazi friends, who also had strong convictions of another kind. A wave of satisfaction at being able to help enveloped her. Simon and Marguerite Bloch were on the list, but had long since departed Paris. It amused her to imagine the Gestapo coming to the fourth floor of her building and be confronted by the SS officers. Her next call to a well-to-do Jewish family didn't go as well.

They didn't believe her.

She returned to the Manoir and gave her mother-in-law the reason for her strange behavior. They agreed to keep Madeleine out of it.

The snow slowed Julie down as she made her way home. A car drove up slowly. She started.

"Let me give you a ride, Julie."

A flash of dislike ran through her. There was no way to avoid it, no store to dive into. "I'm fine, Kurt, and almost home."

"I insist."

She didn't like the tone. "Well, thank you." She climbed into the passenger seat and prayed he'd drive to her building, not take her somewhere else.

"It is too cold to be out."

"It's warm enough in the Métro."

"Do you still work for the Red Cross?"

Was he fishing or did he really not know? She edged. "I am, but there's nothing at the moment. I do some work with the orphanages."

"You could work for me. I need a hostess."

Sure you do! "I much prefer to work with children, Kurt."

He stopped the Citroën in front of her door. "Could I change your mind? It's well paid."

"Thanks for the ride. I see the concierge is waiting. She might want to talk to you about your friends. They don't speak French as well as you do and she can't understand them."

He pulled a face of distaste. "I'm not speaking to that... concierge."

Julie laughed. He took her hand.

"I like it when you laugh. It reminds me of our days in Heidelberg."

She tugged her hand. He released her. She hurried out.

Madame Durand pounced on her before she could close the door. She made a show of wiping her boots on the door mat.

"Getting driven home by those SS?"

"Remember there are things we have to do to remain safe. And refusing to ride with him isn't one of them."

Madame Durand made a throaty noise before speaking normally. "Mademoiselle Yolande came and asked me to give you a message. She heard in the queue that there was meat to be had near the Halles market."

Julie remained impassive. "Nice of her to let me know."

"She didn't have to come in this weather. She could have phoned."

"Remember that the Germans listen in to phone conversations. Not a good idea to tell them meat can be obtained without ration tickets."

"Of course, you're right."

"By the way, I'm expecting a friend. So don't be alarmed if you see a stranger coming up."

"Not a board member this time?"

"Non, just a colleague from the work I do for the Red Cross." The old gossip didn't need to know the job was basically over. "I'll go and see if I can get meat. I'll bring you some."

Back in her apartment, Julie drank a big glass of water. She straightened her clothes, secured a warm cloche hat on her head and set off with a couple of shopping bags. She hoped she understood the message. Yolande had a new address, 4 rue du Bouloi, in addition to her apartment at 88 rue Laugier. A final Métro connection at the Châtelet, and her next stop was Les Halles. After the heat in the Métro, she shivered while she made her way to the building.

"I thought you'd never get here!" Yolande said. "What took you so long?"

"It's an involved story."

A young man stepped forward.

"Meet Roland Dupuis, fighter pilot in the RAF." Yolande said. A saucy smile hovered on her lips.

Julie started. "Don't kid me, the last one to use that identity is safely in England."

"The identity came back in someone's pocket."

"I won't ask who."

"I don't know anyway. Bernard just handed it to me."

"I'm known as Tony Morel in real life."

Julie had to recount her day. "Now, my instructions, please?"

"You need to take Roland to his next stop. A bit different this time. Since he speaks French with almost no accent, he'll be going to Brittany as a farm laborer, but not on his own. He'll have company all the way."

"I'm a lucky man if the company is as pretty as you two ladies."

The tension left Julie's body while they laughed.

"You have to take him home with you until we get the nod for departure. I can't take him to my apartment. My concierge writes letters to the German authorities and tells them about the neighbors who buy on the black market. She's a viper. She'd give me a lecture about an unmarried woman bringing men to her apartment. Maybe even denounce me as a loose woman."

"Despicable. I already told Madame Durand that I was expecting a friend and she expects a piece of meat from me."

"I got that." Yolande put two small packages in Julie's shopping bag. "The Ritz chef had some extra."

Julie laughed. "You devious woman. Thanks, anyhow."

"Let's go. The friends who live here will be back soon. Roland you're my boyfriend till we get past the nosy concierge."

"I'll enjoy that."

She swatted him and they set out toward the Métro.

"Shouldn't we be better take a vélo-taxi?" Julie asked. "Some still run despite the cold and slushy snow."

"If we see one before we get to the station. Let's walk to the Châtelet. If not, we'll take the Métro there."

There was a tandem vélo-taxi and two young men trying to keep warm on the curb. They were glad of the business. Passengers and cyclists alike got splashed with wet snow from the few passing German automobiles. Yolande gave the young men a large tip. Roland took her by the waist and nuzzled her neck. Julie suppressed her laughter and hoped Yolande was enjoying the scene. Madame Durand was delighted with her packet of meat.

In the apartment, they pored over the details of Roland's next step on his journey to his homeland. Yolande left by the servant stairs, across the courtyard and out by the coach door to avoid Madame Durand, even though they presumed she'd be busy cooking her meat.

The next day being a Sunday, Julie invited Roland to the Manoir.

Roland Dupuis, introduced as a colleague, received a warm welcome. He handed the meat to Bérangère and Julie gave the last of her potatoes.

After the déjeuner, Charmaine asked François to play so that the tradition of making music and singing after Sunday lunch wouldn't disappear. He blew on his fingers to warm them up, then performed willingly.

In a bad mood, Gontrand taunted François. "Is that all you learned with your Nazi professors?"

"Enough!" Bérangère's voice was as cold as the weather. "You sound like that old goat in Vichy."

Her barb had the desired effect. Gontrand ranted on about the respect due to Maréchal Pétain, while François, followed by Bernard, escaped to the kitchen.

"Here uncle, I've got the microfilm." He extracted the small roll from under the F scroll of his violin. In a swift movement Bernard made it disappear inside his jacket pocket. François stored his violin and they rejoined the assembly.

Lyse-May hung around the adults. Brigitte hadn't come and the little girl's older cousins were too busy with books to play with her. Julie seized the opportunity to get Roland away before anyone asked too many questions. She asked Lyse-May, "Would you care to come with me?

Julie winked at Roland. While the discussion in the kitchen focused on the increasing number of executions of hostages, Bernard and Bérangère came into the vestibule to help Lyse-May dress for the outdoors. Bernard slipped a piece of paper into Julie's pocket. Her niece was soon dressed and muffled up in a long woolen scarf.

"Are we pretending you're my girlfriend?"

"Of course."

Once outside, Lyse-May bounced between Julie and Roland holding their hands. A German patrol passed on the opposite sidewalk.

"Don't look at them."

"Should I kiss you?"

Lyse-May burst into infectious laughter. She began singing a French Christmas tune where Santa Claus kisses the mother. After a moment's hesitation, the soldiers grinned and continued on their way.

"Beautiful, Lyse-May." How did that child sense the danger of the patrol stopping them? Her little ears must be listening to the adults talking and storing, if not the words, the feelings and using that knowledge in certain situations.

"I like singing. I sing with mémée when we have our piano lesson."

"Tell me, why did you sing just when we met the soldiers?"

"Because they're bad people. But they like music and singing."

Roland nodded several times. "Only four and already grown up."

When they arrived at avenue Victor-Hugo, Julie was surprised by the heat in the lobby. Madame Durand rushed out. "We had a coal delivery!"

"Nice. Must be the tenants upstairs."

"I guess you're right, madame Julie."

"May I ask you a favor?"

"Of course."

"Could you phone my mother-in-law to say that Lyse-May is staying the night with me?"

An air of satisfaction spread over the concierge's features. "I'll do that right away."

Once in her apartment, Julie laughed.

"And what's the cause of the merriness?"

"She forgot that the telephone is only in the mansion side occupied by the general. But she'll give him the message. She just won't be able to tell

Bérangère how appropriate it is for Lyse-May to stay the night when Julie is having a male guest."

"I see. At least I hope I do."

"Propriety is of prime importance for concierges."

Lyse-May hadn't missed one word of the exchange. "I'll go and walk with you tomorrow."

"I think you should go back to mémée tomorrow."

"Non. I'll walk with you because I'm appropriate."

The adults laughed heartily.

"I think it can be arranged," Roland said. "You noticed how she charmed the German patrol?"

Julie picked up her niece and kissed her. "I'm outvoted. You can come. Now let's see what can we cook for *le dîner*."

"Forgive me for asking, why can the tenants get coal but your in-laws can't?"

"The upstairs tenants are German. And my in-laws in the west wing won't accept any help from their uninvited tenants. That'd be construed as collaboration. Now excuse me, I've a note to read." She stepped closer to the window and read the note several times before tearing it into minute pieces which she went to flush down the W.C.

"What was that, or shouldn't I ask?"

"Our instructions for tomorrow."

In the morning, Julie dressed Lyse-May warmly while talking to Tony/ Roland. "We're walking right across the Bois de Boulogne. It's crawling with vert-de-gris but they're usually too busy to pay attention to walkers. The dicey part will be when we cross the bridge to Porte de Saint-Cloud."

"We'll cope."

As Julie'd predicted, the entrance to the Saint-Cloud park and tunnel was heavily guarded. A patrol walked toward them along the same sidewalk. Arms extended, Lyse-May looked up at Tony. He picked her up and she clasped his neck. Her clear childish voice rose to sing *À la claire fontaine*. The soldiers halted. One of them began singing with her. Despite his Teutonic accent, he sang well. When they finished the song, Lyse-May clapped her hands. The soldier offered her a few candies. The walking resumed.

Her heart still beating fast, Julie didn't talk until they reached Sainte-Clodoald church on top of the hill where Tony put Lyse-May down to enter the church. After making the sign of the cross, they knelt on a low bench. They didn't have long to wait. A smartly dressed woman came to kneel beside them. Julie took Lyse-May's hand and, leaving the airman behind, they walked out. No words were exchanged.

Outside, Julie continued to the far side of the hill. She kept her ear attuned to the surrounding noises. Before they'd gone far, she tensed at the sound of screeching car tires, followed by shots. She blanched but steeled herself to talk animatedly with Lyse-May and engage her in a game. No doubt, the airman had been caught. The area was now too dangerous. She deeply regretted having taken the child with her. Julie's game had Lyse-

May run ahead and hide behind a tree while she hurried close behind, avoiding passersby who looked indulgently on the child. She didn't turn when she heard a car behind her. The front-wheel drive Citroën was unmistakably the SS police. On the front passenger seat, the smartly dressed woman from the church craned her neck, scrutinizing the pedestrians and pointing. Rage boiled inside Julie. The woman had betrayed her and the airman. Julie took Lyse-May's hand but there was no running away. A SS officer jumped out. Another car pulled up and four SS men encircled Julie. There was a brief hesitation when Lyse-May burst out crying and Julie picked her up. The car with the woman sped away.

The SS man stepped forward. "Come with us."

"I don't know why you're frightening a child."

"You should not break the law with a little girl. Now come."

Adrenaline flowed through Julie's veins. "I was not breaking any law. We're going to visit my aunt."

The SS officer frowned, searching for the right French words. "You tried to help a man escape."

Julie mustered a surprised air. "I know of no such a thing."

"You told a woman in the church to take the man to safety."

The scenario was playing in her head. She had no trouble assuming her aristocratic air. "No, sir, I never talked to any woman in the church. It is a very ancient and beautiful church and I wanted to show it to my niece. I did not see a woman, just a couple of old ladies."

The officer's frown deepened. "*Papieren bitte*."

"Glad to oblige. I am Julie de Montregard." She put Lyse-May down, opened her purse and handed him her identification.

His attitude was immediately more deferential. He signaled to the soldiers to leave.

"Would you, please, come to my office?"

This would give her more time. "If you insist."

He opened the car door and helped Lyse-May inside. Two minutes later they were inside an opulent villa. Courteously, he asked Julie to sit and held the chair for her.

"You say you are innocent but the woman absolutely recognized you."

"She is lying." Her voice was firm and carried the strength of truth. She hadn't spoken to the woman.

"She has rendered us many services already. She is not lying."

Julie sensed she'd be on losing ground if she persisted. Alone, she'd have given a piece of her mind to the officer before being thrown into jail. But she had Lyse-May with her. Although a wave of disgust engulfed her, there was one person who could get her out of the situation she found herself in. For her little niece's sake, she had to do it. "Please, phone Obersturmbahnführer Meinhard in Paris." General von Trennen would have been only too glad to help, but she knew there was little love lost between the Wehrmacht and the SS.

The officer gave her a strange look but picked up the telephone on his desk. The phone conversation was brief. Whatever was said on the other end made the man redden. He replaced the receiver. “A car is coming for you.” He opened the door and barked a stream of orders to his staff.

Of course, he didn’t know that she understood everything he said, that the SS had the wrong person and that he ordered the arrest of the woman double agent. A moment later, a tray bearing pastries, a glass of milk and a cup of real coffee was brought in.

After a word of thanks, Lyse-May and Julie indulged in the refreshments. They had just finished when the clicking of heels sounded in the hallway. A moment later, the door swung open and the SS officer ushered Kurt Meinhard in.

“*Liebling* Julie. I came as soon as I heard about the mistake. My car is waiting.”

Her smile hid her repulsion. She stiffened her spine when his hand touched her back as he escorted her to the chauffeur-driven Opel. With Lyse-May sitting between them, she sustained light conversation until they arrived at her apartment building.

“*Danke schön,* Kurt. Yes, Lyse-May is staying with me.”

“I’ll see you later.”

She flashed him a smile an actress would have been proud of, and disappeared inside. Doubtless, the concierge observed everything from behind her curtain. The elevator stopped on the second floor. Once in the apartment, Julie flopped on the sofa. Lyse-May joined her.

“It was bad.”

“Yes, sweetie, it was, but we made it.”

“But the man didn’t.”

Julie sighed deeply. This child understood too much. “He’ll have to go to a prisoner of war camp.” At least she hoped he’d be mistaken for a Frenchman genuinely on his way to find work in the country. His papers were real. If not it wouldn’t be a POW camp. He’d have to face interrogations and deportation.

***

Wednesday, March 26, 1941

Bernard came out of the bathroom, adjusting his tie. A furious Marie-Ange threw a handful of papers in his face. He glanced at his briefcase lying open on the floor, the latest issue of Résistance in plain view.

“Do you ever consider the danger of all that stupid propaganda for our children?”

“Sorry, darling. I couldn’t do anything else. The youth who was supposed to pick them up at the office yesterday didn’t turn up.”

Marie-Ange became even more furious. “You should have left them at the office!”

“No, Must not leave any trace.”

“And here, isn’t it a trace?”

“I am assuming I can count on your discretion.”

“What if Paul had found them?”

Displeasure showed on his face. “Paul doesn’t rummage through my belongings." His wife missed the slight emphasis on his son's name. He couldn't tell her that ten-year-old Paul was aware of his father activities and carrying on a few of his own with a bunch of classmates.

"You can't know what children are up to."

An urgent rapping on the door made them both freeze. Marie-Ange looked through the peep-hole and saw Ernest. Bernard had already made the newssheets vanish. She opened the door.

"Monsieur Bernard, you must come to the Manoir, right away. It's urgent."

"What happened? My father?"

"Non, monsieur. It's the general who sent me. His car is downstairs to take you."

Marie-Ange's face turned white. Somewhat anxious, Bernard composed himself. "I'm on my way to work. Is it an order?"

"Monsieur Bernard, if I were you, I'd not question it. General von Trennen has his reasons."

"Right. I'll come." He snatched his briefcase containing the newssheets. "Darling, don't worry. It's probably nothing more than a bit of diplomatic hoopla between my father and the general." He then followed Ernest out.

Leaning back in the comfortable seat of the Mercedes, Bernard sighed. "Now I'll be labeled as a collaborator. Neighbors will think I get taken to work in a chauffeur-driven German car."

"Don't worry, monsieur Bernard. Those who collaborate will think it's good and the others won't believe it."

"Not so sure, mon ami. Maybe I can talk to them about the troubles my father causes the general who occupies his house. Then they might believe I was sent to sort them out."

He didn't have time to ruminate further. The car pulled to the curb in front of the Manoir. Bernard took the stairs two at a time. Günter was waiting for him and showed him into the general's office.

"You asked for me, Herr von Trennen?"

"Yes, please take a seat. I have a few questions for you. First, what exactly do you do at the Musée de l'Homme?"

Bernard hid his surprise as best as he could. "I'm an archeologist."

"Finding old bones and piecing them together?"

"That and a lot of other things, such as trying to determine how people and animals lived in the most ancient times, their social structure, that sort of thing."

"It must be fascinating work. I am interested in ancient history, particularly that of Greece and how far they extended their civilization. There is so much to be learnt. Your museum is a veritable treasure trove. Relax, Bernard. You do not mind me calling you by your first name?"

"Not at all, sir." Bernard wondered where this was leading.

"Please, let's not be formal. Tell me how you got involved in this particular line of study."

"You realize that I am supposed to be at work this morning."

"I shall square it with your boss."

Still suspicious, Bernard began talking about some of his pet topics in Greek archeology. He recognized that the general was an educated man and that his desire to hear more about archeology stemmed, perhaps, from genuine interest.

"I'm quite sure there are more remnants in Marseille, which was a Greek colony. The Crinas Wall was unearthed in 1916 and is now a historic monument. It dates from the fourth century B.C. It's only a small part of the fortifications. On my last dig before..."

"Before the war, of course."

"My team had uncovered a defense tower, next to the Crinas Wall. There must be another one. What is needed now is to establish exactly where the shoreline was back then..."

Noon arrived without the two men having noticed the passage of time. Marie knocked and announced the déjeuner was served in the dining room. They adjourned to the dining room and enjoyed the meal.

At the end of the afternoon, Reynard thanked Bernard and expressed the hope they could continue their conversation some other day. Before going home, Bernard called in to see his parents. Jacques had just arrived in an agitated state. When he saw his godson, he slumped into a chair. "*Cré nom de Dieu!* You're safe."

"What's all this about that you swear in the holy name of God?" Bérangère asked.

"The Gestapo raided the Musée de l'Homme this morning and arrested all the employees. Terrorists they said. Résistants I say."

A stunned silence greeted his words. Bernard closed his eyes and swayed on his feet. He dropped onto a chair and cupped his face in his hands in the knowledge that Reynard von Trennen had saved his life.

END

If you liked this first book, please leave a review.

Book Two: The Rage

The Rage, shows the deterioration of the relations between the French public and the German occupiers as the difficulty of obtaining food increases. The first Résistance movement is dismantled and citizens learn about the Gestapo, but more resistance cells get organized. Women couriers risk their lives daily to help. Adolescents take on responsibilities in the Résistance. The Allies begin bombing industrial sites and railway installations, civilians become collateral damage. Julie continues to lead airmen and children to safety. The first little-known raffle to arrest Jews takes place in Paris in August, 1941. The Germans are no longer so "correct". The United States enters the war.

Kurt Meinhard is still pursuing Julie. Sylvain actively works for the Résistance and briefly reappears. He and Julie meet. He's caught by the

Gestapo. Julie takes time off in the country where she helps with resistance work.

Acts of resistance become more frequent. Relationships break down. Collaboration is rife, splitting families. Food is so scarce, children show signs of malnutrition.

Extract:

In the west wing kitchen, Bérangère sat sewing at one end of the long table. At the other end, Julie showed Lyse-May the different levels of a mountain.

"At the bottom there're trees. When you go higher, there are no more trees but there are pastures. Higher still and you get to the snow that never melts."

"But before the glaciers there were the rocks where the mountain goats live. It says so in my book."

"True..."

A ruckus of shouting voices erupted on the Manoir's side. Instinctively worried, the women raised their heads. Doors slammed, shock waves reverberated through the walls. The commotion moved to Marie's kitchen. The west wing's doors was thrown open. A tall man in a SS uniform barged in.

"Rodolphe!"

Scared, Lyse-May slid under the table.

"Lyse-May come here."

Bérangère stood up. "What's the meaning of all this?"

"I'm taking my daughter home."

"What home? Who's going to look after her?"

"None of your business. Lyse-May, come here!"

Julie straightened. "She doesn't want to. She's settled here..."

Rodolphe strode forward, upended the heavy table sending the sewing machine flying across the floor. Julie fell backward, a terrified child clasped her legs. Rodolphe seized his daughter's arm and lifted her. The girl screamed and kicked. Her father smacked her on the side of the head and wedged her limp body under one arm. Julie got to her feet and grabbed his sleeve. He back-ended her. Gontrand limped in from the bedroom. As his son retreated, he raised his cane to smack him on the head but Rodolphe threw the door open and the cane broke on the side of the panel.

Book Three: The Hope

The Hope shows the resilience of women. The Résistance is now highly organized. Women couriers and liaison personnel carry out the most dangerous of work. The de Montregard women are involved. Marie-Ange betrays her husband to the Gestapo. Food scarcity worsens, as does the shortage of fuel for cooking, and heating. The electricity supply is no longer reliable. The young children and adolescents suffer most.

Julie is apprehended by the Gestapo. General von Trennen intervenes, with an unexpected twist.

François is also caught but escapes to a maquis. Families are torn apart. Allegiances and loyalties are sorely tested. Sabotage hinders the German forces, but retaliation in the execution of hostages increases.

The adolescents are now young men and women, fully engaged in the fight to rid their country of the hated occupiers. The maquis are now organized along military lines.

Paris liberation. Tragedy and happiness mingle.

Extract:

The Maquisards have finished the combat. The German munition trucks are theirs. François walked over to the German soldier he had to shoot in that split second when the brain gives a cruel choice – either him or me. He stopped in surprise.

"Wilhelm!" The young man is bleeding profusely. "I'm supposed to kill you. We don't take prisoners."

"Do François. I'm happy to die. I never wanted to be a soldier. I can't shoot at people. When I crawled up the embankment, I was deserting."

François pulled a length of string from his pocket and made a tourniquet on his friend's thigh to stop the rush of blood from his femoral artery.

At that moment, the Maquis captain arrived to see what was delaying his newest recruit.

"Wilhelm is my friend from before the war. I don't want him to be killed."

"You know better."

"Wilhelm was deserting. He's true to his word. You can trust him."

The older military man's voice boomed across the hill. "Get down and help carry the munitions."

François held Wilhelm's hand for a second. Tears in his eyes, he made his way to the truck through the brushwood. Moments later he heard a shot.

Write to Geneviève Montcombroux at
solitudepublishing@gmail.com
genevieve-montcombroux.com

Follow her on FB

Other books by Geneviève Montcombroux

* **Non-fiction**:
The Inuit Dog of the Polar North – A detailed work about the Inuit dog, its history and provenance, its role in the Inuit life in the Arctic and its place in modern society. The North and South Poles were conquered by explorers using Inuit dogs. Surveyors and geologists mapped Antarctica with the help of Inuit dog teams.

* **Romance:**
Northern Lights and Sled Dogs – Kelly dreams of long distance dog races. Tyler let his problems overcome him, until Kelly comes into his life in a remote cabin in the Yukon Territory. Dogs, puppies, racing, winning, a powerful mix leading to a happy ending.

Northern Skies – Mattiesoon (Mattie), a First Nations biologist in the Canadian North. Josh, a helicopter pilot and owner of a remote fishing lodge. They are at opposite poles. Dramatic events bring them close until they find their happy ending.

Pizza for Two – Piers has known the depth of despair. Nicole carries the burden of a troubled past. Their road ahead is strewn with untruths and deceit until they find their happy ending.

The Magic of Music – Marina, a concert pianist, sees her life shattered. Trent's life revolves around his daughter Sophie who is blind and suffers from selective mutism. Trent carries an enormous guilt. Drama evolves in Otter Lake, a small prairie town. Music soothes the souls and lead to a happy ending.

* Children books
A Dog Named Tezzero – Two smart dogs. Two eager boys. A doggy adventure that brings people together.

Made in the USA
Monee, IL
16 July 2020

35538606R00148